AN ITALIAN ADVENTURE

LEONIE MACK

B
Boldwood

First published in Great Britain in 2025 by Boldwood Books Ltd.

Copyright © Leonie Mack, 2025

Cover Design by Alexandra Allden

Cover Images: Shutterstock

The moral right of Leonie Mack to be identified as the author of this work has been asserted in accordance with the Copyright, Designs and Patents Act 1988.

All rights reserved. No part of this book may be reproduced in any form or by any electronic or mechanical means, including information storage and retrieval systems, without written permission from the author, except for the use of brief quotations in a book review.This book is a work of fiction and, except in the case of historical fact, any resemblance to actual persons, living or dead, is purely coincidental.

Every effort has been made to obtain the necessary permissions with reference to copyright material, both illustrative and quoted. We apologise for any omissions in this respect and will be pleased to make the appropriate acknowledgements in any future edition.

A CIP catalogue record for this book is available from the British Library.

Paperback ISBN 978-1-83603-386-8

Large Print ISBN 978-1-83603-385-1

Hardback ISBN 978-1-83603-384-4

Ebook ISBN 978-1-83603-387-5

Kindle ISBN 978-1-83603-388-2

Audio CD ISBN 978-1-83603-379-0

MP3 CD ISBN 978-1-83603-380-6

Digital audio download ISBN 978-1-83603-382-0

This book is printed on certified sustainable paper. Boldwood Books is dedicated to putting sustainability at the heart of our business. For more information please visit https://www.boldwoodbooks.com/about-us/sustainability/

Boldwood Books Ltd, 23 Bowerdean Street, London, SW6 3TN

www.boldwoodbooks.com

For Sam, the best companion on all my adventures

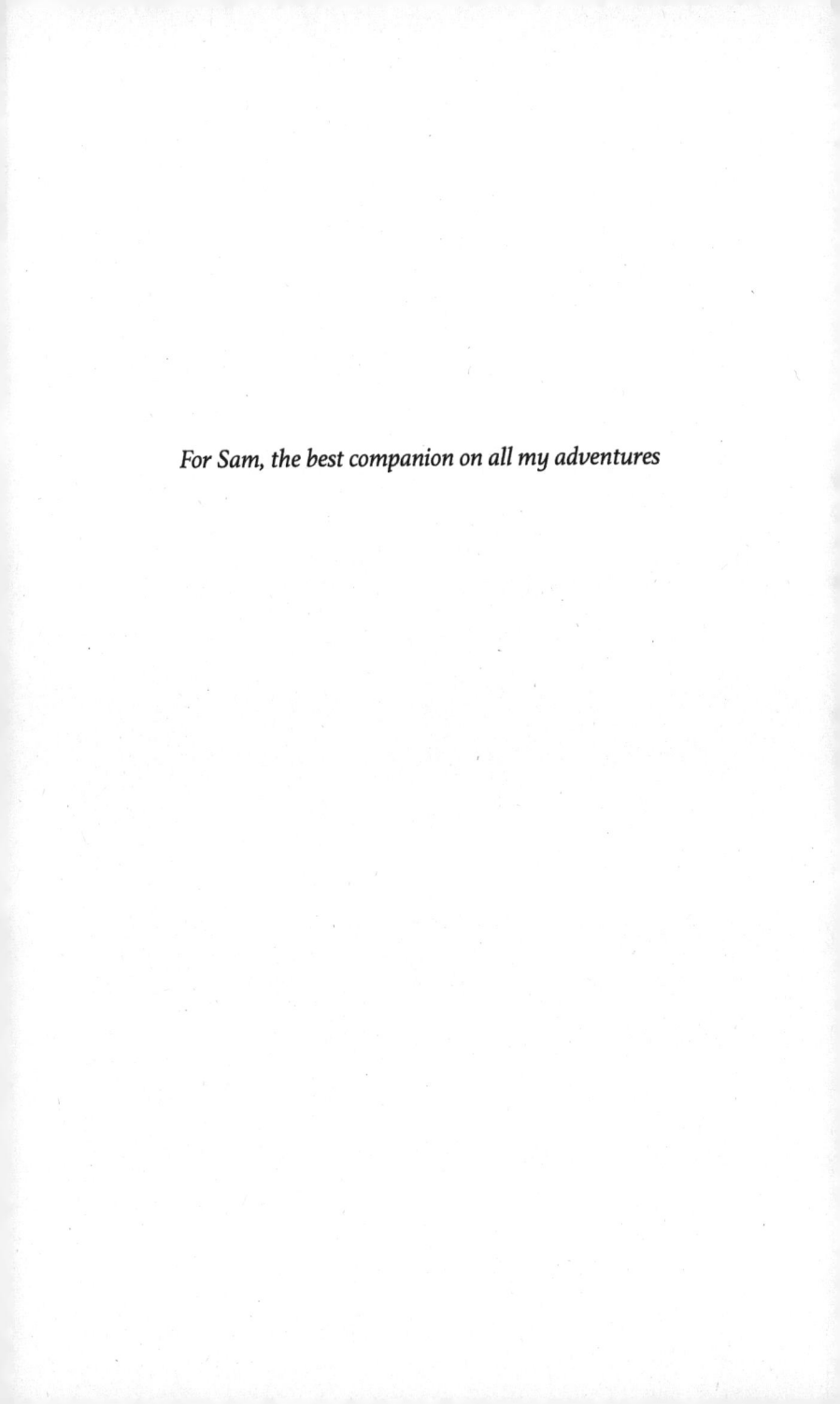

1

When the happy couple arrived for their first consultation, there was no immediate indication that the Tran-Welbon nuptials would be anything other than the usual perfectly planned and exquisitely executed destination wedding.

'Lily, Roman, it's so lovely to meet you in person. Can I get you something to drink? Tea?'

Sophie-Leigh gave the new clients her warmest smile as she ushered them in the direction of the Scandi-design sofa and the minimalist coffee table in the meeting room at I Do Destinations.

Against one wall stood a shelving unit of photography books, magazines and carefully concealed folders of information about getting married overseas – important, even if they didn't enhance the aesthetic. Another wall was frosted glass and on the other two hung photos from recent weddings, printed on shiny acrylic, capturing a moment that contained two lifetimes – and the stunning backdrop of the exotic locations the couples had selected for their big day.

One featured the waterfront on the Italian island of Elba,

the sun bursting over the horizon as the barefoot bride and groom, in all their finery, held hands in the foreground. Santorini was there too (Sophie had planned that wedding. The biggest challenge had been getting the crowds of tourists out of the background of the photos). One of the shots had been taken by a drone camera high above Whitehaven Beach in Australia, the small wedding party captured throwing rose petals into the air.

The meeting room was the heart and soul of I Do Destinations, a cosy place for honest discussion as well as a trophy room documenting the success of the many grand occasions the agency had arranged. It was Sophie's happy place.

'Coffee, please – for both of us.'

Taking the armchair opposite, Sophie set down her tea and reached for her tablet and stylus. 'You mentioned in our call that you haven't decided on a destination, but you have a specific idea for the ceremony,' she began. 'I'm intrigued. Do you want to start there?'

'It's quite... unusual,' the bride, Lily Tran, thirty-two years old and originally from London – according to the profile she'd filled out online – began apologetically. 'We've probably seen too many Instagram photos of couples in stunning locations.'

Sophie flashed them her brightest conspiratorial smile. 'I've planned nearly fifty destination weddings so far and helped my colleagues on at least fifty more. I promise you, whatever you're thinking, it won't be the strangest idea I've ever heard and stunning locations are what we do here.'

The couple shared a smile, their hands clutched between them.

The groom, Roman Welbon, thirty-one years old, from Inglesbatch in Somerset, began eagerly. 'Lil and I met through our climbing group. We both love the outdoors and we just thought—' He gave his bride-to-be a giddy smile, even as Sophie's slipped.

The outdoors. Climbing. Would she be in luck and they just meant stairs down to the beach? It was her job to make wedding dreams come true. She was used to keeping her own past out of it – her own hypocritically disastrous track record on love – but there had been a time when she'd loved the outdoors too. At least, she'd loved someone who loved the outdoors.

Lily nodded and continued, 'A church or an events venue – even a mansion or a fancy villa – those aren't the right places for us to get married. We'd really love that sense of achievement we get from a hike or a climb, so we were thinking—'

Sophie leaned forward to make sure she caught every detail of the couple's wishes – and tried to ignore her tingle of misgiving.

'We'd love to get married at the top of a mountain!' Roman blurted out.

Wonderful. Something that reminded her of the most mortifying day of her life. Sophie hoped they couldn't tell she was gritting her teeth. She prided herself on being good at reading people – it was a necessary skill for her job. But that one man... If she ever needed reminding of her limitations, then that day, that man was enough.

'You know those peaks with a cross on top?' Roman continued. 'We were picturing something like that, with views for miles.'

'I've seen photos of mountain weddings. I don't know if you've done anything like that?' Lily asked.

Opening her mouth to speak, Sophie hesitated, searching for the words to reassure the client, while also admitting that mountains were a long way outside her current repertoire with good reason. But she was saved by the groom's enthusiasm.

'Our friends are mostly outdoor types too and our parents are also interested in an... adventure. Obviously, we couldn't have a party or a meal up there, but that's our dream for the ceremony – something really meaningful for us.'

'Your... parents too?' She bloody well hoped they didn't have any medical conditions. What kind of insurance would she need for this? She was a wedding planner, not a mountain guide! The term 'mountain guide' made her swallow more uncomfortable memories.

'I know we'd have to keep it small,' Lily said with something like an apologetic smile.

Sophie gripped her stylus tightly and dragged her thoughts back to her clients. 'There will be other logistical challenges. In most countries, legal weddings can only take place in designated areas.'

'But on your website, there's a whole section about commitment ceremonies,' Lily pointed out. 'We can get legally married here in the UK and avoid all those problems. And then we could design the day to be really special – and the budget would stretch further, because we wouldn't have those administrative costs.'

'Ah, if you're... um... Yes, of course that's an option. But you can also consider just the photos on a mountain. To be honest, those pictures you've seen online are all staged and taken the day before the wedding or the day after. We can absolutely arrange for that kind of photoshoot and then we don't have to get all of your friends and family up and down a mountain on your wedding day.'

Lily reacted with a slight raise of her eyebrows, a signal of doubt that added panic to Sophie's existing cocktail of unwanted emotions. She was here to make dreams come true, not criticise clients' ideas – or the work of other wedding planners and photographers.

Roman was undeterred. 'We were really hoping for a ceremony right at the top, a long way from any infrastructure. We'd trek up to the summit and that's the spot where we'd promise our lives to each other.' The adoring look Roman gave his fiancée would usually have prompted an indulgent smile from Sophie, but irritation rose up her throat instead. She swallowed it ruthlessly.

'That sounds... very romantic,' she managed to say. 'But are you certain you'd forego the big white dress and the evening wear? If you want to hike up, it might limit your—'

'I was picturing just a wreath of flowers. The big white dress isn't my thing anyway,' Lily explained. 'It's the experience that's important to us.'

'After the scare we had six months ago...' Roman's glance at his fiancée this time was haunted. He turned back to Sophie with an earnestness that was touching, even in her state of distraction. 'We have a lot to celebrate. The doctors weren't sure if Lil would walk again. But she made a complete recovery and we're climbing just like before.'

'Oh, that *is* something to celebrate.' And a reason to get over her own stupid mistakes and make their dream a reality. 'I'm so sorry you went through something so traumatic.'

'As Roman said, I made a complete recovery,' Lily explained. 'It wasn't even an accident or anything. I just developed sepsis from pneumonia – rare, but it could happen to anyone.'

'I proposed to her while she was on life support,' Roman added, his voice weaker. 'But I had to propose again when she recovered, because she only remembered it in a bit of a haze.' He gave a short laugh that Sophie knew hid his lingering trauma.

'Well, I suppose we need to plan a wedding that's at least as dramatic as your engagement,' Sophie said, bolstering her smile. 'Aside from the... summit, did you have any other specifics about the location? A country? I see you're looking at September or October next year, which gives us plenty of time to book a venue – for the reception, I mean. For the Alps, we could look at France or Austria, or perhaps even Slovenia. We had one couple marry near Lake Bled two years ago and their budget stretched a little further there.'

Of course, the Alps ran through one *other* country that she had failed to mention – perhaps on purpose. It was one of the most popular with her clients, the destination for the majority of the weddings she'd planned over the six years she'd worked for I Do.

She was an expert on Italian weddings. She knew all about the 'Atto Notorio' and the 'Nulla Osta' and the intricacies of municipal politics in Tuscany and Verona and she'd even helped a pair of avid history buffs tie the knot near Pompeii last year.

But the combination of Italy and a mountaintop wedding clogged in her throat. She should have been over it. She *was* over *him*. She'd be a fool to still harbour romantic notions when the relationship had never been serious – to him at least. But that day, the 29th of February nearly eight years ago, had etched itself into her obsessively overthinking consciousness. She had to find a way to be a professional about it – although mostly, she was hoping they just picked Austria or Slovenia instead.

'Before Lil got sick, we'd started looking at a holiday,' Roman said.

Sophie's stomach sank. He was going to say it. She could *feel* it. Smoothing her hair nervously, she wouldn't have been surprised to find a wild tangle rather than the neat chignon in her favourite sparkly clip. She slurped her tea to tamp down on her panic.

'And our parents love the idea,' Lily continued, 'of an Italian wedding.'

Oh, boy. 'Who wouldn't? Were you... thinking of the Alps or the Apennines? Piemonte or Tuscany, Dolomites or...' She forced herself to say it. 'South Tyrol?' *Please don't say South Tyrol.*

'Actually, we love water sports too, so we were hoping to find somewhere we could swim and windsurf as well – maybe for the bachelor party. Plus, our parents wanted somewhere to sit and enjoy the beach.'

'Beach *and* mountains.'

'Somewhere with local vineyards would be amazing too,' Roman added. 'We'd love a whole programme of activities for everyone – wine tasting, windsurfing, rock climbing.'

'Beach, mountains – with a cross on top – vineyards and adventure activities,' she repeated, blinking rapidly as she wrote the words painstakingly onto the blank page of her tablet with her stylus. Her script looked blurred and loopy – like these wild ideas.

It wasn't a dream wedding – it was an organisational nightmare. But at least there were no beaches in South Tyrol. As long as she didn't have to face constant reminders of her own stupidity while she planned and carried out this wedding, she could do what she always did: create an unforgettable day for her clients.

'Roman,' Lily chided her fiancé gently, 'that's starting to sound a bit ridiculous.'

Looking up, Sophie contradicted her with a sudden smile. 'Not at all. I can think of at least three options off the top of my head. Let me find some photos for you.'

'Great!' Roman enthused, punctuating his eagerness with a kiss to Lily's forehead.

'Are you serious?'

She hadn't yet earned Lily's trust, but she was determined to do so. Taking down two of the many photo albums arranged alphabetically on the shelves, she opened the first to reveal a panorama shot of a bride and groom holding hands on the shore of a vast lake as sunlight rippled on the surface. Stones shimmered under the clear water in the foreground and in the background, looming green-and-grey mountains rose out of the water.

Lily drew in an excited breath that restored a measure of Sophie's confidence.

Turning the page, she showed them a photo from the reception at a winery. Then she flipped back to the ceremony in the gardens of a villa, surrounded by trimmed hedges and palm trees, with a view of the lake, towering rock faces and a town of dappled clay roofs. Was it too much to hope that they'd change their minds and have a beautiful civil wedding in the villa?

'This one's not exactly "the beach", it's a large lake, but the area is very popular with windsurfers. If you'd like to look at—'

'It's amazing,' Lily said, tugging the album towards her as Sophie opened another.

'Here we have Mediterranean beaches on Elba.'

Roman oohed and ahhed, but Lily was engrossed in the other album. 'Look at these mountains – how high they must be. They come straight down into the water. Is this Lake Garda?'

Sophie nodded. 'We have a hotel we often use in Limone sul Garda, but we have a long list of suppliers we've worked with that you could choose from.'

'Our hiking group went there two years ago, but we couldn't join them,' Roman added, turning to the first album again. 'Lake Garda would be wonderful.'

'And the summit wedding?' Lily asked. 'Would that work here?'

Sophie truly didn't have any desire to trek to the top of a mountain with a wedding party, but her boss had drilled into her when she'd started this job that the client was in charge – or had to feel that way at least.

'We can make it happen,' Sophie reassured her. She just wasn't at all sure *how*. God, she hoped her boss, the queen of weddings Reshma Bakshi, would have an idea – something better than Sophie's first thought: sub-contracting a company like Great Heart Adventures in Weymouth.

Noticing she'd scribbled down the name of the adventure travel agency, she hastily rubbed it out with her finger. Reshma would have a better solution – one that didn't dig into Sophie's past. And besides, there was no chance that *he* still worked there. He was probably at the top of K2 right now, freezing his fingers off for no apparent reason.

Swallowing her uncertainty for the rest of the consultation, Sophie reminded herself that she'd already organised two weddings at the lake and she would find a way to work this out – she always did.

If Lily and Roman wanted an adventurous wedding, they'd get the most adventurous damn wedding anyone had ever seen and it would have nothing to do with the larger-than-life Italian mountaineer who'd been the first to show Sophie how little she really knew about relationships.

2

One of these days, the old Land Rover was going to give up the ghost.

Andreas wrenched the gear stick into neutral with a grinding noise that pounded into his skull. The car park at the climbing gym and headquarters of the adventure travel company was mercifully flat, otherwise the handbrake wouldn't have held. The undercarriage seemed rustier every time he dared look at it and the passenger door didn't open *or* close properly and now boasted several dents from where he'd slammed it.

The old truck had clocked a lot of miles, usually full of ropes and helmets, straps, carabiners and tents. When Andreas jumped out and yanked the door of the boot open that day, the less-than-fresh scent of sweaty socks and sodden wool reached his nose – odours the old Land Rover was more than familiar with.

Pausing to rub a hand over his gritty eyes and grimy face, he hefted four coils of brightly coloured rope and a pile of slings tied carefully together and kicked the boot closed with one foot. The smell stayed with him as he trudged to the glass doors and he realised with a grimace that it was not only the contents of his rucksack that stank. It was him. The Land Rover was used to that too.

The reception area was more utilitarian than interior designed, with hooks for equipment, chipboard dividers and a wall of metal lockers on one side. The logo of the company – a stylised version of the heartbeat electrogram – hung on a slate-blue wall behind the reception desk with the words 'Great Heart' on either side of the spike and 'Adventures' below. As soon as he crossed the threshold and dumped the damp equipment in a free corner, the dusty scent of chalk and the calm shouts from the belayers on the floor enveloped him in a familiar greeting.

Either here in wet and windy Weymouth in February or anywhere else in the world, a climbing gym was a kind of spiritual home. Even if he knew no one, there was brotherhood here – and sisterhood. But the gym at Great Heart was almost literally home. His bedsit around the corner from Asda was more of a place to store his clothes than anything else.

The receptionist appeared through the office door as he was heading out for another load of equipment. She jumped when she saw him, but then a broad smile stretched on her lips. 'Andreas! Griaß di.'

He tugged off his grimy baseball cap, although his hair wasn't much cleaner. 'Hoila, Toni.' It was their little routine of greetings in Tyrolean, although her husband had spoken an Austrian variety, not Andreas's further chewed southern dialect.

Pressing a kiss to her cheek and then looping his arms around her, he gave her a squeeze, letting go when she poked him, wrinkling her nose.

'Have you just got back? You don't need to answer that. I can smell the mountain on you. How was it?'

'It's February in Eyri. How do you think it was?' He'd

adjusted to calling the National Park by its Welsh name. As a member of a linguistic minority himself, he'd embraced the change.

'Any snow?'

He shook his head. 'But it was arse cold in the tent. Clients were disappointed we only got to carry the crampons.'

'Not just the clients, I'm guessing.'

He didn't respond. It did no good bemoaning the absence of real expeditions over the past few years and he knew that fact troubled the founder of Great Heart Adventures – famed mountaineer Willard Coombs – just as much as it disappointed Andreas. At least Andreas also had work as a mountain guide when he was back home in Italy and had been sponsored to open new routes on several six-thousanders over the past few years. Will had got a little old for expeditions even before the bookings had dried up.

Stretching his stiff back, Andreas thought with chagrin that everyone got too old eventually. With his fortieth birthday just passed – here in Weymouth so he could avoid his family and only had to suffer through a pint at the pub with his colleagues to mark the miserable day – he had more and more work to do to stay in shape.

All the more reason why there was nothing in his life except trekking and the gym – exactly the way he wanted it.

'How's Cilli? Getting excited for his birthday party?' Make that work, the gym and his seven-year-old godson, Cillian.

'His birthday isn't for six weeks! Don't dare mention it when you see him, or it'll be your responsibility when he bounces off the ceiling,' Toni said with a grimace.

He mimed zipping his lips.

'But seriously, thanks for offering to help with the party. He wanted to take his friends climbing so much.'

An Italian Wedding Adventure

An Italian Wedding Adventure 13

'It's nothing,' he assured her.

'Your responsibility to Miro, I know, I know,' Toni said with a sigh. Her hand rose to his arm and clutched him briefly. Neither needed to say that before Cillian's party, they had to get through another anniversary that rendered the birthday bittersweet, year after year.

'Andreas!' In a flurry of bare, muscular arms and blue hair, his colleague, British mountain guide Kira Watling barrelled into him. His stench didn't seem to bother her the way it had Toni, but then he'd shared a bivouac with Kira on more than one occasion – and a bed on a handful of others. 'I missed you when you got back from Italy and then you left straight away for Wales!' She gave him a punch in the arm that actually hurt. 'You owe me a pint.'

'I always seem to owe you a pint when I get back.'

'When you learn to say goodbye, you won't owe me any more pints.'

He crossed his arms and slanted her a look. 'I don't do goodbyes.'

'*I don't do goodbyes,*' Kira imitated in a high-pitched voice, using her fingers as extra mouths. She slapped him on the arm again.

He rubbed his biceps with overdone offence. 'Now I remember why I always look forward to you welcoming me back, Watling.'

He heard murmurs behind the door Toni had emerged through and peered at it in confusion. 'Is Will here? I thought he had an appointment with the bank today?'

Toni gave a nod, but her expression turned grave.

'What?' He glanced at Kira to find her staring at her rubber climbing shoes.

'Bookings didn't pick up as he'd hoped,' Toni said evenly.

God knows, she was the one most affected if the business went under, but only a small swallow hinted at what she must be feeling.

'But what does that mean? Problems with the bank?'

'Not any more,' Kira mumbled, now looking out the window.

'What are you not telling me?'

'Will wanted to explain it to you himself,' Toni began, but Andreas was already stalking in the direction of the office. 'Andreas, just wait a minute. Will's found an investor.'

He paused at the door, hearing a female voice. An investor would be better than winding up the business, but if they weren't turning a profit now, there would have to be changes – for Will, for Kira and the other guides, for *Toni*.

'Why would an investor be interested in a struggling business?' he asked baldly.

Kira grimaced. 'Will said it would be a kind of merger, to create a new income stream for both businesses.'

'New... what?' The word 'stream' was supposed to be something beautiful, clear water splashing down from a glacier somewhere in a hidden valley.

'It's a wedding planning agency that wants to buy us,' Toni explained, a wary look on her face.

Andreas opened his mouth to express his disbelief, but his mentor's voice travelled through the door to the office with the spine-chilling words, 'No. Absolutely not! That's out of the question!'

'When we merge the businesses, it's the most logical source of cost savings,' the female voice countered. 'Cost savings' sent another shot of indignation through Andreas – even more than the prospect of weddings. The climbing gym made a profit – a small one. And the only costs involved with the travel arm were the staff. 'We've been through the due diligence. I know exactly how much trouble you're in, Mr Coombs. If I didn't have a vision for how our agencies could work together, I wouldn't be offering you anything. We don't need to double the administration staff for one company.'

'This is a fine way to start working together, by firing my staff—'

Andreas had heard enough. He should have been invited to this meeting. Since Miro's death, he'd looked out for Toni – him and Willard.

When he grasped the handle, Toni stopped him. 'I'm not sure you should—'

He shook off her hand. 'I might not be a permanent employee, but I've been here since the beginning.' And Will would always be his climbing partner – his mentor. Miro would always be his best friend, even though he was gone.

'That's not what I—'

Whatever Toni had been about to say, Andreas ignored it and pushed open the door with a little too much force. 'If Toni goes, *I* go!' he blurted out.

'Andreas.' Will's even voice cut through the haze and a familiar weathered, knuckly hand landed on his shoulder and squeezed. 'You're back.'

'You should have told me about this meeting.'

'Why? So you could rush back from Wales and get a speeding ticket? Or perhaps so you could shower first. This is Reshma Bakshi, by the way, of I Do Destinations, a wedding planning agency.'

'Mr Hinterdorfer.' He turned to find a small Asian woman with a bright smile and a few streaks of grey in her bob, holding her hand out to him.

Suddenly conscious of the grime under his fingernails and the stench of sweat, mould and soil that he'd brought into the room, he shook her hand gingerly – and that's when the other woman in the room stood from her place at the table. Andreas looked up and froze.

His vision tunnelled. He distantly heard Will continuing: '... and I believe you already know Sophie-Leigh,' but her name had been echoing in his skull long before Will had uttered it. *Sophie*... He'd been entirely unprepared for the punch to the gut.

She looked the same – no, some things in her features were still painfully familiar. Her narrow lips that thinned to nothing when she was concentrating, but whispered softly over his skin when she kissed him. Her rounded jaw where he'd enjoyed smoothing his thumb absently while she fell asleep against his shoulder. The ticklish spot on her neck.

But her face was a little more drawn. She wore a few more pounds around her hips. The difference between twenty-six and thirty-four was noticeable, but it didn't stop the sensation of hurtling through a wormhole straight into the past.

His gaze lifted to her eyes – sapphire blue and ringed with thick lashes which he knew were darkened with mascara and not their natural colour – and at her piercing look, he crash-landed on the last time he'd seen her, when he'd laughed in her face and behaved like the arsehole he'd been eight years ago.

Heat rising rapidly up his neck, his chest constricted so much, he wasn't sure how he was supposed to breathe with her eyes on him. She smoothed a hand over her pencil skirt and memories flashed like fireworks in his head: Sophie on the climbing wall, shaking and glistening with sweat as she followed his directives from below; Sophie, her hair mussed and a bright smile on her face for him when they woke up in the tent; Sophie clutching the handles of the raft at the beginning of that first trip, facing her fear, and he'd felt as though his heart had been swept down the rapids too.

Sophie...

Good God, he shouldn't be seeing her again like this. Will prompted him with a look. The other woman appeared to be judging his sanity – and probably finding it wanting. But Andreas wasn't sure if any words would even come out when he opened his mouth – certainly nothing that would make sense. So, with an audible swallow, he turned and stalked back out of the room.

Closing the door carefully behind him, he slumped against the wall, his head falling back with a thud. Sophie-Leigh Kirke. Back in Weymouth. Working for a *wedding planning agency*. Talking about a *merger*. What the hell was going on?

Gentle pressure on his arm made him pop his eyes open to see Toni standing close.

'I tried to warn you...'

3

Shit. Damn. Bloody hell.

Cursing silently helped only a little as Sophie tried to pull herself together. What were the chances? She couldn't believe he was still here. Restless, nomadic Andreas Hinterdorfer was *still in Weymouth* and he'd just made a fool of her again – or she'd made a fool of herself. Whichever it was, she could feel the looks Reshma was surreptitiously shooting her. That Willard Coombs remembered her was yet another nail in the coffin of her dignity.

Mr Coombs would remember her as the groupie who'd hung around the guides, drooling over Andreas with stars in her eyes. The fact that he'd slept with her for months and then discarded her like excess weight before heading off on his next expedition didn't seem to concern his friends – including the receptionist, who Sophie recognised from that time.

Toni, that was her name. She'd been pregnant, Sophie remembered with a twinge. She'd read months later that her husband Miroslav had been killed somewhere in the Himalayas before he'd ever seen his baby – killed while on an expedition with Andreas.

'*If Toni goes, I go,*' he'd said. Maybe *Toni* was what had kept him in Weymouth all these years when nothing had been able to tie him down before. Sophie hated the pettiness in her that resented the possibility. Toni had been a nice woman, from what she remembered. It wasn't her fault that Andreas had dumped Sophie unceremoniously before that expedition.

All fault lay firmly with Andreas himself, including the responsibility for this awkward silence in the meeting room after he'd stormed out without even greeting her. At least she could congratulate herself on not drooling this time, although the bastard had had the nerve to look just as incredible as he always had: craggy features, a lopsided mouth and those limitless green eyes that glowed like copper in the sunshine. Even the shimmer of grey in his beard and the lines on his forehead didn't dim the effect of the man who had climbed Everest with no supplemental oxygen, just the force of his personality.

Sophie responded to Reshma's raised eyebrows with an accusing look. *I told you this was a bad idea.* She would never have casually mentioned Great Heart as an *example* of the kind of company they could work with, if she'd known Reshma would go out and buy them.

'I apologise for Andreas,' Mr Coombs continued in a small voice. 'He's been sleeping in a tent for a week.'

'In *February*?' Reshma exclaimed.

He nodded. 'Our clients aren't usually interested in spa treatments and champagne.' He gestured for them to take their seats once more.

'Would you believe, that is something we have in common,' Reshma said. 'We've seen an increasing trend towards weddings in spectacular locations, or involving adventure activities as part of the celebrations. When Sophie mentioned sub-contracting a company like yours, I decided we should be bold and take it a step further. What do you think of "Great Heart Adventure Weddings", Mr Coombs? We share clients and information, polish up your guides with some new skills and offer a radical travel package.'

Mr Coombs laughed, loud and deep. The hair on the back of Sophie's neck stood on end as she sat silently – miserably – and waited for the next argument. But when he calmed and looked between Reshma and Sophie, there was a twinkle in his eye. 'I'm intrigued. And I think you'll find Toni is a necessary part of the new company, Ms Bakshi. She's the only person I can think of who loves weddings *and* guides.'

He darted a glance at Sophie and it was enough for the prickles over her skin to start up again. He didn't have to say it. She knew Andreas would hate the idea with a passion – the way he was allergic to family and commitment and romance. And apparently personal hygiene.

When the door flew open again, the smell of unwashed clothes presaged his return, his face expressionless this time. He wore a bright-blue technical jacket that did nothing to hide the breadth of his shoulders. His hair needed cutting. It curled golden-brown from under his baseball cap. A silver hoop winked in one ear and Sophie really did *not* need to remember right at that moment how he'd groaned when she'd sunk her teeth into that lobe. Oh dear.

'Ah, Andreas. You are joining us. Sit down.' Mr Coombs gestured to the seat next to Sophie and she was mortified to feel her face heat.

Andreas gave her a measured look and then took the seat next to Reshma instead – pointedly, Sophie imagined.

'Since that was the final detail of the contract, Mr Coombs,' Reshma continued, 'we can probably wrap this up. Sophie is eager to pin down the arrangements for our first couple.'

She was going to kill Reshma – unless the ground opened up and mercifully swallowed her first.

'What contract? What couple?'

Mr Coombs sent Andreas a quelling gesture and turned to Reshma. 'Does that mean we're in agreement? You'll accept a clause protecting my employees?'

'If you can convince them to work for me at weddings on occasion, then yes. Kira Watling and Toni Goschl will remain on staff.'

A huff of laughter erupted from Andreas and he drew up straight from his slump. 'Kira? Working at a wedding? Are you joking?'

'I'm sure Ms Watling will be more than capable,' Reshma said smoothly, eyeing Andreas in a way that gave Sophie a fresh shot of admiration for her boss. 'The fact remains that we have more clients than we can handle and Great Heart Adventures is not so fortunate. I was very much hoping to gain your support too, Mr Hinterdorfer, even though you're only employed on a casual basis.'

Sophie drew her brows together. If Andreas was only casual, then she wouldn't have to see him often. She couldn't imagine him dealing with florists and caterers and fancy hotels and he'd surely refuse even if he was asked. Perhaps he'd just leave the business entirely. She could hope.

He looked ready to laugh again, but paused when he accepted that Reshma might be serious. 'What do you need *me* for?'

Reshma gave him an amused smile and Sophie was appalled to see how easily he'd disarmed her boss with a single, baffled look.

Sophie spoke up. 'Reshma, I think Mr Hinterdorfer,' it was so strange calling him by his surname, 'is allergic to weddings.'

His gaze snapped to hers and Sophie's breath stalled. That had been the wrong thing to say. The memory of their last conversation came alive between them. His expression was dark – unlike the mocking tone he'd used eight years ago – but that was probably because the news of the proposed merger had come as a nasty surprise.

'She's right,' he rasped gruffly. 'The only wedding I've ever attended was Toni's and that was just the three of us.'

Sophie was annoyed to feel the spark of curiosity again at his mention of Toni, his voice softening over her name.

'I don't *do* weddings.' He glanced at his boss accusingly. 'What's going on? What does Great Heart have to do with weddings?'

'Perhaps Sophie is the best one to explain,' Reshma said in a diplomatic tone, but the alarmed glance he shot Sophie filled her with misgiving. He didn't want to talk to her any more than she wanted to see him.

'Reshma—'

'Since she's the one who made me realise there's a market for an adventure wedding package.'

Oh, God. Andreas's gaze had hardened to alpine granite and she wished she'd never mentioned anything about adventure weddings or Great Heart. Then Reshma continued speaking and all of Sophie's hairs stood on end.

'I understand you lead a tour to Lake Garda for Great Heart – one of the activities that reliably books out every year. As you will be able to help with our current clients quite specifically, Mr Hinterdorfer, perhaps you could clean up and then spare Sophie an hour of your time? You will be paid at your normal rate.'

No. Sophie couldn't work with Andreas – especially not on a wedding, no matter how well he knew the area. She needed what little pride she had left.

'I'm not the right person to help plan a wedding.'

'Andreas,' Willard Coombs said in a low voice. 'You know bookings have been dire. Unless you want to fly home for two weeks and pick up some work in the Alps, I don't have anything else for you right now. Maybe you should renegotiate your rate too, since I know you don't charge me enough.'

Andreas shifted uncomfortably, glancing at the door behind which Toni, the receptionist, would be waiting.

'I need to find sponsors for Manaslu – and train. I don't— I can't help with a wedding.' His wild glance was further evidence he was thinking back to Sophie's naïve mistake years ago. The only blessing was that they'd broken contact so completely that he had no idea of Sophie's *other* marriage-related disaster.

'We're not asking you to get married yourself, Mr Hinterdorfer,' Reshma commented, a hint of amusement in her expression as she obliviously made Sophie's embarrassment complete.

'Andreas, this could mean a way forward for Great Heart,' Willard continued. 'Perhaps the *only* way forward.'

Sophie stood, her spine thrumming with nerves. 'Actually, I need to get back to Bath tonight. Perhaps we can arrange a call for next week.' And in the meantime, she'd come up with an excuse for why she needed a different guide.

Andreas scraped his chair on the floor as he matched her stance. 'Sophie,' he said quietly, his emphasis on the wrong syllable sending memories ricocheting through her. 'Come on.' He made an irritatingly presumptive gesture for her to follow him and turned for the door.

'What? Where—?'

He tugged off his cap with a sigh, running a hand through his unruly hair and over his face. 'If you don't have much time, come with me and explain what you need. Maybe we can find another solution.' Without checking to see if she was following, he swept back out of the door.

Go, Reshma mouthed at her. 'This is why you came with me: to start planning your adventure wedding,' she said in a low voice.

'I really don't think—'

'Go on, Sophie,' Willard added. 'You know he'll bluster, but he'll give you any help you need.'

Not wanting to explain her reluctance to Reshma, she followed Andreas into the reception area to find him pressing a kiss to Toni's forehead. Sophie stopped short.

'Let me know what else you need for Cilli's birthday and I'll see you later.'

Blinking, Sophie's breath stalled as she faced the possibility that she had been *right* and not just vindictive when she'd suspected Andreas had cosied up with his best friend's widow. Another woman, slim and energetic, with a bright-blue bob and not very much clothing for a February day, pulled him into a hug and he farewelled her with a very familiar squeeze to her elbow. Had every woman in this place fallen prey to Andreas's careless charm?

When they broke apart, Sophie was surprised by the tingle of recognition. The blue hair was new, but that was Kira Watling. She'd been a trainee when Sophie had met her – far too young for Andreas. Kira gave Sophie a second look, but didn't seem to recognise her.

'Are you coming?' Andreas had paused in the doorway, leaning heavily on the frame and tossing his keys from hand to hand.

'If I have to,' she mumbled.

* * *

Andreas didn't know what he was doing. Scaring her off, maybe – hopefully. Regressing to the cabbage-headed idiot he'd been back when they were together. Whatever his murky motivations, ten minutes in the Land Rover next to him would surely be enough for her to lose all desire to work together.

On a *wedding*.

He slammed the sticky door on her, making her jump. After heaving closed the doors to the boot, he climbed into the driver's seat and turned the key, hoping the old girl would start up cleanly.

'Is this seriously the same old Land Rover?'

He nodded, twisting the key again when the engine merely coughed. 'It works.'

'Are you sure?'

'Yes,' he ground out. 'I drove back from Wales this morning.'

'I noticed.'

He sneaked a glance at her. She was staring out of the windscreen, her arms crossed and a fancy buckled handbag on her lap.

'So, you're a wedding planner these days?' he asked when the engine finally roared to life. He'd been aiming for casual, but felt certain the waver in his voice would have given him away. She wasn't the same girl who'd learned to climb, pitched a tent cheerfully in the middle of nowhere and driven two hours several times a week just to see *him*.

Ouch, he caught himself for the patronising use of the word 'girl'. She'd been a woman then – a young one – and she was definitely a woman now.

'Yes,' she answered defensively – which was fair, because his question had been so obviously barbed. 'And you're still in Weymouth.'

'Some of the time,' he said as he gritted his teeth to take the corner, braking and wrenching the wheel.

Sophie's arms shot out and she grasped the handle inside the door to stop herself flying into him. The handbag tumbled into the footwell and she cursed under her breath, which was cute, because he heard every consonant.

'You haven't managed to fix the power steering in eight years?'

He frowned. 'I forgot this thing even had power steering.'

'What do you mean you're here "some of the time"? Am I supposed to ask?'

'Do whatever you like!' he said, shoving the stick into fourth gear. 'Don't ask, if you don't want to know.'

Her sigh bordered on a growl. 'I didn't think you'd still be here.'

'I thought you needed my help with a wedding.'

'I need a guide, but I didn't come here for you. I honestly thought you'd be long gone from Weymouth.' She mumbled something about K2 which made him want to provoke her into speaking more clearly.

'I haven't climbed K2 – yet,' he grumbled.

'Oh, um, commiserations that you still have all your toes?' She was jiggling her foot in agitation.

'I don't,' he commented lightly.

'What?'

'I don't have all my toes.'

'*Whaat?*'

He was childishly satisfied to have reduced her vocabulary to a single word. 'I lost two on Gasherbrum.' Flicking on the indicator, he threw the Land Rover around the next corner into his street, avoiding her gaze.

Did she even know what had happened after they'd said goodbye? She hadn't kept in touch with anyone.

'They didn't say that in the news reports,' she said faintly.

'They were little ones, so I can still climb,' he said casually as he heaved the car into a parallel park. It would be so much easier with power steering.

'Hurray for that,' she said under her breath. Sitting up suddenly, she asked, 'Where are we?'

'My place. You're supposed to be squeezing me for information for a wedding – not that that makes any sense to me. But if you're just here to chat old times—'

'Andreas, can you stop baiting me for a minute so I can think straight?'

He deserved the hit, but he wasn't ready to let her off the hook. A thick strand of dark-blonde hair had come loose from her clip and he liked her more like that.

'Where did all of this come from? Is it because it's a leap year? You think of me every four years and this time, you realised I might be useful? At least you've stopped with the "Mr Hinterdorfer".'

She turned to him, her eyes bright with indignation. 'The reason I'm here has *nothing* to do with "us". If I'd known I'd have to deal with you, I'd have—'

'What? Run in the other direction?'

'I don't know, but I'm not here to beg you for another chance or rehash what happened. Trust me, I'm the last person who wants to remember *anything* about back then. You don't have to worry.'

He frowned, wondering why she thought he'd be worried about her begging to have him back. 'So, it's just a great coincidence that your company is buying my company? Or did you hear Will was doing badly and tip off your boss? Do you think Kira or any of the other guides are going to be happy about this? Weddings! Um Gottes Willen.' He articulated the curse at the end through gritted teeth.

'But it's not *your* company, is it? It's Willard's. All I did was ask my boss if we could subcontract a company "like Great Heart Adventures" for a specific wedding I'm working on. That's all. The rest is not my fault. I didn't even know what she was planning until a month ago when the due diligence was completed. And it's *definitely* not my fault that Reshma thought about consolidating the admin function, but she changed her mind anyway. Toni's job is safe, so you can quit being a bear with a sore head.'

She reached for the handle to make her dramatic exit from the car, but the door stuck, leaving her pushing ineffectually at it, more curses on her tongue. Andreas had the satisfaction of slamming his own door before coming around to give hers a shove and then jimmy it open. The way she sucked in a breath of fresh air gave him a stab of guilt.

'You don't live at Miro and Toni's place any more?'

He shook his head. 'Toni had to move after...'

'I was sorry to hear about that,' she mumbled.

She hadn't heard about it from him. She hadn't been there when he'd arrived back at Heathrow, Miro in a box – obviously the wiser of the two of them.

He jingled his keys. 'This place isn't much,' he warned her. 'I don't spend a lot of time here.'

'I'm not the one who suggested we come here,' she pointed out.

Wrenching open the boot, he hauled his backpack out, stifling a groan. 'I need a shower.'

He thought she muttered, 'You can say that again,' under her breath as she stamped up the front steps after him.

The house was a 1930s terrace that had been split into four awkwardly shaped flats with only two bathrooms between them. The carpet in the entrance hall was grey and institutional and the facing on his particle-board front door was chipped. As heat stole up his neck, he hoped at least that she could now congratulate herself on her lucky escape from a long-term relationship with *him*.

He let her into the single small room and said, 'Sit down,' before he'd thought that through. The only place to sit was on the dark-blue duvet. By some miracle, he'd made the bed before leaving for Eyri. 'I'll be back in five minutes.'

Snatching a towel from the hook behind the door, he escaped in the direction of the bathroom, hearing the amusement in her voice as she called after him, 'Take your time!'

Only when he was standing in the shower, his hands resting on the cold tiles with the water on full, streaming over his head and slowly stripping the dirt off him, did he realise he hadn't thought to bring any clothes with him.

4

Sophie lasted about one minute before she decided she *really* needed tea. Persuading herself it wasn't snooping, she opened the plywood cupboards of the kitchenette one after another, finding an opened box of instant mashed potato, a pile of energy bars and a hunk of vacuum-packed preserved meat – but no tea. Her hand shook concerningly as she closed the final cupboard.

She jumped when the door banged open, and then she froze. Andreas stalked back into the room, avoiding her gaze. His hair was dripping and the scent of herbal soap finally provided relief for her nose, but the rest of her was far from relieved.

He clutched his towel tightly around his waist, but he was otherwise completely naked, all golden skin and brawn and scars. His chest rose and fell with agitated breaths, drawing her eyes to the play of muscle and sinew, the dips and contours of a body honed for resilience and strength. When he turned away to rifle in his wardrobe, even the bunch-and-release of muscles in his back was hypnotic. Whatever his – many – flaws, Andreas Hinterdorfer still had the most incredible body she'd ever laid eyes on.

An Italian Wedding Adventure

With a rush of embarrassment to her hairline, she remembered all the ways she'd shown her admiration for that body when they'd been together. That had been what he'd wanted from her after all. She'd just been too naïve to see it – and she'd somehow convinced herself she loved the rest of him too.

She forced her gaze down and that was when she caught sight of his feet: pale, lightly freckled and missing the two smallest toes on the right. She swallowed.

'You might want to turn around,' he called over his shoulder, his voice gravelly.

She whirled around so quickly that she had to grasp the Formica bench for balance. She wasn't sure if he meant it for his benefit or hers. She'd certainly seen it all before and he'd never had a problem with nudity. She remembered him leaping into the turquoise water of a tiny lake somewhere in the Dolomites, his naked body little more than a blur with the jaw-dropping backdrop of granite mountain peaks.

'I was looking for tea,' she said curtly, tumbling back into the present.

'I don't have any. And if I did, I wouldn't have any milk.'

His gruff words only reminded her that there'd been a time when he'd kept teabags in his room just for her, milk in the mini-fridge.

'If you want this over with quickly, you could start talking. I will help you if I can.'

She turned without thinking, whipping back around when she caught sight of him tugging a shirt down over his chest, snug boxer shorts the only thing he wore below the waist. The worst part was the pang of familiarity. She shouldn't have remembered the feel of him in such detail.

But she'd been young and impressionable and... he'd made an impression.

'When did you become a wedding planner? I thought you loved being a travel agent.' His tone had thankfully eased to nonchalant, rather than barbed.

'It's not much of a leap,' she said. 'We're not a traditional wedding planning agency. We organise destination weddings – all the travel arrangements as well.'

'And your current clients want to get married in the Himalayas?'

This time when she turned, he was thankfully decent – although still buttoning his supple jeans. But the tight T-shirt from an outdoor brand did little to hide the tough shape of him and when he slipped a patterned woollen sweater over the top, he looked cosier than her favourite sofa.

'It's not as bad as the Himalayas. They're outdoor types and they want to get married at the top of a mountain – a symbolic commitment ceremony.'

'A... "symbolic commitment ceremony"?' He wiped a hand over his mouth, muffling his next words, although she nonetheless heard, 'What's the fucking point?'

'It's one of the options we've developed over the years to deal with the bureaucratic challenges of getting married in another country. Some people call it an elopement ceremony. I officiate myself – I mean, I've qualified as a celebrant here in the UK as well—' She took a deep breath to stop the words awkwardly flowing out of her mouth. 'Look, it's the client's wish and there's no need to disparage them because they're trying to make their wedding day meaningful. I would have thought you'd understand the allure of a mountain summit.'

'Yes, but not to get married up there!'

Her nostrils flared as he ran an agitated hand through his hair. 'Why not? Their relationship means to them what your expeditions mean to you.'

When he laughed, there was a darkness in the sound that made her uneasy. 'Marriage is endurance? Obsession? Pushing the limits of human strength – sometimes too far?'

Her skin prickled. 'Marriage can be about endurance, yes.' Hers certainly had been. 'It's not all easy. And pushing the limits of the human *heart*. When you take a look at all the horrible things people do to each other, I think marriage is a kind of miracle.'

He released a huff of disbelief that didn't seem entirely voluntary. 'What do you know about marriage?' He couldn't conceal his searching glance at her hands.

She tucked her left hand into the crook of her right elbow. Sometimes, the ring finger still felt unnaturally bare. 'This isn't about me. The top of a mountain is the last place I'd like to get married and their plans for a week of wedding festivities involving windsurfing and rock climbing is my idea of hell. But the client is always right and that is why I need a guide. It doesn't have to be you. If you can point out a few places for me to check out, then maybe Kira can help during the actual wedding—'

'You'll need more than one guide. Who's going to keep Aunt Frieda safe?'

'I'm pretty sure Aunt Frieda won't be coming,' she said with a frown. 'It's a small wedding – destination weddings usually are.'

'At Lake Garda, a place I know very well. I'm surprised you didn't suggest the Eggental in South Tyrol,' he grumbled.

Irritation flashed up her throat. 'Why would I, when I didn't know you were still working here and I've never been to your home? Even when we were together.' That word 'together' hung awkwardly in the air when she uttered it. 'Lake Garda is a very popular wedding destination and I didn't even know you take groups there every year. This isn't some elaborate plot to rub your nose in weddings. I learned my lesson. I will never propose to a man ever again in my entire life. I have not been pining for you for eight years and I don't know why the memory even registers with you when you have obviously made an exception to your "no family" rule for your best friend's widow!'

Ohhhhh, shit. The man made her lose her marbles. If there was one thing you could say to convince someone you'd been pining for them for eight years, it was to deny that you'd been pining for them for eight years.

'What are you talking about?' he asked peevishly. 'If we need to go over what happened back then—'

'We don't.' *Ever*.

'Thank God for that. And if you're implying that there's something between Toni and me aside from deep, old friendship, then have the courage to accuse me clearly.'

The steam dissipated from around Sophie's head. How was he suddenly the reasonable one? She opened her mouth, but no words emerged. Andreas seemed to take that as an invitation to continue.

'Miro was my best friend.' His voice had hardened. 'I left a piece of myself on Gasherbrum. I thought you would understand that more than most. I'm Cillian's godfather and when I'm in Weymouth, I teach him to climb – in honour of Miro and also in case he ever gets it in his mind to go up like his Papa. So yes, Toni is family in a way I... didn't necessarily plan. But I haven't taken Miro's place in her life – in her *bed*, which was what you were implying, wasn't it?'

'I'm sorry. It's none of my business.'

'No, it's not,' he agreed emphatically, rummaging in a drawer for a pair of socks and tugging them on, the second over his damaged right foot.

'When Reshma first mentioned consolidating the admin

functions, I honestly didn't know it was Toni's job we were talking about.'

'I believe you.'

'And I'm sorry for jumping to conclusions. I suppose I thought, since your climbing brotherhood is stronger than anything else, it might have happened. I hope Toni's been doing okay.'

'I don't really want to talk about it,' he said stiffly. Wasn't that just typical? Andreas was invincible – or at least he thought he was. He would never admit how much the loss had hurt.

Rolling his shoulders, he stretched his neck from side to side in a movement that sent another shiver of recognition through Sophie. There had been a time when she would have offered to massage his shoulders and stroke her fingertips along his neck to soothe the ache. His muscles would be tight and thick and he'd sigh and groan when she dug her fingers in and then he'd give her a groggy smile and a sloppy kiss in thanks – and then tumble into bed to sleep for eighteen hours straight.

Although a reluctant smile tugged at her lips, she had to wonder why she'd been so caught up in him. Climbers were their own unique kind.

'So, Lake Garda,' he said, changing the subject. He stalked to the sink and filled a glass, glugging half of it. 'There are a lot of summits to choose from, most of them probably reachable for a small group. How are you going to choose? What's important to them? I can't promise to be there for the wedding, but I can help you plan something.'

'I have no idea, to be honest,' she answered quietly.

'You said they want a week of activities? Bachelor party? Hen do? That stuff I'm familiar with.'

'Something like that, yes.'

All he had to do was glance at her for her to feel utterly incompetent. He leaned heavily on his tatty kitchen bench. Outside the single window with its faded curtain, the sky had darkened to slate. 'This needs more than an hour, Sophie.'

Her hair stood on end to hear her name on his lips, the 'o' sound chewed and the 's' a little sharp in his light accent.

'Do you want me to come to Bath next week? Meet with the couple?'

No, she didn't. Not if he was going to look all tired and real and make her feel something. She groped for her handbag, where she'd set it on the bed.

'Maybe this is a bad idea. In fact, it definitely won't work. You and weddings? It's obvious you don't want to and I don't want to force you.'

'Sophie,' he said again, his tone more insistent this time and she had to look at him. Bad idea. He was searching her expression for the source of her agitation. 'I'm sorry I was rude before.'

'Don't worry about it.'

'Can you let me apologise?'

She didn't want to. He was supposed to be the bad guy in her past.

'For today,' he clarified, as though she'd thought he'd apologise for turning her down eight years ago. 'I wasn't expecting to see you.'

'It was awkward. I'm sorry. I didn't intend... any of it.'

His strong brow was low over his eyes. He looked as though he might argue with her for a moment, but then he gave a shrug. 'I know.'

Her phone rang and she fumbled for it, seeing Reshma's name flash up with a mixture of relief and dangerous disappointment.

'Are you ready to go?' her boss asked when the call connected. 'I can pick you up from wherever that Italian mountain guide squirrelled you away to.' The amusement in her voice was clear – and something for Sophie to subtly discourage without piquing Reshma's curiosity.

'I'll meet you at Great Heart.'

* * *

After Reshma navigated out of Weymouth and onto the A-road, Sophie pressed her lips together and tried to ignore the impression that her boss was counting down to an interrogation. The silence barely lasted until Dorchester.

'Did you get some advice for the Tran-Welbon wedding?'

'Enough to know it's even more complicated than I'd imagined.' And that was just her feelings.

'The merger isn't quite finalised, but it won't be long. I want you to do extra research for this one. Since adding the section to our website, I've already had five enquiries. This won't be the last "adventure wedding" at Lake Garda; we'll need a comprehensive file.'

'You put the package up on the website already?'

Reshma continued, undeterred by Sophie's concern. 'Willard – Mr Coombs – mentioned that Andreas usually spends April and part of May in Italy for the ski touring season, but after that, I want him to take you to Lake Garda for research. I'm hoping he'll agree to participate in the wedding itself in September, but I don't want to scare him off.'

Her boss chuckled, probably remembering Andreas's horrified look at the prospect of a wedding.

Sophie didn't respond – she couldn't. Her stomach was

churning and it took all her effort not to get a similar horrified look on her own face.

'Willard thought you'd be able to get him on board.'

'He did?' she squeaked.

'I didn't realise you'd met Willard.'

As long as she didn't realise how well she knew Andreas – *had known* Andreas. 'I told you, I went on a couple of trips with Great Heart years ago. My sister is outdoorsy and she dragged me into it.'

'Ahhhh,' Reshma said, drawing out the sound for much longer than Sophie's explanation warranted. Reshma glanced at her, the glint in her eye making Sophie squirm. 'Let me guess. Your guide was Andreas? That explains a lot. Willard said you knew each other and it was obvious there was... something missing from my understanding of the situation.'

Sophie gulped.

'Is this going to be a problem?' Reshma's voice gentled. 'Sophie, I won't encourage you to do something that makes you uncomfortable.'

Lord, was she uncomfortable, but Andreas wasn't entirely to blame for that. 'There's no problem,' she grated out. 'But I don't know why Willard thought I'd be able to convince him. I'm the last person...'

'There is some history between you two?'

'Some,' she admitted. 'But I was young and stupid and it was a long time ago.'

'You can't have been too stupid. I wondered whether we'd have to fear for our brides with that man joining the team.'

'Reshma! You did not just say that! Besides, I'm sure he'll never join the team.'

'A pity. He'd look amazing in a suit. But first, we need that Garda adventure weddings file and our first event to be a success.

Let me know if you need any support on this, but I have every confidence in you.'

Sophie stared miserably out of the window as drops of rain dribbled down the pane. She was so far out of her comfort zone that even Reshma's confidence wouldn't help her. Only Andreas could do that and it was another thing to resent him for.

5

Six weeks later, Sophie was back on the A350, heading to Weymouth determined to keep her head this time. She'd decided she was looking to the future – she had to. The past was a dead-end of frustration and disappointment, there only to rob her confidence.

Her friend and colleague Virginia Weller was behind the wheel; they'd voted Ginny's bright-blue Fiesta as the best vehicle for the two-hour journey. She wasn't the smoothest driver, but the trip down the A-road was no excursion into the Cornish hedgerows or the Scottish Highlands. Sophie could grit her teeth and bear it, even seated in the back. In the passenger seat was Tita Pirnat, the longest-serving member of Reshma's staff and the self-proclaimed heart and soul of I Do.

'To be honest, if Reshma had expected me to book whitewater rafting or crevicing or what-have-you, I wouldn't have known where to start!' Tita exclaimed with a huff.

'Do you mean canyoning?' Ginny asked brightly. Ginny did everything brightly. Usually, Sophie loved her for it, but that afternoon it was blinding and Sophie needed her wits about her.

'I wouldn't know! I'm glad Reshma decided to keep the other lady on. I always thought getting married was its own adrenaline rush. Who knows why people need to add real danger to it.'

Sophie chuckled, leaning forward to pat Tita fondly on the shoulder.

'If it means we can draw on their staff occasionally for extra hands, then I'm all for it,' the older woman continued emphatically. 'It's the bane of my existence, finding waiters and drivers and assistants in these far-flung places – not to mention the nightmare I've been having with photographers lately – plus we've turned down a client or two already this year and it's only April.'

The extra hands were sorely needed. Sophie was flying to Elba in a few days for her next big occasion. The venue was one they'd used many times and she'd worked with the local businesses before, so she wasn't expecting any hiccoughs, but she had another six weddings booked – including the Tran-Welbon wedding – and they wouldn't plan themselves.

After a few stilted phone calls with her surly mountain guide, they'd blocked out two weeks in May and agreed a rough schedule. Andreas had assured her that was plenty of time before September, especially since the wedding party was less than twenty, but Sophie was itching to tick things off her list. She'd booked the hotel overlooking the lake for the week of celebrations and the historic lemon grove Lily and Roman had chosen for the reception, but the rest of the programme was alarmingly blank.

'I can't wait to meet everyone, now the merger has been finalised. What are they like, our new colleagues?' Ginny asked, prompting Sophie with a look in the rear-view mirror. The labret stud just below her bottom lip moved as she smiled.

They wouldn't be meeting *all* of their new colleagues, thankfully. Andreas should be safely at home in Italy teaching rich people to ski up mountains.

'I don't know them well. I think Toni is nice – that's their receptionist. She's a bit older than me. Willard – Mr Coombs – said she'll like helping with weddings although—' She paused with a grimace.

'Hmm?'

'Her husband died,' Sophie explained. 'I hope it's not going to bring back difficult memories for her.'

'We're all poor advertisements for our services!' Ginny said with a grimace. 'I'm chronically single, Reshma's never been married and you're—' She wisely cut herself off.

'I've been happily married for eleven years,' Tita pointed out emphatically. 'Tied the knot as soon as we were allowed to.'

'That's true,' Sophie said warmly. 'You and Sally restore our faith in relationships.'

It was a wonder Ginny was single, given how much she loved romance. Although now Sophie thought about it, perhaps that was her problem. She still had her ideals.

'And the others?' Ginny asked.

'They're climbers.' That was self-explanatory to Sophie.

'Let me guess, they think we're frivolous stylists more concerned with flowers and flawless place settings than the important things in life.' Ginny seemed more amused than upset at the prospect.

'Getting married *is* one of the most important things in life!' Tita said emphatically.

Sophie wished Andreas could have been there to hear this conversation – actually no, she wouldn't look forward to being in the same room as Andreas again, even with the opportunity to see him fidget.

'And place settings *are* life!' Ginny said with a giggle.

An Italian Wedding Adventure

'Kira is the only other full-time employee and... I can't see her appreciating place settings.'

'I don't mind. I can't wait to meet her anyway.'

Ginny pulled the Fiesta into the parking lot at Great Heart after a trip that had felt too short to Sophie. Willard had apparently booked part of the local pub for an informal dinner and meet-and-greet for the whole team. They were a little early, but before Sophie could suggest they take a walk instead, Ginny headed for the glass doors, full of curiosity.

Even without Andreas's presence, lingering embarrassment rose up Sophie's throat at the thought of spending time with Toni and Kira. She would have to prove that she was older and wiser, now, and then get over herself.

By the time Sophie dragged her feet through the doors behind Tita, Ginny was well on her way to charming Toni, all warm smiles and genuine interest. The Great Heart receptionist looked worn out, with shadows under her eyes and Sophie was struck with a sudden stab of sympathy for the woman who was raising the son of a dead mountaineer with only occasional help from another guilt-ridden mountaineer.

Toni's smile for Sophie appeared authentic. 'It is lovely to see you again,' she said, a wry edge to her expression that acknowledged their awkward history – including the day six weeks ago when Reshma had suggested she might make this single mother redundant.

'You too,' Sophie managed. 'I'm so sorry about...'

'Thank you,' Toni responded, but her tight smile didn't encourage that topic of conversation. She gestured towards the climbing hall. 'Why don't you look around while you wait? For old time's sake.'

As Sophie glanced at the wall of multicoloured grips set into textured grey panelling, it was difficult to believe there had been a time in her life when she'd trained here – when she'd made it to the top of the forty-foot wall, chalk on her fingertips.

Taking up Toni's suggestion – mainly so she could talk down her embarrassment before she had to converse with anyone – she toed off her pumps and stepped onto the springy gym floor, turning the corner to take in the full jungle of verticals and overhangs, studded with hard plastic grips. Then she froze, her mouth falling open.

Andreas *was* here. But she had no time to process her feelings about that, because the sight of him was unexpected for an entirely different reason.

'To your right – find the grip!' he called up, his voice gentle. Ten feet above him, a kid scrabbled and clung and flailed his pale legs. Clustered around Andreas were more children, staring up at their friend in horror and awe – and occasionally sparing Andreas a similar look. 'Reach. Push with your foot.'

He held the belay rope with both hands, crooning encouragement to the child until the boy slipped and swung away from the wall with a cry of disappointment. Andreas let him down gently, then swiped a careless hand over his hair.

'Great job, kid!'

The group of children gathered around him, all talking at once.

'Andreeeaaas!' shrieked one, making him grimace. He held up his hands in defence, but there was a smile on his lips – a smile Sophie would never have expected.

Andreas hated kids. She believed his exact words had been, 'Too much snot and not enough sense.' And Sophie had been such a wet blanket that she'd just laughed at him, while her stomach had clenched in disappointment.

Now her stomach was clenching with hurt and regret and that secret grief that never went away. She was sick of her emotional reactions when she should have left him – and her doomed rebound marriage – in the past.

'Andreas, can I go again?' asked a smaller boy in a T-shirt a few sizes too big, his expression pinched. 'Please!'

'What if your friends want another turn too?' he asked, propping his arms on his knees to bring his face down to the boy's level. 'We have to finish up soon.'

'It's my birthday!'

As Sophie watched, stunned, Andreas snatched the boy to him and gave him an enormous hug, following up with a thorough hair ruffle. That must be Toni's son. 'All right. Up you go.'

The smaller boy was obviously more proficient on the wall and scrambled up quickly enough that Andreas had to keep tugging the slack through the belay rope. He called up a few pointers, but his godson reached the top without too much help and let out a whoop.

The smile on Andreas's face was one Sophie had never seen before – tinged with pride and fear and utter bewilderment.

Just after the boy's rubber climbing shoes touched down on the gym floor, Andreas caught sight of her and the smile vanished. Without offering a greeting to her, he shooed the children back to their waiting parents and grasped the carabiner connecting his harness to the belay rope. But he paused before disconnecting it.

'You want to go up?' he called over to her.

She shook her head vehemently.

'Out of practice?'

'You could say that,' she called back, irritated by the weakness in her voice – in her knees – from the sight of him in gym clothes, wrangling a bunch of kids. She would never admit she hadn't touched a climbing wall since the last time he'd coached her on one. 'But I'm surprised,' she said, approaching slowly.

'Hmm?'

'You didn't use to like kids.'

'I still don't,' he claimed with an infuriating air of innocence.

'What was that, then?'

He pinned her with a look. 'One of those kids, I *love*. The other ones, I tolerated for his sake.'

The word 'love', emphasised in his rough voice, sent a shiver up her spine. But that sentence was all the more reason not to get caught up in this attraction again. There were precious few people Andreas Hinterdorfer loved and Sophie would never be one of them.

'That was more than tolerating,' she accused instead. 'You were great with those kids. They adored you. And you never went so easy on me.'

She regretted the words as soon as they came out of her mouth, hoping he wouldn't interpret them as a complaint that he'd never loved *her*. Two minutes in his company and she was already regressing to the insecure twenty-six-year-old she'd been.

His expression twisted into confusion and he opened his mouth to say something she didn't want to hear, so she made a quelling gesture and turned pointedly away, heading for the reception area. The dampened sound of climbing shoes on the springy floor followed her and she tensed.

'You needed me to be hard on you.'

'Oh, that's rich!' she said, whirling on him, but her consternation dissipated as soon as she caught sight of his face. The shimmer of regret she felt was mirrored there. She wished she couldn't see it, wanted to keep hold of the resentment that grew slipperier every time she saw him. 'That's an excuse,' she managed to say. She glanced away to find Ginny and Tita gawking at her.

Toni came to Sophie's rescue. 'That's Andreas,' she said, introducing him to Sophie's colleagues. 'He's a bit of a fixture here. And this is my son, Cillian.' The small boy who'd raced to the top of the wall squeezed into her side. 'He's just turned eight and celebrated with the party of his dreams.' She caught Andreas's gaze and they shared an eye-roll. 'Did you survive?' she asked in a mock whisper.

He just raised his eyebrows.

'I have to take Cillian home, but my parents are watching him tonight, so I'll meet you at the Admiral in a little bit,' Toni explained. 'Rhys, Kira and Laurie are probably already there. I don't think you've met Rhys and Laurie yet. Laurie is another of our guides and Rhys works with us occasionally as a photographer.'

Tita's eyes lit up.

'I'll get changed and meet you there,' Andreas said. It was difficult for Sophie to tell from his clipped tone whether he was talking to her or to the rest of the group. She felt a light grip around her upper arm – brief and hesitant, but when she turned to him, he was already several steps away, snatching a towel from the floor and heading for the changing rooms.

* * *

He must have looked even more grim than usual when he stepped over the threshold into the taproom at the Admiral. It was raining – again. Drops skidded down the leaded windows, making the fading evening light even weaker inside. He was hungry and restless, but mostly he was frustrated – with everything about that day.

Kira caught sight of him first, but her smile dulled as soon as she took in his expression. She stood, giving Laurie's shoulder a clasp and muttering something to the rest of the group as she hurried over. Slinging her arms around Andreas, she squeezed with her familiar tightness and he returned the hug, his expression reluctantly softening as his arms wrapped around her.

'What's up?' she asked, drawing back, but not letting go. He was vividly conscious of the proximity of her face, but not in the way he'd experienced it before – usually as a friend, occasionally closer. That day, his hair stood on end and he imagined – or felt – Sophie's gaze on the two of them, coming to her conclusions. Or was it wishful thinking that she was watching? If she were, she was probably just disapproving. He was nearly ten years older than Kira.

His head had been a mess ever since he'd walked into that meeting room and seen Sophie's face again after so many years. A clear head was one of the main requirements of his job and he was struggling to maintain one, haunted by her pinched expression, by the suggestion that everything that had gone wrong between them had been his fault. A lot of it had been, he would admit, but he'd thought she'd understood his dilemma. He hadn't meant to hurt her.

'A group of kids is enough to finish me for the day, but the pub with strangers afterwards?' He shuddered for effect, casually disengaging Kira's hands from his waist.

'You can escape to your remote mountains soon,' she reassured him, but then paused, shooting him with an assessing gaze. 'Do you want me to help you out with Sophie?'

He shook his head vehemently, then paused. 'What do you mean? What help do you think I need?'

'You could sit next to me. I'll keep you... occupied. She won't dare talk to you.'

His mouth opened to protest, but he stopped himself, embarrassment tingling over his skin. What could he say to that? He settled on, 'Sophie doesn't want to talk to me.'

'It doesn't look that way.'

The back of his neck burned, but he didn't dare look over at the rest of the group. He could still feel the shock of her statement in the gym: *You never went so easy on me.* While he'd showered, he'd agonised over why she'd said it, what she thought about their relationship. He hated agonising. There was a powerlessness to it that he couldn't cope with.

'She asked when you're flying out again, how long you usually stay in Weymouth these days.'

'If you're suggesting she's still interested in me, I can assure you it's not true,' he said with a dark laugh. 'She's probably hoping to avoid me as much as possible before we go to Italy.' Hoping to avoid talking about the past, as though that would mean not thinking about it either.

'She mentioned an ex-husband.'

'What?' He snapped his mouth shut when the word came out more loudly than he'd intended. His skin crawled at the thought of her married to someone else, but the idea of her divorced didn't improve his discomfort. Of course she would have got married. It had been eight years and she wasn't the one allergic to commitment. 'Who?'

Kira held up her hands. 'I don't know!' She studied him with a wary look. 'Is it *you* who wants to get back together?'

He gritted his teeth. '*Nobody* wants to get back together.' Scraping off his cap and running his hand over the back of his head, dreaming of a hundred-foot wall or, better yet, real granite beneath his fingers and nothing but air at his back, he breathed in and out through his nose and faced up to the truth. 'We just have some unfinished business.'

To his surprise, Kira smiled and whacked him on the arm.

'You think? God, your head is harder than rock. But the merger has happened. If you're so certain neither of you wants to start things up again, maybe you should clear the air?'

He *didn't* want to get back together with Sophie. Those few months with her had been the most intense relationship of his life, but they'd only proven he wasn't built for forever, especially since their paths had diverged so dramatically since. When Kira said, 'Clear the air,' all his hair stood on end and he wanted to run.

But unfortunately, Kira was right. He glanced in Sophie's direction, catching her eyes on him, although she dropped her gaze so quickly, he could have laughed. Colour blossomed on her cheeks. She looked so neat and untouchable, with her gold hoops and chic white blazer. He still wanted to touch her – to ruffle her hair and smear off some of her lipstick until he could see the woman she'd been back then, the woman he missed, even though he shouldn't. Whether she liked it or not, they had to talk.

6

The group was slightly too large for the booth. Ginny was wedged in at the back next to Tita, who was trying fruitlessly to engage the sullen photographer in conversation. He appeared to be a man of even fewer words than Andreas and he'd had no compunction about bursting Tita's bubble in the earliest moments of their acquaintance with his insistence that he wasn't a wedding photographer. He only photographed nature and never people, which Sophie couldn't help thinking was an indication of his opinion of humanity in general.

The other guide, a sandy-haired giant of a man called Laurie, whose upper arms were as thick as Ginny's thighs, had sensibly pilfered a chair and settled himself at the end of the table, rather than squashing those enormous shoulders in next to her. She couldn't tell if he was genuinely intrigued by the idea of working at weddings or if he was mocking them. His banter with Kira suggested the latter.

Sophie's first glass of wine went down a little too easily, even though she knew it wasn't smart to dull the awkwardness with alcohol. Conversation had split into two separate tranches –

climbing and weddings, with no natural crossover – and that was all before the main discomfiture of the evening was heralded by the arrival of Andreas.

She spent all her energy arranging her features to appear normal and forcing herself not to look at him. Of course she eventually did, summoning the frustration that had been simmering for six weeks. Even with a grim expression, he snared her gaze so completely until she found herself tracing the shape of his false smile and the lines at the corner of his eyes.

He looked very cosy with Kira, but she refused to feel anything about that – or at least, not to admit it. That Andreas Hinterdorfer had casual relationships with whoever was available wasn't new information. She forced her eyes away again.

She was staring into her glass, wondering if it was sensible to order another, when Andreas suddenly loomed close. Giving her a nudge that was far too casual – and still sent the nerves in her skin into overdrive – he said, 'Shuffle over?'

Blinking back surprise, she did as he rudely requested, tugging her wine glass with her as though it could protect her. He eyed her as he shrugged out of his quilted jacket. He was wearing a T-shirt underneath, despite the temperature hovering in single digits. When he leaned his forearms on the table, her eyes were drawn to the spiderweb of cords in the muscle, his large, rough hands and blunt fingertips, the nails worn down to stubs and pink sports tape wrapped around his forefinger.

Squashed as they were in the booth with the monosyllabic photographer, Andreas's shoulder pressed into hers, every thought flew from her brain except memories of the times she'd sat tucked under his arm while his friends conversed boisterously around them.

A waiter appeared to take their next drinks order and Sophie's throat was too thick to say anything, so she just clutched the stem of her glass as though she weren't finished. Andreas ordered an unsurprising espresso. His answer to everything was espresso.

'How's it going?' he murmured without looking at her, after the cup was placed in front of him, so tiny in his hands, it looked like a novelty item. She'd learned back then that climbers' bodies actually changed in response to their training. Andreas's prodigious forearms had developed over time to help keep him alive.

'Not exactly a house on fire,' she mumbled in response.

'Give it some time,' he said softly, bringing the cup to his lips and taking a sip.

Sophie couldn't resist eyeing him expectantly as he moved the scalding liquid over his tongue. When he set the cup down again with an accompanying grimace, she snorted a laugh.

'Still not used to coffee made in England?'

He eyed her. 'I keep hoping they'll make a decent one.' He frowned into the cup before knocking back the rest of it.

'Were you trying to reassure me that we'll turn this ragtag band into a wedding dream team just with a little time?' she prompted him sceptically.

'We?' was all he said in response.

She gritted her teeth. 'I— Me, then.' Of course there was no 'we'. She scratched one neat nail over the base of her wine glass, hoping, praying that one day she would no longer be such a wreck simply because Andreas Hinterdorfer was sitting next to her.

He turned his head and sighed, deeply enough that she felt the air moving over her blouse. 'I thought we needed to talk—'

'You thought? I need you to *stop* talking about it – the past.'

'But I can see it in your eyes every time you're thinking about... us.'

Her cheeks burned and she bit into her bottom lip while ferociously focusing on her wine glass to stem the urge to cry – or yell, or any of the emotional reactions that would undermine her much-needed professionalism.

'I thought I'd explained myself back then, Sophie. But if it's still difficult for you—'

'God, thank you *so much* for explaining my feelings to me!' She snapped her mouth shut when she noticed that all conversation around the table had died and there were four pairs of eyes glued to where she and Andreas were sparking dangerously. The photographer just stared awkwardly into his beer.

Andreas stood so suddenly, she had to steady herself and her hand caught, wedged between the back of the bench and his jeans-clad bottom. She hadn't needed to know that part of him was still rock-solid.

'We'll be back in a minute,' he said, groping for her hand and peeling it away from his jeans. Sophie was surprised his stomping footsteps didn't make the building shake. She might have resisted, especially since his hand was still curled around her wrist, except now she *did* want to talk – or she wanted to tell him where he could stuff his patronising bullshit. It was better that they weren't overheard.

But when he propelled her through the door of the pub, the cold breeze whipped some sense into her and she tugged her hand back. 'I left my jacket inside.'

He blinked at her as though he hadn't noticed he was outdoors in a T-shirt in the rain at the beginning of April. With a muttered curse made entirely of consonants, he started moving again, tugging her around to a side entrance and ushering her in with a furtive glance at where the others were sitting. Drawing her into a corner, he took a deep breath through his nose, standing far too close.

'I know eight years ago, everything went wrong,' he began, but Sophie had already had enough.

Leaning back against the wall, she looked away and grumbled, 'I asked you to marry me and you said no. It was a little more than everything going wrong.'

'The proposal came out of nowhere – the day before I was leaving for one of the biggest expeditions of my career! I don't know what you want to blame me for. Besides, I'd told you marriage wasn't for me – at least I thought I had.'

Sophie pressed her lips together, flinching at the reminder of how stupid she'd been. He was unfortunately right. He'd told her near the beginning of their relationship – quite baldly – that he didn't picture himself getting married, ever, and she'd still foolishly believed he might change his mind for her, for the connection she'd thought they'd shared.

'Perhaps the timing wasn't great, but you were leaving and I wasn't even sure if you'd come back to Weymouth!'

'Then maybe you should have asked me to come back to Weymouth instead of to *marry* you!'

The truth was she'd feared he'd say no to that too. Hindsight was sometimes a wonderful thing, but not when it showed her how little trust she'd truly had in the relationship. He'd never felt the same and in response, she'd only held on tighter.

With a shrug she hoped was convincingly casual, she said, 'Because you wouldn't have said yes to that either – or at least, if I had to ask you, then there was more wrong with the relationship than your aversion to marriage. That much at least I learned that day.'

Her pride had completed a long descent when his callous response dashed every hope she'd had for the relationship. *'Look, Sophie. You're a lovely girl and we've had a lot of fun, but that's not what this is about. I'm not that kind of guy. Maybe we should take a break for a while. You've spent a lot of your time this year hanging around me.'*

Like a crazed fan. Or a limpet. She'd never been so mortified.

'Do you want me to apologise? I thought I did enough of that eight years ago.'

'I don't want you to apologise. I want you to understand!' She crossed her arms, although not to protect herself from Andreas. He might harrumph and growl and speak in clipped, rasping sentences, but he was also ruthlessly in control of himself at all times. He had to be.

No, she was protecting herself from this conversation, from the truth that might spill out – truth about her own behaviour that she'd only begun to grasp with hindsight.

'What do you want me to understand?'

That was it – he'd cut straight to the heart of the matter, to her heart, as he always had. 'Me?' she tried, snapping her eyes shut for a moment when that wasn't quite the right answer. 'Yourself?'

'Shall we start with you?' His brow was so low and his eyes so close. 'I embarrass you – or your memories do. But I thought I told you then that you were right and I was wrong. If I was a better man, we'd be married right now.'

Oh, God. His words took the wind out of her.

'I didn't deserve you, Sophie.'

She forced air into her lungs, through her tingling nose. Ah, shit, on top of everything, now she wanted to cry. 'This is where I need you to understand yourself, Andreas,' she managed to say, although her voice wobbled.

'What?'

'You're just shifting blame. You hurt me, you let me believe our relationship was deeper than it was, but you don't want to admit it. It's not about *deserving*. You didn't want me.'

An Italian Wedding Adventure 57

'...Let you believe? What are you talking about? I explained why I couldn't marry you. I won't leave anyone behind. I was trying to spare you.'

He looked hurt at that – haunted, even. She shook her head to clear it, brushing back the lock of hair that fell into her face and ignoring the way his eyes followed the movement.

'Spare me? You broke up with me.'

'I didn't! I said we should take a break.'

She gave a disdainful eye-roll. 'You said no to marriage and then suggested we go on a break. Only an idiot would believe you meant just a break. You were trying to split up with me without taking any responsibility for my feelings – because you don't want to take responsibility for anyone else's feelings. Your "can't" marry me was an excuse too. You wanted to climb mountains and not worry about who you were coming home to. I remember you said that.'

'No, I mean, yes, you're right about taking responsibility for other people's feelings. I tried to explain, but perhaps you didn't understand, because you've never been... up there.'

'I did understand that you would only ever have your climbing and mountaineering relationships,' she said, pulling her arms tighter. 'That was clear.'

'Sophie!' he said sternly, her name this time a curse. 'That's not what I said then and it's not what I'm saying now. My family... it's bad enough with them, but with you...'

Her mind and heart pulled in two directions, but she had to keep her wits about her and ignore the consternation in his expression. 'Perhaps if you could talk in full sentences,' she said, proud of herself for remaining calm. 'And I never met your family, as you know. How would I understand what you mean?'

He swiped his fingers over his mouth, staring at the ceiling for a moment, but when he gathered himself enough to speak, his voice was calm, low and full of conviction. 'It wasn't about you. I take risks. I have to. I don't know how to be another way. And that's not fair to... the people who mean something to me. I can't take those risks for other people, only for myself. To me, the only logical course of action is to refuse commitment.'

The shadow over his features made her think of Miro, of how Andreas's friend had died mere weeks after that disastrous conversation, leaving Toni to give birth and raise their child alone.

'I do understand why you think that,' she began. This time, the tightening of her arms around herself was to stop her reaching a hand out to him as she would have done in another time. 'But we can't choose. I couldn't just switch off my feelings because you wanted to climb a mountain and you...' She dropped her gaze. 'You've made an exception for Cillian, but you wouldn't for me. You just didn't love me, and that is okay. It just hurts... I mean it used to hurt.'

7

If Andreas had needed a reminder of why being in the same room as Sophie was agony, he had it.

You just didn't love me...

What could he say to that? That he had wanted to – so badly? That he thought he probably could have – at least better than whatever Orschkopf she'd married. At one time, he'd even thought he could make it work with Sophie, as stupid as that sounded to him now.

His mind spun with the mess of pride and hurt from the day he'd said goodbye to her – and the day weeks later when he'd realised it truly had been the end.

Damn it, this woman turned him into a reckless fool and reckless fools had no place on a mountain.

So, he swallowed deeply and said nothing, even though he'd never seen her look as compelling as she did in that moment, her lips pressed tightly together and her make-up wearing off to show the pale freckles on her nose.

'I'm sorry,' he whispered – an apology that solved nothing. Her doubtful gaze told him she knew it. He leaned one shoulder against the wall next to her, lifting a hand hesitantly to smooth a strand of hair back. The small touch quelled the agony – at least for a moment.

'What do we do now?' she asked.

'We build you an adventure wedding file.' It was the easy answer. 'And try to be friends.'

'Try? Why couldn't we be friends?'

The consternation in her expression made him smile. He brushed his thumb along her cheek, drifting for the merest second to her lower lip. The way her breath stalled proved his point. No matter how much the past bothered both of them, the pull between them was still alive.

She lifted her chin, the slightest movement, but he saw it, recognised the invitation – the challenge – was desperate to take it. He came closer, each breath heady with memories of a softer, gentler time in his life. But he tipped up his head and pressed a kiss to her forehead instead.

He felt her sway in his direction, her eyes slamming closed, but at least he'd avoided tumbling headfirst back into the intimacy that had ruined them before. She wanted a different life. She wanted marriage, a partner, and repeating history would get them nowhere.

'We'll try to be friends,' he repeated.

She opened her mouth to say something, but a loud buzzing stopped her. Pulling her phone out of her pocket with a frown, she glanced at him apologetically and connected the call, slipping out from under his arm and making him realise how close he'd been standing.

'Rory? What's up?' she answered, turning pointedly away.

Andreas glanced at her out of the corner of his eye. *Rory*. The name reminded him of Rory Brent, the guy from the Sardinia trip where Sophie and Andreas had first met.

'Yes, that should be fine. Just leave food and water for her, because I won't be back until later tonight.' She paused, listening. 'I said it's okay, don't worry. I'm at home until Monday, so I can have her.'

Her?

'Have a good time. I'll see you later.' She disconnected the call swiftly and he didn't quite have time to look away. Her cheeks went pink. 'My dog,' she blurted out in explanation. 'I have to take Betsy from...'

He lifted his brow, wishing he wasn't holding his breath for her answer. Surely it wasn't the same Rory. That would be... significant in a way he didn't want to think about.

She blew out a breath. 'We share custody of the dog,' she said with a dark smile he didn't like. 'My ex-husband and I.' He watched her swallow and then she headed for the rest of the group around the corner.

Grasping her arm, he stopped her. 'Rory?'

When she only nodded, avoiding his gaze, his stomach pitched and sank. It shouldn't have made any difference who she'd married – whoever it was would have been a loser to let her go – but the fact that it might be that stubborn, supercilious Mistkerl, the fact that it might be someone he knew, made him sick.

'You married Rory Brent?' He couldn't quite stop the rather hysterical laugh that emerged from his throat. He waited – hoped – for her to deny it.

'I could have married Mickey Mouse and it wouldn't affect you. You turned me down, remember.'

It damn well did affect him. He just wasn't sure why. 'But... he was such an idiot on those trips.'

'He was *jealous*, which I understand. He was interested in me and I was a lovesick fool over you at the beginning.' Turning away, she fiddled with the clasp of the chain that hung around her neck.

God, she'd been a sweet fool at the beginning. He couldn't think about it without his heart hurting. She'd laughed at his terrible jokes and looked at him as though he could hang the moon and he wished he'd never had to hurt her.

But as much as that, he wished she'd never married Rory Brent.

'*I* should have married you, if only to stop you ever imagining he was the right guy for you!' he growled.

'You're unbelievable, Andreas!' she bit out. 'Feelings are off limits, but locking horns in a stupid contest with another guy is fine? You're just as bad as Rory turned out to be! Maybe you're right, being friends is going to be a stretch, but not because you're so bloody irresistible. You have no clue about how to be a human being!'

She turned and walked away with a toss of her head that sent ripples through him. He stood rocking on his heels for a moment after she disappeared around the corner, knowing he'd deserved every word.

When he reluctantly followed in her footsteps, he found Kira eyeing him with a pointed gaze. All he could do was shrug. He'd screwed up – again. He always seemed to screw up with Sophie.

He had to make sure the trip in May was a success, for her sake, but also for Willard's, for the merger that was his last chance to save the business his friend had spent fifteen years building. If they had to do a few weddings to stay afloat, that was a fair price to pay for the downturn in expedition bookings.

Maybe he'd get a chance to make it up to Sophie.

* * *

Sophie was thankful that the new team of Great Heart Adventure Weddings didn't quite get on. No one wanted to stay after they'd eaten their toads in holes or their fish and chips and Sophie bundled herself into the back seat of Ginny's car with her head still in a fog.

Her coworker didn't even wait until she'd left the car park. 'All right, Soph. Those were some of the weirdest vibes I've ever felt. Spit the whole story – and don't skimp on the details!' she instructed as she closed the driver's side door.

Through the windscreen, Sophie's gaze snagged on the shadowy figures of Andreas and Kira near the rusty old Land Rover and her voice failed her. Despite the fruity white wine she'd just finished, there was a sour taste in her mouth. Kira was welcome to him, but the conversation before dinner had scratched open a wound.

She should look away before whatever she saw stabbed the knife further into her pride, but part of her needed the blow. As long as her skin still prickled and her lungs ached in his presence, as long as that wanting still sprang up, out of her control, she'd be in danger of believing a relationship between them might work. Perhaps she should be glad he'd ruined the fragile truce by laughing at her for marrying someone who had claimed to love her – even if that marriage had turned out to be a disaster.

Sophie was a wedding planner, after all. She peddled dreams and hope and if anyone had the ability to quash those dreams for good, it was Andreas Hinterdorfer. It beggared belief how someone with no clue about emotions could so thoroughly manipulate hers. No wonder she'd married—

Nooo. She'd had more than enough of her past mistakes tonight.

So she forced her eyes wide open and waited to see her ex

kiss another woman. But when Andreas turned to Kira, all he did was cross his arms and lean heavily on the old paintwork. With a small shake of his head, he gave Kira's shoulder a squeeze and then he did kiss her – a light press of his lips to her forehead that flashed through Sophie with something other than the hurt and disgust she needed to keep him out of her heart.

It was the memory of him doing the same to her an hour earlier. It seemed two women had wanted to kiss him tonight and he'd put both of them off with a friendly – and absurdly tender – kiss on the forehead.

The rush of embarrassment up to her hairline was a familiar sensation.

Ginny started the car and the headlights flooded the scene with harsh light. Kira was already walking away, her hand raised in a wave, and Andreas flinched, shielding his eyes. The idiot hadn't even put his coat back on and the light showed up all the furrows of his prodigious muscles.

'The forearms do not maketh the man,' Sophie muttered – not quietly enough, because Tita turned to her from where she sat in the passenger seat.

'But those are not forearms. They are art!'

Ginny snorted a laugh. 'Sophie was not appreciating them aesthetically. He's an ex, right? Before or after Rory? And just how ex-y is he really? Looks like it's not all in the past.'

'Very ex-y,' she insisted through gritted teeth, refusing her brain's request to add an 's' on the front. 'From before Rory. It was a long time ago and it wasn't serious.'

'Really? Andreas looks like he does everything seriously,' Ginny said as she steered out of the car park and away so Sophie could breathe again.

'Not me,' she said emphatically.

'He didn't do you seriously?' Ginny clarified with a wink.

'Oh, shut up,' Sophie grumbled.

'If the colour of her cheeks is anything to go by, he did that part very seriously!' Tita gave her a less-than-subtle thumbs-up.

'Given the way he was looking at you, I think he might still be seriously interested.'

'Ginny! We are a wedding planning agency, not a dating app.'

'Yeah, we're single women who plan other people's weddings,' Ginny said with a dismayed smile. 'Although I suppose at least you got married once.'

Yes, in a small ceremony at the town hall with only his parents in attendance – another reason thinking of Rory always ended with a stab of grief. She didn't need Ginny to remind her of what a joke of a wedding planner she was.

'As the only married one at I Do, I think after everything that happened with Rory, it might do you good to hit the sheets with a gorgeous guy who stares at you as though you're Princess Diana,' Tita said.

'Not Princess Diana! Tita, how old are you? Sophie deserves a guy who looks at her as though she's chocolate cake!'

'I'm not really happy with either of those metaphors,' Sophie mumbled.

'Do Italians like chocolate cake? Maybe he looks at you the way he'd look at cannoli. Mmm,' Ginny licked her lips, touching on the subtle gold piercing below the bottom one. She had a notorious sweet tooth. 'I love cannoli.'

'Andreas doesn't eat cannoli,' Sophie corrected her grumpily.

'What does he eat? Whatever he loves to eat, that's the way he was looking at you.'

'He was not! He eats instant calories out of tins as far away from civilisation as he can get. And besides, he's from the German-speaking part, which means he would have been looking at me like...' She took a second to remember the name of the dumplings he'd insisted were the food of the gods in the typically parochial fashion of a person from a small place. 'Knödel,' she said with a snort of laughter, the name even funnier than she'd remembered. 'That would mean he was looking at me as though I were a Knödel, a big dumpling.'

'That's kind of sweet,' Ginny continued, undeterred. 'He could call you "dumpling". Maybe you'd end up getting married and—'

'I am *not* going to marry Andreas! For God's sake! I was young and stupid enough to suggest that once and then I never saw him again!'

She caught herself abruptly, the heavy silence confirming that she'd revealed too much.

Ginny found her voice first. 'And you have to work with him now? On a *wedding*?' she squeaked.

Sophie buried her face in her hands and wished she could skip ahead a few months, and get Andreas back into her past.

When Ginny continued, her tone was wary. 'Soph, I didn't mean to upset you. I was teasing. I didn't know he popped your heartbreak cherry.'

'He didn't pop my— That is a stupid expression. He didn't break my heart,' she insisted. 'It was all a long time ago. I've been married and divorced since.' And she'd lost a lot more than just a husband, although she'd never wait around for Andreas's reaction to *that* news. 'I am perfectly capable of dealing with this calmly and maturely – and professionally.'

Ginny and Tita nodded, the older woman reaching back to squeeze Sophie's knee.

'But, you know, a little... Knödelling in Italy wouldn't hurt—'

'This is the last time I tell you two anything!'

There would be no Knödelling with Andreas, under any circumstances.

8

On her arrival in Italy at the end of May, Sophie found her professionalism tested numerous times in just the first few minutes. Before she'd even entered the arrivals hall at Verona airport late in the afternoon, memories – mostly of previous Knödelling – assailed her.

She'd been here once to visit Andreas. He'd been late to collect her and when he'd finally swung by in his old Fiat Panda, she'd still been stupidly happy to see him. Any aggravation had disappeared when she'd caught sight of him in a worn leather jacket, peering up with a wide smile just for her. Then he'd kissed her for long enough that they'd nearly outstayed the short-term parking limit.

In hindsight, she could see there was something desperate in his affection. He'd always known there were limits to their relationship. Sophie had still stupidly thought they might cross the lines together and find a solution. She just wished she could switch off the shivers up her spine when she remembered the feel of his hand on the back of her neck as he kissed her.

She'd flown into Verona several times since then. Italy was

perennially popular with her clients for its great food, charming locations for photoshoots and comparatively straightforward bureaucracy around tying the knot. But that morning, Sophie's cynicism – usually kept well under control in the face of her clients' starry-eyed optimism – was flaring and she could only see the questionable symbolism of marrying in the city that was famous for a pair of star-crossed lovers who came to a tragic – and foolish – end.

The words 'tragic' and 'foolish' drew far too many parallels with the last time Andreas had met her here. They'd had several weeks apart, talking on the phone every day – Sophie had always been the one to call, it mortified her to remember – and then she'd taken a few days off work to visit him.

She'd been starry-eyed herself, but she'd also been wrong. She'd imagined him taking her to his home – his real home, not the room he kept at Miro and Toni's – introducing her to his parents and to the mountainous places that were part of him.

None of that had happened. Sophie had never even once set foot in South Tyrol. Andreas had picked her up from the airport and taken her hiking and climbing in the Veneto Dolomites. She hadn't had time to be disappointed, because every view had been spectacular and every day gruelling, since Andreas didn't do anything outdoors by halves. And at night, he'd wrapped his arms around her in the tiny tent he'd carried for them and she'd almost managed to forget she'd wanted an insight into the rest of his life and not just another spectacular adventure.

Now, she was only interested in the adventure – involving a summit cross where her clients could promise their lives to each other while Sophie resisted thinking about everything in her own life that had turned out differently from how she'd expected.

Holding her breath, trying not to wonder whether Andreas

would smile for her, she sailed through the sliding doors and into the arrivals hall. Sophie's eyes found him before he saw her. Although his baseball cap hid the grey highlights peppered through his hair, he still looked strikingly older than he had that autumn day nearly nine years ago. His face was weathered and freckled and she pictured him for a moment as an old man, growing to resemble his stony mountains – and just as quiet.

But neither the evidence that he'd recently turned forty nor Sophie's strange mental image could reduce the inviting picture he made, staring off to one side lost in thought, his hands stuffed into the pockets of his jacket – *that* jacket.

When he glanced over and saw her, he did smile, but there was none of the brightness of the last time he'd collected her here. She knew she looked different too. She'd had her hair styled in a long, layered bob and her fitted dress was one of her favourites for work.

Her heels clicked on the tiles as she approached and he met her in the middle. She clutched the handle of her suitcase as her mind raced, wondering how they were supposed to greet each other. He hesitated with the barest glance at her outfit, before grasping her upper arm and pressing a kiss to her cheek.

'Benvenuta in bella Italia, Sophie,' he said, his voice textured and rough even when he welcomed her in Italian.

'Grazie,' she thanked him with an uncertain look. 'Or should I say "Danke"?' She still didn't quite understand the dynamic between his two languages. He said German was his mother tongue, but she'd rarely heard him speak it and he seemed entirely comfortable with Italian.

He didn't answer – perhaps he'd thought the question was rhetorical – and she followed him uneasily outside after he'd snatched the handle of her case. She paused, nonplussed, when he led her to the same old Panda, the khaki paintwork even more faded.

'There might be a bit of mud on the seat.'

Hoping he wasn't serious, she settled gingerly on the passenger side while he rummaged in the boot to make space for her suitcase amongst his usual collection of dirty boots and pristine ropes. She breathed a sigh of relief when the car started on the first try.

'It still works,' he rumbled carelessly. 'Still got power steering.' He shrugged out of his jacket before grasping the gear stick and shoving it into reverse, making Sophie jerk her gaze up when she caught herself watching the play of bone and ligament and muscle in his arm.

'I suppose I've been doing weddings for too long,' she said, keeping her gaze strictly forward. 'Most couples want a Ferrari here. I have a list of hire companies.'

'Vintage cabrio?' he asked with a chuckle. 'Or would that blow away the veil? Just make sure they don't stop to take photos on the Stelvio Pass. They might never make it all the way up.'

'I did have one couple who wanted to take photos up there, but it was in spring and when they discovered how much snow was left, they decided on Verona instead.'

'I don't suppose the same might happen with your current clients?'

'There won't be any snow around Lake Garda in September,' Sophie said drily. She peered at him. 'You're still sceptical about their plan to get married on a mountain summit?'

'Do you remember when we went hiking near Cortina?' he asked instead of answering.

Sophie resisted rolling her eyes. 'I'm not likely to forget.' As much as she might want to.

'We did the via ferrata Marino Bianchi.'

If she closed her eyes, she could still picture the dizzying drops, the grey limestone peaks that dominated the equipped climbing route. She could hear the clink of the safety equipment and feel the steel cable of the via ferrata – 'iron way' in Italian – under her hands.

Andreas continued, 'I still remember the look on your face when you reached the top of the Cima di Mezzo.'

Sophie hoped he was concentrating on the road, because the multi-lane highway and the toll gates all disappeared from her vision. She was lost in memories of how it had felt to stand on that crag and know she'd hauled herself up, fought gravity literally with all her muscles, with her fingernails and her determination. She'd floated on the crisp air and the sunlight, as though she'd just discovered a new dimension to life and to herself.

'Can you imagine reaching the top and then *marrying* someone?' Andreas snapped, sending Sophie's thoughts crashing back down.

Actually... she could imagine it. And somehow, the only groom she could imagine in that picture was Andreas.

'The bride isn't planning to do a via ferrata in a wedding dress. You won't have to lug the champagne to the top in a cool bag or produce a violin quartet out of your pocket!'

'No, because I'll be long gone by the time they actually get married!' he said, his voice irritatingly light. 'I can just about bring myself to help you find them a place.'

Sophie gritted her teeth. 'I know you'll never get married and don't appreciate the idea of combining a wedding and challenging sports, but surely you can appreciate the parallels. It's all about the big feelings; getting married is a moment of adrenaline too, a destination and the continuation of that journey along the same path. There's symbolism that you should grasp at least intellectually, if you're incapable of appreciating it emotionally.'

He was silent for a moment, his hand gripping the worn vinyl of the steering wheel tightly. 'I can see why you're a good marriage celebrant,' he said eventually. 'If the couples need one last pep talk, you're there to convince them to take the plunge.'

'I do no such thing,' she retorted. 'If someone doesn't want to get married, then nothing I say is going to change their mind – as *you* well know!' She took a deep breath. 'It's not my job to convince people to get married.'

'But your livelihood does depend on it.'

'I wouldn't make comments about my livelihood when yours seems a little tenuous. And I don't know why *you're* criticising *me*. It's been barely half an hour and we've degenerated to this already,' she mumbled at the end.

'What did you expect when you roped me into helping with your wedding research?'

'I thought we'd cleared the air – somewhat at least.'

His injured tone put her off-balance. She still didn't understand why he seemed to resent her for asking him to marry her. He hadn't lost anything by her asking.

'Yes, we cleared the air but it doesn't mean I'm going to cry at their wedding. I'll show you around different places so you can do your research, take your photos. Kira and I can plan the hen and bachelor parties, but the ceremony is your thing. I don't have to like it.'

Sophie blew a long breath out through thinned lips. 'Fine. That's fair.'

She stared out of the window, seeing only streaks of green and the ribbon of the grey road. Hopefully, his disparaging remarks would be the nail in the coffin of this old attraction and she might find some much-needed closure.

'You said the Great Heart accommodation is in Brenzone?' she asked, changing the subject. 'That's about an hour from the reception venue. Kira and whichever other guide we have during the wedding might be able to stay there, but I'll have to sleep at the venue.'

'They're having a normal reception?'

'Since she can't have the nice dress for the ceremony, we've planned a traditional wedding reception. That's my area of expertise, don't worry. I'll need to drop by the venue at some stage, but I can hire a car and go alone.'

'I can be a taxi service.'

'At your mountain-guide rates? You've just taken great pains to remind me how much you hate weddings. You don't have to chaperone me around the lake. If there's a kettle in my room, you won't even need to see much of me.'

He didn't respond, but the bob of his throat suggested he was working up to saying something – probably something she wouldn't like. 'About the accommodation…'

'Oh, God, don't tell me. Is it bunk beds? I knew when you said we should stay at the Great Heart property that there would be a catch.'

'No catch. It's a small place – two bedrooms and a kitchen-diner. We usually use it for the guides before and after a trip, rather than clients, but… when I said it was Great Heart accommodation, that wasn't quite true. The place belongs to my family. My grandparents bought it.'

'To go on holiday? I thought your family didn't like leaving South Tyrol.'

He eyed her. 'They like to come to the water where it's a little warmer.'

'So it's not free accommodation then? You give us mates rates or something?'

'No, I don't charge,' he said with a vehement shake of his head. 'We don't rent out the apartment at all. It's usually sitting empty.'

She stared at him, perplexed. 'Why?'

When he didn't immediately answer, she suspected there was more bad news.

'It's in an old building. It needs renovation, but none of us can afford it, so...' He shuffled in his seat, taking a hairpin curve with practised hands. 'It's liveable. It's fine, just don't expect a nice hotel.'

'I didn't,' she insisted. 'But you should charge. You're not only working for Willard now.'

'Just wait until you see the place.'

She shook her head. 'It doesn't matter what—' The Panda had trundled around another hairpin curve and Sophie's words trailed off. Tall, narrow cypress trees swished past the windows, interspersed with stone pines. Rhododendrons tumbled over the chain-link fence at the side of the road, blooming vivid red. Clay rooftiles baked in the afternoon sun with a little haze that suggested warm temperatures for late May.

But it was the view that forced air into the deepest bronchioles of her lungs, that loosened the muscles in her forehead.

She sighed. 'I always forget.'

'Forget what?'

'How beautiful it is here,' she said with a smile.

Swerving hard, Andreas brought the car to a sudden standstill in a lay-by. Flung forward against her seatbelt, Sophie floundered for purchase against the dashboard, but when she'd steadied herself and given him a sharp look, she remained leaning forward, peering through the windscreen as he turned off the engine.

The lake was wide at the southern end, blue-green water rippling lightly, stretching out under a sky streaked with frothy clouds. Mountains rose into view on the other side, growing higher and craggier to the north, where the ground had been crinkled and concertinaed into incredible shapes over the aeons.

Glancing at Andreas, she found him following her gaze, one arm propped on the steering wheel. As usual, she couldn't read his expression.

'I suppose you come here all the time,' she prompted.

His only answer was a small nod.

'And the views are better at home anyway?'

'The views are better from higher up,' he said after a pause.

Their conversation from the pub back in April came alive between them again. He lived for altitude and adventure. She organised weddings. The gulf between them couldn't be spanned by a simple suspension bridge.

'But I forgot how beautiful it is too,' he said, his voice rough. Turning away with a deep breath, he started the car and backed it out, his arm draped over the passenger seat as he watched for traffic over his shoulder.

Sophie didn't move, his words echoing unexpectedly between her ribs. The proximity of his hand to her neck was palpable. She stared straight ahead as he reversed the car onto the road and drew his hand away, but not before the backs of his fingers whispered over her nape.

She must have imagined it.

9

Andreas noticed that Sophie was trying to keep her expression carefully cool as he led her up the cobbled lane from where he'd parked the car, but her eyes lit up as she took in the crumbling stone walls, the wooden shutters and the planters bursting with spring flowers on every doorstep and windowsill. With the heat from the lake at his back, he was far from the crisp air and wooden gables of home, even though the run-down cabin where he lived most of the time was only two hours away by car.

He probably hadn't needed to warn her about the state of the apartment. No matter how she looked these days, she'd slept in her share of tents at one time. But when he led her up the tiled steps, unease shivered through him, as though he were letting her into more than just his grandparents' holiday apartment.

Through the small front hall, they emerged directly into the kitchen diner, the heart of the place, with its open fire and exposed beams. The cabinet and dining table were of old, scratched wood, heavy and solid – farmhouse furniture from long-dead relatives. Her footsteps made muted clicks on the

An Italian Wedding Adventure

ceramic tiles and she gazed around her – curiously, without judgement – and that was almost worse. He wondered what she'd find of him here and wished he didn't care.

She'd changed a lot since they'd been together. Her hair was shorter, her face sharper – her expressions much sharper. The chic outfits were new, too, although he'd rarely seen her at work back then. He preferred smudged outdoor gear. Then he didn't have to worry about getting her dirty.

Her cream linen-blend blouse was a perfect reminder that he couldn't touch her now anyway.

Forcing his eyes off her for the hundredth time since he'd picked her up, he strode across the kitchen to wash his hands at the farmhouse-style sink, indicating her bedroom, through the door to the right.

'Take as long as you want to settle in and then we can get some dinner,' he said over his shoulder. 'I've got the weather forecast for the week. We can discuss what you need to do.'

'I'm not sure I have the energy for more arguments.' She spoke quietly, her voice muffled by the distance between where Andreas stood and where she'd disappeared into her room.

'I didn't say anything about arguments!' Cutting himself off with a huff when he realised he was energetically disagreeing with her again, he continued more mildly, 'I promise not to take my cynicism out on you any more.'

She appeared in the doorway. 'We don't have to work over dinner – and you don't have to take me to dinner. I'm used to being on business trips alone or in charge of everyone else. Then you don't have to pack away your mood to spare me. I'm sure you'll be sick of weddings by the time we're done.'

He studied her for a moment. 'I'm sorry for what I said in the car. I am trying.' *I want to take you to dinner. I'm happy to see you.*

You look stunning in that outfit. I like your haircut. I like the way you said you're usually in charge. 'And there are only two restaurants in this town, so chances are we'd run into each other anyway.'

She blinked at him for long enough that he felt heat rush up his neck. 'That really *would* be awkward,' she muttered.

The warmth of the day was still hovering over the lake when he led the way down the steep, winding lane to Via Marniga, the main street, such as it was. He felt somewhat at home here, far from the bustling towns of Riva and Garda where throngs of tourists flocked to the waterfront. Brenzone was the name of a cluster of small villages clinging to the hillside on the eastern bank of the lake and this one, Marniga, was barely on the map.

The town was little more than a few cobbled streets, a cluster of multicoloured buildings scattered with cypress trees and tucked into olive groves, with the slopes of the Monte Baldo massif rising behind. Residents strung their washing from the upper windows and the lanes were too narrow for cars to pass.

'Where do you usually stay in this area?' he asked.

'At the same hotel as the wedding party. We've held weddings in Sirmione and Limone sul Garda, as well as a couple in the Valpolicella region and one in Verona itself. I do know the area quite well, just not the...'

'Interesting bits,' he completed for her, with a quick lift of his eyebrows to indicate he was joking.

The restaurateur greeted him with a warm handshake. 'Good to see you again, Andreas!' he exclaimed in German with a hint of an Italian accent. 'Is it business or pleasure tonight?' he asked in a low voice as Sophie drifted towards the terrace with its wide view over the lake, the sun shooting colours across the sky as it set.

'Business.'

An Italian Wedding Adventure

'Che peccato, my friend,' he said with a chuckle. 'Such a shame your colleagues are always so beautiful.'

Andreas grimaced, remembering that he'd come here with Kira several times over the past few years. But the owner thankfully said nothing as he went to sit down. It was early for an Italian dinner, but at least the temperature was still mild enough to sit outside on a spring evening.

Sophie ordered a glass of Valpolicella and the owner disappeared again, leaving only the two of them and the familiar sensation that he'd never worked out how to do romantic dinners. Not that this was romantic.

'You didn't order anything?' she asked.

He just gave her a smile and blew out the candle on the table, moving it aside to unfold the map he'd brought with him. Best stick to business. 'I've marked several summits on here, but we'll need to narrow it down to the ones most likely to be what you want.'

The restaurant owner reappeared with two glasses of red wine. 'Your schiava,' he said pointedly.

'Grazie,' Andreas replied, exaggerating the pronunciation of the Italian. At Sophie's curious look, he explained, 'This is what we call Vernatsch. It's quite unusual to find it outside of South Tyrol or labelled in Italian, but this one is both. It's my usual order, since he doesn't stock any St Magdalener.'

'You don't want to try a local variety?'

'No. Why?'

'Are you going to order Knödel too?'

'He doesn't serve Knödel,' Andreas grumbled. 'If he did, I would order it – or maybe not, because I'm certain the chef wouldn't get it right.'

'It needs a certain tang of alpine meadows in the butter, does it?' The smile that touched her lips drew his eyes.

'That's it exactly,' he quipped, wrenching his gaze back up.

They each ordered a single course and dessert and then Andreas raised his wine, prompting her with a lift of his eyebrows until she tapped her glass against his.

'I can't believe you,' she began lightly. 'How many continents have you travelled to and you're secretly a homebody?'

'I'm not a homebody,' he insisted. 'I just know where to find the best food and wine.' He stuck out his chin.

'Ah, I see.' She took another sip, watching him with a look he wasn't sure was meant to be provoking, but definitely was.

He could only hold out about a second. 'What do you see?'

She leaned across the table and whispered, 'It's pride.'

He fiddled with his glass to distract himself from her lips and the itch over his skin, as though they were flirting. He was certain that wasn't what she meant to do, but given their history, his brain kept taking him in that direction. That and her face was a masterpiece of dips and curves in the evening light, the differences between this Sophie and the Sophie from eight years ago – *his* Sophie – subtle and tantalising.

'To be honest, it's probably a little of both,' he mumbled. 'I... appreciate familiarity.'

'I remember the octopus salad in Sardinia, after we got back from the four-day hike. You looked green when I offered to share.'

'You offered me a tentacle.'

'And you rather rudely refused,' she countered. 'I thought I'd been getting... you know, "vibes" from you for a few days. You were sitting so close, but then you were grossed out. I thought I'd misread you.'

The hair on the back of his neck stood on end. 'You still kissed me later that night.' A kiss that had haunted him with its sweetness.

She froze, as though she hadn't expected him to continue the story – or as though she'd forgotten that the tentacle had been a strange preamble to their first kiss. After ten days of trying to ignore her while he led the group, telling himself there couldn't be anything so special about the back of her neck that he kept wanting to touch her there, as soon as she'd lifted her mouth to his, he hadn't wanted to stop.

So they hadn't stopped. Andreas had never been so thankful for a private leader's cabin at that camping ground. By the time they'd emerged the following morning, he'd discovered just how heady it was to touch her – and all the places that made her feel good.

Including the pulse point under her jaw, the one that was fluttering right now. She swallowed heavily and he didn't dare glance up. He focused on the collar of her linen shirt to remind himself that this was wedding-planner Sophie, not lightly sunburnt, infectiously cheerful Sophie.

He'd missed that chance...

She cleared her throat, a small, neat sound that nevertheless held a hint of the same potent memories. 'I'm surprised you let me, given I'd just been eating octopus salad.' She forced a laugh and took a long sip of her wine. 'Tentacle kisses.'

He snorted his wine, spluttering a cough. 'That wasn't necessary,' he said with a pained sigh. 'I had fond memories of those kisses, but apparently I'd forgotten about your bizarre sense of humour.'

'Bizarre? Mine? You used to joke about people falling off cliffs and if that's not poor taste...'

Sitting back in his chair and crossing his arms, he said, 'Dark humour is a self-preservation tactic.'

'You didn't think weird humour might be as well?'

He stilled, his mind racing as he watched her across the

table. He suspected he knew what she was protecting herself from. Dinner together had been a bad idea. Sitting across the table from each other, talking while avoiding the many topics that would lead them into trouble, was exhausting.

A waitress arrived with their mains, bringing the scent of spring onions and fresh fish to tease his nose and trigger his appetite, but he only reluctantly cleared away the map that lay ignored between them. It wouldn't be wise, but he wanted to keep wallowing in the memories – make her remember.

He wanted to make her regret – even if it was only for a moment – giving up on him, on *them*. But, God, that was selfish. He'd pushed her towards the exit and even though he'd had a wobble after he got back from Gasherbrum, the fact remained that he still couldn't give her what she really wanted.

Marriage. Maybe a family. At the very least a partner who put her first and came home to her. Whatever she'd been looking for with Rory Brent.

His thoughts must have shown on his face, because she eyed him before swiping her wine glass and taking a deep sip. 'Buon appetito,' she mumbled, picking up her knife and fork and flaying her lasagne with gusto.

Taking his time, he tucked his serviette into his collar and sliced his first piece of fish. 'Guadn,' he replied mildly in Tyrolean.

They managed to eat silently for several minutes, but he could see Sophie getting fidgety with no safe topic of conversation. In the past, she would have asked him about the word he'd said, peppered him with questions about home and his family – which he'd answered cagily, because the combination of Sophie and his family had felt like walls closing in on him.

But this time, when she finally gave in and opened a new topic, it wasn't what he'd expected. 'Do you want to tell me about the peaks? Lily and Roman are quite keen on one with a cross to mark the summit.'

Lily and Roman? Ah, right. The bride and groom. The reason he was here. A safe topic of conversation. They had business to discuss. He was *not* here to remember little details about Sophie that would drive him crazy while he lay in bed that night.

10

Sophie had thought talking about the end of their relationship had been mortifying enough, but when Andreas had sat calmly across from her and mentioned their first kiss? She was still squirming.

She'd been so naïve back then, pursuing him, believing her feelings meant great things, when they'd been blurred by adrenaline and hormones. But that kiss had been a decisive moment in her life; the way she'd combusted with him had shocked her, like waking up. She might have pursued him first, but he'd responded with vehemence and everything about that night had been more than she'd bargained for – more than she'd been ready for, although she hadn't realised that at the time.

Perhaps everyone felt as though they would burst the first time they fell in love. Sophie couldn't picture herself doing anything like that again, no matter how attractive Andreas still looked across the table from her.

She forced herself to pay attention to what he was saying – to the wedding plans – not the slant of his mouth as he spoke or his rough, clipped voice.

'Not all summits have crosses, but many do. How big will the wedding party be and how long will they need to stay up there?'

'I don't have the final numbers, but we're looking at fifteen to twenty people, about six each at the hen do and the bachelor party. Four parents, all very fit and mobile apparently. *Not* Aunt Frieda,' she added, one more awkward joke to try to keep her on an even keel.

'If they have to get up and back in a day, plus all of the... not-marriage stuff—'

'You mean the vows? The commitment ceremony?'

'Is that seriously what you call it?' he asked, his voice high. 'It sounds like a ritual that might involve blood – or lawyers.'

'Usually, I just call it a wedding,' she said witheringly.

'Fine, but stopping for a wedding in the middle of a trek...' He cleared his throat. 'I still can't believe what I'm saying.'

'I still don't know what your point is.'

He glanced up with an amused glint in his eye. 'Even if Aunt Frieda isn't coming, a long hike is going to be too complicated.'

'As I understand it, they're after that sense of achievement to mark the occasion. If I suggest a nice Sunday walk, it's not going to be what they want. They mentioned they climb too.'

His expression was pained. 'All right. What condition are you in?'

'What do you mean?' She drew back defensively.

'Physically. What can you handle? If we want to tick off a couple of summits a day, I need to know how fit you are.'

Not as fit as she'd been eight years ago, that was certain. 'I can walk all day.'

'Speed? How much altitude gain?'

'I have no idea,' she bit out. 'I don't hike much any more.' She didn't like the wary look he gave her. 'Who am I supposed to go hiking with? And to be perfectly honest, I haven't missed it much. I quite like showering and sleeping in an actual bed too.'

He sat perfectly still for a long moment, his gaze reflective, as though he were analysing her down to the finest detail. It was disconcerting, especially since she'd expected his gruff disapproval. 'Fair enough,' he said, his voice low. 'You mentioned a via ferrata? Is that something we should be looking at? They'd get their feeling of achievement. Climbing is ruled out with a group that size, but a via ferrata could be a compromise to get somewhere really spectacular in a short time.'

Sophie looked down at her lap to hide her grimace. 'I think they'd love a via ferrata.' Sophie on the other hand... 'As long as it's not too challenging for the rest of the party.'

'Don't worry,' Andreas scoffed. 'I've got no desire to lead a large, mixed-ability group up a difficult route either. When was the last time you did one?'

'With you,' she answered in a small voice.

His brows shot up. 'You stopped climbing... entirely?'

She just nodded.

'What about with Rory? He seemed keen. He even said he'd consider training as a guide.'

'He didn't,' Sophie said with a gulp. 'We were just quite... comfortable in our spare time.'

Andreas looked as though 'comfortable' was up there with bad coffee in his books. 'Are you sure you're still up to it?' he asked evenly.

'I'll manage,' she insisted. They'd agreed he wouldn't choose anything difficult. Although it sometimes felt surreal, she had dangled from ladders and scrambled up plenty of precipices that summer they'd been together. She might not be looking forward to it, but she would manage. She had to.

An Italian Wedding Adventure

'Okaaaaay,' he agreed – a little doubtfully, but that only hardened her resolve. 'We should find some place.'

'Some place? People don't usually plan to get married "some place". We need to find somewhere perfect – a few options that are perfect – and soon. I know we don't have to make any bookings, but they're getting married on the nineteenth of September!' She was already getting nervous about a four-month turnaround for arranging the ceremony, but Andreas had assured her it was plenty of time and coming any earlier would have been too cold.

'The nineteenth is the day booked for the reception, is it?'

'The wedding, yes. They arrive on the Monday. Pre-wedding events are scheduled for Tuesday and Thursday, with a rest day on Wednesday and then Friday is the big day. I avoided the weekend to minimise the number of other hikers—'

'I can't guarantee it can happen on the Friday,' he interrupted her. 'Don't you remember our pre-departure briefing for Sardinia?'

Sophie remembered arriving for that meeting and having every molecule of breath punched out of her lungs when she met their adventure guide. She'd been worried she'd have to peel her chin off the floor and mop up the drool. When he'd shaken her hand with an impersonal smile, she'd lost the ability to form words, so distracted by his rough fingertips and rasping accent.

She took a deep breath, clearing her head enough to work out his meaning. 'Safety comes first. The most important tool is good planning and the key to good planning is adapting to conditions.'

He huffed a laugh. 'You were a good student.' Hopefully, he didn't mean she'd hung on his every word, because she'd hoped he hadn't noticed. 'But the other lesson from every briefing: the guide is in charge. No one gets married until I say so.'

She stifled a chuckle at his dramatics. Biting her lip and keeping her gaze on her lasagne, she ordered herself not to point out that he'd put himself back in the picture.

'Was something funny?'

Oops, busted. 'Nope.'

'Safety is not a joke.'

She couldn't stop the next snort of laughter. Trying to hide behind her wine glass, she only succeeded in choking on her sip.

'Sophie.' The way he said her name this time, with a shake of his head and an exasperated smile, sounded even more like an endearment. 'You know I'm serious, hmm?'

'Very serious,' she agreed, still trying not to laugh. '"No one gets married until I say so,"' she imitated him, pitching her voice low. 'I couldn't help it,' she defended herself when he pinned her with a dubious look. 'I get it. Their dreams of getting married somewhere unique aren't worth twenty people slipping to their death – or one person breaking their leg. We can have a special signal. "Are we all clear for the wedding?" "Roger that, all clear. Code green. They're getting married." "Copy that, code green."'

'Have you ever spoken into a radio?' he asked doubtfully.

Sophie snatched a piece of bread and tore it apart as she answered. 'I have, actually.'

'Ah, wedding radio? A big event where you had to keep in touch with your minions to avert the champagne emergencies.'

'The best tool for avoiding champagne emergencies is good planning,' she imitated him. 'And I don't have minions. It's usually just Ginny with me or one of the casual managers and occasionally, we wear portable radios.'

'Ginny's the one with the—' He gestured to the spot on his

own chin where Sophie's colleague wore a stud in her labret piercing.

Sophie nodded.

'This wedding will be a bit different to your usual.'

'There is no "usual". That's what I like about destination weddings. But yes, this is quite a bit more complicated than the other outdoor weddings I've arranged.'

He drained the last of his wine, his knife and fork lay neatly on his plate. He didn't quite have a smile on his face, but he was leaning back in his chair, his posture relaxed. Perhaps this was the right time.

'You do realise,' she began, not meeting his gaze, 'that you said no one gets married until *you* say so.'

With a long sigh, he rested one hand on the table. 'I did notice that.'

'Reshma is keen for this wedding to be a success – a blueprint of sorts. Proof of concept. I'm pretty sure Willard is eager to see everything turn out well too, as a sign that this merger could actually work.' She paused. 'And I don't think you're going to be able to bow out once you've helped me plan this part. You'll need to see it through to the end.'

When she risked a glance up, she found him watching her thoughtfully. 'Do you want me to? Really?'

No. Yes! She paused to gather her thoughts, marvelling at how quickly he'd turned this back on her.

'I want this wedding to work.'

'It'll work, with or without me. Kira and Laurie are both experienced guides and Willard has another twenty names on his books. It doesn't have to be me.'

His words took her back to that disastrous day when she'd asked him to marry her. She couldn't remember exactly what he'd said, but the sentiment had been the same, as though she'd be able to replace him with a snap of her fingers. She bristled at the memory.

'You're right, it doesn't have to be you. But my boss is also right, you are the best choice for this area, this situation. You know that. Whether I want you on my team for personal reasons is beside the point.' She caught herself, wondering if those words had come out wrong. 'As long as you refrain from mentioning your views on marriage – and we don't start... reminiscing in front of the wedding party—'

His eyebrows shot up and Sophie could have choked on her words – definitely poorly chosen this time.

'I don't mean—'

'I didn't think you meant—'

'I was obliquely referring to our arguments, not... getting reacquainted.' She blushed so completely, even the tips of her ears burned.

'You're full of pretty ways to say things this evening,' he said with an irritatingly straight face. There was a softness in his eyes that drew her in, as though the good memories of their time together could banish some of the bad – for him at least.

The restaurant manager who'd taken their order set their desserts on the table with a flourish – tiramisu for Sophie and panna cotta for Andreas. He leaned his elbows on the table and studied her, obviously taking his time to formulate his next sentence.

As punishment for his lengthy hesitation, she stole a blueberry from his bowl. But instead of a scowl, he smiled and pushed his dessert in her direction.

'Have whatever you like.'

Lifting her spoon hesitantly, she gestured to her bowl. 'Do you want to try—?'

He shook his head. Waiting until she'd taken a spoonful of

strawberry and thickened cream – okay, two spoons – he said something she would never have expected. 'Euphemisms aside, I think it would be good to get reacquainted.'

'You do?'

'We've obviously both changed.'

She couldn't tell if he meant that as a good thing.

'But I have an expedition to the Himalayas. There's a team taking shape. We were looking at going in autumn this year – I don't know exactly when.'

Sophie stilled, waiting for him to continue, although a ripple of unease went through her at his further plans to scale dangerous mountains for reasons she'd never really asked – or at least he'd never satisfactorily explained.

'If you're here, you won't like handing it over to someone else. You'll want to be the one to lead.'

She expected him to bluster and deny it, but he just smiled, a closed-mouth twist of his lips that was mirrored in his eyebrows. 'Maybe. But if I do it, I'm not going to say "code green" into a radio and I am *definitely* not coming to the reception.'

'Roger that, over and out.'

11

Andreas mourned the old Sophie the following morning as he nudged his rucksack impatiently with his toe. He'd piled up the equipment ready to take out to the car, checked and re-checked his emergency kit and now could only stand restlessly by the door with his hands on his hips. When they'd been together, she'd scrambled out of bed as soon as he had in the morning, stumbling after him even though she'd looked like a zombie until about nine.

That last part hadn't changed. She'd made a beeline for the kettle first thing, with puffy raccoon eyes and a cardigan pulled over her patterned pyjamas, but half an hour after her sacred tea, she still wasn't ready to go.

That she hadn't gone hiking or climbing *at all* over the past eight years gave him an uncomfortable twinge between his ribs. Had he put her under pressure back then? He couldn't rule it out. He'd struggled, wanting to spend time with her whilst also feeding his rock-based obsessions.

But she'd enjoyed herself on those trips. He remembered the light in her eyes, the growing confidence in her fingers as he taught her to tie knots, the sounds of wonder she made when she looked out at the view. He was tempted by the thought that she might enjoy it again.

'Sophie?' he hollered from the front door when he didn't see her in the kitchen.

She poked her head around the door of her bedroom. 'There's no need to shout. I'm nearly ready to go.'

'We have to hurry to catch the next ferry. There's a chance of rain late this afternoon and I want to reach two summits before it hits. We need to get moving.'

'When were you planning to tell me this?'

He drew himself up. 'I didn't?'

She shook her head. 'I can't read your mind. I can barely read your expressions.'

'Ah... Sorry.'

She disappeared again before emerging with a day pack and a pair of pristine hiking boots. 'Don't worry,' she anticipated his words. 'I broke them in walking the dog. I did have a good teacher and I haven't forgotten everything.'

Every sentence from her seemed to land on him like a flaming arrow.

The lake was looking fickle as they took the traghetto vehicle ferry across. He peered out of the windscreen at the slanted limestone cliffs, draped in cloud. The heaviness in the air hinted at instability. He would never depart for a high-altitude trek with a client in this weather.

'So, what's the plan?'

'The peaks on the western side are lower altitude, but the ascent is steep and the views are good. If the weather holds – and you can keep up a decent pace – we can tick off Monte Castello di Gaino and Cima Comer.'

She retrieved her tablet from her bag and scribbled something with the stylus, flicking through multiple windows and zooming in on a map that she marked meticulously.

'Is that thing an extension of your body?'

She barely spared him a glance. 'My brain, actually.' She lifted the tablet to snap a photo of their approach to Toscolano Maderno, a riviera oasis of warm colours and clay roofs with a line of stone pines along the promenade and cypress trees rising into the jagged hills above.

'To keep your memories?' he asked mildly.

This time, she turned her gaze on him. 'Something like that.' Then she lifted the device again – between them this time – and snapped another picture. 'To remember you by, when you're up on Mount Everest later this year,' she said with a smile.

Andreas tugged off his cap and belatedly smoothed his hair and rubbed at his three-day beard. 'Our goal isn't Everest,' he said with tolerant smile. 'It's Manaslu. And you don't need a picture. You won't forget me.' He winked at her.

The ferry docked before she could formulate a response beyond an eye-roll and he started the car, revving the engine as he navigated off the ferry and then turned north on the Gardesana, the main road around the lake.

She waited until the engine had quietened to a mumble. 'As much as I might like to.' Forget him. She meant forget him.

'As much as I'd love to have the last word, this time, I'm happy it goes to you, Miss Kir— erm...'

'Miss Kirke,' she said with a sigh. 'I changed my name back.'

'But you did take his? How long were you married?'

'Only three years.'

'Only?'

'I suppose in comparison to how long you and I were together, Andreas, it's a long time,' she said with an indulgent sigh. 'What's the longest you've ever been with someone?'

An Italian Wedding Adventure

'Ten months,' he answered matter-of-factly and waited to see how long it would take for her to work it out.

'Wha— You're not serious.'

'Why wouldn't I be?' He kept his gaze on the road. 'I thought you knew that.'

'Your longest relationship was... with me?' she clarified.

He answered with a shrug. 'Relationships aren't my thing. I didn't get married to someone else since I last saw you.'

'Obviously not,' she said, her tone peevish, although he didn't understand why. She was the one who'd stayed away when he'd returned from Pakistan and he had a gemstone to prove it – a reminder of his moment of weakness – hidden in the back of a drawer at home. 'What about Kira?' she asked.

Heat rose to his cheeks and he briefly considered denying there was anything between him and Kira, but Sophie had obviously picked up on something. His skin felt tight as he answered, 'We're friends. Every time we sleep together, we remember we're better as friends and it's been a while anyway. She would kill you if you suggested it's a relationship. She's worse than me.'

She sighed, but a fatalistic smile touched her lips. 'And this is the future of I Do.'

'It's the future for Great Heart Adventure *Weddings*,' he added gruffly. 'Leading a tipsy wedding party on a hike with a long stop at the top for empty promises that no one can keep.'

'You have to admit the name of Willard's company is perfect.'

'It's supposed to be a heart with chambers and blood vessels sticking out of it, the thing that keeps you alive, not a cute symbol for emotions.'

'You might be surprised at the real emotion in a wedding ceremony,' she said carefully. 'There's adrenaline there too.'

'Waiting to see if your partner will actually show up?'

'I've organised fifty weddings and only one of them hasn't

gone ahead, and not because of cold feet. People usually solve their problems long before they get to this stage – or they never get to this stage,' she added with a pointed glance at him.

He raised his eyebrows in acknowledgement. 'You're the expert. I suppose that's an advantage of getting married after a via ferrata. If they unclip, they could fall. They're literally attaching their lives to the same cable.' His voice trailed off. When he glanced at her, she was scribbling on her tablet again and she wasn't looking at him, but her small smile made him uneasy.

'That's very romantic, Andreas,' she finally said with a grin.

He sighed as he pulled the Panda off the Gardesana and up along the winding road to the tiny town where they would start their ascent. Sophie appeared to be concentrating on her tablet and Andreas found himself wanting to point out the view, nudge her into appreciating the sheer enormity of water and rock, but they weren't here for that.

She wasn't the eager novice she'd been when he first met her. She was a wedding planner struggling with her own cynicism – although she'd never admit that – who was so capable, it was a turn-on. He did want to get to know this new Sophie, and also dig out the pieces of the old Sophie that were hiding dormant inside somewhere.

One summit at a time...

* * *

Andreas kept up a murderous pace – at least she would murder him if they didn't stop for a rest soon. His 'easy hike' had Sophie's hair hanging limp in her face from sweat and now her thighs were screaming from the steep altitude gain and stony conditions. She had to keep her wits about her or she'd turn her ankle

An Italian Wedding Adventure

– or worse, she thought every time she caught a glimpse of the steep drop.

At least Lily and Roman would love this. Despite the fact that they'd only walked an hour from the quaint hamlet where they'd parked near a pizzeria that was now calling her name, the landscape was scrubby and wild. They were navigating a craggy ridge that loomed over the towns dotted along the lake far below.

'Doing okay?' he called back from where he was waiting for her, his foot propped casually on a limestone outcropping. 'We'd obviously take it more slowly with your wedding group.'

'I'm fine,' she lied, just seconds before her foot slipped and she clawed at the rock face to stabilise herself. Andreas made no attempt to help her. She remembered that from when they were together. She'd pictured him coming close to show her the handholds when they climbed, but he'd just yelled at her like a drill sergeant and then expected her to get the hang of it.

'This last part is the hardest.' He gestured to the path, which swerved steeply across the rock. He hefted himself up the first few steps, using his hands.

'Let me take a picture for the file,' Sophie called out, retrieving her phone from her pocket. He straightened and peered down at her as she snapped the shot. He looked so at ease with nothing but air at his back, his posture perfectly balanced with the angle of the rock. He wasn't smiling, but there was an energy to him that was compelling, even in a photo.

With a flash of embarrassment, she remembered looking up a spread in a mountaineering magazine when they were first getting together. Despite the stunning photographs of dizzying drops and dramatic landscapes, she'd only seen bright-eyed Andreas, calmly fitting into the world around him. She wasn't sure she was prepared to have a whole folder of photos of him on her own hard drive, including the one she'd snapped in the car, capturing every rough detail of his face and his slightly sheepish expression.

She shook herself, needing to stay in the present, not only to take her next steps safely, but to ensure she didn't fall under his spell again. That he still had this effect on her, even though she was older, wiser and more assertive, was concerning.

Scrambling over the rocks after him, gripping the steel cable that was bolted in at the most dangerous parts, she glanced down once and immediately regretted it, forcing her gaze back to the safety of the stone. This might have been 'just' a hike, but she suspected it could be adventurous enough for most clients.

There was only sky when she looked up. Hauling herself to the top using the cable, her knees scraping on the rough limestone, she emerged onto the narrow summit puffing and groaning. She didn't have a chance to catch her breath. Every angle of the 360-degree views was awash in colour, bursting with drama.

Patches of blue sky were interspersed with swollen clouds. The weather system was visible and fluctuating wildly, moisture hanging over the lake like a bubble. Straight ahead, a tall summit cross rose towards the clouds from the highest point – a protrusion of rock that seemed to hang suspended. Behind the cross, nothing, just a sharp drop-off and then the distant water and the miniscule clay roofs of the towns far below.

Inland to her right, another summit ranged even higher, with steep, wooded ridges and an outcropping on top. Sophie stared at the peak that seemed almost close enough to touch, but she knew it would be a long and hard climb to reach it.

'Monte Pizzocolo,' Andreas supplied for her. 'Probably a little difficult for your wedding party. I've done the alpine route up there once with a group of trainee mountaineers. Want to try it out one day?'

He must have been teasing, but she couldn't tell from his

tone. Clutching his arm, she urged him in the direction of the cross. 'Stand there for me, just in front of the cross.' She held her phone up to adjust the camera settings, testing several angles. 'It's marvellous,' she commented absently. 'I can picture a wedding here.'

Bride and groom would face each other with the stunning backdrop of the lake. She could see it already, even with only one person in the shot – the wrong person.

'I didn't know you were the photographer as well as the celebrant.'

Her gaze shifted from the image of him on screen to the real Andreas. 'Your face is ruining the shot.'

'I'm sorry?' he replied belligerently, crossing his arms.

'I'm trying to create an idea of how the ceremony would come together up here. You look like a cranky adventure guide, not an elated groom.'

'I am *not* pretending to be a groom for you!' His voice was scratchy.

'You don't need to pretend. Just look a little less scary, hmm?'

He bared his teeth in something that looked more like a visit to the dentist than a smile.

'Okay, forget the smile,' she grumbled. 'Look somewhere else. I'm just trying to get a feel for it.'

Despite her grouchy subject, the familiar shiver up Sophie's spine told her she was on the right track. This was a part of the job she loved: putting together a picture of the client's hopes and dreams about their big day and finding a way to make it happen.

Lily and Roman would love this place. It would be a little tight with twenty people, but they could hold their short ceremony in front of the summit cross and it would be just as beautiful as they imagined – perhaps more beautiful.

'Sophie, stop! Watch where you're walking!'

Trust Andreas to snap her out of her wedding daydreams. She glanced at her feet to discover she'd strayed into a patch of uneven rocks. Another step and she might have tumbled over – and then down the side of the mountain.

'Damn it, a whole wedding party up here sounds like a nightmare!' He swiped off his cap and ran a hand through his hair.

'I was just thinking it looks like a dream.' She snapped one more picture with his mussed hair in honey-coloured waves, his expression wry as he looked into the camera. If only she had an excuse for him to take his shirt off— Sophie bit her lip to stop a smile at that thought.

A scraping sound distracted them both and Sophie glanced down to see a hand and then a bright-red helmet emerge from the cliffside near the cross. The climber whooped as she hauled herself up, two ropes attached to her harness. She called down to someone below before turning to give Andreas a polite smile.

'Ciao, amici,' he said, his grin wide as he chatted with the woman in Italian. Sophie caught a few words, but she was too tired to concentrate on the meaning. The woman's climbing partner emerged and both of them shook Andreas's hand firmly, the conversation animated with sweeping gestures at the wall of rock and the wide view.

Sophie was trying not to begrudge him those smiles that he wouldn't give her when the woman turned and asked in Italian, 'Did you want to get a picture of your boyfriend? I'm in your way. I could take a picture of you both if you like.'

Flustered, Sophie replied in English. 'Oh, he's not— Actually we're working. I'm a wedding planner and I'm trying to see if it would be possible to hold a small ceremony up here. I was just getting a few mock-up shots using him as... um... a groom.'

She didn't dare meet Andreas's gaze.

'I love that idea! Allora, let me take a photo with the two of you and you can take a photo for us.' She gestured for Sophie to hand over her phone, but Sophie could move only sluggishly as she processed the suggestion. Andreas as a fake groom was amusing, but the two of them together? She made the mistake of meeting Andreas's equally horrified gaze as the woman continued, 'Then there can be a bride *and* groom in your photo.'

12

'Bellissimi! You are beautiful!'

It turned out the climber, who had introduced herself as Cristina, was an avid amateur photographer – and Sophie had a penchant for torture that Andreas had never suspected. She must realise the pang of emotion that shot through him as she faced him in front of the cross.

His life flashed before his eyes: the jubilation of summiting an eight-thousander; the apple farm where he'd grown up, always looking up and away from the valley; pain and bitter cold that was somehow addictive; Sophie's face. *Sophie's face.*

There'd been a stage in his life when he'd seen her every time he closed his eyes.

Now, he was looking at her again – slightly rumpled, the way he liked her best. Her top lip was finely drawn, narrow and expressive. Verdammt, he shouldn't be looking at her lips while they acted out a bizarre non-wedding in preparation for another non-wedding.

'You hold hands for a wedding, yes? Try that!'

Hoping it would all be over soon, Andreas snatched Sophie's

An Italian Wedding Adventure

hands from her sides, gripping them more tightly than he'd intended. How he'd come to stand in front of this cross, facing Sophie while his heart drummed a driving rhythm in his chest, he still couldn't fathom. It wasn't a church altar, but it felt every bit like a wedding – which was why his throat had closed and he wanted to crawl out of his skin with discomfort.

'I *definitely* want to be married like this!' Cristina gushed as she peered at the screen, lining up a new shot, pausing only to wink at her partner. 'A little closer together I think. It's more natural. And don't stare at your feet! So many more beautiful things to look at!'

Andreas followed both instructions at the same time, his gaze colliding with Sophie's just as they found themselves standing as close as they'd been that night in Weymouth when he'd nearly kissed her. She wasn't smiling. Her eyes were wary, but that only sharpened the impression that this moment meant something.

He gulped, the sound loud in his own ears. He'd just taken a drink from his canteen, but now his mouth was dry as he wondered what she'd look like if she were truly standing up here facing the man she loved – someone who deserved her and would treasure her properly. He wondered if she'd looked happy with Rory and clenched his jaw at the thought that she might have been at one time.

Then he wondered what she would have looked like if he'd just said yes eight years ago, if he'd stood in much the same way in a chapel somewhere back home, taken her hand for real and showered her in promises.

The clarity of the image shook him, as well as the way he could picture raising his hands to her head, gently holding her still while he kissed her and kissed her.

He was light-headed, as though they were at altitude rather

than the measly 870m this summit actually was. He had to put some distance between them before he removed all distance entirely.

Sophie's sudden laugh – breathy and a little wobbly – snapped him back into the present. 'Your scowl makes this look like a ritual human sacrifice. Only, I don't know whether you're sacrificing yourself or getting ready to toss me over the side.'

His hands tightened on hers reflexively as he made a frustrated groan. 'I'm not thinking about tossing you over the side,' he growled, pulling on her hands for emphasis and accidentally dragging her closer. Endorphins rushed in his brain in anticipation.

'You may kiss the bride!' Cristina announced with a chuckle. 'It's going to be a beautiful wedding.'

To Andreas's horror, he thought for a moment that she really meant a wedding between him and Sophie and the rollercoaster in his chest started off again. All this talk of weddings was making him lose his mind. Sophie's cheeks went pink in an instant and Andreas stepped back hastily. But he tripped on a stone and teetered alarmingly close to the cliff edge.

With a cry, she fumbled for him, her hands swiping over his chest as she gripped his shirt in two fists and hauled him to safety. She could probably feel his heart bouncing against his ribs, but she'd assume it was because he'd lost his balance. He squeezed her hand with his.

'Thanks. I'm okay.'

She let go with a grimace. 'I hope that's not a sign of what's to come.'

'I'm sure it's just a sign of what would happen if I were ever a groom.'

'Marriage would kill you, huh?' she said with a withering look. 'Maybe I need an "I survived" T-shirt.' She patted him condescendingly on the chest and he wanted to snag her hand and keep it there – and land a good one on Rory Brent's nose.

Instead, he turned away, perching on a stone to wait while she snapped a few shots of the two climbers in front of the cross – smiling like normal people, instead of pretending to be a bridal couple.

He had old photos of him and Sophie that looked like that: colourful helmets and wide smiles, a smudge of dust on her cheek, occasionally with Sophie poking out her tongue because she'd been embarrassed by the image of herself on the phone screen. As he watched her wipe sweat from her forehead with the back of her hand, bringing her water bottle to her lips, he suspected she wouldn't be embarrassed like that any more.

'We should keep moving,' he said. Ignoring the curious gazes of the climbers, he gave them a firm wave and hefted his pack before swinging himself down the rocky trail they'd climbed half an hour – and a lifetime – ago. They needed to descend quickly if they were going to make the second summit before the weather turned.

He glanced back at Sophie's progress and found her stepping gingerly down, a long way behind him. She'd done well so far. She was level-headed and sure-footed. He'd noticed her flagging just before the summit, but she'd been able to push through, as he'd known she would.

'Use your left hand on the rock,' he called up to her. 'There's a foothold below you – a bit further. That's it.'

She seemed a little shaky when they reached the safety of the saddle and the forest path.

'You did well,' he said gruffly.

She just eyed him with a frustrated noise he'd heard a lot from her and she mumbled something that sounded suspiciously like, 'Drill sergeant,' under her breath.

* * *

'This is your definition of the weather rolling in?'

Sophie leaned casually against the sturdy wooden railing of the lookout and lifted her nose in the air. She was teasing him, but Andreas couldn't bring himself to care when she looked so content, sunshine in her untidy hair.

The billowing clouds of the morning had burned off completely. Instead of the forecast rain, Lake Garda was sweltering in unseasonably warm spring weather.

'I'm here to keep you safe, not predict the weather,' he said. 'Give me your phone.'

She handed him the device and he lined up a photo of her with the backdrop of the Monte Baldo massif and water stretching south to the horizon. Handing the phone back, he joined her by the railing, his forearm next to hers.

'What do you think?'

'There's a lot more space up here than at Monte Castello di Gaino. The view is more spectacular too.'

'We're quite a lot higher in altitude. Do I sense a "but"?'

'It seems a little silly, but the summit cross was nicer at the first one. And it's kind of weird that there are two crosses up here. Where's the actual summit?'

'It's not silly. You're a purist. If you're not standing on the actual highest point, then it doesn't count.'

'You *do* understand,' she accused him gently, apparently too relaxed to spar in earnest. 'There's symbolism in a summit.'

'I still don't think you need to get *married* up here.'

'Because you prefer the symbolism of getting married at the bottom of the lake with weights attached?'

The tension of the day snapped over him and he laughed,

dropping his head, his shoulders shaking. 'Is that one of the packages on offer?'

'Fuck, I hope not,' she said through pursed lips.

He grinned at her again. 'I only have to get you to 1,200m for you to start swearing?'

'I only have to say "fuck" to make you smile?' she shot back.

'I smile all the time,' he insisted.

It was her turn to laugh. 'You have the biggest scowl on your face right now. And we're not even up to the bit where you have to play the groom.'

'You're not going to make me do that again, are you?'

'Unfortunately, you are the only person I have to work with right now. You're my "Andreas for size".'

'I'd rather be Andreas for size than the groom.'

'I know. I'm sorry,' she said, patting his arm. 'I get that it's awkward for you.'

It was awkward how his brain had gone straight to kissing her – awkward how he still felt as though they weren't standing close enough, as though part of him had forgotten they'd broken up years ago.

'Do you think they'd like this lookout for the ceremony?' he asked.

'Maybe. But we should grab some shots of the crosses and then I'm dying for a swim and a pizza, in that order.'

'I like your thinking. I might join you, for both.' He followed her along the rocky path down to the spur that boasted a small metal cross and a white Madonna.

'As long as you keep your clothes on this time, Hinterdorfer,' she called over her shoulder.

His steps petered out as he was struck by memories, by warmth at the realisation that she'd shared all of those moments and filed them away as he had. 'I don't remember you complaining.'

'I will certainly complain if you scandalise the families at the beach in Marniga.'

'Don't worry. I like freedom but I'm not an exhibitionist. I only swim naked with people who've seen it all before.' He winked at her as he passed, taking up his position in front of the cross, hands behind his back, so she could snap her photo before they tramped back to the car.

She fell asleep on the way back to Marniga, after fighting it for a good ten minutes. He'd pushed her today and he wasn't sure if he felt guilty about it, especially now the rain hadn't materialised. She'd been much brighter on the way down from the second peak than the first, but he wouldn't point that out to her. If she needed to grumble during the lows, when her muscles screamed and her motivation dipped, then she was welcome to do it. He knew she could push through it. He remembered...

Too much. He remembered far too much about the woman snuffling softly in the passenger seat.

Shaking her gently awake when he reached the car park, that ache in his ribs started up again when she sluggishly opened her eyes.

'Oh, shit, I fell asleep.'

'Still swearing at sea level?'

She scowled at him.

'Blame me if you have to, but out you come. Avanti! Hopp hopp! It's time to go swimming.'

'Don't you "avanti" me! I'm coming!'

13

Do you remember when we went swimming on the last day of the Selvaggio Blu?

Sophie kept her mouth shut and stared up at the sky as she reclined on the pebbles, the cool water lapping at her waist. Since she hadn't exchanged any harsh words with Andreas for several hours, it was far too dangerous to start reminiscing about the trip to Sardinia where they'd got to know each other, even though the water and the rocks and the shirtless man with golden skin took her right back.

The lake was several degrees cooler – a blessed relief for her sore legs – and the man several years older. But metaphors about fine wine meandered through her thoughts as she sneaked a peek at him.

Rory had been on that trip too... That thought poured cold water over her reminiscences. She didn't remember struggling to peel her eyes off Rory, finding every little thing he did attractive. But, damn, she'd been on fire for Andreas by the third day. He'd licked his thumb once after eating the fish they'd cooked on the camp stove and she'd felt the action in her stomach. One word from him had burrowed deeper than all of the friendly conversations she'd had with Rory on the trail.

Her fascination hadn't been a good basis for a relationship. She'd dived in too deep and learned that lesson the hard way, but that didn't stop the renewed tug now, when she was supposed to know better. She was still fascinated by the twitch of wistfulness on his face as he strode through the water in her direction. His face. She was fascinated by his face, even as droplets streamed down his body and the muscles in his torso bunched and released, sunlight caressing the dips and swells of his chest. Okay, she was fascinated by a little more than just his face.

'Feeling better?' he asked, swiping his wet hair off his forehead.

She smiled and nodded as he sat down beside her, resting his arms on his knees.

'I think we should do Cima Rocca next – the via ferrata,' he said decisively.

Her stomach clenched. There had been a time when the thought of a via ferrata hadn't given her a spike of fear, but that time had been short and was firmly in the past. 'Shouldn't I work up to that?'

'It's a very basic route, not much more difficult than what we did today. You'll do fine.'

'I'm not twenty-six any more, you know,' she said, aiming for peevish, but not quite managing it.

'You're pretty fit. You had no problems on two moderately technical hikes, despite the lack of practice. I wouldn't worry about it.'

She sighed deeply. 'You always did push me out of my comfort zone.'

'Do you mean that as a bad thing?' His tone was even, as

though he'd accept her opinion if she were criticising his methods.

'Not necessarily,' she acknowledged. 'I did have problems today. I felt as though my legs were on fire during the last part of the first ascent. I got wobbly climbing down from Monte Castello di Gaino and the thought of a via ferrata makes my stomach churn.'

He shook his head, dismissing her concerns. 'You weren't close to your limit. I was keeping an eye on you.'

'How do you know what my limit is? *I* don't even know any more.'

Turning to her in an irritatingly matter-of-fact manner, he began, 'Sophie, it's been a while, but you still approach a challenging hike the same way you used to. I'm a mountain guide qualified in two different countries. You were fine. And the only reason the thought of a via ferrata makes you nervous is that you've forgotten what you're capable of.'

'Maybe I don't want to be challenged any more!' she blurted out, disliking the cold, sinking feeling that accompanied her admission. Had that been Rory's appeal?

But there was no disappointment in the way he studied her. If anything, there was just a touch of sympathy. 'Maybe you're just out of practice at that, too,' he said.

'I'm not Kira,' she insisted. 'And I'm not the same person I was eight years ago.'

'No one is the same person they were eight years ago.' The only evidence that he was smiling were the little brackets at the corners of his lips.

'You must have been bored today,' she insisted, raising her chin.

He regarded her intently, the sheen in his eyes turning to copper as the sun dipped low and reflected off the water. 'I hope

I didn't give you that impression. I couldn't take you up Manaslu, Fini, but... it was good today.'

Fini... The old nickname gave her goosebumps.

'What was it, 1279m of altitude? How high is Manaslu?' she asked, changing the subject.

'It's an eight-thousander,' he said, biting his lip as though he was trying not to smile. 'But if I can't be up there, I may as well be here.' *With you.* Surely he couldn't have meant that. 'What did you do on holiday with Rory then? He seemed a hardcore outdoor type on that trip.'

'Possibly we were both pretending,' she said grimly.

'Pretending? You weren't pretending.'

'I was trying to impress you! It was silly, I know.'

His brows lifted as he processed what she was saying. 'You didn't enjoy the cliffs in Dorset?'

'God, it was always so windy!' Sophie said. 'You had to patch my wounds every time. That rock was sharp!'

'I have good memories of that,' he said with a rueful smile.

'Me too,' she said with a chuckle. 'I played a damsel in distress a little too eagerly.'

'The Dolomites? You didn't enjoy that?' His tone was pained.

Sophie stared out over the gently lapping water. There was a light breeze, just enough for the windsurfers gliding smoothly in the distance. 'I did,' she confessed. 'And I was glad I'd had the climbing boot camp beforehand, because those routes were incredible. But... I had thought maybe I was finally invited to meet the family.'

She was embarrassed to admit the truth, but it was a relief as well, in the same way it was a relief to look at him and see a flawed man and not some kind of god. He grimaced and followed her gaze to the other side of the lake: lush hills, crooked peaks and sun-baked villages below.

'That was my issue, not yours.'

'What's wrong with your family then? The little things you mentioned sounded pretty normal.'

'My family is completely normal. Parents married for forty years, they live in harmony with each other and the world. They're so normal, they don't understand why I climb mountains.' His smile was tight. 'And they would have marched you to the church in my hometown and emotionally blackmailed me until I married you.'

'Ah, so I had a narrow escape.'

'Exactly!' he said with emphasis, not looking at her. 'How's your sister? I hope she didn't say, "I told you so," when we broke up.'

'She's good. She took up trail running and now has a superfit husband and two super-fit kids and lives in Scotland.' She glanced at him. 'Of course she said, "I told you so." It's her responsibility as the older sibling.'

'She never liked me,' he commented mildly, as though Tash had been right to be sceptical of their relationship.

'You know she dragged me on that trip to Sardinia? I'd never done anything like that before and didn't particularly want to. "Kicking and screaming," was how she put it.'

To Sophie's surprise, Andreas smiled broadly. 'I know.'

'You know?'

His hand hovered over her calf, as though he might give her leg a squeeze, but he quickly reconsidered. 'Of course I know. You screamed, "Tasha, this is your fucking fault," all the way down the zipline on the second day.'

She stilled, stunned that he remembered that.

'And the boats... You thought the rafting would kill you – at least it sounded that way. I know just how quickly you learned to deal with your fear. I had thought you'd learned to love outdoor sports, but...' He gave a shrug and picked up a stone, brushing his fingers over it before flinging it into the water. It skipped four times because skipping stones was exactly the sort of thing that Andreas was good at: distractions from difficult conversations.

She was surprised they'd lasted so long in this one.

'But what?'

He glanced at her with half a smile that would have been cheeky on anyone else. 'Na,' he said with a shrug, a German word he'd once explained as something between 'so' and 'well'. 'Maybe you did learn to love it and you've just forgotten. Maybe you wanted to forget because of me.'

Her brows flew skyward. 'Is there no limit to your conceit?'

'I saw you today,' he insisted with an expansive hand gesture to assert his innocence. 'You were looking at Monte Pizzocolo with that glint in your eye.'

'Maybe because the name almost has "pizza" in it and I was starving! But the part I took issue with the most was the suggestion that I gave up something I enjoyed simply because you left me.'

'I didn't—'

'Break, break-up – whatever. I resent the suggestion. I might have been a moron back then where you were concerned, but I never missed it – climbing, the mountains.' *I just missed you.* And maybe missing him had got rolled up with the mountains and the squeezing feeling in her chest whenever she thought about ropes and climbs and dizzying drops.

A rock formation on the opposite shore caught her eye and she inclined her head to study the ridges and forested gullies, the prominent spurs and jagged mountain profiles.

'Is that where we were today?'

He leaned in to follow her gaze, the fresh scent of the water and sunshine on his skin. 'Mmhmm. There's Cima Comer directly across from us, the highest point.' He gestured further to the left. 'And there's Monte Castello di Gaino, and Monte Pizzocolo.' He snapped his fingers. 'We didn't get your Gipfelstempel!'

'My what?'

'At each summit, there's a box with a stamp in it for you to collect in your Wanderbuch – your hiking book. We missed two today.' His teasing smile grew wider.

'I don't have a hiking book.'

'Na, maybe you should get one.'

* * *

When Andreas offered to collect pizza for dinner, Sophie assumed it was because he didn't want a repeat the awkwardness of their 'date' from the evening before. They were spending a lot of time together and she wouldn't be surprised if he was uneasy – *she* was uneasy.

But when he arrived back with two flat boxes and then immediately shed most of his clothes and his shoes, peeling off his socks and slipping into a pair of Birkenstocks, she wondered if his real reason had been nothing to do with her.

The late-May evening was cool and Sophie had retrieved her favourite oversized cardigan, but Andreas sat in a vest top and cargo shorts, eating salami pizza straight out of the box with a knife and fork.

After dinner, Sophie set up her laptop at the kitchen table and loaded the photos from the day. She knew from bitter experience that it was easier to sift through the shots regularly than deal with thousands when she got home.

The lighting at the top of Monte Castello di Gaino was questionable. The weather had been undeniably weird: menacing in the morning and then a surprise heatwave in the afternoon. The dark clouds billowing behind Andreas in the first shots were mirrored in his facial expression.

'What?' he asked, looking up from his book when she didn't manage to stifle a chuckle.

'I'm sorry I made you be the groom,' she said with another snort of laughter. 'You look so pissed off.'

Setting his book down, he came around the table and peered at his image on the screen.

Then he said the last thing she expected. 'It's an amazing spot for a wedding.' He rubbed the back of his neck with one hand as he propped himself up on the table with the other. Leaning across her, he tapped at the arrow button with one finger, scrolling through the many photos of him scowling, until he reached the first one of the two of them in front of the cross and his hand stilled, hovering over the screen.

Sophie froze as well. They looked wooden and miserable, Sophie cringing and Andreas recoiling. With a sigh, she flicked to the next picture and her brow furrowed. Andreas appeared to be staring at her mouth. In the next one, they were standing closer, and the deep twist in Sophie's stomach had nothing to do with embarrassment and everything to do with longing.

The picture cut them off at a strange spot just below their entwined hands and the whole image was slightly on an angle, but it was so clearly a *wedding* photo that she couldn't help herself. She zoomed in until their faces were in sharper detail – Andreas's eyes glinting, his mouth slanted and tight, but not with disgust this time. It was the expression he'd had on his face in Weymouth when they'd talked about everything that had gone wrong in their relationship.

Sophie clicked ahead quickly, wanting to give each picture only a cursory look so she knew where to file it – under 'never again', she decided – but each one contained some kind of truth she didn't want to see but nevertheless found enthralling.

In the next shot, Sophie was laughing, Andreas watching her wryly. Then they were even closer.

'God, it really looks like you were about to grab me and kiss me!' she attempted to joke, but her voice squeaked. He made a choking sound next to her. When she glanced at him, his head was bowed and he was leaning heavily on the table. Her gaze returned to the picture and she felt the prickle again, the merging of past and present. 'I don't know if these photos are marvellous or... kind of incriminating.'

Sophie snapped her mouth shut. How exactly would the photos be incriminating? There was nothing between her and Andreas and hadn't been for eight years.

'I mean... I don't know what I mean. You don't really—'

Andreas lifted his head, his expression vivid with frustration. 'I don't really what? Want to kiss you?'

Her mouth dropped open and her ribs felt as though they were pressing on her lungs. His gaze fell to her mouth and the hiss of air out of his lips made her brain check out for the evening.

'Where have you been all day?' he muttered, his voice rasping.

'Erm, with you?'

He eyed her with a quick grin that turned into a chuckle. 'Yeah, I noticed that.' He stretched his neck as though something pained him. 'I'm going to bed.'

'Already?' Clearing her throat, she quickly changed tack. 'I mean, oh, right, yeah. Buonanotte.' Of course he didn't want to stay up to chat.

But instead of disappearing through his bedroom door, he paused with one hand on the frame, his posture tight. Then he turned abruptly with an audible grumble and stalked back to where she was sitting, hauling her out of her chair with insistent fingers on her upper arm.

'Do you truly believe I don't want to kiss you? Do I have to prove it?'

Her head swimming, the only response she could manage was a nod, but that was enough for him.

His hands lifting to either side of her face, he kissed her – really *kissed* her – hard on the mouth, then pulled away immediately. As Sophie gasped for breath, reeling and off-balance, he turned and stalked off just as quickly as he'd come.

'What was that?' she blurted out after him.

'A kiss!' he snapped, throwing an arm up for emphasis. But he paused again, his shoulders rising and falling and a moment later, he was incoming again.

Slinging an arm around her waist, he pulled her in close. 'No, that was a poor excuse for a kiss,' he said. Then his eyelids fluttered closed and he stooped to bring his mouth back to hers. He paused for a breath, as though waiting for her to pull away, and when she didn't, he kissed her again.

14

Sophie's chest was too small for her heart as it leaped and raced. She was light-headed, but she didn't want to breathe; she wanted to keep kissing. The languid, aching rasp of his mouth over hers turned her knees to liquid and her brain to porridge.

She'd forgotten it was like this when they kissed: the world ceased to exist, only sensations and emotions, heat and connection. Although, perhaps it had never been quite so charged in the past. The rawness, the insistence in the way he kissed her triggered more than just memories and when he leaned in, almost bending her back over the table in his attempt to draw even closer, she fisted her hand in his top, angled her head and deepened the kiss.

He stumbled, throwing an arm out to stop them from toppling onto the table. The action wrenched his mouth from hers and his eyes flew open, wide and a little haunted. He was about to pull away – Sophie could see it. Her hand slipped around to the back of his neck, unconsciously trying to hold him where he was.

But that was the action that made him stiffen and slowly draw back. His chest rose and fell heavily. Emotion rippled across his expression, so much that she couldn't hope to interpret it. Then with a deep breath, he turned and left the room without a word, the door to his bedroom closing with a muffled click.

Sophie stifled a groan. 'God damn you, Andreas Hinterdorfer.'

* * *

She didn't say a word about the kiss the following day. Of course she didn't. Even though he could see it in her eyes when she was thinking about it – a glint of panic – she wouldn't bring up the subject. She was here to plan a wedding, not kiss her ex-boyfriend. Or colleague – or whatever the hell he was. Andreas had been surprised to realise he didn't care about their current professional relationship. She would always just be Sophie in his mind and apparently, he would always want to kiss her.

He wanted to kiss her again in the morning when she emerged from her room in loose pyjamas and peered doubtfully out of the window. The pane was streaked with droplets and the cobbles outside were dark and slick with rain.

He wanted to kiss her when she settled into the passenger seat of his old Panda and pulled out her tablet. She was wearing a grey skirt and a white blouse with a cropped jacket. The sleeves weren't short, but they weren't long either, leaving a stretch of wrist and forearm that he couldn't stop looking at. A fine silver bracelet would look distractingly attractive right there – especially if he was the one to give it to her.

He still wanted to kiss her when they dashed into the reception venue, a historic limonaia, a lemon garden, on the other side of the lake. He especially wanted to kiss her when he heard her speaking decent Italian as she greeted the middle-aged woman behind the counter.

He wondered what she'd sound like speaking German and reined himself right back in. Giving in to a kiss last night – a kiss that had felt so natural, so good it had shaken him – had been bad enough, but imagining her slotting into his life was a recipe for heartache.

Manaslu was calling him, the first real expedition for a couple of years. He knew a guy who was putting together a team for the Polish Glacier Traverse of Aconcagua early in the new year too. Now Toni's parents were moving to Weymouth to help with Cillian and Willard had this wedding shit to deal with, he could stay in South America for half the year. There were still so many unclimbed peaks in Bolivia and Peru.

Imagining saying goodbye to Sophie again as he set off on an expedition, as he had eight years ago, was enough to stop him dreaming about turning kisses into something more. Even without the stilted proposal that he'd had to turn down, it would tear him in two.

He mumbled an excuse and left her there to organise her wedding admin and hightailed it to the nearest bar to down a couple of espressi. That was one Italian ritual the Südtiroler had adopted with enthusiasm: the quick espresso at the counter.

Because Lake Garda was a tourist magnet, his cheap espresso was a slightly pricier €1.20 and rather than the comfortably shabby bar he'd hoped for, he drank it at a gelateria while the visitors licked their morning ice cream.

The weather continued to be foul and they filled the afternoon visiting a vehicle-hire company to arrange a quote for Vespa-rental options for the hen and bachelor excursions.

'Do we need to do a test drive?' he joked, shoving his hands into his pockets.

'You're welcome to. You can borrow my rain poncho. It'll suit you,' she replied without even looking at him.

He wanted to shoot back a witty quip, but she'd caught him on a rare day when he hadn't bothered preparing for the conditions and he deserved the mocking.

The following day, he still didn't trust the weather. A storm was forecast and this time, the air was already heavy and charged when they woke up. But Sophie had a seemingly endless list of local businesses to visit for this wedding and another she had pencilled in for the following year.

Meaning to just drop her off and find something else to do, he found himself tagging along, juggling samples while she tapped on her tablet: two bottles of Valpolicella from the vineyard restaurant, three sample corsages, two mini wedding cakes; and a heavy book of fabric swatches for something he hadn't quite caught, even though he'd understood all of the words.

He didn't speak wedding.

As they waited to chat to one of the stylists on her list, he leaned on the back of her chair and tweaked a lock of her hair. 'Do you have to try out the hairdressers, too?'

The stylist chose that moment to appear with a warm handshake for both of them. 'I'm happy to demonstrate!'

So it was his own fault when he found himself in the leather chair five minutes later, a plastic smock around his neck, staring at his own scowl in the mirror while Sophie grinned in the background. Her hair was shorter than the bride's, had been her excuse.

But it was a passable cut – at least Sophie seemed to think so. She brushed her fingers through his hair, pulling her hand back quickly, but not quickly enough to prevent the shock of gratification at her petting.

He must have still been in a daze an hour later at another florist's up in the hills behind Bardolino. The storm had passed with more bluster than actual weather and the afternoon blazed hot over the clay roofs of the town. The florist led them to a balcony with a view over the vineyards and a glimpse of the lake, served a fairly good espresso and then brought out her parade of samples.

'You have to see someone wearing this to truly appreciate it,' the florist was saying as Andreas was distracted, studying the terraced vines, cypress and olive trees, the brightly coloured render on the houses and the pink rhododendron below. He was only two hours from home, but summer came earlier near the lake. He'd been skiing at altitude a week ago – which only made him wonder if Sophie had skied again since he'd coached her onto her first red slope. Probably not.

'My assistant has been very hands-on today, so perhaps we can try this.'

Andreas snapped his gaze up, at first wondering what Sophie meant with 'hands-on' and then recoiling when he saw what she intended. But his back met the railing and he had nowhere to run, so he dipped his head with a grumble and allowed her to place the floral wreath on his head.

'On me, it's going to look more like Julius Caesar than a bride.' But he enjoyed her smile as she snapped a few pictures.

'Julius Caesar probably isn't the right look for clients, though,' she said with a sigh. 'Here.' She thrust the tablet into his hands and plucked the arrangement off him, setting it on her own head.

That was worse. The wedding nonsense made him feel restless – useless. He didn't care if those flowers were roses or gardenias. The fuss was stifling, claustrophobic. But when Sophie stood in front of him looking like that, he ceased to function. The neurons in his frontal lobe all panicked and he didn't know whether to haul her over his shoulder like a caveman or run the other way.

'Are you going to take a photo?'

He managed a grunt in response, but he was in a foul mood by the time they drove back to the apartment.

He managed to keep quiet until they were getting out of the car, packing the samples into a collapsible crate he usually used for ropes. 'Do you really enjoy this stuff?'

'Yes,' she answered stiffly, her top lip thin. 'I did suggest getting a car myself. You were hired to be my guide... and not my test subject. I'm sorry you've had a miserable two days, but don't take it out on me.'

She hefted the smaller box of samples and turned away. Juggling the crate under one arm while he closed the boot, Andreas had to hurry after her, the words rushing out before he'd thought them through. 'I haven't had a miserable two days.'

'What?' Her tone was peevish.

'I didn't mean to criticise you just because—' *I freaked out when I saw you looking like a bride.* 'Because you enjoy your job. And I didn't mind coming along.'

'It's all right, Andreas,' she said with a glance heavenward. 'You don't have to pretend you like weddings any more than I'm going to pretend to enjoy the via ferrata.'

He wanted to insist that she *would* enjoy the via ferrata, but he knew she was afraid and telling her what she felt would only be counterproductive. So he restricted himself to an inarticulate grumble and then said, 'I don't understand why you have to loot the garden centre to get married, but the past two days with you —' *have been amazing. Ohhhhh, porca di merda, halt's Maul, du*

Lopp. Cursing, calling himself a fool and telling himself to shut up helped calm him down enough to finish the thought more sensibly. '—have been fine. And we got cake. Are we allowed to eat the cake?'

She regarded him as though he had a screw loose, which was fair. 'I'm not going to take it back to the UK in ten days' time. Yes, we can eat the cake.'

He rubbed his hands together. 'Good. Do you want the millefoglie or can I have it? Wait, you should have it, since it's the classic Italian wedding cake.' Brushing past her to unlock the door, he kept his face averted, not wanting to know what sort of look she was giving him.

When they set the crates on the kitchen table, he couldn't avoid her gaze any more.

'How do you know that?' she asked, a hand on her hip.

'Hmm?'

'How do you know about the classic Italian wedding cake? You haven't been to any weddings.'

'TV?' he tried. 'Movies?' His voice trailed off. 'You've been to a lot more Italian weddings than I have, haven't you?'

She nodded, obviously trying not to smile, which was unfortunately a very sweet expression on her. 'I've been to a few,' she said lightly.

He took a deep breath and straightened. 'Does that mean I can have the millefoglie?'

'No way!'

'Half?'

'You could just go to more weddings and then you'd get some. You must have had friends or family get married.'

He gave an eloquent shrug.

'You always make sure you're in the Himalayas on the big day?'

'Something like that,' he mumbled.

With a long huff, she rummaged in the crate until she found the little gold boxes with the cakes inside. She peered into one and he caught a glimpse of the honey-brown pastry of the millefoglie, dusted with sugar and bursting with cream and berries. 'Andreas Hinterdorfer would rather climb Everest than go to a wedding,' she muttered. 'I think you're just afraid you'll cry.'

'I would not.' He snatched the box from her and fetched a knife from a drawer.

'You don't know what to do with your emotions,' she accused him, softening her words with a smile. 'I bet you, our mountaintop wedding will make you cry.'

His response was a snort. Why would he cry at some strangers' not-legal promise ceremony, where they vowed to do all the things they probably already did without the vowing? 'This isn't convincing me to commit to September, but what would you bet? What's your prized possession?'

'You sound a little bit sensitive about this, Andreas,' she teased. 'But okay. I bet my signed Foo Fighters T-shirt.'

His eyes widened. 'Fini, I'd forgotten you had good taste. I hope it's my size,' he said with a wink.

Crossing her arms, she pinned him with a look. 'What do you bet? What will *I* win when you bawl like a baby at, "You may kiss the bride"?'

'Do people actually say that?' he asked with a scoff. 'But my prized possession is easy.' As the words tumbled out, Andreas knew that under no circumstances should he continue, but he was feeling a little reckless. 'It's a Pakistani emerald, three-quarters of a carat, round cut.' Currently sitting in a plastic box in his sock drawer.

Her smile vanished. 'You're not serious,' she said eventually.

'I'm pretty sure I won't cry.'

She paused for a wary intake of breath. 'Fine,' she said, her voice tight. 'You're on, but if you escape to the Himalayas instead of coming to this wedding, I'll know you chickened out. Now give me my half of the cake!'

It was his turn to regard her in silence. *Well played, Sophie-Leigh. Well played.*

15

'A mountaintop wedding is the stupidest idea I have ever heard!'

'You don't mean that,' came the crooning response from several feet above her.

'Don't tell me what I mean!' Sophie snapped. Her fingers ached and sweat dripped from her forehead. 'You know Reshma is advertising this as a special package? "Adventure weddings"?'

'I think you mentioned that.'

Sophie leaned her helmet on the thick cable bolted into the stone and closed her eyes, but she could still see the sharp drop on the inside of her eyelids, even though she knew better than to look down. 'What will the next couple want? A bungee ceremony? Jet skis?' The rock was jagged under her bare fingertips – good for grip, she remembered Andreas telling her years ago. But that didn't help her find her missing courage. 'Did you know a couple got married underwater? They were keen divers. Get your PADI licence at the same time as your marriage licence. Reshma could advertise that! Can you dive?'

'Mmhmm.' She knew that patient tone from Andreas, but

she hated to think what opinion he had of her, freezing up on a basic via ferrata.

'Why would someone want to climb up here to get *married*?' she continued, venting her frustration.

'We're not up there yet.'

'Oh God, do you think I don't know that?' Her voice sounded shrill even to her own ears. 'Why are you so calm?'

'I've taken a lot of people on vie ferrate before, Fini. Only a handful of times we haven't made it, and usually that was because of the weather.' His voice was smooth and slow.

Whether he was purposefully mirroring her words about weddings from a few days ago, she wasn't sure, but it felt easier to get married than to find footing on the rock.

But then she'd already failed at marriage once and despite her panicked words, she didn't want to give up on this via ferrata. It annoyed her that Andreas knew that.

The rainy weather had given way to bright sunshine that day. Andreas had insisted on setting off early and they'd walked nearly an hour, clambering over rocks, to reach the bottom of the route. For all Andreas's insistence that this was a popular climb, it had felt as though they were the only people for miles in the scrubby forest, the red-and-white way markers their only company, although the galleries and hides from World War I hinted at the darker history of the mountain.

Then they'd reached the bottom of the via ferrata. Sophie had managed to scramble up the first part that was little more than a steep walking trail, but as soon as they'd reached the initial vertical section – where she now clung to the cable – she'd lost her nerve.

The lake was so far below her, the cliff so steep, she could have been flying – or weightless. But she was acutely conscious of her mass, of the vortex of gravity that seemed to suck her in when she looked down. She was clipped into the safety cable. Andreas had taught her painstakingly – both back when they were together and again that morning – to unclip one carabiner at a time at each bolt to ensure she always had at least one strap tethering her to the steel.

All she had to do was grip the brackets and climb, but she was frozen with fear.

'Remember Cristallo di Mezzo?' Andreas called down cheerfully. He was waiting for her, casually hanging off the rock, unconcerned that her knees were shaking and her hands clutched the cable so tightly, they hurt.

'I remember the ladders,' she said, her voice weak. Ladders over nothing, suspended from rocky outcrops.

'I was thinking about when you got to the top.' She could hear the smile in his voice. 'You yelled like an Amazon at the top.'

'A battle cry,' she snorted, searching for a foothold in the jagged rock and finding nothing. 'Andreas, I was a lot younger then,' she said with a sigh.

'And you're even tougher now.'

She looked up and narrowed her eyes at him. She was tougher than he realised – inside. She'd lost a lot more than just a dodgy husband and a slippery mountaineer boyfriend and she was still here to fight to enjoy another day. But her body...

'My muscles aren't.'

'I know,' he said, still smiling. He was so damn tranquil up a mountain. 'But this is an easier route than the Marino Bianchi. You've got the muscle for it.'

'I can't believe this is an easy route,' she grumbled.

'Allora,' he said expectantly.

'Well what?' she prompted him peevishly. 'Don't you mean, "Avanti, hopp hopp"?'

'I'm trying to be gentle with you for now.'

That 'for now' was ominous, but she slung her leg to a higher notch this time and hauled herself up. Her safety straps were level with her waist, so she unclipped one and hooked it into the cable above the next bolt, repeating the process with the second.

There was memory in the action, in the feel of the carabiner in her hand, the gentle clink of metal, the creak of the straps of her harness – even the way her skin prickled on the back of her neck, knowing there was nothing but air behind her, came with a deep-buried affinity.

She focused on the rock in front of her, on breathing in and out, footholds, ascent, clipping one carabiner back into the cable, then the other. She wasn't climbing. She was just taking small steps, feeling the equipment in her hands – *having a fun day out*, she thought snidely.

'I can't imagine the wedding party doing this.'

'Fair enough,' came Andreas's reply. 'But you're the one who has to tell them that.'

She chuckled as the clambered up another few feet. 'Are you using emotional blackmail to get me up?'

'I didn't think it was emotional. Just the usual sort of blackmail. I'll bribe you, too, if you like.'

'Or a bet?'

He grumbled inarticulately and she wasn't sure why his tone had suddenly grown belligerent.

'A bribe,' he repeated. 'I'll take you out for Knödel tonight to celebrate reaching the top. I know a place.'

Sophie had to stop climbing while she laughed.

'Something funny?'

'It was just something Tita said after we met you all in Weymouth. She thought it sounded like canoodle,' she explained with a snort. 'You know what canoodle means? It means—'

'No,' Andreas said with a groan. 'I mean, yes, I know what it means, but no – just no. That's not funny.'

'*I* thought it was.'

'Because you don't speak German. We have a perfectly good word for "canoodle" and it's "knuddeln", not "Knödel".'

She snorted another laugh.

'What is it now?'

'Because "knuddeln" and "Knödel" are sooooo different,' she said with what sounded alarmingly like a hysterical giggle.

'They're entirely different!'

'Okay, fine. I understand you're very serious about your dumplings.' She shot him a teasing look, but wrenched her gaze right back down, then unfortunately caught sight of the distant, deep blue of the lake, so far below her that the town of Riva was in miniature and a mountain range took shape behind.

She heard voices below and the clink of carabiners.

'Should we let them overtake?' she asked Andreas. She remembered him telling her that allowing faster climbers to overtake was one of the rules of the vie ferrate.

'Not here. Up there will be safer. Buongiorno!' he called to the other climbers. While he discussed the plan for overtaking, Sophie tucked her tongue between her lips and hauled herself up after him. 'Clip in here, past the pole at the top,' Andreas called down to her from where he was partially obscured by the rock.

Sophie was surprised to realise she'd been planning to do exactly that. He'd taught her well all those years ago, when she'd hung on his every word. He spoke more on the mountain than in the valley. After he'd ended things, she'd been embarrassed to realise that he'd treated her like a climbing partner and not a romantic one, but that seemed for the best, now.

As she clipped her carabiners above her head, she realised Andreas treated *everyone* that way. Was he close to anyone? She thought of Miro with a twinge. She hadn't been there when Andreas had returned from Gasherbrum and it was a gap in her understanding of him that she suddenly resented – not that he would ever talk to her about it.

But two nights ago, he hadn't treated her like a climbing partner. She shook off the memories of that scorching kiss before her knees turned weak. Andreas had kissed her hundreds of times. What was one more?

Ever since they'd kissed, her stomach had been in a slow freefall, buffeted every time his gaze connected with hers. Something about their time together hadn't been closed off yet – a thought that sent twinges of remorse through her and triggered other feelings she hoped would stay buried, feelings about marriage.

Dragging Andreas around to discuss ribbons and boutonnieres had only made everything worse, reminding her why she shouldn't want him.

Now he was praising her in his smooth, mountain-guide voice and she didn't understand how that sound could both melt her bones and turn her spine to steel.

Gripping the cable that ran along the ridge, she scrambled all the way up, hauling herself to her feet, and then the world began to spin. She slammed her eyes shut, but it turned out the spinning was actually in her head and didn't stop, so she forced them open again and then her stomach dipped at the same time as her heart leaped and for a moment, she wondered if she were falling.

But she wasn't falling. Her hands were firm on the cable. Her feet were planted on rock. The slightly delirious feeling was the world expanding around her, her heart expanding in her chest and her blood pumping. Although the mountain crags rose higher on one side, at the top of this spur, she was surrounded by sky. The world revealed its extremes of colour and form and she was part of it.

'It's so damn beautiful up here!' she blurted out. She couldn't have stopped herself.

Andreas watched her closely, a grin forming on his lips, and she couldn't help matching it, laughing because her chest was so tight and she was so full of emotion.

She waited for him to say, *I told you so*, but he remained silent, studying her with a glow of approval. Giving her upper arm a quick squeeze, he pressed a kiss to her cheek – softer and more tender than the smacking congratulatory peck she would have expected, but nowhere near enough to settle the flutter she'd been experiencing since he'd kissed her properly two nights ago.

The other climbers were right behind them and without any more time to examine the threads of emotion coiling inside her, Sophie moved further along to make space.

'It's probably safe enough here to unclip, but let's have a little overtaking practice, shall we?'

'Because I'm so slow, another group might appear at any time?'

He wisely didn't respond.

When the first climber from the other group emerged at the top, Sophie was shocked to see a woman with a grey ponytail sticking out from below her helmet. She wore a compact rucksack with a pair of telescopic hiking poles tucked on one side.

'Buongiorno,' she said, not even breathing hard after the ascent. 'Mi scusi, bellissimo,' she said to Andreas as she clipped one of her straps around him, following a moment later with the other one.

It turned out there was an entire seniors' day outing behind them and they waited while eight older people emerged onto the ridge and passed them with a smile.

'Wow, they showed me,' Sophie commented, shifting her rucksack on her shoulders. 'But no one called *me* beautiful!'

'Did you want a stranger to call you beautiful?'

'Not really,' she admitted reluctantly. 'It's just a bit awkward that you're apparently so blindingly attractive.'

'I can't help that,' he said with a wide shrug. 'Let's go,' he continued, gesturing her ahead of him, 'bellissima,' he added quietly after she'd turned away.

After another short clamber, she emerged through the bushes at the first summit of the tour, Cima Capi, a protrusion of rock that ranged above everything in its immediate vicinity. The dramatic slope of the landscape, the enormous lake and the mountain panorama that extended with every metre of altitude gain struck her powerfully.

'Na?' she heard as Andreas came up behind her.

'Bellissimo!' she said with a smile. 'Wedding photos up here would be one-of-a-kind. The photographer I've booked also uses a drone.'

'But there's no cross,' he pointed out, gesturing to the wonky Italian flag that marked the summit.

'No cross,' she agreed glumly. 'But the next summit has one?'

Andreas nodded. 'And the view is just as good – better even.'

'I don't think we'd fit the whole wedding party here at once anyway,' Sophie said thoughtfully, teetering when she peered down one steep drop for too long. She saw Andreas lift a hand to steady her, but he dropped it again when she righted herself.

She took a deep breath, feeling the strength in her limbs in the slight soreness of her muscles.

'You okay?' Andreas asked. 'Can we keep going or do you want to rest?'

She nodded hastily. 'I'm okay. Sorry I freaked out.'

'It's all right. You probably needed it. Next time, I recommend swearing and keeping going.'

She headed for the path down the other side of the peak where the seniors' group had gone ahead. 'That's your mountain-guide advice? Break open the curse words and keep going?'

'Yep,' he said cheerfully, clipping in his carabiners ahead of her. 'It's worked for me so far.'

'I'll give it a try,' she said drily. 'But do you know what, I actually think I can do this.'

16

'I can't do this. Fuck.' She followed up that sentence with a few more curses that struck Andreas as rather unimaginative. She stood stiffly on an iron bracket bolted into a rock face, the Val di Ledro far below, the only way forward was to traverse the exposed vertical.

He didn't contradict her, even though he knew what she said wasn't true. She'd work that out herself soon enough. He wished he could read her as well at sea level as he could on the via ferrata. But that was his life. Everything made more sense up high – everything was just *more* up high.

His breath was more precious, his body stronger, his thoughts clearer. Sophie was more beautiful. Although, she'd been beautiful by the lake, too. It was his response that was harder to ignore up here. For an easy via ferrata, his heart had certainly been pounding a lot today.

The low technical skills required for this route were usually advantageous because the views were incredible. There were regular spots with secure footing to stop to breathe in the clear air and take photos of the lake. That wasn't the view that drew his eyes that day.

He couldn't remember wanting to memorise every detail of her eight years ago. If anything, he'd dragged her out into all sorts of inhospitable places so he *didn't* get caught up in his feelings. Perhaps he should have chosen a more difficult via ferrata, since all he'd seen that day was her: Sophie's wry smile; Sophie's silver studs; the way her hands looked simultaneously fine and strong in fingerless climbing gloves. She had a strand of hair on her cheek that he *would not* brush back.

When they'd been together, she'd been so willing to try everything and he'd enjoyed watching her growing confidence. Today, he didn't care as much about developing her skills. Perhaps that was part of their relationship back then that hadn't survived. But the fascination was alive and well and distracting him just as much as he'd feared.

'Did the swearing help?' he asked.

'Not really.'

'Maybe you need to swear in Italian like I do.'

'Cazzo!' she cried, so suddenly that Andreas jumped.

He stifled a laugh. 'That helped, right?'

'Maybe a little,' she grumbled. 'There aren't enough footholds. I can't see how I can get across.'

'The extra footholds are in the rock. See?'

'I'll slip and hit my head.'

'You won't, but that's what the helmet is for anyway – and the straps.' He eyed her. 'One foot at a time, remember?'

She swallowed, squeezing her eyes shut. But she didn't move.

'Do you trust the equipment?' he asked.

She nodded wordlessly.

'Sophie, you won't fall. I won't ask if you trust me, because I'm not sure I want the answer, but your equipment is all in order.' He came closer as he spoke, giving her carabiners one more rattle to check.

She nodded slowly. 'I used to be so focused on trying to impress you,' she said suddenly.

Her words pricked him. 'You don't have to—'

'I know,' she said again, her voice no longer reedy.

He tried again. 'Actually, what I meant was... you are impressing me. There's a side of you...'

'...I didn't want you to see back then,' she finished. 'Maybe I was pretending more than I realised.'

'I hope you weren't pretending *everything*,' he said emphatically, then choked on his own words when she burst out laughing. 'I meant... I didn't mean *that*.'

'You'll never know if I was pretending *that*.' The playfulness in her expression drew him in. 'Andreas,' she said, her voice low, a small smile on her lips, 'I didn't intend that as a challenge.'

He lifted his brow. 'I'm trying not to take it as one.'

'Are you just distracting me so I forget to be afraid?' She was so close now. Their hands on the cable were almost touching, her body changing the air around his.

'I'm successfully distracting myself,' he said in dismay, his gaze dropping to her mouth and bouncing back up again. 'But only because I know you can do this.'

'What do you think would have happened if I hadn't shown any interest in following you on all those adventures?' she asked quietly.

Andreas froze with a flash of understanding for how she was feeling. He could cross a ravine with ropes and anchors, scale an ice-covered mountain summit, but answering that question scared him.

'To be honest,' he said quickly before panic gripped him, 'we probably would never have got to know each other. That's what you thought? You're right. You've got me.'

Her lips thinned. 'And then I got a little hooked on the adrenaline high and mixed it up with you.' She nodded slowly, as though the realisation comforted her.

It didn't comfort Andreas even though it should have. The wash of guilt at hurting her he'd felt when he'd seen her again – guilt he should have shed in the course of eight years – could be assuaged if her feelings for him hadn't been so deep after all. But he wanted her to insist there had been something more.

'I've told you before I didn't want to end our relationship.'

A nod. A hint of a smile. 'Just pause it while you climbed another mountain and we waited to see if you'd come back down alive.'

Which was exactly why he'd never risked another relationship. He'd had no right to send her that message when he got back. It wasn't fair to leave her figuratively hanging and she'd been right to ignore it, even though he'd blamed her for a few years afterwards.

'But it's not your fault if I didn't realise things were casual,' she said lightly.

'They weren't! I mean... you were important to me.' More important than he could tell her without starting the whole cycle again.

'I know, I know. I bet you love Kira, too, in your way. You told me what your limits were and I shouldn't have tried to cross them – or got angry at you eight years later. I can see now...' Her throat moved as she gazed at the exposed traverse before her. 'It's powerful stuff, adrenaline.' Her smile gained a little strength.

'It is,' he agreed emphatically.

She studied him, her expression this time enigmatic. 'Okay,' she said quietly, loosening her body. 'Let's do this.' And she stepped towards him into the small cleft in the rock.

He waited until she reached the first bolt and clipped her carabiners over one at a time. She glanced up with a hint of uncertainty as he shuffled further along to give her space.

'I'm not going anywhere,' he murmured.

'Except Manaslu,' she added through gritted teeth.

Before he could work out what was behind that comment, she was moving again, sideways along the rock, her feet scrabbling for the steel brackets when the sheer limestone had no natural footholds.

It was a long traverse and they inched across, Andreas always one bolt ahead of her. Her chest rose and fell; he could almost hear her heart racing. He'd loved watching her learn years ago, but his memories were coloured by her admission that she'd forced herself through some difficult moments simply to keep him in her life.

The thought made him weak. He'd lost her devotion, never even mourned it because he hadn't recognised it. He was mourning it now, but with a curious feeling of detachment. They'd both screwed up eight years ago. But she was here, now, and she wasn't pretending any more.

Perhaps this new phase of their relationship, even if it wasn't romantic, was better.

'Want me to take a picture?'

'Right now?' she groaned. 'I suppose we need to show this part to the bride and groom, even if I look half-dead.'

'You're hanging off a mountain, Fini. You look amazing.'

She laughed and he managed to capture the image on his phone. 'That's your fantasy, huh? A sweaty woman in a harness? You will definitely love these extreme weddings!'

'Give you a crown of flowers and I'll fall at your feet,' he joked.

'The flowers looked better on you!' she shot back, still making slow progress in his direction while he stowed his phone again.

'You don't look half-dead,' he said with a smile. 'How do you feel?'

'Wildly alive,' she answered drily.

She climbed doggedly, up and down and across, gaining confidence with each step. By the time she scrambled down the last gully to the next section of hiking trail without safety cables, she was glowing with energy.

After waiting for her to descend the last few steps and unclip her straps, he should have pushed on, set a fast pace to the summit, which was their goal after all. But she stood close on the narrow path and he paused.

Should he give her a high five? A friendly slap on the back? A hug? Her chest heaved as she stared up at him, almost as though she were wondering the same thing – and coming to the same conclusion.

She moved before he did, slipping a hand around his neck. He only had a moment to accept that this had to happen before she tugged him close and kissed him.

Adrenaline shot through him. His hands slammed into the rock on either side of her for balance. His helmet knocked into hers, but he was too overcome to do anything about it. The heat – the softness. Her lips moving over his, drawing him out and pulling him in. The fire in his skin, the fog in his brain. Her fingers insistent on the back of his neck.

The drag of her mouth over his, her shudder of response when he pushed back, when he inclined his head and opened his lips, sparking a heavy craving. One hand made it to her head, his thumb chafing her cheek as his fingers curled under her ear.

God, he'd forgotten how he could lose himself in kissing her – or he'd blocked it out. She'd always been so sweet and eager and he'd wallowed in the simplicity of it.

She straightened, lifting her head as she deepened the kiss further with a tease of her tongue. A rasping, pent-up groan rose from his chest and he let her drag him closer, her hand curling in his harness.

He was light-headed, his blood rushing, his mind full of Sophie and his lungs protesting the lack of air. When her lips broke away from his, he should have been relieved. His body felt lit up like the June bonfires back home. But he wanted her.

Her face was close enough that he could see the imperfections in her skin; he noticed he'd smudged dirt on her cheek.

'Andreas,' she said, her voice low. Whether it was a warning or an invitation, he couldn't tell. 'Do you think that was a bad idea?'

'I've been thinking about kissing you all day.'

It wasn't an answer, but she took it as one, lifting her hands to his face and starting the process all over again.

Her fingertips light on his cheeks made him lose orientation. All he knew was that he needed to stay right here where she was. The second kiss was slower, without the bite of adrenaline but with an aching tenderness that stripped him of some necessary safety equipment and sent him freefalling.

He wanted to wrap his arms around her, but the path where they were standing was too narrow, so he propped himself up on the rock again and leaned close, letting her hands glide over him.

'Achtung Stein! Attenzione!'

Hearing the shout from above, Andreas reacted in a heartbeat, tugging Sophie away from the bottom of the via ferrata as a shower of rocks clattered down. They weren't sizeable or dangerous, but the climber above had done the responsible thing and shouted the usual warnings in German and Italian.

When the danger had passed, he found Sophie watching, trying to stifle a smile. 'Maybe it's a good thing they dislodged some rocks,' she whispered, 'otherwise they might have got a surprise when they reached the bottom.'

He could hear the other climbers scuffling down quickly. 'They can still go to hell for interrupting,' he grumbled in response. He settled his helmet against hers and breathed out deeply. 'I don't care who sees us.'

'We have a whole apartment back in Marniga, Andreas,' she said with a smile. 'We don't need to make out on the via ferrata.'

His gaze snapped to hers, amused, hopeful, slightly wary. He pressed one last, heavy kiss to her mouth. 'Are you serious? You want to do this again back at the apartment? What about—?'

'I'm not going to ask you to marry me afterward,' she said drily.

'That's not what I meant,' he protested. 'But what happens when we leave here?'

'I'm not the fangirl I was back then. I understand you don't want commitment and for a week in Italy, I can forget that I do. For one week.'

Andreas tried to ignore the way his stomach dropped at her words, the way memories from the day everything had gone wrong shivered through him again.

The first climber from the other group took the last few footholds down, unclipping her carabiners. Andreas pulled Sophie to the side of the path, his arm around her waist – *where it belonged*, some forlorn part of him added. Three climbers squeezed past with casual greetings in two languages, which he acknowledged absently in German.

'Are you absolutely sure?' he asked softly.

Her brow quirked. 'Are you?'

'How quickly can we get back to the apartment?'

17

Andreas fumbled with the keys when they raced up the steps to the apartment door later in the afternoon. Sophie laughed at him and he shot her a wry grin in return. When he finally got the door open, he drew her inside with firm hands around her waist and kicked the door shut behind them.

Without another word, he was kissing her.

While Sophie was certain this had been the plan – her idea even – she hadn't expected measured, practical Andreas to immediately fall on her like a starving man. But starving he appeared to be. His hands on her face, he pressed his mouth to hers, quickly deepening the kiss as his fingers speared through her knotted hair.

It was rough, desperate and the hottest kiss of her life.

Sophie had shed those foolish fangirl tendencies. It was reassuring to see him as he was, instead of with stars in her eyes. She could walk away again. It wasn't first love. It was *sex* – great sex, if the kiss was any indication.

Andreas could still stir up her desire with the simplest

things: a smile; his gnarled, capable hands; the efficient way he moved. And boy, the man could kiss. She hadn't remembered kissing specifically as something they'd indulged in often. He'd kissed her in congratulations on summits, they'd definitely kissed in the bedroom – all over each other. But making out the way they had at the bottom of the via ferrata today?

The feeling of being pressed into the limestone, his hands near her head, was something she'd store away for future lonely moments. *I've been thinking about kissing you all day.* Now he seemed to want to kiss her all night and she grabbed his shirt at the waist with both hands, demanding he come closer.

His response was to hoist her onto the side table by the door, his hands slipping down her back and beneath her waistband. She had blocked this out somehow, the way he made her feel as though no one had ever existed for him before. Perhaps the focus was part of what made his personality magnetic. Perhaps she should have been a little worried about losing her head.

But she didn't want to be sensible right now. She wanted to run her palms all over him, tighten her legs around him and soak up the deep kisses that grew clumsy as he seemed to want to touch her everywhere at once.

'Shower?' he asked between kisses and a fresh surge of memories made her skin hot. Showering together when they got home had featured in many of their adventures. She'd been so young, experienced so many firsts with him as the water poured over them both.

A bedroom door flew open. Sophie froze, her eyes widening, as the figure of a young woman emerged, looked up – and also froze, her mouth agape.

'Andreas?'

He jerked away from Sophie so quickly, the side table rattled.

'Caro?' he said with a grimace, his voice high. He said something else in German, but all Sophie caught was the word 'Mama'. As she shuffled to the edge of the side table, her feet feeling for the floor, the other bedroom door opened and a lively older woman appeared – a woman with the same green-gold eyes as Andreas. Sophie was close enough to hear the groan that rumbled deep in his throat.

'Hoi, Mama,' he ground out, rubbing fingers over his brow.

Curiosity warred with mortification and maybe also a touch of schadenfreude when she noticed Andreas swallowing heavily. Her own cheeks were hot and her knees were still wobbly from the thorough – and unfinished – make-out session.

Both women began speaking at once, crossing the kitchen towards them. Sophie finally made it off the table, which made an embarrassing creak. Andreas rushed to head them off, speaking in rapid German. When she smoothed down her shirt and shorts and stepped up to his side, all three of them fell silent.

'Hello, I'm sorry for the... mix-up.' She winced at her inadequate word choice, but 'mix-up' was better than 'eyeful of your son with his hand on my boob'.

'It's not your fault!' Andreas snapped.

'We thought you were in England for work,' the younger woman said. 'So I was very confused when I found the bed unmade and your stinky socks in the washing.'

'We're *here* for work,' Sophie said before she'd thought that through and her throat closed.

His mother's eyes were dancing. 'Are you one of the British guides at Willard's company?'

'I *told* you – both,' Andreas said eyeing them. 'Sophie is a wedding planner. We're planning an outdoor wedding.'

His tone was grumpy and dismissive. Sophie expected a

comment about how unsuited he was to planning a wedding, how he was allergic to commitment, but his mother and the other woman – presumably his sister – gasped.

His mother stepped nearer, her expression strangely luminous. 'Sophie?'

Andreas stared at the ceiling and sighed. Sophie looked warily between them. 'Yes, I'm Sophie, Sophie-Leigh Kirke.' She extended her hand but snatched it back again when his mother didn't seem to notice.

She looked to Andreas, prompting him with a lift of her brow that reminded Sophie of him.

'Yes,' he grumbled an answer to her unasked question. 'This is the same Sophie.'

Sophie's hair stood on end as Andreas's mother studied her. With two more halting steps, the older woman was in front of her, a smile on her lips. She grasped Sophie's forearms briefly, then let go.

'It's lovely to... finally meet you,' she said, her voice not quite steady, although English didn't seem to be a challenge for her. 'I'm Petra, his mother.'

'I'm so sorry—'

The younger woman laughed. 'Don't worry because of us. We should thank you for giving us this insight into his private life.'

Sophie could almost see steam coming out of his ears.

'I'm Caro – Carolin – his sister, much younger of course. Let me guess, you didn't even know he had a sister?'

'Maybe he—' She cut herself off. 'You know Andreas,' she mumbled instead.

'My bad luck,' Caro agreed with a lopsided smile. 'But we should be apologising to you two, I think. Mama, should we go back home? Leave Andreas to...'

'Goodness me, no!' Sophie said emphatically. 'I can stay at a hotel. My employer will pay. There's no reason for you both to drive all the way back.'

Andreas gritted his teeth as though he wanted to disagree, but Petra's eyes lit up.

'Please, don't go to a hotel on our account,' his mother said graciously. 'There's an extra bed in the attic, which Caro can sleep on in my room, and we can all have dinner together.' Andreas again looked ready to protest, but his mother cut him off with, 'Speckknödel? Your favourite? I brought the Speck from home.'

Sophie's stomach growled and she pressed a hand to it to try to stay out of the argument, but she'd tasted lo speck, the distinctive cured ham from South Tyrol, and it was delicious.

Andreas said nothing, which Petra seemed to take as assent.

'You did promise me Knödel,' Sophie commented, then nearly choked again when she remembered Tita's joke about canoodling. Andreas's blazing expression suggested he thought she'd said it on purpose. Trying not to laugh, she turned to Petra. 'That's very kind, thank you.'

It was only afterwards, when Petra moved her things into the room with Caro, that Sophie realised exactly what sharing the apartment meant: Petra had assumed Andreas and Sophie would share a bed. The thought made her pace her bedroom floor, arms crossed, as she waited for Andreas to appear.

They'd been planning to share a bed that night, anyway. It shouldn't have sent goosebumps up Sophie's arms. But they couldn't exactly continue where they'd left off when Caro and Petra went to bed, which meant... they'd spend the night cuddling and that felt like a worse idea than sleeping together in the other sense.

Plus, they'd be giving his family the wrong impression. She

was desperate to know what he'd told them about her to provoke such a reaction.

Andreas strode in, dumping his rucksack in the corner without looking at her. He stared out of the window, hands on hips, and even that was attractive. 'You can have the first shower.'

She swallowed at the reminder that they'd been about to share the shower stall and thanked him. Peering at his profile, she asked, 'Is this okay?'

'It's a bit late for that, isn't it? Anyway, I should be asking you that question.' He glanced at her, his expression grave.

'Do you want me to make it clear that... *this*... is nothing serious?'

He grimaced. 'That might be worse.'

'Worse than them marching us to the nearest chapel? Or were you joking about that?'

'Of course I was joking – in a way.'

'I get that you didn't want to introduce me to them back then. I do understand.'

His gaze snapped up, full of consternation. 'What do you understand?' He rubbed his hand down his face.

'You struggle with how much you love them. You don't want to imagine someone delivering the same news you had to give to Toni. With me, you had a choice. With them, you don't.' Sophie was startled by her own words, but they settled in her mind like a missing puzzle piece.

She wasn't a pre-marriage counsellor, but she'd done some training when she'd started at I Do. She'd learned the theory of attachment styles and the challenges of the various combinations of anxious and secure, attached or avoidant, but she'd never applied it to Andreas – or herself in combination with Andreas.

What a disaster they'd been, her attached, him avoidant,

both of them anxious. But the realisation didn't stop her wanting to get to know Petra and Caro – to know everything about him that he held back. It didn't explain why he still felt like part of her, all these years later.

Part of her past, she reminded herself fiercely. And maybe part of the next week or so of her life. But that was all.

18

Speckknödel usually made everything better, but the meal was unbearable.

First, he'd brooded for half an hour about Sophie's calm accusation: *You struggle with how much you love them.*

Then he'd had to watch Sophie and his mother laugh and joke – occasionally at his expense – while Sophie helped to make the South Tyrolean speciality. He had sat at the table sharing a beer with Caro and avoiding her meaningful looks.

The necessary conversation had been whispered while Sophie was in the shower:

'You didn't mention you were back together!'

'I'm *not* – we're not. Not really.'

'Oh, Andreas, "not really," isn't going to stop her breaking your heart again!'

'She didn't break my heart!' He obviously hadn't convinced his mother and unfortunately, she had reason: she knew about the blasted emerald, had more of an idea than anyone else of exactly what he'd been through after Miro's death.

Now they were one big, happy family around the scarred

wooden table, but at least his mother had brought a nice bottle of St Magdalener from home. He just had to make sure he didn't down his glass too quickly.

'I always thought it must take forever to shred cabbage like this,' Sophie commented with a tight smile when the silence stretched a little too long for her British sensibilities. She scooped up a forkful of Krautsalat, the cabbage side dish his mother had brought from home. The tangy vinaigrette with caraway seeds was another of his comfort foods, but he nearly choked on it when he caught himself staring at Sophie's mouth as she took a bite.

'There is a tool for that,' his mother explained. 'The Krauthobel. But I have a machine.'

'A cabbage-slicing machine?'

'All the benches in the kitchen at home have machines on them,' Caro said with a smile. 'We have a machine for bread, for mincemeat, for sliced meat, for peeling fruit, pitting olives, spraying cream—'

'I think she understands,' Andreas grumbled.

'So, you're here doing research for a wedding?' his mother asked with more than a touch of scepticism.

Sophie nodded. 'We've held a few weddings in the area, but this client wanted something special involving outdoor activities, so...'

'Ah, that makes more sense. I was picturing Andreas helping you pick out flowers!'

Sophie mercifully kept her mouth shut, although he could tell she was stifling a smile.

'What are *you* doing down here?' He tried to keep his voice casual, without much success.

'We're going shopping tomorrow in Verona.'

'Do you want to come?' Caro asked teasingly. 'Your last pair of Armani jeans must be about ten years old now.'

'Twenty,' he corrected her. 'I'll pass. I have to sort out our equipment stores anyway.'

Then his mother opened her big mouth. 'Would *you* like to come, Sophie? Do you have Saturdays off while you're away?'

'You know, actually I'd love to.' She sent him a sidelong glance and then leaned over the table to speak softly to his mother. 'But we might have to promise not to talk about... him.'

'You can talk about what you like,' he snapped.

'Perhaps you could meet us for lunch?' his mother suggested, ignoring his grumpy outburst. He should have made an effort to be civil, for Sophie's sake, but company was not what he wanted right now. He needed to get up a mountain and stop the churning in his stomach at everything that had happened over the past few days.

'A late lunch, maybe.' He could do a few climbing routes from Arco in the morning, clear his head. Then see Sophie again on her day off. Damn, he wished they could have got this unexpected crackle of desire out of their systems before his family had appeared.

'Tell me about the weddings you plan,' Caro asked Sophie. 'Are they all over the world? Where's the most exotic place you've organised a wedding?'

'Most of our clients don't have an unlimited budget, so European destinations are most common, or holiday destinations in the UK, but I have been to the Caribbean and Australia for beach weddings.'

'Beach weddings,' his mother repeated with a nod that he nevertheless interpreted as disapproving. 'I suppose that's what some people want. I got married in the same church as my parents *and* grandparents.'

Andreas didn't look up from his Knödel, carefully slicing into the spongy dumpling and focusing on the simple flavours of onion refined with salt, rather than the unspoken words in the air around the table.

Surprisingly, Caro had mercy on him. 'I think a beach wedding sounds lovely.'

'Since when do you like the beach?' he teased her, hoping to change the subject.

'It's true,' she said, turning to Sophie. 'Most of Mama and Tatta's friends have holiday apartments on the coast near Rimini, but our grandparents couldn't stand the sea, so they bought this one.'

'How can you not like the sea?' Sophie exclaimed.

'Our family,' Caro continued, 'gets uncomfortable when their familiar mountains aren't visible any more – Tatta especially. We have a German word that means home and tradition and comfort, familiarity and history – "Heimat". Tatta's big on Heimat. He can name every peak around our house and he likes it that way. When you grow up cut off in deep valleys, you don't always like to leave.' She rolled her eyes as she said it, but Andreas knew she was carved from the same wood. 'But not Andreas, of course,' she added.

His mother's expression pinched and he stifled a sigh. When she opened her mouth to speak, he cut her off, 'Maybe we can skip the criticism of Andreas tonight? Especially since Tatta would miss out.' He felt Sophie's curious eyes on him as though they scratched his skin.

'I was going to say that you haven't been away as much recently. Perhaps you've discovered the value of home and don't need to prove yourself in the earth's most isolated corners.'

His leg twitched and he had to fight to stop his knee bouncing restlessly under the table.

Then Sophie opened her mouth and said entirely the wrong thing. 'But what about Manaslu?'

Caro's head jerked up. 'Manaslu?'

His mother went white.

'You're going again?' Caro prodded. 'When?'

'In the autumn,' he answered as casually as he could.

'Who with?'

'Brzezinski and Kastelic so far – Dexter might join. We don't have a firm plan yet.'

'We need Andreas in mid-September to be one of the guides for a wedding party,' Sophie added, trying desperately to smooth over her mistake. 'I hope he'll be able to. I made a bet that he'd cry at the wedding,' she added with a smile, but his throat closed all over again. If she said anything about the terms of that bet in front of his family...

He stood abruptly, his chair scraping on the terracotta tiles. He would have had another dumpling or two, but the conversation had turned into a treacherous snow bridge on a glacier, where one wrong step could see him falling into a crevasse.

'Andreas at a wedding?' his mother commented lightly as he dumped his plate in the sink and started running the water. 'You must be very persuasive.'

'No, he's only doing this for Willard – his overdeveloped sense of responsibility.'

'His sense of responsibility doesn't extend to *some* things,' his mother said tightly. 'No mother likes to imagine her son frozen or in pieces, in some place on another continent that God left behind. We have plenty of mountains right here at home and they're not enough. Nothing is enough for my son.' Her voice trailed off.

He'd heard it all before, but this time, he was desperate to know what Sophie made of it all while dreading finding out. He glanced at her, but she had that expression of wide-eyed dismay on her face that reminded him of the day he'd told her he wouldn't marry her. She would understand his mother's sentiment. *Nothing is enough for Andreas.*

But she also understood more: *You struggle with how much you love them.*

She stood, grasping her plate. 'Can I help with the washing up?'

'No, we had a big day. You should rest, if Caro and Mama are going to drag you around to a thousand shops tomorrow.'

'I do have quite a lot of stamina when it comes to shopping, you know.'

'Well, I'm glad I don't have to take you,' he quipped, but kicked himself when her cautious smile slipped. *But I would, if you asked me. I'm going to drive an hour and a half to meet you for lunch. I want to spend all the time with you, except my mother's right and you're right and I can't give either of you what you need.*

She stifled a yawn.

'Go,' he said gently, 'read your book. I'll be there soon.'

* * *

When he slipped into the bedroom an hour later after nursing a schnapps on the balcony, the room was dark and Sophie was a stretched-out shape on the far side of the bed. He should have come earlier so they could talk, rather than being the coward he usually was when it came to feelings, but there were just too many feelings, all conflicting.

When he peeled off his T-shirt and jeans and slipped into the bed, his thoughts unexpectedly calmed to a still day on the lake, rather than the stormy sea he'd been since his family had interrupted them. Sophie rolled over, her hand landing on his bare arm and absently stroking his skin, making the warm, calm sensation spread through him like syrup.

'Andreas,' she sighed sleepily.

'I'm sorry.'

She stilled and he wanted to take her hand and move it along his arm until she understood that she should keep touching him. 'For what?'

'Everything,' he said with a sigh. '*Me.*'

The sheets rustled as she propped herself up on one elbow and peered down at him. The dim glow through the shutters illuminated only patches of her face. 'You don't need to apologise,' she said, her voice even. She was fully awake now. 'I shouldn't have said anything about Manaslu.'

He liked her remorse even less than his own. 'I should have told them already. I just didn't want—'

'That reaction from your mum. I get it. I really do.'

'She's right, though,' he added softly. 'I don't even know why I put them through it. Did you know the death rate for Gasherbrum is 9 per cent?' His voice trailed off. 'Nine in every hundred people who attempt it never come back.' Miro had been one of them. 'When we lost Miro—' His throat closed. It was a miracle he'd got the first four words out, that a concerningly reckless part of him wanted to keep talking.

'You had to tell Toni.'

He crumbled, pulling away from her unconsciously. 'I had to tell her over the phone, from the hospital and then... bring him back to her.'

'But it wasn't your fault, was it?'

He shook his head.

'You did what you could.' The conviction in her voice faded the longer he was silent.

Rubbing a hand over his face, he replied, 'I don't feel guilty.

It's not as simple as that. He was killed by falling ice – a risk that's always present and impossible to predict. We all take responsibility for ourselves on the mountain. In the death zone, you even have to leave the bodies. I managed to get Miro down with ropes and a plastic sheet for a sled, but I would have left him if I'd had to. He would have left me, if our positions had been reversed.'

The wobble in his voice alarmed him and he willed Sophie not to touch him. He wouldn't cope with that undeserved tenderness right now.

'If you don't feel guilty, why the turmoil?' she asked, thankfully matter-of-factly.

He paused, hesitating one last time before admitting the truth – the reason she should stay well away from him. 'I don't feel guilty because I understand the choice he made. I've made that choice hundreds of times myself. I can't control the elements, but I go up anyway. I just don't know if it was fair to Toni.'

'Ah,' she said softly, although he was bewildered by what she thought made sense in his admission. 'You're scared of yourself.'

'What does that even mean, Sophie?' he harrumphed.

'Would you prefer it if they didn't love you? If you could just go up a mountain and no one would miss you?'

'Of course not!' But it would be simpler.

'You feel responsible for their worries.'

'I *am* responsible for their worries – as they constantly remind me. I could just stay down.'

Her reaction was not what he'd expected. 'No, you couldn't.'

'You're right. I couldn't.' He stared at her, what he could see of her face. He thought she was frowning, but something in her tone, in the way she defended him, reminded him of the old Sophie. 'Nothing really makes sense to me in the valley,' he admitted. 'People. They don't make sense to me.'

'I've seen you, Andreas,' she said, a smile in her voice this time. 'Not right up high, but I've been with you in the valley and up a mountain.'

'But with my parents, they don't see me up a mountain. I used to climb with my father, but we did the same routes, the ones he learned on when he was a boy, the routes he taught me when he was young. It's not the same as the split-second decisions, the confrontation with the fragility and resilience of life.'

'That could be the name of your biography.'

He scrunched his brow. 'What biography? I want a climbing route named after me and that's all.'

'That's *all*?'

'I'll leave my invisible footprints on the mountains, the bits of my soul. But I'm a disappointment to my parents. I'm a disappointment to just about everyone. Even my sponsors want me to post on Insta-whatever and I disappoint *them*.'

'You didn't disappoint me.'

Although her words crawled into a dark space inside him and nestled there, his first reaction was a snort. 'Sophie, I turned down your marriage proposal. There's no bigger disappointment than that.'

'I meant today,' she clarified. 'You really don't have to apologise. I wanted to meet your family when we were together for the wrong reasons – as a statement you didn't want to make. But I know, now, that nothing's perfect. My eyes are open. No disappointment, just enjoying this between us for a little while, having my nosy questions answered. You're not responsible for me and I won't expect commitment.'

'I thought you liked commitment? You plan weddings. You married Rory Brent.'

'I keep my hopes and dreams for other people these days,'

she responded drily. 'And you can shut up about Rory. I did a lot of stupid things when I was younger.'

He got the message, but the idea that Sophie had no hopes and dreams for herself didn't sit right with him either.

She flopped back onto the bed. 'But if you want to apologise for something, then apologise for your mum's terrible timing. They couldn't have arrived an hour later?'

He met her gaze across the pillow, his eyesight now adjusted enough to make out her lips, curved into a smile. The valley air pressure, the feeling that he couldn't breathe properly eased and his chest rose and fell with deep breaths.

'An hour?' he responded, his voice pitched now. 'You're optimistic. Don't you know climbers are shit in bed?'

'For someone who believes he can climb any mountain on earth, you are remarkably humble about some things – that or you're just scared.'

It was his turn to hop up on an elbow. 'Scared? Of what?'

'Great sex,' she replied cheekily, draping her arms around his neck. 'Good enough to keep you in bed in the morning instead of heading out to scale a rock face.'

He lowered his head until he was a breath from her lips. 'I am terrified of you,' he admitted, safe in the knowledge that she didn't understand how deeply he meant the words. 'Terrified of wanting you so much that I could ignore the presence of my mother in the other room.'

Pressing a kiss to her mouth, he lingered for a long moment, savouring the softness, but he didn't push deeper.

'It's better if we don't, isn't it?' she asked with a gratifying note of frustration in her voice.

'They won't stay long.' He would make sure of it. 'I don't think I'd be able to keep you quiet.' A grin stretched across his mouth when she rolled her eyes. But his smile faded as he studied the shadowed lines of her face. 'I don't want to be thinking about my family if we... cross that line again.'

She nodded, threading her fingers in his hair until he wondered if he'd melt from the affection. 'Then I do hope they don't stay long.' She pressed a light kiss to his lips. 'Because as soon as they leave, we're crossing that line.'

With a groan, he collapsed back onto the bed and tugged her close. Her head settled on his shoulder, the past and the present mingling in him with that simple action. Despite the heightened emotions of the day, he drifted off easily. Even his final thought before sleep claimed him couldn't disrupt the warmth of well-being glowing in him: *You struggle with how much you love them.*

19

Sophie woke up disoriented and sweaty – and squashed. Andreas had curled his limbs around her in the night like a giant squid and his leg was heavy. But when she glanced across the pillow and caught sight of his face, lax with sleep, a glow spread through her.

His lashes were dark and thick, his lips broad and lopsided. And he thought he disappointed everyone. He felt unsure of himself in the valley. He came alive on the mountain, but there was trauma in him too, that he clearly hadn't processed.

Trauma, she recognised, although he knew nothing about hers and it was probably better that way, especially given his odd reaction every time Rory came up in conversation and his own attitude to marriage and families.

But Sophie wasn't a psychologist. She couldn't advise him – she could only accept him, for a little while at least. She knew this time, she couldn't tie him down. His family took their worry out on him and it only did damage. If he needed to shake off gravity and commitment occasionally, then she couldn't change that.

Which meant they had a week. A safe timeframe – far too short to fall in love again. In a week, she would go back to her normal life and he would go back to his and if they didn't keep in touch, she might be able to get over him enough to one day find someone else, as much as that thought felt distasteful when she was awash with gratification to be tucked up against him. Lying next to him, snuggling like a puppy, it felt as though she'd missed him every day for the past eight years.

Including the days she'd spent as Rory's wife.

The disturbing thought made her ease away as gently as she could. How he turned her from a sensible person into this sentimental mush of a human being, she didn't know, but it was dangerous how good it felt to touch him.

She draped her cardigan around herself and tucked her feet into Andreas's enormous Birkenstocks, to shuffle into the kitchen, where she found Petra putting the moka pot on the stove, already dressed for the day.

'Buongiorno— I mean—'

'Buongiorno,' Petra replied reassuringly. 'And griaß di. Would you like some coffee? We can go soon. We live farm hours and might have the city to ourselves before anyone else leaves the house. I assume Andreas left to go climbing already? I didn't hear him.'

Sophie realised with a start that Andreas usually did get up with the birds on his free days to enjoy the sacred hours on a rock face somewhere. 'Actually, he's still asleep,' she said with a frown.

He wasn't for long, emerging wearing only his loose boxer shorts and a scowl. He filled a glass of water at the sink and Sophie tried not to stare. He was more dishevelled than usual, groggier than he'd been the other mornings, even though she didn't think he'd drunk too much wine the previous evening.

Dishevelled was unfortunately a good look on him, as though his hair was mussed from her fingers and they'd stayed up late last night doing more than just talking.

Sophie rushed to wash and get ready so she didn't hold up Petra and Caro and Andreas waved them off, still looking oddly disoriented.

The shops in the centre of Verona were just opening their doors as the trio arrived at the Via Mazzini after parking the car – a slightly newer Fiat Panda.

'We have to visit the shops here before the crowds arrive,' Caro said.

Even for early in the morning, the pedestrian zone was buzzing with shoppers walking beneath the wrought-iron balconies that inevitably made visitors think of *Romeo and Juliet* in this town. The Gucci store in a historic stone building with arched, stuccoed windows was still closed, which didn't bother Petra and Caro, as they seemed to have their favourite smaller boutiques.

By the time they emerged onto Piazza Erbe, the Saturday-morning bustle was in full swing. Petra seemed a little stressed by the crowds – as Sophie knew Andreas would have been – but Sophie enjoyed the buzz of conversation in Italian, the stall-holders selling scarves and hats, jewellery, souvenirs and towels with the image of the Venetian winged lion. Behind them, the Mazzanti houses took the scene five hundred years back in time with their decorative patterns and frescoes of long-forgotten figures.

The buildings on the square were tightly packed, the morning sun picking up the yellow and white and terracotta of the render. The crooked balconies overflowed with plants and two historic towers of ancient brick rose above the long square, into the blue sky.

'A bride and groom had photos taken here last year,' she said as they passed the Domus Mercatorum, the striped brick structure on the corner with crenellations and arched windows. 'We came here at six in the morning to whirl past all the sights with the photographer.'

'Ouch, that's early!' Caro said emphatically. 'Our farm hours aren't that bad.'

'The photos were amazing, though,' Sophie said, smiling as she remembered the bride's serene smile as she posed in her flowing dress in front of the Roman arena as the sunlight burst across the sky. 'Let me show you.'

She unlocked her phone and tapped the gallery app, but then froze when she noticed she'd forgotten to close the app and instead of the little grid of thumbnails, a larger photo appeared on her screen – a photo she wasn't quite fast enough to shut down.

Of course Caro was too quick to have missed it. 'Was that Andreas? Did you have him practising a wedding with you?'

'What's that?'

Sophie held her phone to her chest, her mind racing. 'I just needed to check how it would look – for my clients!'

'May I see?'

Sophie wasn't sure how she could refuse that request, asked so softly by Andreas's mother, so she swallowed her cringe and unlocked her phone again. 'The framing isn't great. A stranger took it. The cross should be slightly off-centre. And the bride is going to have flowers in her hair and hopefully look a bit fresher than me—' She cut off her babbling, not sure if Petra and Caro were even listening.

When Petra looked up, she had a light in her eyes that made Sophie's stomach dip. Taking a deep breath, she blurted out the words she probably should have said last night. 'I should tell you that we aren't together and we have no intention of being together despite... everything you've seen.'

There was only a nod in reply.

Sophie decided it was better to imply that the reasons they weren't together lay with her. 'I mean, after what happened eight years ago, there's no way I could consider a relationship with him again.'

'After what happened... You mean with Miro?' Petra asked.

'I meant between him and me. The twenty-ninth of February thing.' She mumbled the last part.

'What happened on the twenty-ninth of February?'

Didn't they know? Or had she confused them? 'It's the... date where traditionally, women have been able to ask men to marry them.' It sounded so foolish. Her cheeks were hot and she wished she'd never been that twenty-six-year-old idiot who'd taken those traditions seriously.

Caro clasped her forearm. 'You asked him to marry you?'

Oh God, she needed a hole to fall into right now. She gritted her teeth, cursing Andreas.

'Wow, I'm impressed,' Caro continued.

'He said no,' she added, only realising the absurdity of that comment far too late.

'But what about—?' Caro bit her lip and glanced at Petra. 'I thought you broke up after he got back from Gasherbrum? That's what he said anyway.'

Sophie stifled a grumble at Andreas and his 'break' versus 'break-up' pedantry. She'd never seen him again. That was clearly enough of a break-up.

'No, he turned me down and then we broke up. It was probably for the best.' She should have said, *It was for the best*, but that continuing pull between her and Andreas wouldn't let her.

'I felt certain we'd meet you one day, but I didn't imagine

these would be the circumstances,' Petra said smoothly, glancing at Sophie's phone. 'It was partly my fault that he never brought you home.'

'Why? Andreas is the one who didn't want to introduce me to you. I mean, I know he had his reasons, but I don't understand why you would blame yourself.'

Petra's cheeks went pink and Caro laughed.

'Because Mama overdid the drama when he told us about you,' his sister explained.

'I was happy for him,' Petra insisted. 'He's always been so lonely – you know he'd never admit it. He never felt he quite fit in at home on the farm. He had Miro, but Miro always had Toni. But then he had… you, Sophie.'

The goosebumps that skittered up her arm were out of place on the hot day. 'Surely he's had other girlfriends – before that and since?'

When Petra shook her head, the goosebumps dug in. 'Very few we'd heard about and no one he really loved.'

She didn't mean Andreas had loved her, Sophie was certain.

'He was living at home at the time, saving money for Gasherbrum,' she said, her tone growing dismissive as she said the name of the mountain. 'When it got to around six o'clock each day, he'd start glancing at his phone obsessively, picking it up and putting it down and going out to the garden and back inside. Then the phone would ring and he'd disappear upstairs, like a child going to the Christmas tree.'

Sophie's stomach twisted as the image burrowed into her heart in vivid focus.

'I did wonder whether you'd come – after Gasherbrum, after Miro—'

'Mama,' Caro scolded gently. 'It's not Sophie's fault, especially after what Andreas did, turning her down.'

'He took it hard didn't he? Miro's death?' Sophie asked, thinking of Andreas's tone the night before. He was still grieving, as much as he'd tried to reason with what had happened.

'Very hard,' Petra confirmed gravely. 'For a little while, I hoped at least one good thing might come of it: that he'd stop taking these risks. But he was even worse after he recovered from Miro's death as well as his own injuries.'

The renewed twinge in Sophie's stomach was uncomfortable, especially with her mind running wild with images of Andreas sick and injured. She'd read reports about the expedition, but she'd never allowed herself to picture what it had meant that he'd lost his best friend and sustained injuries himself. Part of her wished she'd been there for him, but she was trying to be sensible about her feelings and nursing him through a difficult time would only have dug her in deeper.

'We really thought you'd broken up with him then, during that awful time,' Petra said with a grimace.

'Although I wouldn't have blamed you,' Caro added. 'He was a wounded bear, nipping at everyone who came too close.'

'I still don't know why he led you to believe I broke up with him.'

'He said you weren't at the airport to meet him when he got back.' Petra looked as though she could have added more.

'I didn't even know when he was coming back. He never contacted me a—'

An uneasy thought struck her, a split-second decision she'd made with her heart bruised from his rejection, convinced he'd only been letting her down gently by suggesting they go on a break. But surely he wouldn't have tried to contact her after the way they'd parted.

'He hasn't told me a lot about that time,' she said. 'Not that I expect him to. We're colleagues now – friends.'

'Friends, hmm?' Caro said with a chuckle as Sophie shook off her confusion. 'I think you're the only person who could convince him to attend a wedding!'

'I haven't convinced him yet,' she insisted, catching sight of a three-piece suit in a shop window. 'And I don't think there's any way I could convince him to come to the reception. Does he even own a suit?'

'I think Andreas would go up in flames if he ever touched a suit,' Caro said wryly.

Sophie managed a distracted chuckle. 'I think you might be right.'

20

'And... buy yourself a suit, Andreas,' his mother said in a withering tone the following morning as she was about to leave for home.

He wasn't sure where the idea had come from, but his collar felt tighter just hearing the word. He'd walked Caro and his mother to their car, hoping they didn't work out he was ushering them off quickly so he could get back to Sophie.

As he'd fidgeted all the way through their late lunch in Verona the day before and lost every round of cards against Caro last night, they could probably guess he wanted them gone.

'It won't hurt you to help Sophie with her weddings, confront your fears,' his mother continued.

'My *fears*?'

'Yes. It would do you good to watch people defying their pride and their doubts and choosing love.'

Andreas needed to end this conversation before he started brooding about Rory Brent again. He didn't want to know how much Sophie had loved him. 'What I've gathered from Sophie is that weddings are about symbolism and floral arrangements. The love happens before – hopefully.'

The way his mother shook her head, he felt ten years old again. 'You test yourself – over and over again – against geography, the elements, the natural world. You prove yourself that way, as much as it worries me that you never seem to have finished proving yourself. A wedding is like that, except for two people, for love. A wedding is proof.' She sighed, pressing a kiss to his cheek. 'I hope that if you see the proof, you might believe in love after all.'

'I know love exists. I don't need proof,' he insisted. The proof was back inside the apartment, having a cup of tea. He'd loved Sophie. There was no other explanation for that squeeze of desperation and that was how he knew it couldn't be a long-term state for him. 'Going to a wedding in Italian tailoring isn't going to change anything.' He thought briefly about that reckless bet he'd made.

'Then it won't hurt you to attend one – for her. I can only imagine how much your disdain for weddings hurts her feelings.'

He frowned, curious about his mother's tone. She didn't know Sophie had proposed marriage and he didn't imagine Sophie would have brought it up while they were shopping. She had a point about hurting Sophie's feelings, but that had always seemed inevitable.

'One shopping date and you're on her side? She knows it's not personal,' he ground out.

'All right Andreas,' his mother said with a deep sigh. 'I know better than to argue with you. But if you won't make compromises for Sophie, you have to let her go – for your own good as well as hers.'

'I know,' he said grimly. 'I understand *that* much better than you do.' He'd let her go once and it had hurt like hell. Whatever they were doing right now – fooling around, being intimate again – he was dreading the end of it but determined to do it anyway.

After waving off his mother and sister where they'd parked their car, he trudged back through the narrow streets to the apartment. He was sick of making trouble for Sophie. She'd claimed he didn't disappoint her, but how could he not? He wouldn't even commit to attend someone else's wedding when she might need him.

The Manaslu trip dangled in front of him as though it held the secrets to the meaning of life – his life. That's all he was committing to right now.

Stomping up the old stone steps, he managed not to shove the door open despite his mood. Sophie looked up from her computer and a thousand thoughts rippled over him. Her smile was uncertain but so damn beautiful, his knees wobbled.

She wore a floral dress that draped over her shoulders. She'd tugged her short hair up with a clip and he just wanted to take it down and fist his hands in it. He wanted to fight with her – or have her fight with him, more specifically – and then kiss her, let this smouldering thing between them catch fire and worry about what would be left later.

With slow, purposeful steps, he approached her and drew her up out of the chair with a firm grip on her upper arms. Her gaze clouded, but she didn't say anything, even when he drew so close, he caught the subtle scent of rose, which took him right back to that first trip together. He'd thought he'd gone crazy for that sweetness with a spicy, earthy note underneath, until he'd realised he'd just gone crazy for Sophie.

Stroking up her arms, across her shoulders up to her face, he felt her shudder. Maybe this would end in heartbreak sooner rather than later but touching her was the only way he could soothe the ache right now. When her hand came up to clutch his forearm for balance and her eyes shut, he knew exactly how she felt.

Her mouth dropped open and after one mingled breath, his lips found hers.

The kiss was long and slow and indulgent. They'd kissed thousands of times, but the wanting in this one made it feel like something new. He'd thought perhaps she should stop him, but she encouraged him instead, opening her mouth and making him groan, part of him still stunned by the fact that this was *Sophie* letting him touch her.

He hadn't quite intended for it to happen, but a moment later, they found themselves exactly where they'd left off on Friday before Caro had interrupted, except on the kitchen table instead of by the door. And Sophie was wearing a soft dress instead of heavy-duty trousers.

His thoughts were mush as his hands tightened on her skin. It wasn't supposed to feel so good. But when she clutched at him, he only felt better with each moment.

The zip of her dress came down and he found more skin to stroke and enjoy as the neckline followed.

'I love this dress,' he murmured as his teeth grazed the little bow on the strap of her bra, where the cup began.

She started to say something that he guessed would be nonsense, given the glaze over her eyes, but he hoisted her against him and she finished on a squeak. Tugging her arms out of her sleeves, she clung to his neck as he bore her into the bedroom, dumping her at the foot of the bed where he could continue exploring.

'Tell me any time if you want to stop, Fini,' he said, his hands inching the hem of her dress higher.

'Don't stop,' she said emphatically.

* * *

Sophie's head was muddled, her thoughts sweet and syrupy, as though Andreas had such a potent effect on her that she was drunk. She distantly remembered that there was supposed to be some danger here. She couldn't fall in love with him again. Her heart couldn't take another round against Andreas Hinterdorfer.

But whatever this round was – *not* love, she insisted – he was winning it completely and utterly, and she was happy to surrender. They were *both* winning. So much for Andreas's joking claim that climbers were bad in bed – always distracted or dirty or tired. He was none of those things as he dropped down between her legs and teased her and coaxed her to a peak that seemed to shudder through him as well.

She panted, getting her breath back, but she wanted him close, now. Forcing herself upright, she found enough presence of mind to help him with his jeans, her hands suddenly fevered.

He caught her chin briefly between his thumb and forefinger. 'Hey,' he said gently. 'We can stop there if you like.'

Shaking her head vehemently, she peeled his T-shirt off, then pulled him onto the bed by his wrist. She paused to kiss him there, by the tattered leather bracelet, then in the middle of his palm. His unsteady breath sent a fresh shot of adrenaline through her.

He tumbled onto the bed and she came with him, his mouth finding hers again for a searing kiss as he grasped the back of her head. He had to reach down beside the bed to fumble in his bag for a condom, but he kept a hand on her thigh as though he couldn't let her go.

'Okay?' he asked one more time when he was ready.

An Italian Wedding Adventure

There wasn't even a hint of uncertainty as she answered, 'Yes.'

It was eight years overdue as he fitted inside her. Sophie hung on and struggled to remember to breathe as an ache she hadn't acknowledged, the unexploded bomb of her feelings resolved – for a moment at least.

His expression was taut – his muscles too. She could tell he was trying to hold back, draw it out, but everything felt too good and his determination crumbled before her eyes. Propped up on his elbows with his fingers tangled in her hair, he shut his eyes while hers soaked in every detail of him beginning to come apart.

The climax swept them both away, rising through Sophie until her vision blurred. Then there was just the weight of him, his head on her shoulder, blissfully heavy.

Now was the time to talk herself out of falling in love. He'd expressed passion, fervour – nothing more. But wow, he felt amazing against her: soft, relaxed – vulnerable. She ran her fingers through his wiry hair and down to his sculpted shoulders. His groan was muffled in her neck.

'Ahhh, Sophie,' he mumbled. With what sounded like superhuman effort, he propped himself up again and peered into her face. 'Okay?' he asked again.

She nodded hastily.

'I didn't mean to... the instant they left.'

She smiled faintly and traced his strong brow with her fingertip. He caught her hand and kissed it before hauling himself upright to take care of the condom. Sophie sat up, tugging the bedsheet over herself, and stared at his back, safe in the knowledge that he wasn't looking at her as more troubling thoughts descended – unwelcome thoughts about her four years with Rory.

After spending those years convincing herself that she'd got everything wrong with Andreas, those opinions seemed upside down, now, after only one week with him. Rory had never strode around their apartment casually naked. He'd never asked her if she was okay after sex, even at the beginning.

He'd never fallen on her the instant they were alone.

When Andreas came back into the room a few minutes later with a cup of tea, Sophie had to gather all her wits to stop herself bursting into tears.

'Hey,' he prompted, brushing a hand over her hair and cheek. Setting the tea on the bedside table, he sat on the bed next to her. 'Did I hurt you?'

She shook her head. 'I don't really want to talk about it.'

His eyes clouded. 'Are you thinking about Rory?' His tone was indignant, no trace of his earlier uncertainty.

'Yes, but it's nothing to do with you. It's me and my decisions, so don't lose your shit.'

The puzzled frown he gave her almost made her laugh, as though he thought he would never lose his shit. 'I thought the "it's not you, it's me" was my line. And when we've just slept together, it's a bit difficult not to think it's about me.'

She gave his shoulder a shove and he grabbed her hand and held it. Staring at her hand in his beaten one, Sophie's breath was short again. She felt too close to him, but she didn't want to back away again – not yet.

'I suppose that's fair enough,' she murmured. Resting her head on his shoulder, she continued, 'Was it always that good? Or have you improved with age?'

He chuckled, his muscles moving under her cheek. 'I don't know whether to be flattered by the compliment or to tell you off for forgetting how we were back then.'

'I think I forced myself to forget,' she admitted.

Swallowing heavily, he replied, 'I never managed to.' His breath tickled her forehead as he turned to her. 'But it was a little different today – better, yes, although those memories of you are important enough to me that I don't want to touch them.'

A shiver raced down her spine. Being together that day had held a sharpness that hadn't been there years ago, a push-pull of emotion, blurry, flawed wanting. But the rawness hit deeper somehow. Sophie had tried to give him everything eight years ago, without knowing how – without knowing *him*?

But today…

He pressed a quick kiss to her forehead. 'Let's eat some lunch and then I want to show you something – something your wedding-loving soul will appreciate.'

She gave him a doubtful look, but nevertheless dressed quickly and followed him into the kitchen.

21

'Where exactly are we going?'

Following a stone path through twisted, silver olive trees, Sophie followed Andreas up the steep slope. Marniga was only a cluster of clay roofs below them, the belltower of the church of San Giovanni Battista a bright white in the sunlight. Heat shimmered over the lake, the mountains appearing to snooze in a delicate haze.

Nothing moved except a bird of prey – a falcon or a kite, she wasn't certain – soaring and swooping in the updraft. The hillside glistened with the freshness of spring before the sweltering summer.

'A ghost village,' he replied with a grin. 'Have you ever organised a wedding for supernatural enthusiasts?'

'No, but Reshma has. Sometimes, I think she's seen it all, when it comes to weddings – except her own, of course.'

'She's not married?'

Sophie shook her head. 'None of us are, except Tita. But luckily, places like this do our advertising for us.' She paused to take a breath of the grassy freshness of the air, with a hint of pine.

'What was your wedding like?'

Her gaze whipped back to him, but he wasn't looking at her. His tone was neutral – carefully neutral.

'I'm not judging you,' he continued mildly, taking his cap off and settling it on his head again after rubbing at his hair. 'I'm trying to... You're obviously good at what you do and it's important – very important to your clients. I'm sorry I was dismissive. You and weddings hit a nerve and my reaction reflected more on me than on you.'

She was speechless for several seconds and had to scramble to catch up with him when he continued ambling uphill, his boots scuffing on the white stones.

'Thank you,' she responded. 'I didn't mean to touch that nerve.'

He glanced at her ruefully and she had the reckless thought that she *did* want to touch that nerve. She wanted to get into his system and ruffle them all up, make him feel something he wasn't ready for. But he wouldn't let her and she was worried about untangling it all when he put distance between them again.

'So, what was it? A grand affair with two hundred guests in a quaint farmhouse in Somerset? Or a chic hotel in Bath? Or did you have a commitment ceremony too?'

Sophie grimaced. 'Well, it was in the Guildhall in Bath, but we just sat in the registry office with our parents and my sister and went to the pub afterwards.' The familiar stab of grief accompanied the explanation.

'You didn't want a big wedding?'

'Of course I did,' she admitted. There was only one way to explain herself and perhaps it was better to mention it and move on, so she rushed into it before she could get stuck in her tangle of feelings. 'We didn't have much time to plan it. I got pregnant while we were engaged and... But we... And then... I miscarried, but we had the date booked and thought it was best...'

With a snort that was still preferable to a sob, she swiped at her eyes and stomped ahead before he fully comprehended that she'd had the most miserable wedding in history – before she did something stupid like fall apart in his arms.

'Sophie.' The shock in his voice stopped her. Several tears fell and she couldn't stop them. Then he enveloped her in his arms, his arms that seemed perfect for hugging, even though she knew they existed to drag him safely up mountains. 'I'm sorry.'

She gave half a shrug and forced herself to let go of him. It wasn't his grief. 'We always said we'd celebrate the wedding properly one day – I'd plan it to be perfect. And then we'd start a family – on purpose this time. But I got so busy at work. Probably, I was trying to deal with the... loss the only way I knew how. We never did either of those things. We just got Betsy – our dog. It's kind of strange how easily the marriage was erased at the end, without even any photos of me in a white dress. But I still... Maybe I hung onto the marriage for too long because it was all I had to remember the... Oh, *shit*.'

Now she was bawling in earnest, batting away Andreas's hands as he tried to comfort her.

'It's fine,' she said, her voice as wobbly as her steps. 'I mean, it's fine that it's not fine. You didn't know I'd lost... someone and I didn't—' She cut herself off. Perhaps it wasn't wise to express that part.

'You didn't what?'

His voice was so gentle, so unlike the defensiveness that had been the hallmark of their reunion, that she allowed the words to tumble out. 'I didn't realise how much pain you were in after Miro died.'

He froze, a flicker of surprise in his eyes – and uncertainty. 'I didn't think you—'

'Your mum mentioned something, but don't blame her. Maybe I should have—' The end of every sentence felt like a trap.

'You thought we'd broken up. I get it now.' He seemed to understand more than she did. 'I wish I'd— I don't know. Been there for you?'

She blinked, his words prickling over her. 'It wasn't your baby, Andreas,' she blurted out, grimacing when the sentence felt bald and hurtful. She hadn't intended that.

'I know, but... Ach, forget it. I'm just sorry. If you want a family so much, I wish it had worked out.'

'It's not that I'm desperate for a baby,' she said bluntly. 'At least, not just any baby. But *that* baby will always feel absent. I couldn't just go out and replace him or her and maybe that was part of the problem. I don't think you could understand.'

'Maybe not,' he said grimly.

Before the thread between them pulled too tight, Sophie hastened her steps. They'd only slept together again – after agreeing that they weren't rekindling their relationship in any other way. Neither of them should imply that they'd had any responsibility to each other during the past eight years.

He caught up to her quickly, his Adam's apple bobbing and his expression harsh, but he snatched her hand and held on, looking ahead, rather than at her. The path curved up the hill, a steep drop-off on one side, and when they turned a corner, Sophie saw it – the ghost village.

Nestled amongst the foliage – olive and oak trees, a single, spindly cypress and lush growth of ivy – was a cluster of crumbling stone and dappled clay roofs. An electricity cable strung across the shallow gully was the only sign she hadn't gone back in time in this secret hollow over the lake.

'This is the village of Campo – population around five,' Andreas said as he squeezed her hand to urge her on.

The impression of entering a secret, forgotten place grew stronger as she took the uneven path after Andreas. Dilapidated walls with vacant windows loomed on both sides, shutters hanging by a single hinge. Many roofs were missing. The mismatched houses were built onto each other or separated only by narrow streets that pre-dated the invention of the automobile.

Archways, hidden steps and short tunnels led them through the tiny town, with constant glimpses of the hillside and the lake. A pot plant or two suggested the presence of the few residents, but the place was eerily quiet.

A carriage wheel was propped under an old stone balcony. An archway led from nowhere to nowhere, but framed a stunning view of olive groves and still, turquoise water. The roots of old trees tangled in the bricks of ancient walls.

Everywhere Sophie looked, she could picture unforgettable wedding photos.

'Look,' Andreas said, gesturing through the arch. As Sophie stepped closer, she saw that someone had mounted a red sign at the edge of a little clearing that read simply:

LOVE

Her chest hurt. The sign was trite at best and at worst tasteless, but to stumble upon love in this secluded ghost town struck the sentimental part of her she refused to give up, even after everything she'd been through. But that sentimental part had no business imagining she was here with Andreas for a reason.

It didn't change anything that he now knew about the lowest time in her life. Today had to be a part of her own story, not their doomed romance.

Perhaps she had to admit that their relationship had meant a lot to her – everything, at one point. She hadn't been only young and stupid; she'd been genuinely in love and she shouldn't throw away the memories, the experience, as much as she might want to when it hurt.

'Not "*amore*"?' she asked with a chuckle that probably didn't quite disguise her emotional state.

'Take some pictures – for your clients,' he suggested, possibly as a coded instruction for her to calm the heck down. She was on a business trip. 'Then we can see if the lady is around to open the café, such as it is.'

She gave him a tight smile, pulling her phone from her rucksack. He drifted through the arch towards the sign and paused, his hands in his pockets and his foot propped up on a log, gazing out at the view over the water.

Sophie suspected she'd regret this – all of it – but she lifted her phone and opened the camera app. With a tap of her finger, she framed and saved forever the image of Andreas, straight-backed, tranquil and probably dreaming of mountains, with the word 'LOVE' in huge letters next to him.

* * *

'Is this enough of a view for you?' Sophie teased.

She stood resting her arms in the straps of her rucksack, feet wide on the loose rock debris, and gazed at the 360-degree vista. The entire lake was visible, from a hazy Sirmione in the south all the way to Riva in the northern corner. But even in its entirety, Italy's largest lake looked small from over 2,000 metres up, high enough that the Alps ranged into the distance, a few peaks still snow-covered, even at the beginning of June.

But Andreas struggled to tear his eyes from another view – one he'd missed for eight long years. A view he would miss again for he didn't know how long – because she was going home tomorrow and so was he. He was trying not to resent her smile, when he couldn't muster his own.

'What will Lily and Roman think of it?'

Sometime over the past week, he'd developed a little grace for the wedding Sophie was planning. The bride and groom had become people, as Sophie spoke of them. Lily had been gravely ill and they wanted to celebrate her return to health as well as the strength of their commitment. After the gnawing ache he'd felt when he'd heard about Sophie losing a baby... He was more prone to sympathy than usual right now. He was more prone to everything emotional.

'To be honest, I don't know if it's what they were hoping for,' she said, the wind whipping her hair in her face as she picked her way back over the rocks to him. She was beautifully surefooted, his Sophie.

'Why not? Like you said, the view is almost unbeatable, as this is the second-highest point around the lake. There's a croce di vetta.' He gestured to the rounded metal cross marking the summit the way a used-car salesman presented his wares.

'It's a bit of a moon landscape,' Sophie said, gazing around her again in wonder at the sweeps of rubble from previous rockfalls, the looming stone with slanted strata where only the hardiest bushes clung to life. 'I think a little wedding would be overwhelmed up here, where geology and geography are the main show.'

He approached her slowly, waiting until she prompted him

with a look. 'Are you suggesting that there might actually be bigger things in life than a wedding?'

'I walked into that one, didn't I?'

Nodding, he pressed a quick kiss to her lips. 'We've both come a little closer to understanding each other's point of view.'

'Close enough that you're guaranteed to cry on their wedding day,' she quipped.

His stomach flipped. They'd both mentioned the bet in passing over the past week, in banter. But every time, it made him wary of the consequence of losing the bet. He'd happily give her the stone, but how would he explain why he had it?

The point was moot because there was no way he'd ever cry. He hadn't cried at Miro's wedding – he hadn't even cried at Miro's funeral.

'We should head down before the wind gets worse,' he mumbled.

22

He was purposefully quiet as they tramped back to the top of the chair lift, reminding him of their first two treks, where he'd tried so hard not to dwell on what she made him feel. He was dwelling, now – brooding, even.

She'd said one week. He had three months – perhaps four – before Manaslu and whatever came after that. He'd already started thinking of how he could spend more training time in Weymouth – or Bath. He wanted to meet her dog. He wanted to look Rory in the eye with the hint of a thousand broken bones.

'You're quiet,' Sophie said warily as the rocky summit ridge gave way to rolling meadow.

He would rather have her teasing. 'Aren't I usually quiet?'

She inclined her head in acknowledgement. 'I suppose the past week was the anomaly, not this afternoon.'

'What do you mean?'

'I mean the smiling, the... displays of affection.'

He snatched her hand mainly to make a point. 'I can be quiet *and* display affection.'

'So you can.' She paused. 'As long as everything's okay.'

'How can everything be okay when you're leaving tomorrow?' he blurted out. '*You* seem pretty peaceful.' She peered up at him in confusion and he bit his lip, wishing he hadn't said anything. 'Sorry, you didn't deserve that. It's my problem.'

'Where have I heard that before?' she said with a sigh. 'Is this to do with the wedding? Have you decided you're chickening out?'

'I don't know,' he answered woodenly.

'If you are, it's better to just tell me, Andreas. It's called "planning" a wedding for a reason.'

'I don't know!' he snapped. 'I want to help you, but I'm committed to this expedition and there's a chance they'll decide on the September window. I'll let you know as soon as I can.'

'Okay, fair enough.'

That was also more grace than he deserved.

Over dinner at the same restaurant as the first evening, they casually discussed the drive to the airport the following morning while he tried desperately not to picture her walking through a set of departure gates without him and then called himself all kinds of hypocrite for putting his family through that exact scenario so many times – except worse, because of the chance that he'd never come back.

That was his real life, not lounging for an hour in bed with Sophie every morning, discovering new ways to make her laugh – and moan. He was a mountaineer, not a guide for a Sunday stroll with Aunt Frieda. It might be best for both of them if he didn't do the wedding. He could suggest to the Polish team that early September would be a better time to depart for Nepal.

He could disappoint Sophie once and for all.

'Andreas,' she said, her voice firm. 'I can see something's bothering you.'

'When we get back to England, do you want me to come up to Bath to meet Lily and Roman?'

She studied him. 'If you like, but if you can't commit to the wedding, I'm not sure if it would be worth the trip.'

'If I was... in Bath...' Now she was looking at him as though he had a screw loose and he wasn't sure she was wrong. 'I want to see *you* in Bath.'

She blinked. 'I'm not sure that's a good idea.'

'It's a terrible idea, but I still want to.'

'For what? More sex? Casual, the way you're used to?'

'No!' He got as far as the denial, but then he hit problems. The conversation teetered on a precipice and gravity was tugging at him. 'A week hasn't been long enough. You're... *Sophie*.'

'Yes, I'm Sophie,' she repeated doubtfully when he couldn't get any further.

He ground the heel of his hand into his forehead. He wasn't built for these conversations. He should have done it on a mountain. God, if he ever got married – which he wouldn't – it would have to be at the top of a mountain where his head was clear.

'I've never— You're the only one I—'

Her shoulders sagged and he saw as though in slow motion that there was no way for this conversation to end well. 'You can't finish that sentence,' she said – too gently. 'You couldn't eight years ago and you can't now. At least this time, I understand why you can't but continuing to see each other is only delaying the inevitable. My feelings for you are real, too, but we want different things and maybe a clean break would be best for both of us.'

With a flash of memory, he saw her giddy smile, felt her arms draped around his neck and heard her soft voice. '*I'm in love with you.*'

His world had tilted when she'd said it, as though his centre of gravity had tried to shift. He'd almost felt himself falling – desperately falling.

Sophie hadn't noticed. She'd just smiled widely, hopefully – naively – and continued, *'When you get back, will you marry me?'*

He'd never felt panic quite like that – until today. So, he'd laughed, as though her brave statement of feelings was something insignificant, when the opposite had been true. He'd covered his pounding, panicking heartbeat with the most casual tone he'd been able to muster and dashed her hopes to nothing.

'You asked me to marry you eight years ago, but this time, you're suggesting a clean break?'

Perhaps that pointed reminder was unfair of him, but it had the desired effect. She glanced up with resentment. 'I was stupider – and stronger – back then. Can you imagine if you'd said yes out of responsibility – or guilt? How long do you think we would have been married? A year? A month?'

Ouch, they were both throwing punches. 'Maybe we would have worked things out.' He didn't know where those defensive words had come from – or what he was defending. God knows, she was probably right.

'Maybe we would have, except you would have been miserable. Either I would have asked you to stay home more often because the months were so long without you or you would have been distracted and guilty while you were away. You warned me of the consequences of that! You don't belong in the valley.'

You make the valley more tolerable. 'It worked the year we were together. I was away a lot, but you were always there when I got back.' Until that last time, when he'd finally had to accept that it wasn't fair to keep her in his life.

'We weren't much more than a year-long fling.'

He tried not to flinch.

'I've been married. Marriage is a whole lot more than

climbing lessons and going on holiday together. I spent all of my time and money that year chasing you and you never made a step in my direction. Afterwards, I thought the relationship had been all in my head. You didn't exist in real life, no matter how much it felt like you did.'

His vision tunnelled, memories from that year tarnishing as he appreciated just how badly he'd screwed up back then.

'I never imagined... I hurt you that much.'

'I'd asked you to marry me! Of course it hurt. And then you never contacted me again!'

'I... *What?* I contacted you – and you never replied, you never came. I understand that's fair, now, but *you're* the one who had the last word.'

* * *

Sophie gripped the tabletop tightly as the world seemed to start spinning. He thought she'd been the one to break contact?

'I never came where?' she asked, clinging to her understanding of what had happened before she lost her orientation.

His gaze snapped up, his eyes blazing. 'To the airport – to Heathrow.'

'To wave you off? You'd just suggested we go on a break. Why would I think you wanted to see me? I didn't even know which flight you were on!'

'I mean after the trip!' he said, still staring at her as though she were being purposefully dense. 'When I texted you – from Pakistan.'

Sophie's muscles went slack. She managed to prop her elbows on the table and catch her head, but her body was rubber. His information didn't compute, contradicted everything she'd convinced herself of over the past eight years.

'You texted me?' she managed to say, her voice mostly breath.

It was his turn to freeze. 'Twice. Are you saying you didn't get them?'

She nodded her head weakly. 'I blocked your number. You'd just dumped me and it hurt. But you never mentioned it before now!'

'I thought you knew, that you'd ignored my texts on purpose.' Something in his strangled tone reminded Sophie of Miro's death and dread settled in her stomach. Exactly what had he texted her?

'It doesn't matter,' he assured her, settling a hand over hers. 'I was... in a mess at the time. I probably would have made everything worse if you had come.'

She would have come; she wouldn't have even hesitated. Her lungs were tight as she tried to work out what this meant for the future, but still couldn't calculate the end of their relationship any differently.

'You spent all this time thinking I never contacted you ever again?' he asked. 'I mean, I *didn't*, after those two texts. How much difference can it make? I was oversensitive when you didn't respond.' He gave a humourless laugh.

'I would always have responded, Andreas.' The words were out before they scared her, but when they did, she wasn't sure if she was ready for his response.

'You would have answered, even if it was years later and you were with Rory? I can't imagine *he* would have been happy for you to be contacting me.'

'That's an impossible question!' she said, lashing out. 'I didn't know you'd texted me. I'm sorry I wasn't there if you—'

'It was probably better the way it turned out,' he said through gritted teeth.

He was right. They always circled back to the same place: no matter how much he meant to Sophie, the practicalities would crush their relationship sooner or later.

It still felt like she was losing something even more precious than that gemstone he'd recklessly wagered.

'If you don't want to help at the wedding, you don't have to,' she said, her shoulders slumped. 'I hope you don't feel I was manipulating you. I would have been glad of your help, but I do respect your position on marriage – and I know how important this expedition is to you.'

But instead of relief, her words seemed to agitate him even more. 'Sophie,' he said, his tone the same as earlier, as though she was supposed to understand something important merely because he said her name.

'It's all right—'

'It's not all right. *Nothing* is all right,' he growled, taking his wallet from his pocket and throwing a few notes onto the table. Grasping her hand, he hauled her up, calling a farewell to the restaurant owner.

As he stalked back to the apartment in such typical Andreas fashion, Sophie was pricked with the sensation of missing him already. One day, she'd find a way to move on, but today was not that day – especially when he pressed her into the front door as soon as it was closed and kissed her as though he were a long way underwater and she were the air.

He said things with his hands and his lips that her heart was too afraid to hear. The consuming physical sensations of being together were difficult enough to bear, but at least she could hide in her own desire, pretend he was just the most explosive lover she'd ever had, which muddied her thoughts.

But her cover slipped that evening, knowing it could be goodbye, at least for a while. She couldn't hold his heart, so she held him everywhere else, her hands fisting in his hair, her mouth on his skin.

And when she awoke the following morning to see him sprawled out next to her, hogging the bed, she felt everything at once: annoyed, indulgent, needy and tender. She was so tender, so soft for him and so sore from trying not to hope.

She couldn't stand it. She slipped quietly out of bed, dressed, and called a taxi. Sometimes, a person had to make their own clean break.

23

They left him alone for nearly a week, which was a week longer than he'd expected. The delay was a reprieve, a chance to regroup – and catch up on preparations for Manaslu. Filip Brzezinski had sent him several messages with leads on sponsors that he needed to follow up and the question of a departure date had already been thrown out.

Andreas avoided that one. Whenever he was tempted to bash out an email suggesting they leave before mid-September, his heart raced and the honed panic centre in his brain warned him that he wasn't acting with a clear head.

A clear head was what he wished for most and couldn't seem to find.

He had several bookings now the snow was gone from the lower peaks and climbing could begin in earnest. He even had a group of apprentice guides to keep him busy for a day of training that he always enjoyed.

The trainees were fit and capable and straightforward to instruct – as well as fun to challenge – and seeing his experience put to use to teach them about keeping clients safe, about managing risk and facilitating achievements was more satisfying than he'd imagined.

But when they sat together to discuss the ethics of risk and personal responsibility, his brain fired with images of Sophie, imagining how it would feel to push himself to the limit on a desolate ridge in the Himalayas, knowing she was at home worrying about him.

You didn't exist in real life for me, no matter how much it felt like you did.

Her words had come back to him in unexpected moments since she'd left – since she'd sneaked away, rather than face goodbye, which was supposed to be his modus operandi. He'd rarely wanted to exist in real life. School had been torture and his parents' hopes for him leading a normal life a noose around his neck.

Instead, he'd found his true self among the peaks, in that altered state of mind, where his peculiar drive was an asset rather than an oddity. But that week, he was still adrift, despite the chance to head up into the thin air.

He returned to the cabin in the forest he called home lost in thought, hanging up ropes and straps in the lean-to before he even noticed the beat-up Fiat 500 parked around the side. While he kept his equipment securely locked, his house rarely was and he pushed open the door to find Caro stretched out on the sofa reading a magazine.

Despite the lurch of discomfort in his chest about why she might be there, he smiled and wrapped her in a hug. She pulled back and eyed him.

'There really is something up with you.'

'It's nice to see you, too, Schwesterherz.' The endearment 'sister-heart' was a little light mocking between them, but that day it tumbled out of his mouth with a sheen of truth that made him uncomfortable.

'You never mean it when you call me that,' she said with a roll of her eyes. 'And for the record, I resent this. I'm ten years younger than you and I'm supposed to be the one without my shit together, but instead, your weird behaviour turns me into the dutiful daughter and I follow Tatta's bidding and check up on you.'

'What a surprise he didn't come himself,' Andreas mumbled, before pausing in thought. Perhaps he'd learned more at his father's knee than how to tie knots and place anchors in limestone. 'Does he really think I'm going to talk to you?'

She shrugged. 'You don't have to. I came here. We could just drink beer – and please skip the joke about me being old enough to drink. I just turned thirty and that baby-sister crap is getting old – like you.'

He responded with a grunt and shuffled to the fridge to fetch two bottles of Forst, popping the caps against the countertop. They sipped in silence for several moments, Andreas leaning against the bench and Caro perched on the sofa. His mind wandered, realising he didn't even know if Caro was seeing someone – or if she wanted to be. Her longest relationship had been a long-distance thing with a woman she'd met on holiday who lived in Hamburg, but the break-up had seemed amicable and he thought Caro had had the occasional boyfriend from the neighbouring villages since then.

As a brother, he probably should have known these things.

'This place is a bit of a dump, Andreas,' Caro commented, her doubtful gaze skimming over the chipped laminate and the threadbare rug on the floor. 'What would Sophie think, if you ever actually brought her here?'

His sister's use of the hypothetical was conspicuous. 'She saw my bedsit in Weymouth. It's worse.'

'Did you let her think it's all you can afford?'

'It *is* all I can afford,' he insisted.

'Only because you have to pay for the privilege of freezing your toes off on some Godforsaken—' She cut herself off. 'I mean... Figuratively. It wasn't supposed to be—'

'It's fine,' he said, smiling around the neck of the beer bottle as he took a swig. 'Everyone knows I'm not a whole man any more.'

Her eyes flashed. 'That's not funny, you know. You might enjoy taking risks, but we can't stand it.'

Andreas sighed, the usual steel in his spine softening to putty. Collapsing onto the sofa next to her, he leant his head on the back and stared at the ceiling. 'I understand better than you think. It tears me in two, sometimes. I want to be who you all need me to be, but it never works.'

'That's not all your fault. I know how our parents are, how Mama overreacts and Tatta doesn't know what to do with his feelings.' Her head touched down against his shoulder, lightly, as though she was trying not to scare him off. Another day, he might have been spooked, but he'd been aching a little all over since leaving the lake – vulnerable, when he'd lived his whole life as though he were impervious to everything, especially love. 'Is that what worries you about Sophie? That you're not who she wants you to be?'

'I'm not who she needs.'

Caro lifted her head to give a frustrated huff. 'I hope you didn't say something like that to her. You can't tell her what she needs like a patronising cabbage head. She knows well enough herself!'

He ignored the insult. 'You're right. I suggested we keep it going and she said no.'

Caro blinked, once, twice – slowly. 'Keep what going? Sophie told us you weren't in a relationship.'

Pressing his lips together as though sucking on a lemon, he sifted through his thoughts and feelings, searching for an answer.

'Did you mean you suggested you get together for real? Build a relationship? Because that might have been the most intelligent thing you've ever done, Bruderherz,' she said, her tone heavy with sarcasm.

'I didn't suggest that,' he admitted.

'Ah, I see it all now. You told her you wanted to keep having sex and when she said no because she loves you too much to keep her heart out of it like you do, everything went to shit.'

'That's not—' He couldn't get any further. His heart hammered as Caro's words rang in his ears. That wasn't what Sophie had meant, was it? 'She doesn't love me,' he insisted, barely even convincing himself. 'Maybe she did back then—'

'But she could, Andreas,' Caro interrupted. Her words pried the chasm in his chest a little further open. 'Give things a chance between the two of you – a real chance, with time and compromises and planning – and she could! But you already screwed things up once, so she's not going to go there again unless you take the first step.'

He waited a few breaths for his heart to settle back into rhythm. 'How do I do that?' He'd meant the question to come out belligerently sceptical, but instead, he sounded desperate. 'I'm leaving for another expedition in a few months.'

'You are planning to come back down, aren't you?' Caro said, crossing her arms.

'Of course!'

'Then it's simple. When you go, you kiss her goodbye and when you get back, you kiss her hello. At least that seems to be what other people do about occasional absences.'

He shoved her with his elbow. 'You know what I mean. I have to have complete focus on the mountain. If I'm worrying about what's happening...'

'Do you think she'll run off with someone else?'

'No! I mean, not if...'

'Not if you've actually admitted that shrivelled-up organ in your chest has always belonged to her – such as it is.'

His second shove was more pointed and she yelped and scowled at him. But although her words annoyed him just as much as she'd intended them to, her description also made his throat close and the air in the cabin suddenly feel too thin.

His gaze swerved to the chest of drawers just visible beyond the room divider, to the top drawer that housed his socks and that unassuming little box from a gemstone trader in Islamabad. He knew why he'd taken on her bet and it hadn't been recklessness.

Caro studied him warily and recoiled at whatever she saw in his expression. 'If this is about to get emotional, I should go. I am a Hinterdorfer, after all. I gave you the kick in the arse you needed, so I'm out of here.' She drained the last drops from her beer bottle and hauled herself off the sofa. 'Say hi to Sophie for me, when you see her.'

When you see her...

He barely acknowledged Caro's departure. He reached for his laptop on the coffee table and powered it up. Navigating to the email from Brzezinski, he started a laborious reply with his two-finger typing.

With a faint smile, he thought of Sophie and her stylus and he knew he was doing the right thing. He couldn't predict or control the future. He'd screwed up so badly with Sophie that he was only inviting further heartache.

But they'd made a bet. They weren't finished – yet.

24

Sophie was busy with two weddings in quick succession in the weeks that followed her trip to Italy as well as a dog who'd missed her daily walks along the canal near her house – and Reshma's coddling on the days when Betsy was allowed to come along to the office. But Bath looked different, as though the direction of gravity had shifted slightly and the Earth turned on another axis. Her life felt different.

The first wedding was at a stone cottage in Normandy, replete with a thatched roof and fields of poppies. But although Sophie and Ginny spent hours adding the final touches the bride and groom had requested, including a bower of pink, fragrant roses in a circle – to symbolise eternity – and a rustic, wooden chair design for guests, which had to be rented from two towns away, the day itself had felt off to Sophie.

The residence requirements for getting married in France were complicated, so the couple had already married at the Bristol town hall. The commitment ceremony she had helped them develop felt laboured and she was terrified it was because of her delivery. Not only was she a divorced marriage celebrant, but now she was a divorced, broken-hearted one.

Or perhaps she always had been but was only now admitting to it.

As she fixed a smile to her face for the reception – nearly a hundred friends and family had made the trip, just to test Sophie's endurance – she wondered for the first time if she'd had enough of weddings, if she could keep doing this without being a hypocrite.

Noticing Sophie's exaggerated sighs on the drive back, Ginny assured her that all weddings were different – as Sophie well knew. Some couples wore their hearts on their sleeves and some were more concerned with chairs and place settings and they usually knew better than to judge.

The second wedding, the following weekend, was somehow worse. The grooms were a pair of sweethearts who'd been together half their lives and had finally decided to get married even though one of their families still refused to attend. As the wedding was in New York City, Sophie travelled alone to save expenses. That meant a desperate hurry sorting all the final preparations and she found herself constantly in a yellow taxi, rushing to collect the licence and then the hors d'oeuvres for the twenty wedding guests.

But running the wedding alone turned out to be a blessing when she was dabbing at her eyes along with Jacob, as Chris stuttered through his vows. All the meetings she'd had with them over the past year, where they'd bickered gently but been so easy and lovely with each other after all their years together, got under her skin and she wondered if all couples should actually get married when they were in their mid-forties and had been together over twenty years.

Perhaps she needed to switch to destination anniversary celebrations until her hope was restored.

She hadn't heard from Andreas. Toni from Great Heart had assured her that two guides would be available for the week of the wedding. She'd mentioned one of the guides was Kira, but not the name of the second, so she had to assume that Andreas either hadn't decided or wasn't coming. Sophie wasn't sure which was worse.

She'd wanted a clean break, but it didn't feel clean. She wanted to hear *something* from him.

By the time June was coming to a close and the next appointment with Lily and Roman loomed, Sophie knew Ginny and Tita had worked out something was wrong, but she'd dissuaded them from asking so far by projecting a subtle aura of stress.

As she brewed coffee and set up the screen in preparation for the meeting, she tried to consciously suppress that aura and found it more difficult than she'd hoped. Sophie didn't get stressed. She thrived on the tiny details and preferred to be busy than not.

Ginny came in to ask her a question about a venue in Tuscany and Sophie wasn't sure what kind of nonsense came out of her mouth, she was so distracted.

'Is it Lily and Roman you've got coming today? Shall I send Kira in to you afterwards?'

'After what?'

'Kira and Willard are here talking to Reshma. She mentioned she's doing the Garda wedding and sounded a little nervous, to be honest.'

'Um, yes, sure. She should come in and meet the couple – and I can talk her through her nerves afterwards over a cup of tea. If she drinks tea.'

Ginny peered at her warily. 'I'm sure that'll do her some good.' She paused. 'Do you want me to stay in the meeting, too? I could help write stuff down.'

As much as Sophie wanted to assure her that wasn't necessary, she had to admit her thoughts were a mess and it would be better if they didn't screw up Lily and Roman's wedding, so she nodded with a grateful smile.

'I know Reshma's keen to make these adventure weddings a thing, but don't put yourself under more pressure than necessary. The adventure part is Kira's job.'

She nodded again, hoping her expression showed enough relief that Ginny would continue to assume that was Sophie's problem.

Lily and Roman arrived early, hurrying inside from the car park in a light shower of rain. Ginny served them coffee – and tea for Sophie, which saved the day.

After a few fortifying sips, Sophie started her curated photo presentation and opened her mouth to introduce the first one, but Roman's reaction cut her off.

'Oh my gosh!' Roman exclaimed. 'We could say our marriage vows there?'

The picture showed the peak of Punta Telegrafo, the last hike she'd taken with Andreas. 'There or any of the other spectacular places for the ceremony around the lake.'

Lily laughed in delight. 'This is incredible. I know we said we wanted a cross on top of a mountain, but... wow, the idea of it is so much more powerful, seeing that picture.'

Sophie smiled helplessly, all her discussions with Andreas coming alive in her mind.

'How do you get up there? Would we need ropes?' Lily asked.

'It's just a hike from a cable car, but the landscape is fantastic the whole way,' Sophie reassured her.

'Ah, okay.' Lily's tone held a hint of disappointment. 'I suppose that's for the best.'

Sophie bit her lip, her finger hovering over her tablet. 'I've been working quite closely with one of our adventure guides—' She swallowed, remembering just how closely. 'He has a very good idea of what's possible, what's safe – for everyone. And there is…'

She flipped through the photos, passing briefly over Monte Castello, the first summit where she'd stood across from Andreas and made him pretend he could be a real groom – her groom – and Cima Comer, with the wooden lookout.

'It's all so beautiful!' Lily commented as she watched the photos change quickly on the screen.

But Sophie stopped scrolling when she reached Cima Rocca with its metal cross set into the boulders at the summit. She'd taken a panorama shot of the looming rocky peaks and the lake, dizzyingly far below.

'This one,' she began, pausing unintentionally before realising Lily and Roman were holding their breath. 'This summit is accessed by via ferrata, a fixed climbing route. If you're sure your wedding guests want to slip on a harness and a couple of straps and scramble up for your ceremony, then this might be the place. There's an alternative route to the top on foot if some of your party aren't willing to climb.'

The look Lily shared with Roman was so eager, Sophie had to forget her own reservations – and her own memories of adrenaline and kisses.

Roman clutched his fiancée's hand in both of his. 'We had all those plans to do the via ferratas in Austria last year and then you got sick. How amazing would it be…?'

'Obviously, a wedding dress won't be an option, but the wreath we discussed will look absolutely gorgeous and with matching corsages for the wedding party that you can preserve afterwards, it will be stunning.'

'You lost me at the corsages,' Lily said with a grin, 'but that's why we hired a planner. I don't know anything about that stuff.'

'A woman after my own heart!'

Sophie glanced up to see a flash of blue as Kira poked her head around the door.

'Come on in, Kira. This is Lily and Roman, our Garda couple. This is Kira Watling. She's a qualified guide and will be with us for all the activities.'

Kira shook their hands firmly. 'I'm more familiar with bachelor parties, but I reckon we can pull this off.' Glancing at the screen, she said, 'Ah, Andreas told me about the via ferrata. Is that what we're going with?'

'It looks that way,' Sophie said.

Roman thankfully picked up the thread of the conversation while she dealt with the twin blows of the prospect of doing the via ferrata with Kira instead of Andreas and the fact that he'd been talking to *Kira* and not to her.

Picking up her tablet to distract herself, she flicked through a few more pictures, looking for the shots of the reception venue, when she swiped to a photo she hadn't been expecting: she and Andreas on Monte Castello di Gaino, holding hands, Sophie stifling a laugh after that spine-tingling moment where her brain had tricked her into thinking it could be real.

'What's *that*?' Ginny blurted out, staring at the screen.

Sophie mashed the button to turn off the tablet, forgetting that wouldn't affect the image on the bigger screen. Frantically tapping buttons, she swore under her breath.

'Oh, I must have... put that one in by accident.' Sophie cringed, cursing herself for the oversight and itching to transfer the file out of her work folder and into the forbidden Andreas folder she'd been trying to stop looking at.

'Is that you and—? Are you two—?' Ginny continued.

'No.' She cleared her throat, feeling Kira's gaze on her. 'It was just for the photographer to... an example of the—' She swiped the photo away, at least a minute too late.

'It really does look like a wedding,' Roman said, looping his arm around Lily and pressing a kiss to her hair when she shared his grin.

This was *their* wedding and Sophie was doing a damn good job organising it. Her own feelings could get lost and she didn't need to worry what Kira thought either. The awkwardness would fade by the time they had to work together in September.

When Lily and Roman left, Ginny went to make tea and then Sophie was alone with Kira, desperate to ignore the tingle at her hairline.

'I thought something happened while you and Andreas were away,' Kira said as soon as Ginny was out of the room.

'It didn't mean anything.' It was so obviously a lie, Sophie couldn't say anything further. She risked a glance at Kira and her new colleague's scowl made her wish she hadn't.

But when Kira spoke again, what she said wasn't what Sophie had expected. 'I don't want to see him get hurt again, okay? We look after each other at Great Heart.'

'You don't think he can look after himself?' Sophie asked in a small voice.

'Of course he can, but you've always been like a summit he failed to reach and you know what he's like with a summit.'

Sophie frowned. She'd thought *she* was the one who needed closure. 'He's got another summit to focus on right now,' she said, alarmed by her bleak tone.

'As long as he is focusing on that and not...' Kira made a frustrated noise. 'I don't want to talk about this crap. But I also don't want to scrape him up off the floor again.'

'I'm sure he's not...'

'God, the both of you are idiots,' Kira mumbled and flung herself onto the sofa, leaning her forearms on her knees. 'Let's just talk about the hen do.'

'That sounds like a good idea,' Sophie agreed, trying to shake off the uncertainty. A wedding planner needed to be the one in control while the bridal party broke down in tears. Her own emotional turmoil was a moot point – especially since Andreas seemed to be honouring her request for a clean break. 'What have you got planned? And which of the other guides have you got booked in to come? Is it Laurie or one of the casuals?'

'What do you mean? Do we need a third person? I think Andreas and I can manage.'

'But... I thought Andreas wasn't coming? It might clash with the departure for Manaslu.'

Kira didn't respond, she only peered doubtfully at Sophie. 'He's not leaving for Nepal until the middle of October.'

'Oh, well...' She tried to ignore the flicker in her stomach. *Clean break, clean break, clean break.* 'He'll have to train and prepare though, right? You can't just stick some crampons on and off you go.' She crossed her arms tight.

'Andreas probably could, but I thought you wanted him?'

Did she?

'For the wedding, I mean,' Kira added, which only made Sophie flush.

'Of course, I—' She swallowed. 'I just got the distinct impression that he didn't want to do any weddings at all and this one – with me – in particular. I'm not going to force him... or *expect* anything.'

The way Kira looked at her, Sophie must have sounded like a fool. 'Sophie, he's already accepted the booking in our system and we've thrown around some ideas for the bachelor party.'

'You've... He's actually booked in?' She tried not to be excited at the prospect of seeing him again. At least she hoped nothing showed on her face – not eagerness, nor confusion and especially not hope.

'Sorry, I thought he'd told you.' Sophie heard Kira mutter, 'The muppet,' rather fondly under her breath.

'I'll get the name updated on the hotel booking then,' Sophie said with a nod she hoped looked final. Topic closed.

But Kira grimaced. 'Do we have to stay at the hotel with the wedding party? We usually stay at Andreas's family's place where have more space to store the gear and we don't have to babysit the guests out of hours.'

An unwelcome shiver ran down Sophie's spine when she pictured Kira and Andreas sharing the flat where she'd made so many memories herself. But Kira had been there before – and probably slept in similar positions to where Sophie had found herself.

Swallowing her discomfort, she said, 'No, only I need to be at the hotel for last-minute problems, but you and Andreas don't have to be.'

'Oh, good. I can tolerate the idea of being an assistant, but you won't want me anywhere near the fancy decorations and the chair sashes and that other stuff you and Ginny were talking about. Knots, I can handle, but bows are really not my thing.'

Sophie smiled faintly, remembering similar sentiments from Andreas but also the image of him with a wreath of flowers on his head, contrasting with his grim, lopsided mouth. She wanted to look at the photo again, even though she could picture it perfectly in her mind.

Damn, she missed that man. The ache only seemed stronger now she knew she'd see him again in September.

But all he'd agreed to was a job he'd get paid for, probably only because the timing of his trip allowed it. He hadn't even got in touch to tell her himself. Nothing had changed. She couldn't allow herself to hope that anything had.

25

'If you don't take it easy, I'm going to lose my lunch!' Kira braced herself against the dashboard with one arm as Andreas dodged a cyclist in hi-vis wear on the narrow single carriageway lined with stone walls and hedgerows, heavy with late-summer greenery.

He eased off the accelerator. He'd just lost concentration for a moment, that was all. He was usually a good driver, although he'd never worked out why English people liked hedgerows so much when they were a deathtrap if you drove at – or slightly over, which was still fine – the speed limit.

With her foot propped on the seat, Kira swivelled to face him. She was always putting her feet all over the furniture.

'If you take your shoes off at weddings, too, you're going to end up as Cinderella one day.'

She snorted a laugh. 'You think I'll marry a prince?'

'You'd die of boredom,' he said, checking his blind spot before turning.

'You're funny, but I'm not letting you off the hook. You're nervous about seeing her. You're never yourself when Sophie is in the picture.'

The lump in his throat grew bigger. That much was true; he was a much better person when Sophie was around. But he didn't want Kira to suspect how mushy he'd been feeling since June. He didn't know if Sophie had been thinking about him as much as he'd thought about her.

'I'm just worried about you,' she said.

'Don't be,' he said, flashing her a reassuring smile.

Another snort of laughter, this time full of scepticism. 'Well, that was expected. You don't let anyone worry about you. If we were talking about climbing a rock face, I wouldn't be, but Sophie's your weakness, so don't do anything stupid.'

'What stupid thing am I likely to do? Buy a suit and ask her to marry me?' His hair stood on end as he uttered the joke, but it had the desired effect on Kira.

'Ha. Ha. The necktie would strangle you before you ever got to the altar.'

She directed him through the backstreets in the south of Bath and he pulled the Land Rover to a stop outside a red-brick terrace, its sparse design tempered by a bright-green door and an orchid on the ground-floor windowsill.

He was just trying to resist thinking something stupid like, *So this is where she lives*, and imagining her greeting him with a smile, when the door opened and a man appeared – a man Andreas recognised.

He set a white, fluffy dog on the ground and turned back as Sophie appeared in the door. Lifting a hand to her head, the man leaned up and—

Bang.

Rory jumped in surprise, dropping his hand as Andreas slammed the door of the Land Rover so hard, it was a miracle the glass didn't shatter.

'We need to go,' Andreas said, jerking his arm up to glance at his watch, but seeing nothing. When Rory's eyes widened, Andreas recognised his mistake.

'It's not... What are—' Rory turned back to Sophie as the dog yapped and pulled at the lead. 'What is Andreas doing here?'

'Driving to the airport,' Sophie said tightly, settling the dog with a hand on its back before fetching a suitcase and locking the pretty, green door. 'Good morning, Andreas,' she said when she turned to him and with a sinking feeling, he realised he hadn't even uttered a greeting.

She looked good – she always looked good. Her hair was a little longer and held back with a clip. She had a pair of star-shaped studs in her ears that he liked. The curve of her ear he liked even more.

The dog continued yapping, but Rory did nothing about it. 'Why didn't you tell me you were back together?'

'Why does she have to tell you?' Andreas shot back before he'd thought it through.

Sophie made a tight, frustrated noise and shook her head. 'Let's just go,' she said, giving him a nudge to his chest when he didn't respond.

'I think it would be a common courtesy!' Rory replied, finally trying to shush the dog as the eager barking reached fever pitch. 'Especially since she *always* denied she still had feelings for you.'

Even the dog fell silent at that.

'Rory—' Sophie warned in a choked voice.

'God, after all these years, I can't believe I was fucking right,' Rory said, his voice high. 'I knew you never really committed to me because of him. It was all because of *him*!'

The next nudge Sophie gave Andreas was harder and with a quick, shocked glance at her, he took the hint and tumbled back into the driver's seat as Rory's words echoed in his head. *Because of him...*

'Goodbye, Rory. Thanks for taking Betsy. I'll be home on Sunday,' Sophie called out in an attempt at a dismissive tone.

'How long?' Rory persisted.

Andreas waited silently, ignoring Kira's pointed look, for Sophie to tell her ex they weren't together, that he'd got everything wrong. But she didn't.

'Goodbye, Rory!' was all she said before heaving on the door handle to make a dignified exit.

Except, because his car was a pile of shit, the door stuck, leaving her jerking at it ineffectually, strands of her hair coming loose. Andreas scrambled to open it from the inside – and accidentally knocked the door frame into her face.

'Ow!'

'Porzehittn! Sophie!'

She batted him away when he got back out of the car and grasped for her.

'Let me see.'

Flashing him a dark look, she nevertheless stilled and let him tip her face up to the light to check for scratches.

'I'm sorry,' he whispered, trying to focus on something other than the sensation of her skin under his fingertips – after three of the longest months of his life.

'Two minutes back together and you're already apologising— I mean, back in my company, not "back together",' she qualified uneasily.

A smile twitched on his lips. 'Of course not,' he said, brushing his thumb down her cheek one last time. 'Nothing broken, I don't think.'

She squared her shoulders. 'That's lucky. A black eye would have been the *perfect* start to this wedding.'

The wedding wasn't what concerned Andreas. The happy couple could make their promises in a bivouac if it came to that.

He wanted to put things right with Sophie – whatever 'right' looked like to her – but seeing Rory had riled all his feelings up again.

And what had her ex-husband meant, *'You never really committed to me because of him'*?

'Just don't expect me to be here to comfort you again when he dumps you, Soph!'

Andreas stiffened. Giving Sophie's shoulder a quick squeeze, he took slow steps towards Rory until he was close enough to speak without her hearing – and had taken a moment to settle his racing thoughts.

'Andreas,' she called, a warning in her voice.

But of all the choice words he had for Rory Brent – including several colourful insults in dialect about cabbage and cucumbers – the calm, considered ones he actually said hit deepest.

'Being there to comfort her was an honour you should have appreciated.'

* * *

Telling herself this would be the most awkward wedding of her career would help no one, so Sophie brushed away the thought as soon as it assailed her. She wished she'd handed Betsy over last night so there would have been no chance of Rory seeing Andreas – or Andreas seeing Rory, or whichever was worse. And she should have better prepared herself for the reality of sitting in close quarters with Andreas and pretending she'd managed that clean break.

She didn't know what he'd said to her ex-husband, but he'd been particularly grumpy when he'd returned to the car – perhaps because he'd kept his big hands to himself, not that Rory was worth a punch when he had an expedition coming up.

She felt Kira's curious looks as they held a stilted, casual conversation on the way to the airport and then the wedding guests descended, leaving Sophie hyper-aware of everything Andreas did, but with a strong imperative to ignore all of it.

When they all landed in Verona and Kira and Andreas headed to Marniga in the old Panda, leaving Sophie with the guests in the hired minibus, she could finally calm down and focus on her clients.

But her brain kept hanging on the image of Andreas, silver hoop winking in his ear, giving Rory a terrifying look and asking why he thought she had to explain herself to him. For once, she was glad she'd peeked at the pictures from their trip a little too often, or the sight of him might have made her do something stupid like throw her arms around him.

Now they were back at the lake for Lily and Roman's big day, not to reminisce about her own romantic trip. Usually, she thrived on the business end of weddings – both the literal business side of budgets and bookings, and the figurative business end, when the big day loomed and there were a thousand small errands to run.

But that Monday, her head felt concerningly foggy and she itched to pull her tablet from her bag and recheck her lists, because she couldn't seem to remember the work that awaited her once she'd got the wedding party settled into the hotel. She already felt slightly out-of-control, which wasn't normal.

Thirteen guests had arrived on the flight today with another three expected tomorrow. The minibus made its way along the winding Adige river from Verona, cutting through sweeping, trellised vineyards with looming hills on both sides, and finally approached the lake. Olive trees flashed by on the side of the road and a town in the valley below them baked in the warm sun, the slanted lines of Monte Brione appearing hazy in the sunshine.

The parents of the bride and groom had their faces glued to the windows and the wedding party seemed to be in high spirits. It would all work out.

Then the bridesmaid, Lucia, opened her mouth and Sophie's tension zipped right back up again. 'Please tell me we have that guide for the hen do!'

'Lucia!' the maid of honour admonished her. 'It's not like he's a stripper! We're going kayaking for the hen do.'

'If he's shirtless in tight swimmers, it'll be even better than if we'd booked Lily a stripper.'

Sophie counted silently to ten. If this was what the bridesmaids were like without alcohol, it was a very good thing they were kayaking for the hen do and not doing anything involving shots – or strippers.

'I thought by bringing everyone here, we'd manage to avoid all that stuff,' Lily said with a huff from her position at the back of the minibus.

Sophie breathed again. Gently reprimanding a group of bridesmaids for objectifying her... colleague wasn't something she'd wanted on her to-do list for the day.

Roman turned around and asked, 'Are you talking about Andreas Hinterdorfer?'

Oh God, if only everyone would stop talking about Andreas Hinterdorfer, she might have a chance to clear her head!

'I can't believe Andreas Hinterdorfer is coming to our wedding! He's climbed Everest six times! I went to see an exhibition of photos from two of his expeditions by that famous nature photographer.'

Ah, Rhys the nature photographer who refused to take

pictures of people – apparently unless those people were at foolishly high altitude.

'I was just looking at how big his hands are!' Lucia said emphatically as the minibus disappeared into a tunnel.

Lily sighed, putting Sophie on alert. 'Lucia, I really want you to have a good time—'

'I know what you're going to say, so don't bother,' Lucia cut her off, her smile vanishing. She glanced out of the window at the glimpses of turquoise water through the arches. 'I won't ruin your wedding, don't worry. Besides, it's Sophie the wedding planner who's got something going on with our mountain guide – right?'

Heat rushed to Sophie's cheeks. She always tried to be open and friendly with wedding parties so she didn't feel like an awkward addition on the big day, but the question pushed her to the limit. 'I— Erm...'

The minibus shot out of the tunnel into the sunshine, the road running right along the waterfront with a sheer rock face on the other side. With gasps and sighs, the wedding guests were thankfully more interested in the view than Sophie's questionable love life and she couldn't blame them when the stony mountains tumbled theatrically into the rippling water and every shade of green and blue – and the orange of the clay roofs – was enhanced by the late-summer sun.

Lily and Roman shared a grin. The awkward moment had passed without Sophie having to decide what on earth to say.

After twenty minutes of breathtaking views and stern reminders to herself not to seek out glimpses of the places she'd visited with Andreas, Sophie and the guests arrived at the hotel in Limone sul Garda to a chorus of happy murmurs.

Sophie loved this place. The hotel was tucked against a rock face at the edge of the town, above old, terraced gardens of olive trees, spreading stone pines, palms and tall, thin cypresses. A curving swimming pool occupied one end of the largest terrace. The clay roofs of the town of Limone were visible to the south and directly in front, the lake glittered and the sun hit the sloping meadows and jutting rock of the Monte Baldo massif on the other side.

She'd worked with the hotel on three weddings now and she knew prosecco on the roof terrace awaited the guests. Then they'd enjoy the pool or walk down to the shore while Sophie met with the hotel manager to tackle any last-minute problems.

Once all that was achieved, she'd wave off the guests as they walked to the Romantica restaurant for their seafood linguine or grilled whole lavarello with lemon and herbs with a glass of chilled soave, while she breathed out with an aperitif on her own tiny balcony on the top floor of the hotel, before ordering some stuffed gnocchi to take away for herself. Amidst the stress of the events leading up to the wedding, that time was precious to her. She needed it more than usual that day.

As soon as she saw Elena, the manager, coming out to meet her, a world of worry in her tight expression, Sophie suspected her wind-down time wouldn't be coming as soon as she'd hoped.

She was thanking her lucky stars that Lily and Roman were so happy and easy-going an hour later as she juggled a stack of pizza boxes with the receipt clutched between her lips. A voice called out from behind her.

'Looks like I arrived right on time.'

Sophie stumbled, feeling the boxes slide, her thoughts racing forward with the image of them taking a nosedive and ending up crumpled on the ground in a fragrant pile. But before any of that could actually happen, another pair of hands steadied the precarious pizza tower – unmistakably large hands, with a braid of leather around one wrist.

'I thought your weddings were supposed to be gourmet events. I would come along for takeaway pizza. Oh, here. Let me help you.'

Instead of him taking the pizzas, as she'd expected, he snagged the receipt out of her mouth and prompted her with a look.

'We had a problem with our usual restaurant,' she mumbled, her lips dry. 'They had an electrical fire yesterday. No one else could accommodate such a large group at short notice, so they opted for pizza rather than splitting up.'

'Do things like this happen a lot?'

'They happen,' she snapped, 'but not a lot. What are you doing here?'

'Paperwork,' he said, brandishing a sheaf of print-outs. 'We need release forms on file.'

Sophie stopped so suddenly, the pizzas slipped again and she staggered drunkenly in an attempt to right them. 'Are you going to help me? Or is balancing a tower of pizza boxes all on my own a skill you think I need to master for my own good?'

He stopped short and she had to turn to look at him. With an alarmingly perceptive spark in his eye, he slapped his release forms on top of the boxes and then took the whole stack from her, capturing her arms briefly against his.

'You asked for help,' he observed. 'Well done, Sophie.'

'Give me a break,' she muttered. 'You could have told me you were coming with paperwork. I need to know these details. What if we hadn't been here?'

'I'm sorry I forgot to tell you.'

Sophie's misgiving swelled. Lily and Roman's wedding was the first of its kind for I Do – or for Great Heart Adventure Weddings, she should try to remember to say. She hated that she had no idea what other problems might crop up.

'This wedding has not started well,' she groaned.

'It'll finish well.'

'I bloody hope so.'

Andreas shrugged, rattling the pizza boxes and making Sophie's heart leap in alarm. 'They'll get married and it'll be their wedding – whatever happens. It would be boring if everything went to plan.'

She scowled at him. 'That's easy for you to say.'

'I thought weddings were all about the emotion.' His voice was gentle and it put her off balance because she hadn't expected it.

'You're right, which is why you'll cry like a baby when they promise to always be partners on life's adventure.'

His footsteps stalled for a second, as though the words had touched him, but when she glanced up, his expression was doubtful. That was better – familiar ground. 'Is that really the wedding vow?'

'One of them. Do you know how difficult it is to write wedding vows that *don't* sound like something out of a Christmas movie?'

His brow was thick. 'I've never watched a Christmas movie.'

'That figures,' she mumbled, opening the door for him.

'Hey, ähm...' He paused. 'Do we need to talk? About this morning?'

'This morning? No,' she said quickly.

'Are you... Do you mind that I'm here?'

'It would have been good of you to tell me you were coming yourself, rather than letting me make the wrong assumptions and find out from Kira.' She hoped her voice was even and that he didn't notice she'd avoided the question.

'Sorry, I... the "clean break" thing...'

Her cheeks grew hot and she thought again about those text

messages that had got lost all those years ago. He'd said things were better the way they were. Thinking about what might have been was pointless when he still couldn't commit.

'Roman is thrilled to have you here,' she said, forcing a smile. 'He's lucky your departure date for Manaslu turned out to be later.'

The expression that flickered on his face was confusing.

'You are still going to Manaslu, right?'

'Yes,' he said, with less conviction than she'd expected. 'In three weeks.' Sophie wished her stomach hadn't plummeted at that.

'Well,' she said with a carelessness she didn't feel, 'enjoy your time at sea level while it lasts.'

She showed him into the breakfast room and he set the pizzas on a table. His mouth was twisted, as though he wanted to say something.

'I can get them to fill in the forms for you,' she said before he had the chance. 'You don't have to hang around.' She didn't want him staying to study her with that much intensity.

With one last nod, he turned to leave, settling his cap more firmly on his head.

26

Sophie awoke less-than-refreshed after a night of tossing and turning, her brain running scenarios of what Andreas had wanted to say, from, *'You must allow me to tell you how ardently I admire and love you,'* to, *'Just so you know, I've got back together with Kira and we're banging like rabbits in the apartment where you thought we "made love".'*

Jarring fully awake at that last one, she felt as though she'd run a marathon in her sleep and she groaned, tempted to curse something full of consonants – something from Andreas's vocabulary of unintelligible swear words in his dialect.

But she was determined to be the usual Sophie today, smiling at her really rather sweet client couple and doing everything she could to make their time here memorable.

She floated into the breakfast room and headed straight for the hot-water dispenser because Sophie was nothing if not an expert at prioritisation. Unfortunately, Lucia, the troublemaking bridesmaid, and maid of honour Adelaide stopped her before she could get there.

With one longing look at the teabags in their fancy paper

envelopes, she turned to her guests with as much of a smile as she could muster – which quickly drooped when she saw their expressions.

'We haven't mentioned this to Lily because we don't want to stress her out,' Adelaide said in an exaggerated whisper.

Sophie moved them surreptitiously out of sight of the bride. 'What's happened? I'm sure we can work it out.'

'It's my fault,' Lucia said in a small voice.

'It was an honest mistake,' Adelaide reassured her, making Lucia look a little green.

The bridesmaid took a deep breath. 'I broke up with my boyfriend a month ago. He's arriving today. You might have noticed I've been a bit of a cow.'

'As long as you can keep it together for the wedding, you have my sympathy,' Sophie said, remembering her first few weddings after she'd separated from Rory.

Lucia's expression wobbled as though she hadn't expected the kindness. 'It didn't occur to me that we'd booked one room for the two of us, but now the manager said they're fully booked.'

Alarm raced up the back of Sophie's neck. 'He doesn't have a room. Oh, shit.' She bit her lip, ignoring the surprised looks from the bridesmaids at her language. 'Don't worry. I can fix this,' she said, feeling wobbly on her feet, but with a sense of inevitability. 'He can have my room. That way, you're all still at the same hotel.'

'Wow, that's so kind!' Adelaide exclaimed. 'But what will you do?'

'There will be space somewhere.' And if there wasn't, there was a trundle bed in the attic at Andreas's apartment, she thought, as she resisted the urge to laugh from her belly – or cry, she wasn't sure which. 'Let me pack my things so Elena can get the room cleaned.'

The wedding guests split up for the day's activities – windsurfing for the more adventurous or markets and sightseeing in Limone. Sophie was thankful to discover that the parents of the bride and groom were just as active as Lily and Roman had assured her, but even they faded after two hours of admiring ceramics and tasting olive oil in thirty-degree heat.

Sophie herded the group towards a café with tables by the harbour, sheltered by white umbrellas, potted palms and a lush grapevine, while her mind whirred with arrangements for the rest of the week. With a sinking feeling, she realised she needed to discuss the schedule in detail with Andreas and if she hadn't been so nervous last night, she could have at least got his confirmation that the weather forecast was favourable.

There was some rain due on Wednesday and Thursday, but Friday looked clear – Friday, the day she'd pencilled in for the climb to Cima Rocca and the ceremony by the summit cross, the part she'd been quietly blocking out since they arrived and she saw the familiar soaring peaks. The week had turned out even hotter than usual for mid-September. It would be nearly ten degrees warmer on the via ferrata than the day Andreas had kissed her against the rock – although she wasn't supposed to be thinking about that.

She'd been out of her comfort zone with Andreas; she was even further out, contemplating leading the bridal couple up the via ferrata. Although three of the parents had opted for the steep hike from the other side instead of the climb, there were still far too many variables. An entire massif of release forms wouldn't make this any less stressful.

Flicking briefly through a few booking websites to find a hotel, by the time she'd filtered out places like the Imperial and the Elite Resort, which had lofty prices to match their names, and also the run-down caravans at the other end of the scale, she never quite got around to selecting and booking a room before she was interrupted.

When they arrived back from the city walk, it was almost time for the winery tour in the hills, which hopefully would be a few degrees cooler. Lily and Roman were absent when the appointed time came and Sophie worked very hard not to indulge her anxiety. It wasn't uncommon for engaged couples to want to steal a little extra private time.

But she was surprised when Lily phoned her, asking if the minibus could collect them in town on the way through. Although pink-cheeked from the hours of windsurfing, Lily looked off when she ducked into the minibus and Sophie's stomach dipped. The bride was definitely avoiding her gaze.

The drive took them up high, the road winding through villages perched on the steep, green hills overlooking the lake, to a charming, stone cantina surrounded by bushy olive trees, hanging with green fruit. Grapevines snaked along the hill in terraces, creating orderly stripes of lush leaves.

Lily's steps faltered as she climbed out of the minibus and stared at the sign for the boutique winery so Sophie was relieved when Lily came straight to her after greeting Signor Cozzaglio, the owner. Looking furtively for a quiet spot, Sophie led her to the corner of the terrace that was set up for the wine tasting while the others headed into the olive grove, Roman urging them on when they looked back for Lily.

Sophie tensed, awaiting her next challenge.

With her arms tight around herself, Lily blurted out in a whisper, 'I'm pregnant!'

For a moment, Sophie couldn't respond. It wasn't the first time this had happened during a wedding she'd planned. She'd experienced that tightness in her throat before as memories assailed her and she shoved them right back down again. But this time, her stomach swooped with worry – worry upon worry that had been building since yesterday, since June – since those brief weeks six years ago where she'd also carried the beginnings of a small life inside her.

'Are you okay?' she managed to ask. 'Shall we find a doctor?'

'No – I mean yes, I'm okay and nothing seems to be wrong I'm just—' Lily couldn't seem to find the words. Sophie knew how she felt, unable to stop her own memories – shock, fear, excitement. There had been joy in there, but it certainly hadn't been the only emotion.

Joy was far from what she was feeling now, as much as she wished she could be happy for her client.

'You only just found out?' she guessed.

Lily nodded vigorously. 'It sounds terrible, but I wanted to drink and enjoy my wedding – and the climbing! And now I don't know—'

Oh shit, the climbing. Sophie didn't even know what was appropriate for a pregnant woman. She needed Andreas, as much as those words made her uneasy.

'I don't want anyone in my family to know yet,' Lily said through her teeth. 'I can't even get my head around it myself. We kind of vaguely wanted kids, but not this soon. I had a suspected chest infection a month ago and the doctors don't take chances with me any more. The medication must have interfered with the pill.'

The practical challenges were at least something Sophie could cope with. 'Don't worry about that. I'll help you cover your tracks – you can spit during the wine tasting and I'll make sure we have some discreet non-alcoholic options for you otherwise and if there's anything else you need, come straight to me – anything.'

Her tone must have given something away, because Lily

studied her curiously. 'I appreciate it. And I'm sorry for upsetting all our plans.'

Tears pricked behind Sophie's eyes. Damn it, she wished she hadn't been right about weddings always making people cry. 'Don't apologise. You and Roman have been a dream couple to work with and even if you weren't, this is my job.'

Lily shook her head. 'You've gone above and beyond, Sophie. It's like your calling.'

Lily had to stop talking before the urge to cry grew unbearable. A few tasteful tears during the ceremony were professional; bawling when the bride told her she was pregnant was not.

'But do you think I can still do the via ferrata? I really want to!'

Sophie's head spun. 'Honestly, I have no idea, but I'll find out for you as soon as I can.'

* * *

Andreas wasn't answering his phone.

Sophie paced the beautiful terrace with ancient grapevines creating a thick canopy of shade. The wide waters of the lake shimmered far below while a falcon played on the breeze in her eyeline. The contented murmur of the guests enjoying sips of wine and morsels of homemade bread with olive oil reached her ears from behind her and in front of her, the Monte Baldo massif with its gullies and ravines and the enormous row of peaks filled her vision.

But Sophie could only appreciate it abstractly as her phone calls rang out in her ear, over and over. Kira's phone appeared to be switched off. Andreas might be driving back to Marniga and unable to use Bluetooth – she would have been more surprised if he *had* managed to connect his phone to the old Panda with his technological prowess, or lack thereof. Or he could be back already and simply not answering his phone. He might be busy.

Her stomach twisted as her fevered brain pictured all kinds of ways he could be 'busy' right now, no matter how unlikely those scenarios were.

Hoping her smile held up, she made her apologies to the wedding party and rushed to where the minibus was parked on the gravel drive. 'Could you take me back to Limone?'

Pulling her rented Fiat 500 into the car park in Marniga an hour later, a few drops of rain plopped onto the windscreen, as though the weather was reflecting Sophie's dread. Billowing storm clouds churned over the lake. She should have hurried to the apartment before the rain started in earnest, but a glimpse of her reflection in the mirror revealed just how many tears she'd swiped off her cheeks on the drive here, so she took a moment with her make-up remover wipes and concealer.

Keeping everything together in front of Andreas would not be easy. She should never have told him about her own experience, or had to listen to his gentle voice telling her he wished he'd been there, although she knew he avoided emotional entanglements. By the time she was ready – not *ready*, but resigned to the awkwardness of the next few minutes – the rain was falling in sheets.

Holding her handbag over her head, she rushed up the cobbled lane to the stone steps that led to Andreas's apartment and paused, the irrational images of him with Kira still stabbing her brain.

She tried Andreas's phone one more time, but there was still no answer.

What if they *were* 'occupied' right now? Chances were low. He'd told her clearly that he hadn't been with Kira like that for a few years. Why would they start up again right now?

But why weren't they answering their phones?

Grumbling quietly at herself, she set her shoulders and stomped up the steps as loudly as she could, rapping sharply on the door.

'Andreas? Kira?'

At first, there was no answer, then when she was about to knock again, she heard light, quick footsteps approaching. The door swung open to reveal exactly the scene Sophie had been trying not to imagine: Kira, her blue hair mussed, wearing a kimono robe and apparently nothing else.

It was all too much. Calm, collected Sophie was going to snap. She froze on the doorstep, grasping desperately for the threads of her dignity and expecting any moment for Andreas to appear, also half-dressed and dishevelled, and make her misery complete.

And that's when the lightning flashed, a crash of thunder alarmingly close.

27

'Sophie! Get inside!' Andreas called.

What was she doing?

He rushed along the lane in quick strides, arriving at the door to find Kira staring doubtfully at Sophie and the pretty, put-together wedding planner looking a little wild and increasingly wet. He ushered her inside with a firm hand on her back, almost expecting her to protest.

Instead, she blinked at him in surprise as he closed the door, shutting out the hiss of rain on the clay roofs and cobblestones.

Tugging off his damp cap, he asked, 'Are you all right?'

'Yes, I—' She swallowed. 'Where have you been? I've been calling you for over an hour.'

Setting the bag of groceries on the table, he tugged his phone out of his back pocket, finding an alarming number of missed calls when he woke up the screen. 'Sorry, I went for a run and then grocery shopping and left my phone in the car.'

She was still blinking at him as though something had confused her. He hurried to put the kettle on, stealing one of Kira's teabags.

'I'll go get dressed,' Kira said, glancing between the two of them. 'You caught me in the shower,' she said to Sophie. 'Sorry it took me a minute to answer the door.'

Sophie grimaced, looking as though she wanted to say something, but he set a cup of tea in front of her, earning him a sigh of relief that made a smile tug at his lips.

'Just to be clear,' Kira said, pausing in the doorway to her room, 'I'm not sleeping with him. Not now. Not ever again.'

Sophie spat her tea. Holding a hand to her mouth, she spluttered and coughed. 'I didn't—' she choked out.

While Andreas's heart pounded in his chest, he busied his hands searching for a cloth to clean up the drops.

'Sorry, was that too blunt?' Kira asked with a wince. 'I could see what she was thinking and I wanted to set the record straight. God, I always screw this stuff up.' With a dismissive gesture, she disappeared into the bedroom, closing the door behind her.

Wiping up the tea while his mind raced, Andreas glanced at Sophie to find her cheeks pink and her brow knit and all of her expressions seemed to be tailor-made to get under his skin.

'Did you really think I wasn't answering my phone because I was... in bed with Kira?' The pressure that had been building behind his eyes since their stilted conversation last night swelled again.

Her cheeks went from pink to white. 'Not really.'

'"Not really"? Or "No"?'

'Maybe a little.'

'Sophie,' he began, sounding pained even to his own ears, 'I would never do that to you.'

'Look, I couldn't have blamed you, if you two were... We broke up – again – three months ago. We were never back together.'

'That's not what you told Rory,' he said before he'd thought it through.

Her eyes flashed. 'Because you were right and it's none of his business!' Her chest rose and fell erratically. 'I said I wanted a clean break and you are within your rights to sleep with anyone you want.'

'I still wouldn't do that, right in front of your eyes.'

'Oh, come on, Andreas! You're not going to be a monk for the rest of your life. One of these days, you'll get together with someone and if we're still occasionally working together, then it'll be in front of my eyes. It wasn't that much of a stretch to think it might be happening now.'

'Except there's no way it would be happening now!' Something hot and uncomfortable bubbled in his chest. 'I'm not over *you* yet!'

If she'd been holding her mug of tea at that moment, he'd bet she would have spilled it.

He groaned and ran a hand over his eyes.

'Please don't, Andreas.' She sounded hurt, but he had no idea how to undo what he'd said when it had been the truth. 'Not now.'

'Please don't what? Think about when we were here together back in spring? It's kind of hard when you show up.' He collapsed into the chair opposite her. 'But I am trying.'

She sipped her tea, clutching the mug like a defensive weapon. It pricked him that she looked vulnerable in her bedraggled state, her eyes glazed with stress that he was adding to. He wanted to ask her about Rory, what her ex-husband had meant by blaming their break-up on Andreas – to work out why that made such a difference to his own feelings – but now was obviously not the time.

'I assume you didn't come here to discuss our break-ups.'

'No, definitely not.' She paused for barely a breath. 'Lily has just found out she's pregnant.'

Oh. Was this why Sophie looked brittle? Staring at her hand, limp on the table, he knew he couldn't hold it, but damn, he wanted to.

'Are you okay?' he asked quietly.

Her gaze snapped to his. 'This isn't the first time I've had a pregnant bride. I'd appreciate it if you didn't say anything to her.'

'Of course not.' He also heard what she hadn't said: *I'd appreciate it if you didn't remind me that I told you.*

'But it *is* the first time I'm supposed to take one up a mountain! I don't even know if it's allowed – if we're insured. Do we have to change plans entirely now? That's what I need you for.'

He nodded slowly. 'I see. How many weeks is she?'

'Only five. She doesn't want any of the guests to know.'

'Okay, I'll have to talk to her and Roman. There's nothing stopping us from going ahead as planned. Pregnancy isn't considered a medical condition and at five weeks, she wouldn't need any special equipment, but obviously a fall right now could have consequences – not that there's much likelihood that she'll fall.'

'It's an unnecessary risk,' Sophie said quietly. Her gaze lifted to his, full of past conversations.

'All of this has been an unnecessary risk – controlled, but unnecessary. Do you think they'll want to go ahead?'

'I'm not sure, but Lily was disappointed with the timing.'

'Were you? When it happened to you?' The question was out before he could stop it.

'This isn't about me.'

An ache started up inside him. He shouldn't push it – push *her* – but he did anyway. 'No, but it might help me understand Lily.' *It might help me understand* you.

Her brow furrowed but she didn't immediately shut him down. 'I certainly wasn't ready, when it happened. Do you know people who climb while pregnant?'

'I don't know anyone who would stop, but...'

'What?'

He gave half a shrug. 'The people I know are used to taking risks that affect others. Normal people aren't.'

'One of the many reasons climbers aren't normal,' she said faintly, repeating what he'd told her years ago. 'Does knowing she's pregnant change anything for you? What if it was... your child?'

The lump in his throat expanded at her words. 'I never... I've never thought about having my own child. I suppose for the exact reason that I thought it *would* change everything.' He paused, the storm gathering in his chest needing the outlet of words he might want to take back at a later date. 'I don't want to be changed.'

She studied him with eyes so steady and sensitive and sad that he was afraid to look into them for too long.

'So you'll understand if she wants to change plans and hold the ceremony at the reception venue instead – or somewhere safer.'

'Of course. They can pledge their love wherever they like,' he said drily. It was the wrong thing to say, because Sophie drew back with a nod and a withering smile.

'What if they want to continue? Do you think it's irresponsible?'

'You're asking me what's irresponsible?' He gave her a long look. 'I've spent ten hours in the high altitude death zone without oxygen tanks. That's the most irresponsible thing a person can do, according to my mother.'

Her shudder spoke volumes.

'I know what I'm capable of myself, but taking risks for other people... I don't have the faintest clue, Sophie. I've never had an answer.'

She must have heard his agitation in his voice, because she regarded him critically. 'The answer is easier when your only consideration is yourself.'

'Of course! How would you have felt if I'd said yes to your proposal,' he began tightly, 'and left immediately for Gasherbrum? One false step and it could have been me coming home as a corpse. How would you have felt?'

The question turned back on him, asking *him* how he would have felt on the Japanese Couloir, the wind whipping his clothes, snow up to his knees and his eyes peeled for signs of an avalanche, if he'd known Sophie was worrying about him at home, waiting for news. Everything seized up inside of him.

But her answer was even more terrifying. 'Andreas,' she began softly with a shake of her head, 'how do you think I *did* feel?'

He couldn't reply. His mind was too busy rewriting his understanding of the past — and how he'd underestimated the woman in front of him. She was the real daredevil. She'd risked her heart and he hadn't understood. He hadn't been ready for her.

'I'm so—'

'Oh, not another apology,' she said, swiping at her nose and shaking herself, as though that could hold back her tears. 'My safety might occasionally be your responsibility, but my feelings aren't — *weren't*.' She winced and ran an agitated hand through her hair. 'So basically what you're saying is that the decision is Lily's, and Roman's, to make?'

'Everyone takes responsibility for—'

'—themselves on the mountain. I remember.'

When she peered at him in that moment, he was afraid of

what she saw, as though she might be able to unravel the hurt and responsibility, drive and compulsion that made him the mess of a man he was.

He spoke before she could express any of those dangerous thoughts. 'How about we take them out to dinner, the two of us and the two of them, and we talk it through?'

He would do a lot to receive more of those affirming nods from Sophie. Sneaking his hand across the table, he clasped hers and squeezed because he needed to touch her. He very much was *not* over her.

But he was at a loss to know what he should do about it.

* * *

'Take some time to think about it, but from my point of view, we can proceed as planned. It's not a difficult route and I can stay close and make sure you're clipping in at the best place to minimise the risk of even a minor fall. You're both experienced. But ultimately, you have to feel comfortable. There's always the option of hiking up with your parents from the other side.'

Sophie watched him with half a rueful smile. There was something about Andreas when he spoke like that, smooth and low, that made everything seem possible. He could be gruff and even downright rude, but if he wanted you to feel safe, you felt safe.

The long day was catching up to her. Emotions always ran high during weddings, but usually, they weren't her own. Although she'd been kidding herself for thinking this one would be business as usual when it involved Andreas and his volatile mix of danger and reassurance.

She'd been so naïve when she'd leaped without looking and asked him to marry her. She couldn't help thinking he might not have realised how serious she was because she hadn't appreciated back then how serious a question she was asking him.

Allowing someone into his heart was a fraught and difficult process for Andreas and she was beginning to understand why.

Taking another sip of her floral white wine, she allowed her shoulders to sink against the seat and watched the last glow of daylight fade on the peaks of Monte Baldo across the lake. The water was still and dark. There were no white sails cutting across in the wind; the hydrofoil and the big traghetto ferry were docked for the night.

Lily and Roman would make their promises to each other in an unforgettable ceremony, one way or another. And Sophie admitted to herself where she most wanted to spend the night, now it was eight o'clock and she had no hotel booked.

'I thought you weren't even supposed to climb a ladder if you're pregnant,' Lily said with a frown.

'A fall from a ladder is more serious than slipping while using via ferrata safety kit,' Andreas told her.

'Really? That's kind of cool,' Roman commented. 'What about the expeditions you do, though? How dangerous is it really to climb Everest?'

Sophie sat up, leaning her elbows on the table to watch him closely. When he glanced at her, she knew he was thinking about the baggage between the two of them, his guilt about his family and his way of life.

'The danger is part of the attraction,' he said thoughtfully. 'No, not the attraction, the purpose.' He studied his hands, before closing them into fists. 'The struggle is the point – to struggle and achieve something and be the tiny spot of a human being that you really are in all the space and time around you. If it was easy, if there was no cost, you wouldn't get that perspective.'

An Italian Wedding Adventure

Roman and Lily stared, their food forgotten. Then all of a sudden, Lily burst into tears. Roman was out of his chair in an instant, crouching next to her and draping his arm around her. 'Shhhh, sweetheart,' he crooned softly, his mouth against her forehead, and Sophie had to look away before her own eyes pricked.

'That is' – she hiccoughed – 'exactly the feeling I had about our wedding. Our lives are short – small – and they could end at any moment. But if we put in the effort together, we can make something beautiful.'

Those should have been Sophie's words. She was a marriage celebrant after all. But she was grappling with her mistakes, some of which she was only just realising she'd made. What right did she have to espouse the beauty of marriage when she'd wanted to rush into one that neither of them were ready for and when she'd actually got married, it had been for the wrong reasons.

'Maybe Andreas should be a marriage celebrant,' Sophie said lightly, catching his dubious glance at her. 'Maybe he will cry at your wedding after all.' Except she understood now that he wouldn't – she'd lose the bet along with any lingering, stupid feelings. He wouldn't let anyone close, even her, even though he'd tried to insist he felt something for her.

Maybe she could finally accept that – and they could enjoy what little time they had and the chemistry that had been one of the highlights of her life, without her agonising over losing it forever.

After dinner, they strolled back to the hotel between the olive trees and the old walls on the waterfront, vestiges of the historic Limonaie, greenhouses used in the past to grow lemons at this northern latitude. Waving Lily and Roman inside, Andreas shoved his hands in his pockets and turned to Sophie, apparently expecting a farewell.

'Is that why you go up?' she asked instead. 'You need to find perspective?'

'Maybe,' he answered after a long moment simply studying her. 'There are no logical reasons to climb a mountain. I know that. But without it, I'm... a bit lost. That scares me more than dying in pursuit of a summit.'

'It takes a big man to admit he's scared,' she said with a smile.

'Only a stupid man pretends he isn't,' he replied with a snort.

'Perhaps you're just more aware of it than most people,' she mused. 'Taking your life into your own hands at a young age must have given you an interesting education.'

'I was certainly happier on a rock face than at school when I was growing up.'

She had a sudden hankering to have seen him as a teenager.

'Thank you,' she said softly, 'for tonight.'

He shook his head, but she stopped him with a hand on his cheek.

'Not only for putting your own reservations aside and being so capable and honest with Lily and Roman. I was panicking today. I don't know how I'm supposed to make this wedding happen when everything's gone wrong and we haven't even reached the difficult part.'

He took her hand from his cheek but didn't let it go. 'You *are* making this wedding happen. It's difficult because it's something special – exactly what they want. You're holding it all together beautifully because this is what you do. Despite all your own grief, you're showing Lily the grace she needs.'

It was too much – his earnest, rough voice, the hard look that brooked no argument, his unshakeable belief in her, well-founded or not. She stretched up and kissed him. She'd intended to pull back and assess the damage, but he melted under her hands, a groan rumbling from his chest.

She wished she could still ignore the simmering, but the kisses were proof that the clean break had been nonsense and closure was a long way off. She snaked her arms around his neck and hung on as he pulled her close. She was even a little bit glad he knew all the reasons why she was struggling so much today.

'Is this a good idea?' he asked, his mouth at her jaw.

'No,' she said emphatically, her arms tightening around him. 'But I don't know what else to do with you.'

'I can just hold you, like this,' he said, his arms gently around her. But she needed closer. 'Whatever you n—'

Her mouth found his ear, cutting off his words and making him shudder. Even after three months, every little detail of him was so familiar, as though she could feel his spirit in his body as she'd always been able to.

'I had to give up my room,' she murmured between kisses.

'Hmm?'

'There was a mix-up – a couple broke up and needed an extra room, so I checked out.'

He drew back to study her. 'You don't need to kiss me to stay at the apartment. I'm happy getting out the extra bed if necessary.'

'I know,' she said, drawing him back to her. 'But having you in the bed is a nice perk.'

Wrapping her in a cocooning hug, he rested his jaw against the top of her head. 'Two days,' he murmured.

'What's that?'

'Two days is as long as we lasted before getting back together.' His arms tightened.

She stilled, soft and calm against him, but with a ripple of unease at just how good she felt. 'It's not "back together". Just because we—' She'd been about to say, *love each other*, but the words alarmed her enough that they got stuck in her throat. She had to remember that for him, love was a weakness. She had to remember how he'd dismissed her so thoroughly eight years before and ignore the little voice that insisted something had changed. He'd never claimed that anything had changed – the opposite, in fact.

Besides, this wasn't love. Love was... She had no idea what love was – another check-box on her 'Sophie is a hypocrite' worksheet – but it couldn't be this. She didn't believe in love stories with sad endings.

'Understood,' he said with a nod, smoothing his hand over her hair. 'It's just a messy break.'

28

Andreas had not expected to awake on the morning of the hen party with his mind and his heart – and his arms – full of Sophie. God, she was beautiful when she slept, her hair a mess, her face slack, pressed into his shoulder, one arm slung over his torso.

He possibly shouldn't have let it happen, especially when she'd had a shock to remind her of her own loss and he was still smarting from her assumption that he was sleeping with Kira. Objectively, it hadn't been an unreasonable one. He didn't usually tie himself up in knots over relationships, kept his head clear for self-preservation, but she should have known his head wasn't clear.

Please don't, Andreas, she'd said when he'd tried to tell her he'd never felt this way about anyone else. Sophie did weddings and commitment and lifetimes and he knew, when he left for Manaslu, he'd upset her and he hated the prospect.

Enough to cancel the expedition? He was starting to consider the possibility.

His skin went cold at the thought, restlessness, anxiety,

images of her marrying and divorcing Rory Brent surging through him. It was enough for him to gently remove her arm and haul himself out of bed. He'd never brought anything good into her life or given her a reason to forgive him for rejecting her so baldly all those years ago.

Kira eyed him when she came out of her room at the scent of coffee, but he silenced any questions she might have with a shake of his head. She hadn't seemed surprised when he'd arrived home last night with Sophie and her suitcase in tow.

By the time Sophie emerged, looking disoriented, he'd already checked the equipment for the day and stacked it by the door, as well as filled Kira in on Lily's pregnancy and the safety adjustments required.

'There are eggs in the pan on the stove,' he said to Sophie by way of good morning, running a hand over the back of his head instead of obsessing about whether to kiss her.

'Thanks.'

He tried to shake his mood when they got to the car, but the frustration rose in his throat again when Sophie climbed into the back, as though she thought he'd rather have Kira in the passenger seat, when he'd been looking forward to admiring Sophie's bare legs and her look of concentration as she worked on her tablet.

Hen parties were familiar ground both in Weymouth and at home, but he felt a shiver of unease that day when he pulled up in the car park in Riva to see Lily and her five friends in their swimsuits and wraps and kaftans, already pouring sparkling wine into tumblers. He'd experienced the odd tipsy client making eyes at him in the past and the prospect made his skin crawl that day.

Sophie was out of the car like a shot, immediately on duty to help Lily hide the fact that she wasn't drinking.

An Italian Wedding Adventure

Andreas greeted the women briefly, ignoring a lingering look from the tall bridesmaid he thought was called Lucia, and went to where the owner of the kayak hire business was waiting by the water's edge with five boats.

'Filippo! Buongiorno.'

'Ciao, griaß di, Andreas.'

While the hen group chattered and applied sun cream and tried on the life vests, Andreas noticed Sophie standing to the side sending wary looks at the kayaks. She was still wearing her shorts and the soft blouse with embroidery along the hem that made him want to brush his fingers along her buttons. Her gaze snapped up and she caught him watching her. She hurried over.

'I was just thinking, you don't need me to come, right?'

He crossed his arms. 'I thought you were supposed to take photos.'

'You or Kira can manage that surely.'

'Kira and I are going to be managing the group. You'd get more photos, better footage. What's really the problem?'

She didn't immediately answer.

'You still don't like small boats,' he supplied for her, trying not to smile at the memory of her rafting in Sardinia.

'I never have,' she said through gritted teeth.

'That didn't stop you before.'

'*You're* the one who told me about listening to your fears.'

'Listen – and then do it anyway. I think that's what I would have said. You just need to get used to it. I could take you out to practise capsizing. That would show you how safe it really—'

'Nooo, thank you. I'll skip the capsizing. I just— There are a lot of other things I could be doing.'

'You've got it all under control.'

She scowled, blowing her hair out of her face as she did so, and she looked so sweet, his mood lifted against his will. 'Don't use your mountain-guide voice with me. *I* know you're human and you're just saying that.'

He grasped her hand, squeezed and let go again when it was obvious that she didn't want the others to see. 'At least they didn't ask to have the ceremony on the water.'

Her eyes widened in horror.

'Get dressed!' He peeled off his T-shirt for emphasis, but the effect was ruined by a titter from the women behind him and he inwardly groaned when Sophie's smile faded.

'Okay, everyone!' Kira called the group together.

Andreas glanced back at Sophie to find her shrugging out of her light blouse to reveal a black one-piece with two cut-outs at the hips and his mouth went dry. Kira's voice became nothing more than a buzz in his ears as his thoughts travelled back to the night before, when he'd used his hands and his lips on her skin – all over her skin.

'Andreas? *Andreas!*'

Blinking to clear the fog in his brain, he turned reluctantly from the sweet view of Sophie's frown to work out what he'd missed. Hopefully, Kira hadn't called him too many times.

'We might need your help to push off. We'll go in pairs and I'll lead in the single kayak.' Kira hefted her paddle like a spear.

'Who are you going with?'

At least Lucia resisted a wink, but Andreas still stiffened at the question. 'Äh—'

'He's going with Sophie!' He could have given Lily a kiss on the cheek. 'She's taking photos, so he'll need to paddle for her.'

'Yes, I'll be Sophie's chauffeur,' he managed.

Lucia still requested his help to climb into the plastic boat. Kayaks were notoriously wobbly and most accidents happened while getting in and out, so he supported her as gallantly as he could.

'Arse first,' he instructed her in a clipped tone.

'Did you just say, "arse first"?' she repeated with a snicker.

'If you try to step in, you'll rock the boat, so...'

'I suppose it's arse first then,' she said with a smile, plonking her bottom into the seat as he held her arms. He repeated the process with Lucia's boatmate.

'What's your name, sorry?'

'Katie.'

He gave Katie a tight smile. 'There you are. All okay?'

When she beamed up at him, he gave them a push to shove the boat off the crunching shingle and all the way into the water.

When he straightened, he realised a queue had formed for his help and Kira was rolling her eyes from her position, sitting at ease in her single kayak as it bobbed on the clear, blue water.

'I'm Chigozie,' the next member of the hen party introduced herself with another bright smile. She held out her hands and he helped her into the boat.

'Rita,' said the next one and with a grunt, he pushed them off.

'Does anyone want to have a go themselves?' he asked no one in particular.

Lily appeared next to him and mouthed, 'Sorry,' but he reassured her with a shake of his head and a genuine smile.

'Here, let me help,' he offered quietly, settling her into the front of the kayak.

She looked up at him. 'I'm not sick.'

He gave her a nod in acknowledgement.

'But Sophie might be sick with jealousy,' she added in a whisper.

'I hope not,' he grumbled, helping the other bridesmaid into the boat behind her.

'I'll manage myself.'

He froze at the sound of Sophie's voice, cool and calm. But her steps wobbled a little as she picked her way over the shingle and into the shallow water.

'I can't believe you said, "arse first" to my clients,' she muttered.

He grimaced. 'What should I have said? Bottom first? We're not precious about the word "Arsch" in German.'

As she leaned over to grip the sides of the plastic boat, there were a few more jokes he could have made about his view, but he looked away and bit his tongue.

When she slipped one foot gingerly into the boat that was bobbing in the gentle waves, Andreas saw a flash of what was about to happen, but he was too far away to stop it.

The boat tipped and then shot out of her grip, leaving her teetering in the water on one leg for a moment before she came crashing down with a shriek. A cheer went up from the hens out on the water and they raised their paddles in salute as Sophie spluttered.

Andreas fetched the kayak before it floated away and then crouched next to her, where she was sitting in the water hanging her head, the waterproof camera clipped to her life jacket. 'I hope that thing isn't recording,' he said gently, tipping her head up and brushing a few drops off her cheeks.

'I'm guessing that's not what you meant by "arse first".'

A smile touched his lips and it felt like the first genuine one all morning. Sliding his palm down her arm, he gave her a squeeze because he couldn't give her a kiss. 'No, that's not what I meant.'

29

Sophie had the perfect view for keeping calm. The blue-green water lapped at the kayak. Sunshine warmed her skin. Mountains rose on three sides, enclosing the lake in their protective magic, and the water stretched out as far as she could see to the south.

The movement of the boat was a gentle bob, not the frantic wobble she'd pictured. Unlike the shrieking and giggling hens, Sophie's kayak moved smoothly and powerfully through the water – thanks to Andreas acting as the engine and captain in the back.

But Sophie was still struggling. She had a pregnant bride, an emotional bridesmaid, a small boat and a raging bout of irrational jealousy.

'Have you done this before?' Andreas asked her.

She shook her head. 'Not here. Hen parties are usually spa days with pedicures and facials. This isn't the kind of hydrotherapy I'm used to at Lake Garda.' As though to emphasise her point, her paddle clattered against his and was nearly wrenched out of her hands. 'Sorry,' she mumbled.

'It's okay,' he said smoothly. 'Tandem kayaks aren't called divorce boats for nothing.'

'Divorce boats? This is the last time we go kayaking as part of a wedding.' She peered over her shoulder at him and immediately regretted it. He wore a red life vest but it couldn't hide his broad, tanned chest. And the way his arm muscles bunched as he rowed was enough to make her woozy.

But as they made slow progress across the vast water, she had to admit there was peace in the quiet co-operation of paddling. Lily and her friend Adelaide followed Kira with firm, co-ordinated strokes, occasionally oversteering and straightening up with a laugh.

A woman buzzed past on a hydrofoil surfboard, causing Lucia and Katie to shriek as they steered out of the way. They turned to watch the surfer come to an elegant stop and then sink into the water. Sophie took the camera from its clip on her vest and snapped pictures of Lily smiling, talking to her friends and soaking up the sunshine.

'Sometimes, I imagine I can see in her expression that she knows she's pregnant,' she murmured to Andreas, glancing over her shoulder at him when he didn't respond.

He wasn't looking at Lily, but at her, sending a shower of misgiving over her skin. 'It's a special moment to capture, I suppose,' he said. 'Are you okay?' he added softly.

'What kind of question is that?' she scoffed.

'You just seem...'

'Whatever word you can't find, I'm not that. I'm a little stressed, but it's nothing I can't handle.'

'If it was the ladies pretending they needed help—'

'You can do whatever you want with whoever you want and I'm not going to stand in your way if you want to flirt with half the wedding party,' she blurted out.

Oops. She stopped paddling entirely, resting the pole over her lap. The view was too beautiful for what was going on inside her, so she squeezed her eyes shut against the vivid colours and tranquil landscape.

'Sorry, I know you weren't flirting. You *don't* flirt. You're just doing your job.'

He was silent for a long moment, but when he spoke, the bastard splintered her open even further. 'If it helps you to know, I asked them to delay our departure for Manaslu – back in June.'

'Who— What are you talking about?'

'We were discussing dates for the expedition and I said I wasn't available until October.' His tone was casual, but in the silence that followed, she heard him swallow heavily.

'Huh.' Her ears rang as she struggled to interpret what he was saying. He'd chosen to be here – for a *wedding*, when he could have had the perfect excuse not to be.

'Just remember I'm only here for you, because you asked me.' With that statement, his voice roughened and he cleared his throat.

'There was a time,' she began carefully, 'that asking you to a wedding would not have produced this result.'

'I know, Sophie,' he said gruffly, as though he couldn't quite believe the change either. 'But I'm looking forward to winning your Foo Fighters T-shirt. I hope you brought it.'

'Ha!' She figured it was safe enough to peer over her shoulder at that and found him with a faint smile on his lips, peering right back. The lump in her throat expanded. 'Maybe you'll lose. Weddings do tend to be *very* emotional in the moment.'

'I've got an idea of that already. I don't know how you do this several times a year.'

'Emotions are my speciality,' she said lightly. 'I hope *you* brought your forfeit?' She used a teasing tone to hide her genuine curiosity, but she didn't expect that he'd be prepared to give her a gemstone. An explanation would be preferable to the object itself. She couldn't decide which she was more likely to receive.

He hesitated for a moment, a flinch rippling across his facial expression. 'I did,' he said evenly.

Sophie wasn't sure how to respond. She eventually decided on, 'I hope you remembered to lock the door.'

Straightening her shoulders, Sophie returned to the task at hand, shelving her own angst for the time being. Setting the camera to record video, she clipped it back into her vest and hefted the oar again as Andreas steered them effortlessly after Kira. They paddled lazily away from Riva heading south-west, where the cliff faces ranged steeply up out of the water. Orientation was different on the lake and although Sophie knew that the mountain slanting up on the shore behind them was Monte Brione, Riva's landmark peak, she'd lost her grip on north and south.

As the cliff faces drew nearer – or their little boats drew nearer to the cliffs, but movement felt relative to Sophie out on the water – the steel terrace of an abandoned building came into focus, clinging to the rock. It was draped in vines and a rusty sign that read backwards from this angle announced it was a hotel, or had been at some point in the past.

Kira steered for the hotel and then veered right, heading for a low arch supporting a hiking and cycling trail above.

'We're going in there?' she asked, turning to Andreas with wide eyes.

A smile pulled up one side of his mouth as he nodded. 'The Ponale waterfall is only accessible from the lake.'

Her breath caught as she gazed at the imposing rock walls.

The water seemed to draw the boats towards the opening under the arch. She told herself that couldn't be the case, as the water was flowing out *into* the lake and not the other way, but there was nevertheless a sense of being inexorably drawn to the secret entrance of a mythical place.

The group was silent as the rushing water grew louder. Sophie squinted against the sunlight, searching for the waterfall that must be the source of the sound, but she saw only rocks and vines. Then Kira slipped between two outcroppings and disappeared into the shadows. One by one, the other boats followed, punctuated by gasps and shouts of delight from the hen party.

'Here we go,' Andreas said, paddling strongly against the current and steering the light craft around a protruding rock and under a lush vine.

Then Sophie caught sight of the waterfall. Through a fissure, she could make out the cascade of water glowing white in the dappled sunlight from far above, tumbling into a rippling pool.

Kira got out of her kayak in the shallows and helped Lucia and Katie to navigate the narrow opening between the rocks. Sophie leaned forward and gazed upwards. It was a cave of sorts, partially open to admit light from above, but secluded in the rock face so it was barely visible from the outside. The inside was airy and sun-kissed, the shallow water shimmering aqua, the pale stone covered in places with moss and vivid-green epiphytes.

Andreas manoeuvred through the opening using his hands to push off the rock and jumped smoothly out of the kayak into calf-deep water, holding his hand out to help Sophie do the same. She hesitated, remembering her rather juvenile jealousy when they put the boats in and wishing it could be just the two of them in this place.

'I won't bite, Sophie,' he said softly.

Giving him a narrow look, she put her hands in his and slipped her feet into the water, appreciating the delicious cool on her skin after the harsh sunlight. 'Arse last, I'm assuming?' she muttered.

He smiled faintly. 'You got it.'

They were very much not alone. The cavern echoed with exclamations from the guests, which would usually have filled Sophie with satisfaction.

'It's amazing!'

'So beautiful! We could be on a tropical island!'

The little humph that Andreas made coaxed a smile on to Sophie's lips. 'A tropical island would be too hot, right?' she teased.

'And too sandy,' he said with a nod.

'Südtiroler don't like to go too far from home.'

'Why would you need to?'

He pushed the boat to the side of the cave and sloshed back to where the hen party stood around the waterfall, raising their arms in the spray and laughing. 'Is anyone going under it?'

Kira stepped through, pausing to let the heavy gush pummel her shoulders, then emerged out the other side with a whoop, shaking her hair back.

'I'll do it!'

The hens took turns to run through the waterfall, squealing at the shock of the cool temperature and the pressure of the water. Lily held up her arms, a wide grin on her face.

'Wow, I have to come back here with Roman!'

'Ah,' said Lucia, with a pained smile on her face. 'That's love, huh? You haven't really seen anything until the other one has seen it too.'

Sophie bit her lip as the poignant words pricked her. Her gaze strayed to Andreas and she jumped when she found his eyes already on her. He quickly looked away, staring up into the patch of sky visible at the top of the waterfall.

He'd seen many things without her – would see many more things without her. So why had he looked at her as though he'd stood at the top of a mountain and wanted to show her the view?

She enjoyed her own view five minutes later when Andreas shrugged out of his life vest and took his turn under the waterfall. He stood under the cold spray as though it were a luxury multi-head shower system at a five-star hotel. A cold waterfall fed from his precious mountains probably was his preferred method for washing. She took her time, inclining her head to take in every detail of muscle: not just the biceps, that continually attracted attention, but also the triceps on the back, thick and overdeveloped like the rest of his arm muscles.

Sophie marvelled that he had such a capable body, built to survive the impossible, but with his own emotions, he was lost.

'We're going to have a lot of footage of Andreas on there, aren't we?'

Sophie whirled to face Lily, approaching from the side. She blinked, glancing down at the camera clipped to her life vest, as her cheeks heated. 'Sorry,' she whispered, hurriedly switching it off.

'It's fine,' Lily said with a chuckle. 'But when are you going to tell him how you feel?'

'Oh, I'm—' She swallowed. 'Not,' she finished. 'I tried that once and it didn't end well.'

Lily briefly grasped her arm. 'But that wasn't the end,' she pointed out.

'Your turn, Sophie!' Andreas called out, deepening her blush even though he couldn't have heard anything Lily had said over the sound of the water.

'Yeah, Sophie!' Lily added with a whoop, laughing when Sophie scowled at her and shook her head.

Andreas strode through the water with enough purpose for Sophie to take a wary step back, but when he paused, his eyebrows raised, she allowed him to tug her in the direction of the pounding waterfall.

But instead of dragging her all the way there, he slipped an arm around her waist and hauled her up against him, making her squeak. His skin was slippery and warm. His hold was firm. And although she squeezed her eyes shut and cringed as the first drops of water stung her skin, she also laughed, the action bubbling up from the mixed-up place deep inside.

'Argh, cazzo!' she squealed as the water drenched her, dumping onto her back and battering her head.

Just as quickly as it started, it stopped again, as Andreas bore her to the other side of the waterfall where only steaming spray remained. Hoisting her up higher in his arms, he kissed her – light and fleeting and nowhere near enough.

'How was that for flirting?'

A smile stretched on her lips. 'Not bad for a beginner.'

'That should stop the others anyway,' he said with finality.

'Is that what that stunt was about?'

'Partly. Mostly, I just wanted a kiss.'

30

Andreas leaned on the bar at the hotel with an espresso cup next to him, lost in thought as he waited for Sophie in the early evening the following day. The wedding was tomorrow. After a washout today that had meant a change of plans for the bachelor party, the forecast was better for Friday, as though Sophie had submitted a weather request as part of the wedding paperwork. It would be hot and he'd warned the group that they needed to depart early, but otherwise conditions looked fairly harmless for this wild wedding.

Lily and Roman had decided to go ahead with the Cima Rocca climb. They'd wanted to celebrate what Lily was capable of and she wanted to see her pregnancy as part of that strength, not a return to ill-health.

Andreas had to admit the week had been something special. He was in awe of Sophie for making it happen, so quietly and efficiently, and yet with her whole heart.

Roman wandered in from the terrace and caught sight of him, approaching with a smile that Andreas warily returned. A giddy groom was not usually his idea of good company. Bachelor parties were often raucous and occasionally bawdy, but Roman was so gratingly in love with his fiancée that when the others had joked about girlfriends past and present, they'd watched their words around him.

He'd noted the tension in Tom, the late arrival who'd caused Sophie to give up her room. Andreas would have to make sure Tom and Lucia were nowhere near each other for the via ferrata tomorrow.

Shaking Roman's hand firmly, Andreas offered the groom an espresso out of habit, but Roman demurred. 'Thanks for today. It was a shame we had to cancel the climb, but I always wanted to try canyoning, so maybe the rain was a blessing in disguise.'

Andreas shrugged and mumbled something about doing his job.

'I'll have to go again with Lily when... you know.' He leaned his forearms on the bar but straightened again. Then he copied Andreas's stance, elbows back, reclining. He sent Andreas a sheepish look. 'I am a bit nervous, to be honest.'

'Why?'

Roman laughed and slapped him on the arm. 'Because it's my wedding tomorrow.'

'But aren't you already legally married? And you and Lily... you're like an old married couple already.'

'Yeah, signing the marriage register was a pretty big moment too, but there's something about the words, about speaking them aloud – especially up there in nature, somewhere important to both of us.'

Andreas wished the words hadn't touched him. *There's something about the words...* Legal documents could be legally struck down. Marriage could be undone, but words could never be unsaid.

He continually wanted to *say* things to Sophie, but the words were dangerous.

'And we'll exchange the rings, of course – something traditional to show it's really serious.'

Andreas understood that statement too. He'd understood it in that market in Islamabad eight years ago, although he'd called himself a fool a hundred times afterwards for buying the stupid thing – the stupid thing he'd taken out of his sock drawer and brought with him, even though there was no chance of needing it.

'And you're off on an expedition after the wedding?' Roman asked.

Andreas answered with a nod.

'How does Sophie feel when you're away?'

He froze, his jaw working. He wanted to insist they weren't together, that she wouldn't feel anything, but after the past few days when he'd barely been able to stay away from her, Roman would never believe him. 'I don't know,' he said, rather foolishly.

Roman eyed him. 'You know life is short, right? You of all people should understand that.'

Knowing his voice wouldn't work if he tried to say anything, he just nodded again. He experienced the fragility of life every time he scaled a rock face – every time he thought of his best friend.

'I nearly lost Lily last year,' Roman continued.

'I know,' Andreas replied.

'It was awful. We'd just moved in together and we couldn't agree on anything. I wondered whether we'd made a mistake, committing to each other. Then suddenly, she was lying in hospital instead of our bed and to be perfectly honest, I didn't want that either. There was a moment I wished I'd broken up with her before it happened.'

Andreas flinched, more disturbed by the honesty than he would have expected.

'But it didn't matter in the end. It was too late. I missed the little arguments about the dishwasher. I realised it was her way of problem-solving and it worked and I missed how we were together. That sounds selfish, but grief is selfish. It has to be.'

That sentence was another punch in the gut. Andreas's grief had been extremely selfish. He'd taken a lot of responsibility for Cillian and Toni, but that was practical responsibility. Emotionally... he'd not managed more than self-preservation since he'd feebly tried to reach out to Sophie and she hadn't received his message.

God, what an idiot he'd been, blaming her for his own fear – his loneliness. He'd spent eight years trying to convince himself he'd been wrong to reach out to her, that he couldn't have felt for her everything that he'd thought he had.

But he'd been right, the day he'd landed in Islamabad and realised – a few days late – that he should have married her, should have done anything to keep her in his life.

'I was lucky,' Roman said with a distant smile. 'But I wish she hadn't had to go through all of that before I realised how much she meant to me.' He eyeballed Andreas. It wasn't a subtle hint, but Andreas suspected subtle wouldn't have been enough to punch through his tough hide. 'Are you going to talk to her?'

He'd already done more talking than he'd known he was capable of. He thought of the bet, the gemstone that represented all his hurt pride and fear – and grief. He'd never cry at a wedding and he hadn't intended to tell her those secrets.

But part of him wanted to, even though he was terrified of what would happen if he admitted how he'd felt when he'd left for Gasherbrum. The confession would be eight years too late. Sophie wanted a husband and a dog – and maybe a child, if that happened. He wasn't sure how he felt about that. Maybe she wanted him enough to give him some time to think about those possibilities? Maybe she'd be there when he came back, even though it pained him to ask that of her.

He clapped Roman on the shoulder. 'Let's get you married first,' he said gruffly. 'She'd kill me for distracting her at work.'

'And you think Lily and I are like an old married couple!'

* * *

Andreas was quiet on the drive back to Marniga in the Panda. He'd answered in monosyllables when she'd asked how the bachelor party had been. His expression was even grimmer than usual. Sophie tried to ignore him as she swiped through tabs on her device.

As she'd spend most of the day tomorrow up a mountain, she had to make sure the last-minute arrangements for the reception were in place. She'd spent the day collecting decorations and the wedding favours the couple had selected from a local artist, making payments and last-minute checks with the caterer and florist.

'Have you sorted out the equipment?' she asked absently.

'Kira's doing it now. She said she'd pack some stuff into your rental car, since we're still on our way.' Kira had taken the rental car back to Marniga earlier while Andreas had waited for Sophie to finish at the reception venue.

'I'll need to head up to the florist first thing tomorrow. I hope she's left space in the car.'

'I can drive you up.'

'I need to leave at six.'

'Six?'

'I didn't think that was early for you. It's not a summit push leaving at 2 a.m.'

He eyed her. 'What do you know about summit pushes?'

'There are things called outdoor magazines. Some of them even occasionally feature things about you that you don't talk about.'

His lips thinned even further.

Sophie gritted her teeth and explained. 'The collection time is so early because you insisted we need to start out from the hotel at eight. I had to make special arrangements with the florist.'

'I won't risk being on the via ferrata above thirty degrees with that group,' he said defensively.

'I know. Safety first.' She breathed out through her nose. 'Is it the wedding that's bothering you?'

His response was barely half a shrug. She shouldn't have expected anything more. This was Andreas, after all. The anomaly had been the past two days. She was still surprised he'd admitted changing his plans to fit in the wedding.

'How's it all going?'

She blinked at the unexpected question. 'If you're asking about the arrangements, they're all fairly straightforward. The advantage of this wedding adventure idea is the necessity for simplicity. No need to set up chairs, no chance the bower will blow over in the wind, no last-minute delays when Grandma misses her bus. It's like an Agatha Christie wedding: all the guests are already gathered in a single hotel and all we have to do is marry the right ones.'

She snorted a laugh at her own joke, but Andreas just glanced at her doubtfully.

'I know, you and Kira have the difficult job of keeping everyone safe.'

'It won't be a problem. The worst that will happen is that someone will get lost because they're not paying attention and miss the ceremony. Once they're on the via ferrata, at least they're stuck where they are.'

'So we can make sure we marry the right ones,' she joked again.

He still didn't laugh. 'You're marrying them.'

'That's right, while you stand to the side with a box of tissues to mop up your tears.' She'd expected him to at least react to her teasing, but his expression only tightened further so she changed the subject. 'Roman was a little disappointed you aren't intending to come to the reception.'

'I would have thought he'd appreciate saving the money.'

'I'm pretty sure he'd think it was worth it for the great Andreas Hinterdorfer to attend his wedding.'

The sound Andreas made, between a scoff and a snort, was pained. 'He's well aware I'm not "the great" anything.'

Sophie peered at him. 'Did something happen?'

'No,' he insisted too quickly. 'But *you* know I'm not so great in real life.'

She considered his words, thinking back to when he'd walked into the meeting room at Great Heart and effortlessly turned her life upside down again. 'I suppose people can't be good at everything and you've chosen what you want to succeed at.'

His quick glance was dark with meaning. 'And what I've chosen to forego.'

'Yes, exactly.' Her voice lost strength. He was thinking about them again. She didn't want to go there yet. She only had two more nights to pretend and tomorrow, she'd be so tired, she'd barely notice her last night in his bed.

'Did you really...?' He trailed off.

'Are you going to actually finish your question? Be brave,' she prompted him with a dry look.

'Did you really break up with Rory because of me?'

That was not what she'd expected him to say. Her heart stuttered. 'Andreas, do we have to—?'

'I've been wanting to ask since Monday. I keep thinking about it.'

'Why? What difference does it make?'

'I don't know,' he snapped. 'When did you separate? How many years was it, after I... turned you down?'

'Five,' she answered peevishly. 'But don't worry. It's *not* your fault.' She didn't want him digging into her motives right now, when she was walking a tightrope of her own feelings. She'd loved him – she might still love him – but it would never be enough.

'Did you get together with Rory because of me? Because I hurt you?'

Oh God, she hoped not. 'I'm not that much of an idiot.'

'I'm not suggesting you are,' he said. 'It's just that things between us are different from how I thought back then. I'm trying to understand what it all means – the fact that you would have come to the airport if you'd got the message. That maybe you still thought about me years later.'

'Of course I thought about you! It's natural. We had a pretty intense relationship, but we can't change the past. Maybe at first, Rory and I bonded over a mutual resentment of you,' she admitted in a small voice. 'But we didn't talk about you at all after a while. Only at the end...'

'The end?' he prompted.

With a sour taste in her mouth, Sophie forced herself to continue the explanation. 'Rory accused me of never getting over you. I wasn't the same, bright person I'd been when we met and it wasn't fair of me to pretend all those years.'

'That's bullshit,' Andreas said, so vehemently, she jumped.

'I know he was making excuses. He wanted to break up without shouldering all the blame, so he lashed out with something that didn't make sense, something from the very beginning. But maybe I made a mistake, too – misjudged a rebound relationship because I didn't know which way was up any more, when it came to love.'

He seemed to choke when she uttered the last word and she wished she could call it back.

'We were both pretty stupid, then,' she said softly.

'We were,' he agreed.

It was clear to her now that whatever she felt for him, he couldn't love her back. He felt enough to feel guilty while still walking away from her – but it wasn't love. And what she felt for him couldn't be love, no matter how right that word felt to describe her precarious state. Love was like Lily and Roman – love was reciprocated.

One-sided like this, it was just pain.

'We won't repeat the same mistakes this time,' she mumbled, speaking more to herself than to him.

'No,' he agreed firmly. 'We should not repeat the same mistakes.'

Sophie wished his words comforted her, but they did the opposite. And when he grasped her around the waist and pulled her close as soon as they closed the bedroom door for the night, she was even more adrift. She guessed he was trying to say something with his hands and his lips. As she dropped off to sleep afterwards, his fingers traced lines on her back, along her shoulder blades and down her spine and she had the sad thought that if this wasn't love, she didn't know what love was.

31

Andreas couldn't have put his finger on why the people waiting in the car park of the hotel in Limone didn't look like a usual group of clients. They were perhaps slightly more smartly dressed than most sporting types, wearing hiking skirts with built-in shorts instead of heavy-duty trousers, ties peeking out of the men's pockets. But he'd worked with enough Italian clients in Dolce & Gabbana and designer sneakers over the years that the difference was minimal.

He'd led many multi-generational family groups, so the presence of the parents – only three at the moment, as Lily's mother wasn't to be seen – also wasn't anything to remark upon. With their caps and backpacks, some with hiking poles attached, they should have looked like any other group heading out for a day in the outdoors.

But this group was so clearly something more. There was a giddiness in the parents' smiles and high spirits amongst the younger people. The groomsmen appeared to be taking turns to slap Roman on the shoulder and the groom himself was barely able to contain his grin.

This struck Andreas deeply.

Objectively, he knew it was foolish to try to control every variable. Lily and Roman obviously didn't expect a picture-perfect experience – and they were guaranteed some great pictures up at Cima Rocca. Today was about the marriage and not only about the wedding and that was what they wanted.

But the pressure was still getting to him. He hated weddings, distrusted people who made promises they couldn't keep and yet he was rather hoping this one turned out to be something special. All of this was for a promise Roman and Lily wanted to make to each other – a promise he'd been certain *he* would never be capable of making. One that had always felt foolish to him.

If promising to spend your life with someone was foolish, he felt like a fool that day. He'd proven it that morning by slipping the little zip-lock bag into the buttoned pocket of his trousers, next to his multitool – the Pakistani emerald. A reminder of another moment in his life when he'd felt foolish like this.

He didn't want to be without Sophie. He'd given up too quickly eight years ago. He didn't know what solutions they'd find to the obstacles in their lives, but the relationship they'd miraculously rebuilt – stronger this time – was worth making sacrifices for. He wouldn't make the same mistake by letting her go without telling her everything she meant to him and waiting to see what she'd say in return.

Sophie looked her part today: black hiking trousers that could pass for tailored if you squinted; a loose-fitting white shirt with a patterned scarf she'd put in her bag early this morning to add some flair for the ceremony. She was looking lovely and it was becoming increasingly clear to him that *not* saying something to her would be more difficult than letting out the words.

Words were not his forte but still, he'd packed the emerald. If nothing else, he could give it to her even when she lost the bet, as a hint of everything he needed to tell her.

She had a baseline level of stress several notches higher than her usual, but he suspected she thrived on it. She liked to be challenged and he loved watching her as she looked between her tablet and her clients, in control of all the details.

He'd thought she was prettier now than she'd been at twenty-six – although she'd been damn beautiful back then. But how was it possible that he enjoyed looking at her today even more than he had a week ago?

The bride appeared, looking a little flustered and fanning her face. She rushed straight to Sophie. 'I'm so stupid. I didn't heed your advice and I got sunburnt yesterday!'

Sophie didn't even hint at 'I told you so'. 'Don't worry, the photographer will be able to touch things up, but I don't think it looks bad at all?'

'Mum had a cream with her and we've slathered on the aloe vera. I'll touch up my—'

'Lily,' Sophie interrupted gently. 'It's a wedding, not a photoshoot. Focus on that. One step at a time, starting your marriage the way you wanted to. I'm here for everything else.'

Lily's expression blossomed instantly. 'You're the best, Sophie. You're right. Mum kept going on about the pictures, but I don't want to spend my wedding day worrying about my appearance. Roman has seen me looking a lot worse!'

'And he still can't take his eyes off you now.'

Andreas followed Sophie's gaze to find Roman studying Lily with a soft light in his eyes that only Roman could pull off. Andreas caught Kira rolling her eyes.

'They'd be sickening if they weren't kind of cool for wanting to get married at the top of a via ferrata,' she murmured.

'Even though that means Great Heart now has a side business in weddings?' he prompted.

She gave a disgruntled sigh. 'It would have been better if I could climb with the main group instead of the boring hike with the parents. But it's not as bad as it could have been so far. If I don't have to put on a dress and choose from eleven different forks at dinner, I could get used to it. I'm sure not all grooms are as soppy as him, anyway.' She eyed Andreas and his hair stood on end as the suspicion assailed him that she was imagining *him* as a groom.

He could see exactly who the bride would be.

With a loud swallow, he forced his mind back to the task at hand, packing copious bottles of water into the back of the minibus. When he'd finished, he searched out Sophie and found her with her phone to her ear, a line etched between her brows.

He wandered over, glancing around to make sure no one was watching before brushing a hand down her back. She didn't acknowledge the caress, but her body leaned into the touch and he lingered with his hand at her back.

When she pulled her phone from her ear without saying anything, he asked, 'Everything all right?'

'The photographer is late and I can't reach her. How long can we safely wait? We have such rotten luck with photographers and it was so hard to find someone who agreed to come up the via ferrata.'

He pulled out his phone in its chunky case and stabbed at the screen that never seemed as responsive to his fingers as it should be. The weather forecast made him pause. 'Half an hour if we have to, but the showers forecast are showing a little earlier now. It's not something I'd usually worry about, but this is a big group and...'

'It's a wedding,' Sophie finished for him with a small smile.

'It's the weirdest wedding I've ever seen, but yes. It's different because it's a wedding.'

'You haven't seen any,' she reminded him drily. 'Rain would be dangerous on the via ferrata right? Today's forecast looked perfect all week!'

'The Garda microclimate strikes again. But light rain is no problem. We're heading up early. Chances are, it'll be fine and it's just the reception that might be a little damp. Maybe they'll get a kick out of it – go dancing in the rain.'

'I'm not going to go dancing in the rain in my dress,' she said emphatically. 'It's crepe silk.'

He had no idea what crepe silk was, but he was desperate to see it. 'You wear a dress when you're working?'

She eyed him. 'What did you think I wear? Army fatigues?'

'After going on about trying to put me into a suit, I thought you wore one of those.'

'I blend in better in a dress and it generally keeps everyone more at ease. *You* could have worn a dress, if the suit was all that was stopping you from coming to the reception,' she joked.

Of course it wasn't the reason why he didn't want to go to the reception, although he struggled to remember what his reasons were, now he was thinking about Sophie in a pretty dress. He'd thought his ideal woman wore a harness and was draped in ropes, and he loved the dust-smudged version of Sophie who followed him up into the mountains. But he was dying to see the version of her that enjoyed the soft material of a nice dress.

Her phone rang and he gathered that the photographer had been located and was on her way after a childcare emergency to do with the early start he'd insisted on. Sophie snapped back into duty mode, but as he turned to go, she shot out a hand and squeezed his arm. It was a light, casual touch, but his chest heaved with the significance of it, that she'd reached for him.

Significance, symbolism, promises... Today's expedition was beginning to feel like nothing he'd ever achieved before.

* * *

The weather had often been an innocent malignant force in Andreas's life. He'd made two attempts of Cho Oyu, both of which had failed – once due to high winds and the other time a volatile icefall. But he'd rarely wished so earnestly for the ability to control the weather as he did that day. For Lily and Roman – for Sophie.

The morning was perfect: vivid blue sky with a few puffy clouds for decoration. It was cool in the shade. Around half the group opted to hike up with Kira, leaving the bride and groom and a handful of friends – plus Sophie and the photographer – to tramp excitedly along the narrow path through the forest, commenting on the remains of the World War I fortifications.

When they emerged from the cover of the trees at the bottom of the via ferrata, the exposed section was thankfully not too hot, but a billowing cloud in the north caught his eye.

There was a ripple of unease through the group as they gazed at the jagged rock.

'Wow,' Lucia said emphatically as she stepped into her harness. 'That's an "easy" climb?'

'There are plenty of handholds,' her ex, Tom, pointed out.

Andreas smiled at Lucia sympathetically. 'A healthy respect for the difficulty of the route is a good thing, but you'll make it.'

'You promise?' she asked, flirting only half-heartedly.

He stilled, glancing from Lily to Roman to where Sophie stood near the back of the group. That word again.

'I promise it's not as difficult as it looks,' he assured Lucia.

'Now, hopp hopp,' he said, clapping his hands for emphasis, 'or Lily and Roman will never get married.'

'Don't you dare even suggest it!' Adelaide piped up, making Andreas smile.

The photographer headed up first, followed by Roman and a couple of the groomsmen. Andreas positioned himself just in front of Lily, with her two bridesmaids next and Sophie bringing up the rear, a grim crease between her brows.

The first cries of delight from above informed him that the group was over the treeline, clambering up the dramatic spur over the lake. They made slow progress. Twice, the photographer stopped in her resting sling to snap a few shots.

Below him, Sophie's expression grew tighter as she clung to the rock, peering up as the rest of the group seemed to take forever.

'Okay?' he called down to her.

'Fine!' she insisted – of course she did.

When they reached the top of the spur, he unclipped and came to help her up the last few steps. 'This really wasn't in my job description,' she said through gritted teeth.

'You're doing great. Just a little further and we'll be at the cabin where we had lunch. Remember that spot?'

'I remember.' She paused for a few deep breaths. 'Let's keep going. I'm okay.'

Memories assailed him when they reached the rock face where Sophie had stalled last time. Roman whooped with excitement at the prospect of the traverse, but Andreas only saw Sophie's laboured swallow.

He came up beside her, brushing the backs of his fingers against hers, and she surprised him with a laugh. 'You always wanted me to be tough, Andreas. I'm being tough today. Don't worry. I'll be there to see you cry at the top.'

She proved it five minutes later when she stepped gingerly onto the rock, clinging to the cable. Her head held high, she made careful progress at the back of the group and he wanted to kiss her again – this time not because of adrenaline.

God damn it, he loved this woman. Sophie, who'd had the audacity to listen to her heart and ask him to marry her, who'd believed in him long before she'd had reason to. Sophie, who imbued her weddings with significance and meaning and purpose. And weren't those things exactly what he'd always searched for?

He'd imagined the invisible marks he left on the gullies and ridges of the mountains he'd climbed, but letting Sophie leave her marks on him – that thought made him even prouder.

As they headed for the bottom of the last via ferrata that would take them to the summit, all he could think about was holding her and letting everything he was feeling bubble out of him, but the rest of the wedding party was there, cooing and gasping at the view.

How quickly could they get Lily and Roman married?

When he took his own look out at the lake and saw the same clouds as before, only billowing rapidly, the answer to that question presented itself: as quickly as possible.

32

The photos were going to be spectacular.

Sophie watched as the photographer, a young woman called Rachele who seemed entirely comfortable in her harness and via ferrata kit, unpacked her drone from her backpack and positioned Lily and Roman in a dramatic position on a ledge.

The background of the lake, the rocks ranging up into thin air, the world in 360 degrees and three full dimensions was stunning enough, but Lily and Roman, so small against the landscape, still filled the pictures with such joy.

To say that Reshma would be pleased was an understatement.

But Sophie was still unsettled – she had been since the strange conversation last night about Rory and the murky motivations behind the beginning of her relationship with him. Why was Andreas suddenly so keen to dig into her heart? He'd been watching her all day with a spark in his gaze that she couldn't interpret.

After the adrenaline and emotion of the occasion, she wasn't sure how she was supposed to calmly wave goodbye to him tomorrow, not knowing when she'd see him again. Possibly never, if the worst were to happen on Manaslu.

As they prepared to set off again, he drifted casually to her side. When he leaned close to say something quietly into her ear, her skin prickled. But his words weren't a gruff confession of his own feelings – she'd be dreaming, if she ever expected that from Andreas Hinterdorfer – or even another of his brusque compliments that sank straight under her skin.

'The clouds are coming in faster than expected.'

Alarm straightened her spine. 'Do we need to change plans?'

He shook his head. 'There are only showers forecast and rushing would be more dangerous than getting wet, but we can't dawdle.'

She blew out a deep breath. 'What did I say about adventure weddings being a bad idea?' They hadn't even managed the wedding part yet.

The group kept moving laboriously along a rocky track. Sophie didn't want to know how hot it was, but the air was heavy and sweat gathered on her upper lip. She glanced continually at the enormous cloud that seemed to be exploding upwards over the lake, but it was a single weather system with blue sky all around. Perhaps it would miss them entirely.

Staring at the weather was only a moment of inattention, but it was enough that she missed a sudden movement up ahead and then a shriek made her freeze in alarm.

By the time she pushed through the wedding party to find out what had happened, she found Lucia on the ground, clutching her knee as blood oozed through her fingers. The bridesmaid hiccoughed loudly, half sob and half something else, her eyes glazed.

'I'm sorrreeeeee,' she wailed, staring at Lily.

The bride crouched next to her friend as Sophie rushed for

the first aid kit. Andreas was already on the job, kneeling next to Lucia and opening the bulky case from his pack. He cleaned the wound with a vial of distilled water and began the process of dressing it.

'What were you even doing, man?' Sophie heard one of the groomsmen behind her.

'Nothing! I only nudged her. How was I supposed to know she's wasted?' It was Tom, Lucia's ex, who earned a dark look from Andreas when he overheard the conversation.

Lucia burst into tears. 'I've ruined your wedding,' she said between gasps. 'I'm so sorry. I didn't mean to do it. But I slept with Tom again last night and now I feel like shit because I know he'll never love me and I don't know why I—' Another hiccough cut her off. 'So I packed a little bottle of vodka and I know I'm the biggest idiot who ever walked the earth—'

Sophie dropped to her knees next to her. Drunk bridesmaids were one of her areas of expertise. 'Here, Lucia, have some water. Nothing's ruined but take some deep breaths and no more vodka – for Lily's sake.'

'Fuck, it hurts,' Lucia said with a grimace. 'How am I supposed to get down?'

Swallowing her own panic, Sophie looked to Andreas. His expression was blank, but she recognised the little flex of muscle in his jaw and when he glanced at the sky, she felt the ripple of unease he was being careful to hide.

'There's nothing broken,' he declared, wrapping a bandage tightly around Lucia's knee. 'When she sobers up, she'll make it down.'

'But it *hurts*!'

'Come on, you heard what he said!' Tom snapped.

'God, I have the worst taste in men,' Lucia said darkly.

'I heard that!'

'He's not even very good in—'

Sophie interrupted, 'Oh! Look at the—' Her words trailed off as she noticed what she'd thoughtlessly gestured to: the swelling cloud rapidly approaching, expanding upward and growing darker every second.

Then a crackle of light flashed through the fuzzy particles at the top.

Andreas leaped to his feet and clapped his hands twice for attention, his expression calm, but grim – his speciality. 'Allora, we need to keep moving.' A quick glance was all the warning he gave her. 'With the chance of lightning overhead, we can't continue or descend right now and we need to take shelter.'

Gasps and murmurs of alarm rippled through the guests. Roman took Lily's hand and squeezed.

'What about the wedding?' Adelaide asked. 'And the others?'

'Safety comes first,' Sophie said, swallowing the lump in her throat. 'We'll contact Kira. I'm sure they're fine.'

'Where are we going then? Where can we take shelter up here without going back down?' Roman asked.

'There are tunnels dug all through this mountain,' Andreas supplied. 'One more short climb and we'll reach the entrance. We'll be safe in there until the storm passes.'

One of the groomsmen groaned.

'We knew this was a possibility,' Lily began, but Sophie shook her head.

'We'll hold the ceremony today, one way or another,' she assured the bride. She was just wary of the 'another'.

'And you'll have a story to tell your children,' Andreas added grimly as he hauled Lucia to her feet and ushered everyone ahead with a firm hand. Sophie eyed him pointedly and he winced. 'I mean hypothetical children,' he added, making

Sophie inwardly groan. 'It'll certainly be... an adventure,' he commented with a sigh.

The first drops fell while they were making their way painstakingly up another climb. Although fingers of gravity dug into her and her feet slipped on the damp rock, she gritted her teeth and moved briskly from foothold to foothold, no time to indulge her fears.

The group was restless, while Andreas grew calmer and calmer until he was drawing out his instructions in his smoothest tone, as though speaking to a herd of spooked deer. Sophie helped Lucia, who hobbled along as best she could, and tried not to take it to heart when Lily glanced back for reassurance, her face pale.

Another flash – closer this time – greeted them as Andreas unclipped his straps from the cable. Gesturing to the hiking trail, he urged the rest of the group ahead as the crack of thunder rent the air above them. Sophie was the last up and he pushed her ahead of him with a hand on her back.

The rain came down in earnest, the dirt between the stones at their feet turning quickly to mud and the trickles of sweat becoming rivulets of cool rain.

Rounding a corner, Sophie saw the members of the wedding party disappearing one by one through a narrow crack in the rocks and into a dark doorway: the entrance to the Gallerie di Guerra, the tunnels dug by the Hapsburgs during World War I.

At another flare in the sky, she hurried towards the shelter, water sluicing off her helmet and her heart beating an irregular rhythm as the darkness swallowed her.

The stone wall was rough under her fingers, the air musty. For a moment, she felt only stillness, heard only the agitated breathing of the ten other people taking shelter in the narrow tunnel and the rain pelting down. In any other situation, the sound would have been soothing, but this was supposed to be Lily and Roman's wedding day.

Now the group was safe for the moment, all of Sophie's other feelings rushed over her. The event was an abject disaster. One bridesmaid was bleeding and drunk. The location for the ceremony was currently being doused in heavy rain and probably struck by lightning. They were trapped in a century-old tunnel dug by soldiers who were treated as artillery fodder and the bride with her recent brush with pneumonia was soaking wet!

To top it all off, Sophie had to say goodbye to Andreas again tomorrow because he didn't believe in weddings anyway and given everything that had happened, maybe he had a point!

With a muted click, a beam of light appeared. Not from Andreas, where she would have expected it, but from the other end of the long tunnel.

'Andreas?' Kira's voice carried on an echo.

'We're here.'

'Oh, thank God!' came the voice of Lily's mother, then the light bobbed wildly as the other group approached. Another torch clicked on, ranging across the group and then flashing in her eyes.

'We're fine, Mum,' Lily assured her mother shakily.

More pale faces appeared, with rustling as headlamps were fetched from packs. Everyone looked grim and ghostly and bedraggled and Sophie had never seen such a sorry sight at one of her weddings. Even the emotional reunion with the other guests only seemed to make the unfolding disaster bleaker.

What bride pictured her wedding day like *this*?

Pressing her hands to her mouth in an attempt to stifle the sob she felt rising in her chest, she only partially succeeded, the sound coming out of her nose in an ugly snort instead.

'Sophie!' Lily exclaimed. One of the lights bobbed urgently in her direction.

Shaking her head wildly, she fended off her client with a hand on her shoulder. 'I'm fine,' she choked. 'I'm just so, so sorry.' Another snort and an odd squeak that she couldn't believe had come out of her own mouth. 'Sorry,' she said again with a cough and tore away from Lily's concerned grasp.

She barrelled straight into Andreas.

'Sophie!' His voice made everything worse. He'd made her question everything – what her job meant to her, her hobbies, why she'd married Rory and mostly, what had really happened between them eight years ago. When he spoke her name in his rough voice, she couldn't help wondering what she meant to him, even though that made her the same sad fool she'd been when she'd asked him to marry her.

'I just need... a minute,' she managed between frantic breaths, pushing past him.

'Not there! We don't want you to get lost.'

Sophie froze, peering at the pitch-black void in front of her with a new rush of fear. Andreas's headlamp picked out the handwritten sign she'd missed:

Pericolo, galleria senza uscita

A tunnel with no exit felt like a bad metaphor for marriage.

It wasn't the celebrant who was supposed to be an emotional wreck on the wedding day. Leaning one arm on the dank, stone wall, she sucked in a breath through her nose to try to stop wheezing.

'God, what am I even doing here?' Unclipping her helmet and slipping it off, she dropped her rucksack to the ground with a thunk and fell back against the wall. 'How did I ever think I could do this – with *you*?'

33

One minute, Sophie was leaning against the rough stone, numb and limp, her reserves of hope and goodwill completely dry, and the next, she was scooped upright and conveyed around a dark corner by the large form of Andreas, his arm curled around her waist.

'What are you—?'

'Shh, we're just going somewhere we can talk.'

'I don't need to talk! I need to get back to my disaster of a wedding!'

'I think you'll find it's not *your* wedding,' he said in a pointed tone that briefly robbed her of speech.

'And I don't need to get lost in a tunnel with you!' she hissed when she'd recovered.

'We're not going to get lost.'

'Because your sense of direction is superhuman and you have a map of these tunnels tattooed on your arsch?'

He stopped, the headlamp turning as if in slow motion until it flashed in her face again.

'Ow!' She slapped a hand over her eyes.

'No, because we've only gone around one corner. The others are safe with Kira for a minute.'

Her nostrils flared as she took a deep breath.

'Besides, you know I don't have any tattoos – on my arse or anywhere else.'

She crossed her arms. 'Did you drag me down here to talk about your arse?' She caught a twitch of a smile on his lips, but she couldn't see much else. 'Can you take that thing off? It's glaring.'

He tugged the headlamp down to hang around his neck, leaving his face with a pasty glow, all harsh lines of shadow. 'What's the matter?'

'What's *not* the matter?' she threw her hands into the air. 'This is *nobody's* idea of a dream wedding!'

'Lily and Roman don't want a dream wedding. They want *their* wedding.'

She eyed him. That platitude was nowhere near enough to combat the truth of how badly she'd screwed up. 'That's rich, coming from you.'

'What about everything you told me back in June – in February? Pushing the limits of the human heart?'

Heat flooded her cheeks and she cringed at her own words. 'What a stupid thing to say,' she muttered. 'It's all for show. People get married for a whole host of reasons, but I don't think anyone does it to prove what their heart is capable of.' She snorted. 'It's just an excuse for a huge party and I haven't even managed *that* this time. I was just looking for meaning where there is none.'

She swiped a hand across her nose, distressed to find moisture on her cheeks that was too warm to be rain.

'A divorced wedding planner was ironic enough, but a wedding planner who has no clue about lo—' She cut herself off with a hiccough that emerged around the lump in her throat.

She wished she'd kept it together until tomorrow, after he was safely gone.

He was standing too close in the confined space, the air around her full of his energy. He was breathing heavily – too heavily to be from exertion – and she noticed his jaw working fiercely.

'Where has this come from? You were so excited about this wedding. The florist and cake and the nice dress. And *them*. The wedding party. You're magic with your clients because you mean it.'

Despite her misery, the sudden chill that made her teeth chatter and the complete failure of the day, having Andreas call her 'magic' lit a warm light inside her that tried desperately to catch.

'You don't believe in weddings, Andreas,' she said flatly.

It was so quiet in the dank tunnel that she heard him swallow. 'I believe in this one,' he finally said. 'And I believe in you.'

There was an unfamiliar quality to his voice. His face was in shadow, but there was something brewing in him that made her wary – and kept her gaze riveted to his features.

'You believe I can climb a via ferrata. But I'm talking about life – I'm talking about commitment and what do you know about that?'

'Nothing.' This time, his voice shook and he propped a hand on the wall behind her, his eyes bright. 'But I'm trying to learn – for you.'

Her knees wobbled as she thought for a moment he meant he wanted to learn to commit – *to* her. But she must have misunderstood. Shaking her head to clear it, she said, 'Is that what you were doing last night when you asked about Rory? I don't think that was a good reflection on me – or marriage.'

'No, that's not what I mean – and that's not why I was asking last night.' He fell silent again, glancing upwards as though the tunnel ceiling could help him find the right words. 'I think *our* relationship – relationships, whatever – were a good reflection on you.'

'What?'

'I was trying to work out if... you really loved me.' He said it with a huff of disbelief.

Her throat closed and she blinked frantically to hold back another tear. 'What am I supposed to say to that? I said it once when it was more a feeling than a conviction and you ran as fast as you could in the opposite direction! You didn't want to hear it – and you've told me a thousand times that you couldn't return it. We *said* we weren't making the same mistakes again so I *don't*...' She couldn't finish the lie.

Andreas straightened, gazing at her. 'Sophie, I meant *I* don't want to make the same mistake again.'

'What... mistake are you talking about?'

He took a deep breath and paused to press a kiss to her forehead that made her knees even wobblier. 'I missed you, really *missed you*, like my keys when I put them down somewhere, except more permanent. No, not like my keys. Ähm...' He blew out a calming breath. 'I wasn't going to attempt this until after the wedding,' he mumbled. 'It's supposed to be about Lily and Roman today.'

'Don't worry about it!' came a voice from where the wedding party was waiting – apparently listening to every word.

Andreas turned with an arch look.

'You can do it, Andreas!' called another, which sounded like Lily.

'You were saying something about losing your keys,' she prompted him doubtfully.

'It's not about my keys! I need to tell you... what happened after I left for Pakistan eight years ago.'

That wasn't what she expected. 'When Miro died?'

He shook his head. 'I told you that part already.'

She nodded tightly.

'This was before that – and after.' He licked his lips. 'I *was* in love, once.'

Sophie swayed on her feet, blinking wildly as she processed the hurt of his confession. He'd been in love before? What was he trying to say?

'I mean, I realised it was love. It was the only time in my life. The only time I wondered if maybe getting married might be a good idea.' He glanced at her sheepishly for a moment. 'I tried to forget again, but I did admit it – to myself at least, and to Miro – at one stage.'

That was another blow that stole Sophie's breath, but when Andreas glanced at her, his expression twisted with wary hope, a suspicion began to blossom in her stomach. Could he mean—?

'Andreas, you don't believe in—'

'I know what I said and now I think I know why I said it. But when the woman I loved was gone – or I was gone, I don't know which any more – I realised what it meant, that I missed her like a part of myself and I hated that I'd left without telling her, without working things out. I was distracted and I needed to settle my head. Miro and I were in a market getting supplies and a salesman offered to take us to buy gemstones. It happens often. Usually, we just say no, but that time, I thought about... her and I went with the man. I bought this.'

He dug into the pocket of his trousers and pulled out a small zip-lock bag, holding it in his palm in the light of the headlamp.

Sophie frowned again, wondering when he would cease to surprise her. But although the bag wasn't a small, velvet box from a jeweller, the object inside the zip-lock bag was just as valuable.

It was a glinting emerald, round cut. Three-quarters of a carat, she remembered. Goosebumps rushed up her arms as she waited for him to continue.

'This emerald has been up Gasherbrum I,' he said quietly. 'Aconcagua, too. Erm, and the Matterhorn twice. Denali – but not the top. We didn't make it. A few others as well.' He trailed off. 'Anyway, I wasn't supposed to keep it and take it up all those summits. It was supposed to be... I don't know. A ring?' He shrugged apologetically. 'A promise, maybe. But when I came back down – with Miro dead – I was a mess and then I thought she'd wisely moved on... To be honest, I was a bit ashamed I'd bought the emerald, that I thought a relationship could work.'

She knew that feeling. 'What happened next?' she prompted him, hoping she knew where he was going with this, that he was telling the story in a way that made the feelings bearable, rather than telling her a story about some other love. 'Did you see her again?'

His gaze rose to hers, his eyes as serious as she'd ever seen him. 'When I least expected it,' he rasped. 'And I didn't deal with it well when I realised she still meant something to me. I thought I'd been wrong when I bought this – wrong to think I could be... *hers*. I thought my choices were made, but it turned out I had another chance – or *might* have another chance.'

It was only when he swiped a hand over his eyes that she realised they were shining with moisture. She'd guessed he was struggling with his feelings, but she'd had no idea how much.

'She's grown more beautiful, more confident, she knows herself better and I love that. She's also been hurt. She's a little jaded and something terrible happened to her that I wish I could have supported her through. But...' He swallowed again, 'if she does still love me, then I'll do anything to keep her in my life this time – anything. I'll cancel Manaslu. I'll stay down and find a way to...'

Sophie's breath caught. Her mind struggled to catch up with the expanding heat in her chest. She'd been preparing herself for a painful goodbye, but instead, he was standing before her thrumming with the same longing she felt, and for once, acknowledging it.

His words were a step off a precipice for him, a fall into the unknown, but he was saying them anyway. He was handing himself over to her, however she would have him.

Grasping two handfuls of his shirt to hold him up, she asked, 'Does that mean,' she began gently, 'you still love her? After all this time?'

34

The words felt like a build-up of pressure behind his skin, but he took a moment to gather himself to say them properly.

Of course I fucking love you wasn't the declaration she deserved, but hearing her ask him, her voice regaining strength, had drawn everything he usually buried deep to the surface.

'Sophie, I love you more than I ever imagined I could. Even more than I did back then – and I loved you a lot.'

A cheer rose from the wedding party he'd managed to forget for a moment, making Sophie jump. He tucked the stone back into his pocket and grasped her around the waist. Her arms fell around his neck, her carabiners clinking with his.

'What about when you're on a mountain? I couldn't live with it, if I really distracted you.'

'I said I'd cancel—'

To his surprise, she shook her head. 'You should know I'd never ask that of you. I know part of your soul will always long to be up high. I wouldn't change that.'

He was almost too bewildered to believe she meant it, that she wouldn't change him. 'I think,' he began, 'that was my fear talking, when I said I needed a clear head on an expedition. I do let my parents' worries get to me. But if I knew you'd be there when I came down, if you told me you loved me and you actually wanted me, then maybe that's a strength I'd carry with me – instead of the stone, that's rightfully yours.' He chuckled all of a sudden, trailing off with a sniff. 'It's yours twice over, since I think I've lost that bet.'

'We're not really at the wedding ceremony yet, but I suppose that's open to interpretation.'

'Do you... Have I restored your faith in... meaningful declarations?' He was beginning to feel in his gut that she hadn't said the words back.

'Are you really saying that, if I hadn't blocked your number, you would have come back and proposed to me?'

His hands tightened on her. 'To be honest? I don't know if I would have got up the courage. I intended to. Before we went up. I even told Miro. You'd put an idea in my head.'

'You thought getting married was a terrible idea. I believe, "I'm not that kind of guy," were your exact words.'

His face heated. 'I didn't mean to hurt you. I didn't believe you could really mean it.'

'Especially because you'd never let me in – not fully. You were still a two-dimensional hero to me.'

'I'm not a hero any more,' he commented with a lift of his brow. 'I don't know about getting married – I still don't know anything about weddings. But I wanted to show you how much I want you to stay with me. If that means marriage—'

'I get it, Andreas.' She gave a strange sort of squeak and he peered into her face with concern.

'Are you laughing or crying?'

'Both,' she explained with a hiccough. 'I can't help thinking I could have saved us eight years of heartache, if only I hadn't blocked your number.'

'You said, if we'd got married, we probably would have split up again. You have no idea how those words haunted me. I was sure you'd given up on us. It was easy to tell myself you were right.'

Her grimace was sweet. 'I was protecting myself – my feelings. I'm sorry I hurt you. It is true that we were both different, when we first got together. You said you weren't ready and I probably wasn't either.'

He smoothed her hair back from her face. 'You're right, we've both changed. I love who you've become, Fini. I love that you see through me and stand up to me and maybe you needed to get there by yourself. But still, if we'd got married back then, we might have had problems, but we'd have made it work. Because I loved you. I *love* you. And I still think we'll make it work – somehow.'

Her lip wobbled. 'I don't know if I could have believed you if you'd suddenly got down on one knee and claimed you wanted to put on a suit and stand at the altar with me, but you being you – being honest – I want to make it work too. We can sort out the details as we go along and being together doesn't have to mean marriage. I won't push you off a cliff you're not ready for.' She nearly choked on her words. 'That was a terrible metaphor, but you know what I mean. That's the mistake *I* won't make again.'

'I appreciate the graphic metaphor. But you won't push me away again, no matter what wild ideas you come up with. You're a wedding planner after all. I realise being your life partner might come with certain adventures.'

'Life partner? Those are big words from you.'

'I have been saying big words in every way I can think of for the past ten minutes. After everything we've been through, it's all or nothing. I won't take a risk on anything in between and "nothing" isn't something I even want to imagine.'

'Andreas, you—' She took a moment to drop her head between them, taking deep breaths. 'Phew,' she said, straightening slowly. 'I thought I was an idiot to still love you so much.'

'Oi, Sophie, I made a mess of this.' He tucked her head into his shoulder and wrapped his arms more tightly around her. 'I don't know how we'll work out the details, but it's just another mountain to climb. Up on a summit or down at sea level, I want you to know that I'm *yours*. I want to come back to you. If you really think that's enough for you.'

Her hands lifted to his face.

'*You're* enough for me,' she said softly. 'Just the way you are. I know your drive to go up. It's part of you and I can't separate that bit. And there's something you don't realise about yourself.'

'What?'

'Yes, you take risks, but you also take responsibility. You keep yourself safe because you love your family. I know there are no guarantees, but there are no guarantees of anything in life – even the promises we make ourselves. I trust you and you're allowed to trust yourself too, the way you taught me to.'

Simple words, but they contained more meaning than anything anyone else had ever said to him. And it was fitting that they were on an adventure, about to make a summit push, if the storm ever let up.

But she wasn't finished altering the foundations of his existence. 'I love you,' she whispered in his ear. 'And if we ever have problems, I'll climb a mountain with you until you can talk about it.'

There was only one way he could respond to that: he kissed her.

It was clumsy like a first kiss but also hot and charged with all of the mistakes they'd made and all of the years they'd waited. Catcalls and cheering made Sophie pull back too quickly for his liking. 'I knew I didn't like weddings,' he grumbled, but he spoke around a smile.

'I thought you might have made peace with sentimentality. You certainly came through with the romantic speech.'

'It wasn't romantic. It was real.'

Pressing another light kiss to his lips, she said, 'And so is Lily and Roman's marriage.'

'Your confidence is restored?'

Her smile was precious. 'It turns out I was right after all.'

'About loving me?'

'*And* that you'd cry at this wedding. You'll have to get your own Foo Fighters T-shirt.'

* * *

'Well, this is the strangest wedding breakfast I've ever attended!' Mrs Welbon sat perched on a damp rock, surrounded by bushes, as she unwrapped her energy bar.

'Cheers!' her husband said, clinking his water bottle with hers.

'It's not the wedding breakfast when we haven't had the wedding yet,' Adelaide pointed out.

'I never understood why people call it a wedding breakfast anyway,' Mr Tran piped up. 'Are we supposed to eat bacon?'

'God, I could murder a bacon roll right now,' Lucia said with a groan.

After nearly an hour of holing up, the wedding party had cautiously emerged up the long ladder out of the tunnels and into bright sunshine that might have felt as though it were taunting them, if anyone had any cynicism left. But despite the smudges of mud, the limp hairstyles and Lucia's bandaged knee, everyone was in high spirits.

Sophie listened to the contented voices with a smile as she fussed over Lily with the help of her mother. The photographer would have to remove the speck of blood on Lily's blouse with Photoshop, but it was near the hem and it wouldn't show up in all the photos. Her face was clean, however, with subtle make-up, and Sophie had fixed her hair and fitted the short veil they'd smuggled up in Lily's rucksack as a surprise for Roman. The floral wreath Sophie had carried was a little wilted, but Lily's bright smile more than made up for the hints of browning on the white rose petals and the odd crushed carnation.

Behind the rocks on the other side of the summit cross, Andreas waited with Roman and the groomsmen. Sophie couldn't stop shooting glances in their direction, wondering what Andreas was doing with the groom, what they were talking about. The photographer had set up her equipment, the drone ready to take group shots from a wide angle after the ceremony.

'I can't believe we made it,' Lily said softly.

Sophie gave a dry laugh. 'I can't either. This has been without a doubt the most memorable wedding I've ever planned, right from the beginning.' She gave Lily an approving smile. 'Mostly because you and Roman are so much in love that you wanted something unique. It's been inspiring working with you.'

'And you worked magic to make it all happen,' Lily replied earnestly.

Remembering Andreas using the same word, Sophie bit her lip against fresh tears. 'Don't start. I'm already emotional.'

'It's a wedding. We're allowed to be emotional, right?' Lily gripped her hand tightly. Leaning close, she whispered, 'If it's a girl, we're going to call her Sophie.'

There was no more resistance. Sophie's hand clapped over

her mouth to muffle a sob as tears made tracks through the dust on her cheeks. 'I would give you a hug, but I'm filthy and we just got you all dressed up for your wedding.'

'But if it's a boy,' she hesitated, 'we both thought Andreas doesn't really work in England.'

Sophie snorted a laugh. 'I'm sure one Andreas is enough.'

'Did you really think he didn't love you?' Lily asked with an amused smile. 'Ever since we met him, he's stared after you with these burning looks. It makes sense now I know you have so much history.'

'Sometimes, you know something with your heart before you accept it with your head. That, and he's the most stubborn person I've ever met.' After giving the bride one last critical once-over, she stepped back. 'Right, give me a minute to fix myself and then let's do this summit wedding!'

35

'They're waiting for you.'

At those words from Adelaide and with one last squeeze of her hand, Sophie left Lily with her mother and her bridesmaids and picked her way over the rocks to the clearing in front of the summit cross. Taking a moment to admire the decorative ironwork, she pressed her hand to the slender cross, rapidly drying in the sun. She drew in a deep breath of moist, pine-scented air, clear and cool at 1,000 metres above the lake.

It was a beautiful place for a wedding.

Turning to face the rest of the party, her eyes immediately settled on Andreas, standing back with his hands on his hips, returning her gaze with half a smile. Kira stood next to him, her arms crossed, her expression less than impressed as she took in the tableau of the giddy groom with his white rose buttonhole and the groomsmen, who'd hastily slung silver ties around their necks.

Roman even wore a blue silk pocket square in his grey collared shirt, embroidered with gold patterns as a nod to the wedding traditions of Lily's Vietnamese heritage.

Ignoring Kira's doubtful look, Sophie retrieved her tablet from her rucksack, already in its formal case for the ceremony, tucked the rings into the leather pocket designed for the purpose and straightened her shoulders. Andreas approached, giving Roman a pat on the shoulder as he did so, then drew Sophie aside for a light kiss.

'I have lipstick on,' she whispered, 'and now is really not the time for us to draw attention to ourselves.'

'I just wanted to say you look lovely as a marriage celebrant. Radiant, even.'

She scowled half-heartedly at him. 'If you think you're getting some credit for that—'

He cut her off with another kiss. 'I hope so. Making you look radiant is my new purpose in life.'

'Go and stand at the back,' she hissed, giving him a gentle push. 'And remind Kira to smile.'

He grinned. 'Kira doesn't smile on demand. She'll be a tougher nut to crack when it comes to weddings.'

She studied him. 'You've cracked? You don't mind weddings any more?'

'As long as you're in them,' he quipped, giving her a wink as he made his way to the back of the group.

When Mrs Tran scrambled over the rocks a moment later, all of the groomsmen stood at attention. The photographer raised her camera. The wedding party held their breaths.

There was no wedding march played jauntily on the organ, no measured steps up the aisle or chaotic children throwing flower petals. But there was a grinning bride in a wreath of white flowers and a lace veil – and a pair of muddy hiking boots. She bounded over the rocks and came to a stop facing Roman.

'I'm the luckiest man alive,' Roman blurted out, sending

titters of amusement through the wedding guests, with a distinct snort from up the back, which Sophie pointedly ignored.

'Are those for me?' Lily asked, gesturing to the simple bouquet of three pale pink lilies Roman was holding.

He thrust them at her with a shaking hand. 'Yes. Three,' he said softly. 'I love you.'

Sophie pulled herself together to intervene before the tears got out of hand. 'Are you ready?' It wasn't quite in the script, but after everything they'd been through that day, she thought it best to ditch the formal greeting.

'Yes,' they said at the same moment, shooting each other a grin.

'Lily and Roman asked me to specifically thank all of you who have come to witness the beginning of their lives as a family,' Sophie began, taking a moment to acknowledge the guests. 'That you have all trekked up a mountain to support them shows the wonderful network they have to walk with them on the rest of their journey together, whatever may happen.'

Glancing down at her script, Sophie was haunted by the time she'd spent trying to write it, stuffing each sentence with symbolism and meaning, when the simple reality meant enough, just as it was. With one last, quick glance at Andreas, she squared her shoulders to continue.

'We all know there are tall summits and deep valleys in our lives,' she began. 'Lily and Roman have already been together through both. Not only is their love for each other strong enough to weather the low times, it's brave enough to grasp the good times. Lily and Roman *dare* to love each other with such acceptance and commitment, that they challenge all of us to discover our summits – to be brave.

'Today, they will speak the promises of a lifetime, in the company of their dearest family and friends, in a place that inspires them. We are all privileged to share in the joy of their moment.'

This time when her eyes snagged on Andreas, his mouth was wobbling and she watched him dab at his eye with a huff of disbelief. Resisting a laugh, she turned to the bride.

'Lily Binh Tran, do you promise to spend your life with Roman Anthony Welbon, through joy and sorrow and all of life's challenges, with kindness, acceptance and respect?'

'I do,' Lily responded brightly.

Roman looked ready to pass out, so Sophie placed a steadying hand on his shoulder as she continued, 'Roman Anthony Welbon, do you promise to spend your life with Lily Binh Tran, through joy and sorrow and all of life's challenges, with kindness, acceptance and respect?'

'I do,' he managed.

She gave him a reassuring pat. 'Lily and Roman have written their own vows and I invite Lily to make hers first.'

Lily squeezed his hands. 'Roman, I promise to be your wife, to stay by your side whatever happens. I'll be your yang, the chaos to your order and your confidence when you're feeling down. I believe in you – always. I love you, from the depths of my heart, but also from my spirit. I choose you and I promise to choose you every day for the rest of our lives.'

Both of Lily's parents were stifling sobs. Mrs Welbon passed Mrs Tran a tissue and one of the groomsmen gave the other one a shove to snap them both out of their sentimental reactions.

'Now you, Roman,' Sophie said gently. Her eyes were dry now. She was proud of herself, of Lily and Roman, as well as Andreas and Kira, standing at the back. Even Kira's eye-roll was forgivable, because she was here and she'd helped make this happen. Sophie only hoped she wouldn't struggle too much as more and more weddings featured in her future career.

Roman cleared his throat. When he started speaking, his voice was unexpectedly strong. 'Lily, it will make me so proud to hold your hand through all the adventures that await us as a family. I promise to cherish you every day for the rest of our lives, to listen to you with my ears and my heart and love you in the ways you need to be loved. You are wonderful just as you are and it's my honour to promise to be your husband.'

A grin broke out on his face as he completed his vow, which triggered a giggle from the bride.

'I practised that until I was hoarse,' he whispered to Lily.

'You did amazingly,' she gushed.

Sophie slipped the rings out and held them up on her palm. They were plain gold bands, engraved with their names – with the date to be added now that they could be certain of it – tied together with a white ribbon.

'Lily and Roman have chosen to wear traditional rings as an outward sign of their commitment.'

Roman reached up to untie the ribbon and took the smaller of the two rings. 'Lily, please accept this ring with all my love and respect.' Holding her hand gently, he pushed the ring into place to an approving sigh from the guests.

'I will be proud to wear it,' Lily replied with the words they'd prepared with Sophie before their departure. Lily took the other ring and repeated the gesture with her husband. 'Roman, please accept this ring with all my love and respect.'

'I will be proud to wear it.'

They both looked down at their joined hands, the two rings visible between their entwined fingers, and for the first time, Sophie imagined her own hand and another familiar one curled around it.

There would be time for that later.

Lifting her chin, she said, 'The vows you have made to each

other today, as well as the legal marriage recorded in the Bath registry office, constitute an earnest and sincere pledge to each other for the rest of your lives. You have made solemn promises in the presence of your witnesses and it is now my great pleasure to declare you joined as a family and invite you to celebrate the beginning of the rest of your lives with a kiss.'

As the bride and groom shared a lingering kiss, the peaks and valleys around filled with whoops from the groomsmen and cheering from the rest of the wedding party. Andreas and Kira had delivered a strict warning against confetti, but there was no rule against clapping and shouting, the echoes returning to lift the mood even more.

'Man, you guys did it!'

'Oh my God, I ugly cried, sweetie!'

'You're hitched! You've got yourself a ball and chain!'

'Why isn't it *her* who's got the ball and chain?'

Sophie tiptoed away, too exhausted to intervene in Lucia and Tom's argument. She came to stand next to Andreas and Kira, taking deep breaths in and out through her mouth as the pressure sluiced off her.

'Another one bites the dust,' Andreas said.

Sophie laughed. 'It's not a victory in battle.'

'They're behaving like it is,' he said drily, watching as the groomsmen threw their arms around Roman a little too wildly. 'They look like they'll need supervision at the reception.'

Sophie blinked, surprised when her brain interpreted that to mean he would come. She eyed him. Surely that's not what he meant. He didn't even have a suit and she wasn't sure she wanted him to turn up in his rugged mountain guide gear, smelling like he'd just got back from an expedition.

He just smiled at her and she looked away, certain she was wrong.

'Do you want a big, fancy wedding, then?' he asked suddenly, his look wary.

His wording, again, put her off-balance. She thought they'd decided to be partners, to deal with the topic of marriage in time – or even never. Peering at him curiously, she said, 'What about the summit of Everest?'

His laugh was full and deep and he paused to press a smacking kiss to the top of her head. 'I've already been there.'

'Well, good for you!'

'But standing up in front of a bunch of strangers and saying something sentimental is... not one of my strengths.'

'I know,' she said mildly. 'I need to get *this* wedding over and done with. Elena at the hotel might be panicking. I need to call her. I feel like today has taken a week, but there's still the whole reception to go.'

Andreas's hand brushing her shoulder and then the back of her neck made her want to purr like a contented cat. She wondered if he knew how powerfully his casual affection acted on her.

Giving her a quick hug, he said, 'You've got it all under control. But we have to get them all down first.'

Ohhh, shit. She'd forgotten that part.

36

After the violence of the midday storm, the lake was tranquil in the evening, reflecting fading sunlight with a lingering shimmer of warmth. The aquamarine water near the shore at Limone was cool and still and the rock faces ranging over the town radiated the heat of the day.

The bedraggled wedding party had arrived back at the hotel for two hours' well-earned rest before the reception – and to wash off the mud. After checking Lucia's wound once more and leaving her with fresh dressings, Andreas had pressed a quick kiss to Sophie's lips and left with Kira, in something of a hurry.

He probably wanted to escape before the men got their suits on. If he'd stayed even a minute longer, Sophie might have asked him if he'd come along despite his objections, but she didn't want to shove him straight out of his comfort zone when he'd only just got up the courage to tell her how he felt. She would miss him, though.

It was only a short walk to the reception venue, but Sophie was glad she'd arranged for the minibus to transport the heavy-footed wedding party that evening. The ancient streets of the old town meant that the minibus could only take them partway anyway and they disembarked at a cobbled intersection of narrow lanes, surrounded by buildings with wooden shutters and balconies bursting with plants.

Sophie led the group along one of the lanes, past rough stone houses with begonias on the windowsills, to a rock wall covered in vines. She was glad her favourite silver sandals with chunky heels were comfortable as she took the uneven staircase up to the entrance of the museum and function rooms. The stairs gave them a gradual view of the town that was tucked between the vast lake and sheer rockfaces. The church of San Benedetto with its domed belltower rising above the speckled terracotta rooftiles, as well as the palm trees dotted along the waterfront, made it easy to forget this wasn't a beach resort on the Mediterranean, but a mountain lake in the alpine foothills.

The venue was a historic citrus grove where lemons, oranges, grapefruit and mandarins were cultivated at one of the northernmost latitudes in the world. Sophie greeted Marcella, the manager, and introduced Lily and Roman, then she stepped back and enjoyed the fruits of her labour. After the wedding party had spent the day in outdoor gear and boots, it made Sophie smile to see Lily in her red wraparound dress, a fresh wreath of flowers in her hair. Roman wore a pale-blue suit and a pair of white sneakers, dressy enough to be special, but comfortable enough to be himself.

Marcella showed them through the stone building and out onto the highest terrace, where bushy lemon and orange trees with shiny, dark leaves grew under a wooden frame that was open for the summer. The sweet-bitter scent of unripe fruit pervaded the fresh evening air.

The photographer snapped candid shots of the family laughing, of Roman pressing a kiss to the backs of Lily's fingers and the bridesmaids smiling and looking chic in colourful dresses that didn't match, but added to the celebratory mood – all with the backdrop of the lake and the cliffs extending above them.

Soft instrumental music played through hidden speakers – not a live quartet for the sake of space and budget, but soothing, nonetheless. A waiter appeared with a trolley of glasses and several bottles of prosecco as an aperitivo and Sophie stepped in to make sure Lily's glass was discreetly filled with non-alcoholic apple spritzer instead.

As dusk fell over the lake, they moved inside for dinner. Two long tables had been set up on the top floor of the museum in the middle of the terrace, decked with white tablecloths and sprinkled with flowers. On a small table in the corner stood the tiered millefoglie wedding cake, piled with cream and late-summer berries.

The cake would be delicious, but she couldn't help thinking it couldn't be as delicious as the piece she'd shared with Andreas back at the apartment the day she'd photographed him with a wreath of flowers on his head and a signature Hinterdorfer frown.

In Sophie's experience, wedding meals were often either forgotten in the whirlwind of the party or became the main focus – sometimes in a negative way – but, as with everything else that day, the tagliatelle al salmone and the sliced beef tagliata with olive-oil potatoes suited the occasion perfectly. The guests had a hearty appetite and the simple, fresh flavours in the rustic lemon grove created the intimate atmosphere Lily and Roman had wanted.

Sophie took a seat on the corner of one of the tables. She didn't always join in with the wedding meal, but Lily had insisted it would feel stranger if she disappeared inside to eat with Marcella and it wasn't the first time Sophie's dual role as wedding planner and tour guide had blurred the expectations of her job.

There were no speeches, just a delicious meal with a view of the lake, the clatter and clink of cutlery and glasses and the easy conversation of close friends and family.

After the main course, Lily and Roman opened the dancing on the floor below and the guests who didn't want to dance spread out along the terrace to talk. Sophie found a space by herself for a moment, leaning on the low wall and staring out at the water that was misting as the temperature dropped.

She couldn't help imagining Andreas at her back, his touch relaxing her body the way the view of the lake in the dimming light soothed her mind.

'Do a toast with me.' Lily appeared by her side, holding out a glass of prosecco.

Sophie mustered a smile for the bride as she took the glass. 'It's been an absolute joy, Lily. And you were right, your wishes were very unusual, even for me, but that's made today even more special.'

'It's not over yet,' she replied with a smile, holding up her glass. 'To love?'

'To love,' Sophie responded with an amused smile.

In her peripheral vision, Sophie noticed a figure filling the doorway and turned, expecting Marcella needing her help, but it wasn't the venue manager. She stilled, blinking away disbelief as her heart pounded an erratic rhythm.

Pausing to scan the courtyard, he rubbed the back of his neck as he searched the group – for her, without a doubt. As a giddy smile stretched on her lips, she took in the golden-brown hair that had grown too long again, the silver hoop in his ear, the leather braid around his wrist. Those were features she knew and loved, but she'd never seen him looking quite the way he did just then.

He wasn't wearing a suit, but his party outfit was still a long way off his usual technical outdoor wear. A pair of buttery-soft, embroidered leather shorts extended to just above his knees and were a touch snug. Grey, chucky-knit socks with a band of green wool around the top were pulled halfway up his calves, and disappeared into a pair of rustic, brown leather shoes with the laces to one side. Instead of the leather suspenders she might have expected, he wore a grey felt waistcoat with buttons, the rough white shirt underneath rolled up to his elbows.

Sophie had no idea how he'd procured Tyrolean traditional dress at short notice, but she was immensely glad he had. She stifled a laugh – of amusement, but also of delight that he was here.

Lily followed her gaze and grinned. 'Ah, finally. He said he might be a little late, but I was starting to worry.'

'You knew he was coming?'

'He asked me if it would be all right to come after dinner. But what is he wearing?'

'Lederhosen,' Sophie said with a giggle.

Kira appeared behind him, looking uncomfortable in a sundress she'd probably picked up from one of the shops along the waterfront.

Still studying him from head to toe, Sophie put him out of his misery by stepping out from behind Lily and raising her hand in a wave. His expression when he caught sight of her – relief, pride and a wide smile of happiness – made her knees wobble.

He approached and caught her around the waist, dipping his head to kiss her and then coming to a halt before he managed it. 'You have lipstick on,' he said, as though that fact confused him.

'A quick kiss won't rub off on you.'

He mumbled a reply and gave her a peck on the lips. 'That will have to do for now. But you look lovely.' Lifting his hand to her hair, he stopped and drew it away again, studying her neat chignon. 'I'm a little worried about roughing you up.' But he smiled as his gaze took in the soft folds of her dress and her strappy silver shoes.

'You can rough me up later,' she said, grinning. 'I'm glad you came. I didn't want to put you under pressure.'

Snatching her hand and threading his fingers with hers, he gazed at the whimsical setting: the lake, the citrus trees and the ancient stone walls. The fairy lights strung along the wooden beams glowed as the sunlight faded. 'I wanted to come and see what you've achieved, and for Lily and Roman. But I also wanted to do this.'

'Hold my hand?' she asked doubtfully.

He nodded. 'And this.' Curling his other arm around her waist, he adjusted his hold and before Sophie knew what was happening, he was shuffling her along the terrace in a rather decent waltz to the music floating around the lemon grove from the speakers. He swayed with her for a few weightless moments, but she eventually trod on his foot and stumbled, sending them both barrelling into the low wall. 'You can't dance?' he asked in mock outrage.

'I can't dance. I did not expect to find out that you could!'

'I have the "Tiroler Walzer" in my blood – and some embarrassing teenage dance lessons in my past.'

She grinned up at him, smoothing her hand around his waist. 'A nice pair of Lederhosen and waltzing: you are very well qualified for weddings.'

'The outfit belongs to my father,' he said sheepishly. 'I asked him to bring it down this afternoon and… he's staying overnight. He wants to meet you.'

'I want to meet him, but I had other plans for our last night here.'

'But it's not our last night together. I'll come to Bath next week and… can you work remotely sometimes if I've got clients here? I'll get you the internet at my cabin.'

'That's real romance,' Sophie joked. 'No flowers or jewellery, just an internet connection. Actually, I kind of like it.'

'Well, no flowers, but I did get you something else as well. The internet connection will take a few weeks – maybe while I'm away in Nepal.'

Rummaging for something in his pocket, he produced a velvet bag and tugged on the drawstring.

Grasping her hand, he draped a fine silver chain around her wrist, fumbling with the tiny clasp. It was simple and elegant, two small, clear stones in silver settings the only added decoration. He brushed his fingers over her wrist.

'The day after we kissed – in the apartment, back in June,' he began haltingly, 'you were wearing a particular top and I kept thinking how lovely your wrists were and how I wanted to give you a bracelet.'

Her brows flew up. 'I thought you were just grumpy.'

'You were right next to me and I thought there was no way in the world you would want this – me.' His smile was pained as he ran his fingers up her arm. 'The stones in the bracelet are rock crystal – we call it Bergkristall in German: mountain crystals. To remind you that you do like to climb mountains, although you also look amazing in those shoes.'

'I do like to climb mountains,' she admitted, twining her arms around his neck. 'But thank you for coming into the valley for me.'

'Always,' he whispered, pulling her tight to him. 'I'll always come back to you.'

37

A hectic three weeks later, Andreas dumped an enormous duffel bag on the tiles of the departures hall at Munich airport, freeing up a hand to greet Karel Brzezinski. The Polish mountaineer had his own bag of equipment and the third member of their team, Jan Kastelic, would arrive any moment.

Andreas had flown to Kathmandu many times over the years, but that day felt like the first time. Not because he was nervous. The ghostly landscape of monumental ice formations, snowy escarpments and bitter cold called to something deep in his nature and he could already feel the ice axe in his hand and the harsh sunlight of high altitude.

But everything was different knowing Sophie stood off to the side, her arms around herself, waiting to send him off. She'd offered to stay away, but a proper goodbye had felt a necessary respect for everything she meant to him.

She was a saint for waiting patiently while they wrestled their equipment into four bags and had the requisite argument with the man at the check-in desk. Then it was time for him to work out how to say goodbye to the love of his life.

This trip definitely felt different.

He dragged his feet as he approached her, reaching out to take her hands. There were dark circles under her eyes; he knew she hadn't slept well the night before, burrowing into him instead of rolling away to get comfortable.

'Six weeks,' he said, mostly for his own benefit. She knew exactly how long he'd be away.

'Maybe seven,' she completed for him with a faint smile. 'Two months if the weather doesn't cooperate.'

'I don't usually count the days until the return flight,' he commented absently.

'Enjoy your summit, Andreas,' she said softly. 'Stand up there and think about how much I love you.'

With a huff of disbelief, he lifted his hands to her face, studying the features that were dearer to him than he'd imagined possible. 'You're a miracle, Sophie-Leigh.' He pressed a tender, lingering kiss to her lips and she leaned into it, drawing out the affectionate touch. 'I'm going to miss you.'

'I'll be here when you get back. Nothing will stop me.'

This time, when a particular memory surfaced, it brought him something like wonder, rather than the familiar shaft of regret. He remembered a younger Sophie, restless with nerves, looking earnestly into his face and asking him to marry her.

She'd had the right idea.

Struggling to pull away from what felt an inadequate goodbye, he made a snap decision as he stared into her face. 'Wait there a minute?'

Rummaging in his carry-on, he came away with the little package he'd tucked into a zipped inside pocket, ready to make the journey with him all the way to the top as usual. The object wasn't its familiar shape; it was bigger, with edges that he'd run his thumb over a hundred times already.

'Don't say anything,' he muttered, reaching for her left hand. Giving her wrist a light kiss, near the bracelet she rarely took off, he took a deep breath and slipped the ring onto her finger.

There. That hadn't been too hard. Except now he had to look up at her face. He'd told her not to say anything, but he'd see in her expression what she felt about the significance of the action he'd just taken.

Swallowing his trepidation, he gripped her hand tightly and lifted his gaze. She was staring at her hand, at the glinting emerald set in a simple white-gold ring – a solitaire, the jeweller had called it.

Her hand curled around his and he searched for the best place to start speaking, but she beat him to it. 'Isn't it supposed to go up with you?'

'I was going to take it up one last time, but... Look, Sophie,' he began, 'you asked me a question, before I left for Gasherbrum.'

Her expression turned serious.

'I know we can't be certain of how things would have turned out, but I gave you the wrong answer. The more I've thought about it since we've been back together...'

She still kept quiet, her hand clutching his.

'You don't have to answer now – and we don't have to do anything soon – but now we're here at the airport, I don't want to wait until I get back to ask you.'

Watching him, her eyes soft, all she said in response was, 'Okay.'

A smile touched his lips. 'Okay? Allora... do people still do the knee thing?'

'I'd rather you didn't,' she whispered. 'Not in a crowded airport.'

His smile stretched. Taking her other hand as well, he said, 'Sophie-Leigh Kirke, will you marry me?'

She tugged one of her hands back to clap over her mouth and then, to his utter surprise, she broke into giggles.

He frowned. 'I didn't think that would be funny.'

Throwing her arms around his neck, she grinned up at him. 'It was wonderful. I just... after all your resistance, you actually said it. It's kind of funny.'

'It's all your fault,' he said with a pout.

'I know,' she agreed too magnanimously.

'Like I said, you don't—'

'Yes, Andreas,' she cut him off. 'Yes. I'll even consider taking your name, even though it would make mine twenty-four letters long.'

He peered at her doubtfully. 'Twenty-four? That's very specific.'

The flush of colour on her cheeks was the sweetest thing he'd ever seen.

A slow grin formed on his face. 'You've counted that before.' Giddiness rose inside him. 'The idea of being Mrs Sophie-Leigh Hinterdorfer really appealed to you, did it?'

She started at the sound of his surname added to her first. It rolled a little too easily off his tongue. 'I thought about it a little.'

'You don't have to take my name.'

'I know.'

'We'll talk about it when I get back, hmm?'

She nodded, her hand closing in his shirt. 'I'll definitely be counting down. I love you. Look after yourself.'

'Always,' he promised, pressing his hand over hers.

With one final kiss, he bent to retrieve his carry-on rucksack and joined the other two, the restlessness in him finally subsiding. He was ready to go.

* * *

Seven weeks later, Sophie was back in Europe, back at a different airport, wondering how many flights arrived from Kathmandu per day and how many airports she was going to pick him up from in her lifetime. It was Schiphol airport in Amsterdam today.

The ring on her finger was a fixture now, although it had been strange getting used to wearing it without Andreas there to receive the copious congratulations along with her. Rory had noticed the ring, but she'd just lifted her chin and not offered an explanation. Reshma, Ginny and Tita had seen it as soon as she came into work after sending him off and instantly guessed what it meant, wrapping her in an enormous I Do group hug and taking turns to say, 'I knew it!'

She'd put off any concrete discussions of dates or planning. Andreas might have decided to set things right by asking the question that had splintered their relationship years ago, but she wouldn't rush him into marriage, knowing he had years of reservations that might not be overcome in a few short months. She was very content to be engaged.

The merger had progressed, seeing Sophie travelling several times to Weymouth for initial consultations with clients there. Kira had stared at the ring for a long moment, before barking a laugh and then drawing Sophie in for a hug that was more fierce than affectionate, but Sophie had treasured it anyway. Toni had burst into tears and run for her phone to text Andreas her congratulations, for whenever he next had reception.

Sophie had gradually put an I Do stamp on the meeting room in the Great Heart gym, much to Kira's distaste at the white calla lilies and the little blackboard with inspirational quotes. She'd been certain Kira would appreciate it when she'd written,

Nothing is impossible. The word itself says, 'I'm possible,' apparently a quote from Audrey Hepburn, but all she'd earned was an eye-roll.

The world had kept turning, Sophie's days still full of people and work she loved and, while she'd missed Andreas every minute, she rather liked thinking of him battling his way to the top, safe in the knowledge that she would be there when he came down.

And he had come down safe. He'd sent her a handful of pictures: a wonky selfie in front of a stone hut strung with coloured flags, dazzling white mountains in the background; several where she didn't recognise him with every inch of his skin covered; and a wide-angle selfie of three grimacing and yet smiling faces on what she assumed was the summit – not sent live, of course, but after he'd arrived back in Kathmandu.

She thought of that day in February, when he'd barged into the meeting room at Great Heart. That jolt of recognition she'd felt had set into motion the most unexpected few months of her life. And yet, she'd known he was the one for her, even when she'd been a naïve twenty-six-year-old with lots of personal growth still ahead of her.

Now he was coming through the sliding doors into the arrivals terminal, his gaze sweeping the crowd of faces for the one he wanted to see. She rushed to greet him, waving frantically and throwing her arms around him when she reached him. Dropping his duffel bag, he wrapped her in a hug, hefting her feet off the floor and burying his face in her neck.

They stood like that for several moments, clutching each other tightly, letting the weeks apart fall away one breath at a time. Then he took her face in his hands and kissed her, long and deep.

'I love you.'

Sophie wondered if she'd ever get used to hearing him say that. 'I love you too.'

'I missed you.'

She pressed her cheek to his chest and squeezed. 'Welcome home.'

EPILOGUE

'Right, so summer next year is looking full,' Sophie muttered, swiping through the calendar on her tablet as soon as the clients had left.

Ginny Weller watched her friend and colleague curiously as she packed up her things. They had a two-hour drive back to Bath ahead of them after their consultations at Great Heart that day.

'But Elba is a good choice,' Sophie mused, talking about the island off the Italian coast which the clients had expressed an initial interest in as a destination. 'We've got a good network there. Gabi, the florist, is a genius.'

'Are you...? Won't you be planning *your* wedding soon?' Ginny asked.

Sophie flushed the way she did when anyone mentioned Andreas. He'd been gone a couple of weeks and Ginny was keeping a close eye on her in case she needed moral support, but Sophie seemed at peace with the situation.

'I don't know,' was all she said in answer to the question. 'I guess not. I'll do this Elba event next summer, otherwise you'll be back-to-back with the Taymar-Sachs wedding.'

'I'm looking forward to that one.' She'd been thrilled when Reshma had assigned her the beach wedding in the Caribbean. She'd rarely left England before she'd started working at I Do, despite majoring in Spanish and Italian at university.

'Right, we should head back,' Sophie said.

'Um, I just need a word with Kira before we go.'

'Oh? Sure. I think I saw her with a group in the gym. Is this about the Lee-Martinelli wedding?'

Ginny nodded and rolled her eyes. Planned for over a year already, the winter wedding on New Year's Eve seemed to get more extravagant every time she opened the file. They'd already chosen an outing to an ice cave in a glacier and now the guides from Great Heart Adventures had joined the team, the groom wanted to add off-piste skiing to the agenda.

Making her way past the reception desk with a wave for Toni, who was on the phone, she tiptoed onto the rubber flooring of the gym, peering around for Kira. The climbing instructor and adventure guide shouldn't have been difficult to find, since her hair was bleached and dyed blue.

'No shoes allowed in this section,' said a gruff voice from behind her.

She whirled to find a familiar figure, standing behind her in a climbing harness and a vest top and shorts, casually coiling a length of rope. This was the nature photographer who refused to take pictures of people – and had been resolute in this refusal even after Tita had gone on about their troubles booking photographers for about half an hour. She forgot his name but she recognised the stark lines of his angular face, the long, brown hair sweeping over one eye.

'Erm, sorry,' she said, slipping out of her trainers and

proceeding in stocking feet. She felt his eyes on her as she walked away.

'Do you need something?'

'I'm looking for Kira, actually.'

He gestured wordlessly to the changing rooms and apparently, that was all he was going to say, as he stood silently in front of her, his eyes dropping to the silver stud in the labret piercing below her lips.

'Thanks.' She managed a tight smile that seemed to make him flinch.

Shaking off the odd exchange, she made her way to the changing rooms just as Kira hurried out, slipping a hoodie over her T-shirt.

'Kira?'

She skidded to a stop like the road runner. 'What? I've got to go.'

'I need your help – with a wedding in December.'

Ginny could see the steam radiating from Kira's head. 'I just did one of those – and it was bad enough.'

'Sophie said you were great at the Lake Garda wedding,' Ginny tried with a coaxing smile she was fairly certain Kira saw right through.

Kira crossed her arms. 'If Will is booking me in, then I suppose he's booking me in. What do you need in December? I assume the bride and groom aren't going to get married on a ski slope.'

'No, but they do want to do some skiing between Christmas and New Year. They're staying at a mountain resort near Mayrhofen in Tyrol and getting married in a little chapel in the snow and when I mentioned about Great Heart, they immediately asked us to organise a skiing day too, so...'

'That's not far from where Andreas lives. Can't he do it?'

An Italian Wedding Adventure

'He's already busy, so you're kind of... my last resort.'

'Well, that's just great.'

'This is a kind of "no expense spared" wedding,' Ginny rushed on, 'and Reshma's cleared it for you to stay the whole time and help me out. I hope that's okay. You might need...'

'A new personality?'

Ginny gave a stilted laugh. 'I was thinking more, a new wardrobe.'

'I have nice clothes,' Kira insisted. 'A few bits anyway. I just don't wear them very often.'

That didn't sound so promising. 'Okay. And there's one more thing. The bride's family is organising the music for the wedding, but the singer they know has got some other event in Salzburg beforehand – a classical opera something-or-other. I'm going to be run off my feet, so I was hoping you could go and collect him. Apparently, he's a little high-maintenance but nothing you can't handle, I'm sure.'

'First you want me to dress up and now I'm supposed to handle the singer too? What if I break him?'

'Not *handle*,' Ginny rushed to qualify but cut herself off. 'You're joking, right?'

'Send Toni the dates to get them into our diary,' Kira replied in a withering tone.

'Great! Thanks. I really appreciate it.'

Kira's response was a snort. 'I'm not sure you should thank me yet. After everything that went wrong at Lake Garda, maybe I'm just bad luck for weddings.'

She had to be joking this time. 'You might be good luck,' Ginny suggested brightly. 'Something blue!' Even Ginny herself realised she deserved an eye-roll for that quip. 'But seriously, just don't drop the rings and you'll be fine.'

Kira grimaced. 'Now you've got me freaking out about the

rings. I'll do my best, but I'd rather have a root canal, to be honest.'

Ginny didn't understand her colleague's aversion, but she couldn't doubt her vehemence with that fierce expression on her face. 'It will be beautiful: a snow-covered luxury chalet; a sauna and an open fire; photos in a real ice cave in a glacier. You'll see. Your second wedding won't be so bad.'

Kira blanched, but Ginny hadn't the faintest idea why. 'Fine, I'll collect the bloody singer and see you there for the wedding shit. It'll be merry Christmas and a happy new year for all! Now I have to go.'

Ginny released a slow breath as her new colleague stalked away. At least she didn't have to sit in the car with Kira and the 'high-maintenance' singer for the three-hour drive from Salzburg. But she was nervous about what state they'd be in when they arrived.

Unexpected things always seemed to happen at Great Heart Adventure Weddings.

* * *

MORE FROM LEONIE MACK

Another book from Leonie Mack, *In Italy for Love*, is available to order now here:
https://mybook.to/InItalyForLoveBackAd

ACKNOWLEDGEMENTS

Extra special thanks to my editor Sarah for getting behind this series idea and performing her usual magic on my words. Also to my agent, Saskia, for being the first to fall in love with Andreas and sharing my excitement about the series concept.

As usual, this book wouldn't have happened without the unfailing support of my husband (and the many loads of washing he does every week – as well as negotiating the rather wild roads of Lake Garda in a seven-seater hire car) and Tatiana, my irreplaceable cheer-reader. Special mention to my eldest son, who came on the via ferrata with me for research! My Lucys (Morris and Keeling) also need a mention for their invaluable feedback this time too, as well as Marina Crouse for your helpful comments from the first act switcharoo. I'm also forever grateful for the comments, expertise and support from Jenny Lane and everyone in the Smutfest 2.0 discord server.

To all the wonderful author friends who know the ups and downs and the utterly bizarre moments involved in this adventure: you are all precious to me!

ABOUT THE AUTHOR

Leonie Mack is a bestselling romantic novelist. Having lived in London for many years her home is now in Germany with her husband and three children. Leonie loves train travel, medieval towns, hiking and happy endings!

Sign up to Leonie Mack's mailing list here for an exclusive bonus chapter to A Wedding in the Sun!

Visit Leonie's website: https://leoniemack.com/

Follow Leonie on social media:

- x.com/LeonieMAuthor
- facebook.com/LeonieJMack
- instagram.com/leoniejmack
- bookbub.com/authors/leonie-mack
- tiktok.com/@leoniejmack

ALSO BY LEONIE MACK

My Christmas Number One

Italy Ever After

A Match Made in Venice

We'll Always Have Venice

Twenty-One Nights in Paris

A Taste of Italian Sunshine

Snow Days With You

A Wedding in the Sun

In Italy For Love

An Italian Wedding Adventure

Boldwood
EVER AFTER

xoxo

JOIN BOLDWOOD'S **ROMANCE COMMUNITY** FOR SWEET AND SPICY BOOK RECS WITH ALL YOUR FAVOURITE TROPES!

SIGN UP TO OUR NEWSLETTER

HTTPS://BIT.LY/BOLDWOODEVERAFTER

Boldwood

Boldwood Books is an award-winning fiction publishing company seeking out the best stories from around the world.

Find out more at www.boldwoodbooks.com

Join our reader community for brilliant books, competitions and offers!

**Follow us
@BoldwoodBooks
@TheBoldBookClub**

Sign up to our weekly deals newsletter

https://bit.ly/BoldwoodBNewsletter